CRAWFORD POWER was born in Baltimore, and received his degree from the Yale
School of Architecture. He worked as an
architect in Washington for some years,
then moved to a farm in Leesburg, Virginia,
with his wife and four children. When THE
ENCOUNTER was published in 1950, Crawford Power was in his late thirties. Although
he was widely praised at that time as a
novelist of distinction and great promise, he
has written no other fiction. "Mr. Power,"
said The New Yorker, "presents his characters with such respect and understanding
that it is impossible to lay his book down
until one discovers what the end is going
to be."

THE ENCOUNTER

Crawford Power

Afterword By Irving Howe

 BARD BOOKS/PUBLISHED BY AVON

AVON BOOKS
A division of
The Hearst Corporation
959 Eighth Avenue
New York, New York 10019

First Printing, (Avon Library edition), October, 1965
Third Printing, (Bard edition), June, 1970

AVON TRADEMARK REG. U.S. PAT. OFF. AND
FOREIGN COUNTRIES, REGISTERED TRADEMARK—
MARCA REGISTRADA, HECHO EN CHICAGO, U.S.A.

Printed in the U.S.A.

THE ENCOUNTER

Part One

1

SUCH A LARGE SUM, IT SEEMS TO ME, might be spent to better advantage somewhere else. Here in Lulworth we really have everything we need. Down South there are colored churches too poor to pay for a new roof, some haven't even a chalice or vestments. Or over in India. A man can live for two years in India on what the cushions will cost."

Father Cawder took a swallow from the six-sided cup. Mrs. Girard felt that her lips, stretched in something like a smile, must have tightened to a mirthless rigor. She burst into a laugh and sat down behind the tray.

"I must have more tea!" She tried to speak with a special ease. As she filled her cup she noticed his eyes, watchful, of a keen blue. They were judging her, she imagined, weighing the extent of her self-indulgence, her no doubt frivolous concern over the proper apparatus of a tea table. That little silver horn which she had discovered in New Orleans and which she used to blow out the flame under the hot water. The sight of it always gave her a quick pleasure. God knows she had supposed she was living in a small enough way for a woman of gentle birth. She lifted up a silver dish.

"Please take one of these sandwiches, Father. They're nothing at all."

"No thank you, Mrs. Girard."

He was conforming perhaps to some fast of his own invention, a private prohibition of cucumbers. He was thin, all skin and bones. He was waiting, she could see, to contest with her. And all she wanted was to be able to kneel, by means of a layer of horse-hair, in his horrible pews without a shooting pain in her legs.

"Another cup, then?"

He refused inaudibly. It was the silence of this priest, erect against her flowered, old, and by no means costly chintz, which was unsettling her. It was a bother now to go on with it. It had been a harebrained impulse. She rose from her chair.

"To get back to the cushions," she said, her hand fluttering nervously. "You don't understand what I had in mind. I have no doubt what you say about the South and India is true, but the fact remains I want to equip your pews here with cushions. You see, I don't care at all for your excellent golden-oak kneeling benches."

Father Cawder's eyes swung sideways as if to examine the lusters twinkling on the mantelshelf. It was obvious that the generosity of parishioners aroused in him no particular interest. How comfortable and pleased Father Magruder would have been. With the gift of blarney. The old-time priests were friendly and easy. Everything was lapsing, changing for the worse, Mrs. Girard thought to herself. The result of the depression, so they said, or war or communism. She found Father Cawder looking at her with a grimace, which, if it had not been for his probing glance, would have been a smile.

"What you mean," he said in a light exact tone, "is that the planks are hard. You find kneeling on them disagreeable, and so you wish to have them upholstered."

After an instant she decided to laugh at his irony. "Yes, that's what I mean. You take a low view, I gather, of my motives."

"I cannot say I approve of your plan for the cushions, Mrs. Girard. All this troubling over bodily comforts—in general, I mean, not this case of yours, particularly—none of it has much to do with what is

12

useful or desirable in a church, it seems to me. As it is, we have a furnace, storm doors, electric fans."

"Then you don't think that too much heat or cold can be a distraction?"

"People are urged on every side to look to their ease. It seems to me the Church ought to be kept clear of this cult of comfort. Christians are getting to be very soft, Mrs. Girard."

His voice had deepened; it grated with entirely unnecessary emotion. Mrs. Girard crossed to the window and looked out into the street. The sun was catching the gold leaf on the cupola of the town hall. This upstart priest with his accusing voice. Impertinently meaning to tell her off. He was telling her that in the eyes of God she was a draggled slattern of a woman. She pressed her fingers against the sill.

"Am I to understand," she said in a tone louder than she intended, "that you won't accept these cushions? You really won't have them at all, Father?"

The priest stood up in front of the coals pinkly flaring in the grate. "I see I have offended you. I am sorry for that, Mrs. Girard. I wasn't questioning your good intentions. I gave you my opinion as your pastor. These cushions in themselves are a small thing."

Mrs. Girard felt an angry warmth tingle in a wave over her skin. Give these priests an inch they try to take all they can grab. If they were left to have their way they would trample one under their feet. But it was thinkable. It was conceivable he was right. She was not too stiff-necked to admit he could be in the right about her. Before God she was a soft sinful creature.

"You have not offended me. What nonsense, Father." She turned back to the hearth. "I don't suppose I can think of any good reason to insist on the cushions. I see your point, if you won't have them."

"I am obliged to think well of self-denial. Even in small matters, Mrs. Girard. We have more reason to seek pain than to avoid it. Since our Lord was done to death on a gibbet as a criminal."

"It's at least natural to avoid pain," Mrs. Girard murmured. She shifted her glance from the priest's steady, somehow repellent eyes. "I will begin to think about something else for the church. Since you hate upholstery. I'm not particular. Anything but a new boiler."

What was it about him that repelled one? His manners were too precise, but not in any way boorish. And he did not spare himself, even if he ground others under his heel. He was far too thin, wasting away. He never ate enough. She ought to write the bishop to send him an order to eat more. "The carnival," he had said.

"The firemen's carnival, over at the fair grounds," Father Cawder repeated. "Have you ever gone?"

"Of course. Living in a clapboard house, it's sheer duty to go. I gamble and shoot off guns. I win great heaps of appalling china."

He had taken up his hat. He stopped at the silhouette of her great-great-uncle and seemed to inspect it above her head. Had she ever heard of a man named Diamond at any of the other carnivals? An acrobat by the name of Diamond? Had he ever come with the carnival before?

"Who is this man?"

"He does some kind of dive. From the top of a pole. Is he new this year?"

"I don't remember a diver last year."

"You never heard the name at any of the previous carnivals?"

"I don't think so. I never heard of him before."

The priest seemed to ponder as he put on his coat. She opened the door to the street and the silver bangles on her arm clashed together. As she spoke she studied her eyebrows in a mirror.

"I want you and Father Moran to dine with me soon. As a special favor to me, you understand. I'm quite aware you don't approve of dining out with ladies."

"I never take dinner away from home, Mrs. Girard.

14

I made it an invariable rule long ago. But it is kind of you to think of it."

"What about poor Father Moran? Is he forbidden my house too?"

"Father Moran is free to come, of course. Goodbye, Mrs. Girard."

"Good-bye, Father. I'm sorry you don't take to cushions. I'll find a substitute."

Mrs. Girard stood on her steps and watched him walk off past the spikes of iron fence. He had scarcely touched his tea. A creature comfort. It was good, in a way, to see and talk to Father Cawder. One got the habit of thinking well of oneself. If a woman had a little money and ran an orderly household sufficiently supplied with handsome silver and had never been tempted to sleep with a man not her husband and mailed in small checks to this and that officious charitable organization and went to Mass on Sunday, one got the habit of thinking and talking as if one were a good woman, whereas in truth she did little of any merit. Her life was merely orderly, made soft with too much heat, too rich food, a slough of bourgeois mediocrity. Before God all human beings stand convicted of sin. With the one exception. Pray for us, Holy Mother of God! Father Cawder was salutary. He made the pleasure of seeing the blue fronds of her Meissen reflected in a slab of waxed cherry, he made that dry pleasure a mortifying lust. There were many things she should do that she left undone. At the last judgment it would be humiliating to find oneself convicted of merely being soft.

Father Cawder had reached the end of the block. There he turned, reading the pink poster pasted across a wall. Mrs. Girard backed away from a gale of cold wind. Buffeting her head, it reminded her, as it always did, of poverty, hardship, and the chill of winter. She went into the house. "If it's hot I'll have another cup," she said aloud.

2

At THE CORNER OF THE STREET, FACING
the wall of green-stained bricks, Father Cawder stared
at the poster a moment without taking in the sense of
the words. Then he set himself to read it from top to
bottom. He saw the black outline of a rearing horse,
a Ferris wheel, a fat woman dressed as a child. From
a few feet away, the bulbous letters had seemed bands
of meaningless ornament. Now the black spots along
the edge fell into the shape of ANNUAL FIREMEN'S
BENEFIT. His eyes ran from line to line. *October
6 & 7—Handsome Assorted Prizes—Straight from
Rio—No Arms No Legs—The Whole Family.* THE
ONE AND ONLY, he read,

THE GREAT DIAMOND
YOU'LL GASP
when he makes that dive of his!
YES SIR!! HE'S A DIVING FOOL!!!
BOTH NIGHTS AT TEN

Diamond, a diving fool; a hired exhibitionist. An
acrobat unimaginable, a phantom. The man whom
God saw as his double, if he was to credit the im-
becilities of a dream. He was giving no credence to
the thing; it was no more than musing, figments of
make-believe. For the man's name, Diamond, need not
even be coincidence. Possibly he had seen the name,
read the poster, without being conscious of the act at
all; then, asleep and at the mercy of his pride, he had

constructed the whole artful parable of divine intervention—the beach of shingle, emerald water, the gray
specter whose name he imagined had been shouted in
his ear. He had seen the poster without knowing it
and the name had lodged in his mind. Or if not,
then it was coincidence; the name was common
enough—he was not obliged to suppose that this acrobat had bearing on himself merely because his name
was stated on a a poster to be Diamond.

The priest raised his head uneasily. This speculation, curiosity rather—was it in fact a neutral thing?
Was it even permissible for him, presuming to master
impulse, to indulge himself in curiosity? Since he
claimed to weigh the good or evil motions of his will,
it could be occasion of sin; it might hide the germ of
some defection. How could it not be occasion of sin,
keeping his mind from God, from his work? God, however, sees men outside of time and space. God does
not have respect to persons. He would let grace fall on
an acrobat according to His pleasure.

But the childish conceit was not plausible, almost—
almost nonsense it was. He chose to put off the issue,
lingering over it. Thus it could be enjoyed, like a
secret gloatingly kept. He did not wish, so it seemed,
to put a stop to this delectation. If a dream, what
then? A dream being the stuff of a brain incapable
in sleep, a phenomenon of no substance. A man aware
of human weakness could not innocently wish to wrest
meaning from a dream—one out of a thousand fragments of illusion remembered or not remembered
on awakening in a bed. If only because it was tempt-
ing God.

Father Cawder walked on, pale leaves crowding in
puffs of wind about his feet. Ella Johnston, diseased
and black—on his visit to her a short while before,
her clawed hands had joined in prayer, her loose lips
had repeated after him, humbly, suavely, the holy
names of Jesus and Mary; with her scaling cheeks
and piebald loathsome gums, Ella was a good woman,

17

humble sack of filth and plague, no doubt well-pleasing to God. If one compared—but this too was empty speculation. Who was able to say how God would distinguish between Ella Johnston and Mrs. Girard? The vain agreeable widow—"Where I was born, you know, Father, at our house on the Patuxent, we had our own chaplain till after the Civil War . . ." Mrs. Girard with her sentimental idolatries, the disreputable Negress enduring the evil of her body in a fusty bed. It was thinkable they were accorded equal rank in the affairs of God. And the diver too, whoever or whatever he was. Only God could assess a man for what he was in terms of reality.

A black shape entered the street at the far corner, struck out in the direction of the church with swinging arms: Father Moran, taking his constitutional —health was of great importance now to Moran. Every day he set himself to jog on the roads four miles or so, a version with him of religious duty. Father Cawder watched his assistant's diminishing back. It would not be necessary to submit to Father Moran's cheerful loquacity for an hour or more. It was just four-thirty. It was the day on which he chose to visit Mrs. Schroeder in her nursing home, listen for the twentieth time to the account of the start of the remarkable bakery she had founded forty years before— "I had just baked a pan of rolls, Father, and a lady came in and asked if they were for sale and I said, 'Why yes!'—"

He heard a faint, unlocalized sound above his head. Peering up into the sky, he walked at a slower pace with his neck thrown back. He saw them at last, geese, a gray foreshortened wedge, vastly distant, flying south by an instinct perfectly indifferent to the fates of men. For a moment he felt the pressure of a superb immensity. Ill at ease, abstracted, he stood and watched them till they were out of sight.

18

3

FATHER MORAN, ENTERING THE STREET, had glanced without recognition at Father Cawder motionless on the further corner. Now his eyes focused blindly on the shapes of white porches and fenced yards. Moving his head in sudden jerks as he paced the broken bricks, he seemed to cast about him glances of quick attention, but he observed nothing. Weariness, a grinding loneliness, something with a Latin name—decidua—acedia—what was it, theologically speaking? He did not remember. It weighed his shoulders, whatever its name; he felt it load his lungs like a weight, it filled veins and nerves, the pores of his bones. If he had been alone in his room he could have thrust his head between his hands and groaned. This pain—was it suffering?—loneliness sharp as a knife, from now on this was to be the core of his life. He would not have believed it possible. A priest lived to love God and for justice. But this ache of emptiness was like despair. What could it have to do with the love of God? He was to be alone until he died. That was the fact of which he had to be convinced. Not only that, everything he might work for throughout a lifetime would be without effect, whatever he might desire would be kept from him. A new world, a just society—certainly that was desirable, a desire put into men by God, a good and holy desire. And it now followed that he would never witness even the remote beginnings of a just society; whatever he might do would have no share in bringing it about.

While walking past the laundry he had thought the idea harmless enough, just to speak to the man behind the desk in the little office—who would object to that? "Making contacts," it was called, in the jargon of businessmen. Then perhaps he might be free to come again. He planned to make some brief reference to the heat and steam the Negresses sweated in, or to the noise, or to living expenses. And from there go on to touch, as if conversationally, on the debt of justice which lies on everybody. Surely if a man has good will he could not object to some such approach as that. In spite of prejudices which persuaded, beguiled everybody into living in injustice to others. Then later on—some extenuation of a sudden crisis, an understanding, some sort of union, a new agreement, maybe, made between the laundry and the colored women, and in the background himself, a tactful retiring arbitrator.

In the cramped office vibrating to the crashes of twenty machines he had to yell at the manager, a much younger, much more genial man than he had thought to see.

"The heat!" he had heard himself shriek. "Don't they mind the heat?"

The young man wrinkled his cleft pointed nose and laughed. "They love the heat!" he shouted. "The hotter the better!" He seemed to have no active dislike of the Church. Smiling, he had dragged forward a chair. He looked curious and amused at the same time. Maybe wondering why this priest had such a thing as temperature on his mind. He pulled out a dollar bill. For church expenses, on the laundry. Just community good will, Father.

The dollar bill was still in his hand, he noticed. There was no common ground, that was the trouble, no conviction shared in common on which you could meet these men. And so no approach was possible. In spite of being men, in spite of the fact that a desire for justice was common to all men. All his life pos-

20

sibly, probably, he would live in Lulworth and never in that time speak to another man who desired a new order, justice in a new society. Meanwhile, with a sermon or words exchanged on a street corner, ridiculously working for a time hidden in the future. But it was hard to expect a man to work all his life for something which could never take place till long after he had rotted back into the earth. How was it possible he could do nothing? What was the shell closing people in from his love of justice? Why was it words alone could not move them to a love of God? Nothing he might say or do could ever reach the wills consenting to so much injustice. It was a mystery, hard to bear. Father Moran, opening the gate in the fence, closed his mouth over a groan. Lumbering, suddenly tired, he went into the house.

He hung his hat on the clothes tree in the hall and started to mount the stairs. He remembered he still had his office to say. On the third step he paused. There is Father Cawder, he said to himself. It was queer, not understandable. Father Cawder was a good man. There were those practices of his which appeared slightly scandalous at first until it was evident that if he disapproved of Father Cawder he would have to condemn most of the saints too. Father Cawder was a priest almost extravagant in mortification which no vow or rule imposed, and yet he took hardly any interest in a new, a just social order. He could endure injustice. When a case was pointed out to him, he took it calmly—with a horrible calm. He had, Father Moran supposed, no natural sympathy toward economic problems. He never discussed strikes, he took no pleasure in arguing the right or wrong of a rate of interest. And as long as he himself was stationed in Lulworth he would never hear from him an understanding word. That, too, was hard to grasp, mysterious.

At the open door of Father Cawder's bedroom he halted for a moment, half-shamefully. The narrow, clean, ugly room contained a chair, a desk, a bed, a chest of drawers. Behind the curtain stretched across a corner he knew there hung a greenish cassock and Father Cawder's second suit, both many times repaired. The iron cot seemed like any other at a glance, but looking closely one glimpsed the boards laid across the frame in place of springs. Over these was spread a doubled thickness of khaki blankets, an arrangement meant not for comfort but to avoid the giving of excessive scandal to whatever aged gossiping female came in to dust the room. There were no pictures on the walls. Only an image of Our Lady of Lourdes on a little shelf, and above the bed a crucifix, a plaster Christ nailed to black wood.

Father Moran moved away into his own room. He picked up the breviary from the table beside the bed and lowered himself, with creaking joints, to his knees. Leaning against the mattress he covered his face with his arms. It was humiliating and painful, it was also an indescribable relief, he found himself unable to keep back the tears starting from his eyes.

4

DIAMOND—TO GIVE HIM HIS DUE, THE
Great Diamond—he could adequately imagine him, if
he chose, a hulking carcass moving wooden arms up a
ladder, plainly defined, except for his face, in a yellow light. Turning into the path to his front door,
Father Cawder observed the image in his mind: a
mountebank whose face was a pasty smudge, dressed
in a suit of black and white lozenges, poised on a
springboard. After the farm hands and schoolboys
gape at his somersaults, back he goes to a tent to
lounge and joke with the touts from the freak show,
shuffling a deck of greasy cards across a suitcase, re-
galing a knot of little boys with lies as to the height
of his pole, previous perilous feats on tightropes and
trapezes. Father Cawder stepped into the hall and hung
his coat and hat on a peg. He started across the floor.
Father Moran's glasses, magnifying pale round eyes,
were trained on him, he saw, from the parlor.

"I didn't have a chance to ask you about Ella,
Father. How did you find her?"

Father Cawder glanced briefly at his assistant's face,
pink and intent. Apparently he could not bear to wait
an instant before mentioning the old woman. In the
unrepressed animal spirits which young men consider
enthusiasm.

"She's got worse, but she seems patient and doesn't
complain much of her pains. I left her five dollars—
you can enter it for me in the accounts, if you will.

She's been living on corn meal. She says she has no money for anything else."

"Don't you think she's dying?" Father Moran craned forward in his eagerness. "That's why I thought you went. I thought sure she was really going this time."

Father Cawder pushed a chair toward the table and sat down.

"No, she's not dying yet. Ella may last a long while. In a day or so I'm going to take her Communion. It's not—"

"I—" Father Moran interrupted, "I'd be glad to take Communion to Ella, Father. I'd be glad to, if it's all the same with you."

His eyes blinked from the other side of the room as if in a glare. Women parishioners, it was likely, were pleasantly stirred by his fresh-colored, earnest face. But with his vice of engrossing impulses he would be improved by a routine of discipline; he gave in to his will.

"It's best," Father Cawder said, "for me to go, Father. Sick calls are among those duties which I believe a pastor should perform himself. They don't give me much pleasure, unfortunately."

Father Moran turned away with a blush which began above his shining collar and spread slowly over his face. It could seem that a strong devotional sensation had been denied him. Pity for the unwary emotions of young men slightly lifted in Father Cawder. To be fair, there was something more substantial underneath the thin show of sentiment in poor Moran. He might be charitably assumed to have recognized an old woman's resemblance in suffering to our Lord, men in pain and want being living mysterious images of the Word made flesh. It was strange how hard it was to do justice to well-intentioned sentimentalists, to poor Moran.

Father Moran had mildly, shyly raised his eyes. "Would you mind very much taking up our argument again, Father? I've been thinking a good deal about our expenses here. I'm pretty sure we've got enough surplus to make some kind of a start—I mean, in a real way, of course."

"Last week I thought you agreed Lulworth was not just the place for a soup kitchen." Father Cawder unlaced his fingers. "Or is it a different plan now?"

Father Moran laughed. "I know I was out on a limb about that soup kitchen, Father. I've been getting around to the other angles—" he paused and got to his feet, awkwardly searching for words. "What's wrong is the way we don't take the form of society into account. When we give out alms it's just as though we had no idea we are living in an monopolistic industrialized society."

"It may be so." A vague unrest flickered through Father Cawder's mind. Was he being inconsistent, he wondered, remembering the pink poster? Could he reasonably despise a diver, the unknown exhibitionist of side shows, one of a whole class of men presumed to be dead in good works, and who therefore were the poor in a metaphysical sense? He was not guilty of despising a man who was poor in worldly goods.

"Would you mind," Father Moran said, frowning, "if I tried a sort of an overhauling on paper? Our expenditures, I mean. I'd like to estimate costs—maybe work up a scheme of new methods. Then you could see whether—" he paused clumsily.

"If you want to do that, go ahead. These new methods—"

"If there were one or two factories here," Father Moran broke in, "we might get a pointer or two by working with the union. But of course, people—" In his eagerness his voice rose and became louder. "I've been thinking we might revamp the Saint Vincent de Paul Society, branch out to take care of sick people like Ella. Feeling our way forward in a small way. Then as we got going maybe we could think about a clinic or some kind of co-operative, whatever seems best."

"Those who help the poor," Father Cawder said,

25

"are expected to render their services in person, according to the mind of the Church." His eyes lifted to a crack meandering across the ceiling. "The corporal works of mercy. Start from them if you want to make changes." He let his glance fall to a patch of blood-red wool worked into the figured carpet.

That afternoon in Ella's hut, a sagging shed built perhaps to house turkeys, the one window nailed up with cardboard wherever panes had fallen out long before. Stooping to enter, he had felt, he remembered, that these casual intrusions were a slightening of the charity owed by all Christians to one another—they seemed . . . magisterial. The methods of some prying official census-taker. It was not clear to Ella Johnston that a priest might consider his visits to her as a means of grace. Yet almsgiving was as essential to salvation as prayer. So necessary that you could reasonably conclude the rich to be damned without it. Saving God's imperceptible mercies. Beyond duty there was also much excellent mortification for the soft and comfort-loving in these filthy hutches. The eyes of the old colored woman rolled up under lids that seemed to be falling apart in a powdery scurf. But Father Moran was speaking. He had become voluble, his voice creaking in excitement.

"——food and shelter," his glasses blindly winked. "They need somebody to come to for advice, for help at any time, not just emergencies. In any kind of trouble. Money and lawsuits and the loansharks, everything like that. They need an organization behind them."

"Organization is not charity," Father Cawder said abruptly. "Our Lord did these things in His own person. He didn't need a committee to decide that a hungry man ought to have food."

Pulling at his collar, Father Moran cleared his throat. He opened his mouth but said nothing.

"What do you suggest about a case like Ella's? Do you think we should hire a professional nurse? Call in

26

some other woman? Or would you be willing to clean and dress Ella's arms yourself?"

"I don't see—why should you or I do things of that kind? Her sister Nettie probably comes in and takes care of her. Or get somebody else. Why not? Why do you think this is important, Father?"

"It has nothing to do with importance." Inflecting this last word, Father Cawder rose to his feet. Acts of charity undertaken by Christians were no more to Moran, it seemed, than any other meddling social service, a primitive, certainly less antiseptic, Red Cross. "It's not important, in a therapeutic sense. But the Church means us to perform the works of mercy ourselves. Ella's neck and arms, naturally, are disgusting. They are broken out with ulcers. But Saint John of God would have cleaned and bandaged them himself if he had been in our place. Even kissed them, if his biographers are to be believed. You find that exaggerated, do you, somewhat morbid?"

Father Moran looked to one side and compressed his jaws. It was evident he did not understand, or perhaps he disagreed. Or he had not been listening. Father Cawder moved away.

"Our Lord and the saints served the poor themselves, they didn't act by deputy."

Moran still sat hunched, quietly uncomprehending. He was frowning, looking intently downward at a thumbnail. If the dream was nothing more than a prank of his own brain, Father Cawder thought suddenly, it could hold no interest, an ironic trick plotted by himself in the idiocy of sleep. An act of will could pluck its fatuous hints from his mind. But there was at least the other possibility—prospect full of terror, since who does not properly fear the motions of God? Admitting that portents have served the ways of God to men. At Bethel Jacob dreamed. And Daniel interpreted dreams without censure. A dream gave warning to Pharaoh and Pilate's wife and Saint Joseph, to Pope Innocent, Oliver Cromwell.

Father Cawder lifted his eyes. "You and I are not saints, luckily," he said after a pause. "You are not obliged to put your mouth to the running sores on an old woman's arms if you find yourself squeamish."

Father Moran leaned forward and pulled out a handkerchief. Over his forehead a moisture glistened like fine drops of rain. Father Cawder noticed he had shut his eyes. He crossed the room to his chair.

"What is it? Can I get you something?"

Father Moran stumbled to his feet in silence, his handkerchief pressed to his lips. Father Cawder turned the pages of his breviary. When he looked up Father Moran had gone round the table.

"I'm really all right. It was just—it was only a second."

Father Cawder glanced beyond him into the shadows of the hall, as if toward a third person. "That was my fault, Father. You should try not to let words affect you so easily. I'll tell Mrs. McGovern to bring you a glass of hot water."

Father Moran shook his head. "No, I don't want anything."

"Very well. But hot water would do you good. If I were you I'd drink a glass. I must finish my office."

Father Cawder pushed a holy card back into place in his breviary. Then he left the room.

5

$\mathbf{F}$ROM THE HEAD OF THE TABLE, ABOVE A plate of collards and hominy, Father Cawder observed Father Moran with a now familiar instant of irritation. His assistant was about to slice off a second helping of meat. The topic, as like as not, had never presented itself—the nightly cramming of his stomach with the blood and tissues of animals. It failed to apply to a parish priest who took it as his due to glut his body after a busy day. Father Cawder saw a bead of gravy glistening on Father Moran's lower lip. He himself had avoided the pleasure of meat for twelve years.

The two priests looked up as the pantry door swung violently open. Mrs. McGovern caught the door against an elbow and surveyed the table. This was her method of hurrying them forward to dessert. As she turned again into the pantry, her rosary beads clattered against the wall. Father Cawder remembered he must speak to the old woman once again about her practices with her beads. It would be for the third, certainly the last, time. At every meal she irreverently banged and clattered about the table, swinging the chaplet of the mother of God from her belt as if it were a toy or some gimcrack bauble. She was an irreligious woman, filled with a rampant self-will.

Father Moran cleared his throat, about to speak; but he looked away in silence, Father Cawder absently noticed. The coincidence, if that was what it was, hinged on the poster, he was repeating to himself. It was due to the poster that the name Diamond skimmed back

29

and forth across the surface of his mind. If he had not chanced to see the word blackly flashing down from the pink billboard, the dream would have had no further meaning at all. There it had been, boldly eyeing him in the beaded lettering of a small-town circus: THE GREAT DIAMOND.

It was a concurrence of sounds. The hard-eyed wraith in voluminous white who may or may not have been Ned Owen, according to the nature of dreams; he had certainly used the word, spoken the name of the gray figure whose face was only a yellowish smudge. In the dream now falling back into nothingness the name "Diamond" had been clearly pronounced, the gray nonentity had been identified. And then on the following day he had passed a poster on the street giving notice that during the firemen's carnival a certain Diamond would perform. That was the meager fact to which he tried to attach the absurd contingency. Would he hear out a penitent come to the confessional with some such tale, dreams and omens, supernatural rank, one Diamond, an itinerant acrobat? He need not search beyond a loathsome spiritual pride, if he wished to interpret the thing. Why did he spare himself?

Wood smartly rapped on wood recalled Father Cawder to the dinner table. Her nun's rosary swinging from her waist, Mrs. McGovern was sweeping the dishes from cloth to sideboard with large gestures. Her bright black eyes fixed on the bowl in her hands, she set down the Spanish cream with a flourish. A report like the blow of a hammer sounded from her crucifix. She wheeled at the door to face the priests.

"Well, Father," she asked loudly, "is there anything else now I can serve you with?"

Father Cawder helped Father Moran to the custard. "Nothing more. After dinner I would like a word with you, Mrs. McGovern."

Her shaggy eyebrows, suddenly rising, suggested she was weighing a proposal of momentous risks. Then she smiled with pursed lips. It was the same smile which had seemed only queer at first but which now struck the priest as an expression of clownish ill will. The old woman was not, perhaps, altogether in her right mind.

"Very well, Father." She made a quick movement with her knees, the sort of bobbing curtsy little girls are taught to make in convents. In the case of Mrs. McGovern, clothed in black serge and contorting her hairy expressive face, the rapid dipping roused, as it had before, a brief vexation in Father Cawder. He waited until the pantry door pivoted shut behind her.

"We will have to see about making a change before very long," he said in an unhurried voice. "In Mrs. McGovern. The longer she stays here the worse she seems to get."

Father Moran coughed lightly into the tips of his fingers.

"She might have a time getting another job, Father. Couldn't you tell her she was to have another month's trial? Maybe she'll improve."

Father Cawder drew his napkin firmly across his mouth.

"I don't think the frame of mind she's in allows her to improve. It was a mistake, I see now, to have brought her here in the beginning. She has no business in a priest's household. We must be looking around for someone to take her place."

"Where will she go if she leaves? Shouldn't she get a month's notice?"

A look of perplexity came over Father Moran's face. Father Cawder, before answering him, disengaged a spoonful of gelatin.

"You can make yourself easy, Father. No injustice will be done Mrs. McGovern. When she leaves she can go to her daughter's, or up to Frederick to her son's."

"I think she's a pretty good cook."

"That may be. But she's not at all suitable for her

other duties here. We must try to find someone else."

Wrinkling his forehead, Father Moran turned back to his dessert.

And yet, Father Cawder mused, it was a thing that could be thought. It was not impossible to God. If it was presumptuous to think the finger of God might point out a circus performer as in a parable, an unknowable portentous gesture—on the other hand it was not permitted to limit God. Forbidding Him intervention, if such was His will. He could make use of a priest in a country town, allying him in some not unimaginable way with a carnival acrobat. If He wished He could make His will known in intelligible form, projecting analogies on a man inert in sleep, inclining a human will to His mysteries. If it was the will of God! Before he slept, once and for all, it must be dealt with—plaguing doubt, ridiculously possessing him like an ache, like a bodily constriction. Before he slept, again loosening his brain from its discipline.

Father Moran rose in front of his chair and mumbled grace. With a flick of his hand he made the sign of the cross.

"Excuse me, Father," he said. "I want to make the seven o'clock mail."

Left alone, Father Cawder leaned back in the oak armchair at the head of the table. For a few seconds he was motionless, his chin pushed down into the slack seams of his neck. Then he rang the brass bell beside the saltcellar.

Mrs. McGovern paced in slowly. She stopped behind an empty chair and folded her arms across it as over a gate in a fence. He took it some inward amusement was enlivening the old woman. Under the black hairs of her eyebrows her eyes flashed as if with a relish of some pleasure before her. A sounding brogue, richly rolled out, filled the room.

"Here I am at your service, Father."

The priest watched her in silence. His glance fell on her massive haunches, her swelling bosom, the shift-

32

ing sharp eyes. Her dark hair was lustrous and combed in waves; it gave her a matronly dignity. Folding his napkin he looked away and began to speak.

"Mrs. McGovern, I wanted to talk to you tonight because tomorrow your new week begins. You remember, when you came, I said I would see after a time how things were going. I have been—"

"So you're firing me, Father," she interrupted. Her smile became broader and more meaning.

"I believe it would be best if you made your plans to leave," he went on easily. "I know the work here is considerable for a woman of your age. As far as the meals go, Father Moran and I have no fault to find with your cooking. But I don't think you will easily learn how other things should be managed here. I want you to make arrangements to leave at the end of the coming week, Mrs. McGovern. That is, a week from this Friday."

"So you're firing me." Breathing deeply, she straightened herself up. "Are you firing me without giving me the information as to how I've done wrong, Father? I'd be pleased to be told, thank you kindly."

"You will have an extra week's wages. That is to say, you have two weeks' notice, starting from this Friday."

Mrs. McGovern still smiled while her voice plaintively rose. "I've done every little thing you tell me and over. What else can I do for his reverence now, I keep saying to myself. And every night I say my perpetual novena to Saint Jude and I always say a little prayer for you, Father Cawder. I want to be told now just what it is I've done wrong."

The priest gazed down the length of the tablecloth. "Your beads, your rosary. Do you remember, Mrs. McGovern? I spoke to you several times about wearing your beads."

"Oh, very well, Father." She settled her hands on the slope of her hips.

"If you remember, I asked you not to wear your

rosary beads when about your work. In your room, I said, if you wish, but not at your work. I spoke of it twice to you, but you chose not to do as I asked. You wore your beads tonight at dinner. There they are still. This practice of yours displeases me, Mrs. McGovern. It is disrespectful as well to the Blessed Virgin. You have not done as I wished."

Mrs. McGovern listened frowning, her eyes cast down. Her voice suddenly spurted in a gasping whisper.

"My whole life I've never done a thing wrong, Father Cawder! I've tried and I've tried till I'm sick of it, trying to please you and the other priest. Little thanks I get! Now you order me to take off my beads. Oh, don't you worry, Father Cawder." As she wagged her head her teeth flashed. "The Holy Mother of God's got her eyes on every little act of yours. She sees the slights some are putting on her here in this house."

Father Cawder looked up at her with a slanting stare. "It will be better for you to leave in the morning, Mrs. McGovern," he said in an even tone. "You will have two weeks' wages. Now get up to your room, as soon as you have finished your work."

The old woman lifted up her large crucifix, kissed it and stuck it carefully into her belt. She smoothed out her waist and hair with composure. Getting ready to speak, she rolled her eyes ludicrously to one side.

"I'll go out of here and glad to, your reverence! Oh, yes!" she pronounced richly, "I'll go. But the Holy Mary's not the one to let herself be slighted. Oh, you'll see. She'll pay you back. She'll pay you back good and plenty."

"Finish what you have to do, Mrs. McGovern, then get up to your room." He moved away toward the door.

She looked as if she was composing a retort, her head bowed in thought. With a sudden smile she reached for the bowl of Spanish cream. Straining back her shoulders she turned and left the room.

Father Cawder watched the door swing inward behind her. How innocent he was in his dealings with human personalities—not to have suspected the mere appearance of the ranting irreverent old woman in the first place, to have judged the woman fit for a household of two priests! "A respectable pious widow" had been the terms in which she had been recommended. A harridan who was no more Christian in her motives than the witch doctor of a tribe of Zulus. And sacrilegious. Contesting with her voice one who by undoubted ordinance was her superior, handling the cross as if it were a clenched fist against the evil eye.

He went into the hall, opened the side door and stepped out to the strip of lawn. He felt a lurking misgiving. He had by no means shown a perfect indifference toward the trivial passions of this old woman. He was a novice still, like any man twisted this way and that by impulse. A chrysanthemum, loaded with cold dew, struck against his hand as he passed. He bent to pull the glimmering flower from its stalk. While his head was lowered his eyes caught the fresh pink of a poster under the light on the far side of the street. *You will be Amazed. Each Night at Ten. A Diving Fool.* He did not need to read it. *The Great Diamond.*

Through the uncurtained window Father Cawder looked up into the parlor. There was Moran ruddy under the lamp, his evening's reading beside him, the comic sheet, the sports page, the new *Commonweal*. The priest gazed overhead at the scudding clouds, he sniffed the air wafted through the leaves. The scent of spicebush rose through the dark as his arm shook a branch.

6

ACCORDING TO HIS PRACTICE FATHER Cawder knelt at the foot of his bed till ten o'clock. His beads revolving through his fingers, straightening his back when he felt his shoulders start to slump, he prayed for the Pope's intention, recited the fifteen decades, the hundred and fifty Hail Marys, meditating, as his lips moved, on the passion of Christ. He examined his conscience. He was able to bring to mind reflexes of anger, avoidances of discomfort, pleasure in foolish fruitless thoughts. He had sinned as always in pride, anger, and sloth. To gratify an instinct of depraved human nature he had freely permitted himself anger toward Mrs. McGovern, an addled creature hardly answerable for anything. He had taken pleasure in pride with respect to Father Moran, dealt with him in contempt. For his sins it was proper to offer God the statement, superfluous though it might seem, that he was sorry. As on every night he could propose to amend. Given the grace from God.

Effortlessly, without his knowing, his mind slipped at ease, he was looking down from a height into a country fair. The side of the night was strung with lights like ropes of pearls; swags of luminous pink balls swayed in a shimmer of vapor. A crowd of men and women pushed under the lights and the vague trees, some were laughing and singing, they ran forward in S-shaped queues, their faces flashing in the glare of sparkling booths. And like a shooting star the diver vaulted from his perch, down into a plain of eddying upturned eyes and open mouths. Soon, he said to himself, rising from his knees, I will settle you shortly, Diamond. He undressed and went into the bathroom.

In the looking glass above the washbasin he allowed his eyes to rest on the greenish reflection of his body. His flesh looked dry. Streaks of blue shadow were cast over the drawn skin by the bones of his chest and his ribs. With the black hairs springing from his nipples, the protruding bones, his body caught for an instant the violated ugliness of a headless fowl, plucked and blue and flung aside on a butcher's block. He picked up the soap and began to wash. He covered his chest with water just tepid enough to make an easy lather.

Washing, although debased to a luxury through the propaganda of soap manufacturers, still had its usefulness. It served the body's ends, it freed the mind from preoccupation with the itch of a dirty skin. But a strict moralist, he reflected, could find occasion of sin in a daily hot bath. And advertisements of plumbing fixtures urged even farmers and factory workers to the habits of a harlot. In the present world a man with dirty nails or face seemed morally at fault. Our Lord, seen as He had lived, would be suspect. Many a humanitarian in clean linen would start back from a sight of Christ as He looked on earth. He and His Mother, paupers in draggled clothes, their undefiled flesh streaked with dust and sweat. Standing on the bathmat, Father Cawder rinsed the suds lathered over his body with a sponge.

When he had brushed his teeth he walked back slowly to his room. He sat down on the cot and covered his eyes with a cupped hand. Now was the time. If he still remembered all of it. Two days before, fitting it together like pieces of a puzzle while he went along a street, he remembered even the searching tone of an ironic or peremptory voice. Now the dream was sliding away out of reach into his mind. As he woke from sleep it had been like the end of a perilous, im-

37

mensely long journey. Waking at dawn, here on this cot, possessed by phantoms. Curious over merit had he been, the quality of his own good works? Ned Owen had called to him, grinning, wearing the cassock of a Jesuit scholastic, beckoning from a cliff's edge. Ned was urging him on. Come here, if you want to find out—was that what he said? Come and see. Ned had smiled, enjoying the spectacle of another's shameless vanity. He saw himself run forward, eager, it seemed, to learn the degree of his favor with God. He stumbled to an edge of shelving grass and looked over into stark colors and vast spaces like another world—all of it converged on a beach of shingle, sheets of emerald glitter, a lake reaching to infinity, to banks of sublime clouds, splendid, pink, massed like citadels. There was a man standing on the pebbles, a lumpish grayish figure with his back turned. In each hand he carried a bundle, a basket or a bag of old clothes. Or it was firewood he carried, scuttles full of coal. In spite of the bundles the gray figure began to move on, lightly, without effort. He had felt afraid.

Ned Owen was at his side. Only he was not the same—his face had darkened, grown longer, and he was wrapped in linen like a toga, voluminous white folds. Taller, in some way threatening, he pointed his arm at the man below them. There he is, he possibly said, there is the one you wished to see, that man and you have equal merit, you are worth what he is worth, in the eyes of God. Perhaps he himself spoke then, he must have asked, "Who is he? What is his name?"

The giant who was certainly no longer Ned Owen raised his inhuman voice, laughed superhumanly. He waved a billowing sleeve. "Diamond! That is Diamond!" The word was distinct, it rang in his ear. He himself slipped downward over rocks; he meant to slide down the scarp of shale, reach the dark-green water flecked with white foam, see this man face to face. For the man had stopped to look round, was looking upward out of smudged eyes in a face blank and

38

blurred. Then all at once the air darkened and he was somewhere else. He was going down a road in the dark, over cobbles, past great walls built of stucco. The plaster had fallen off from damp and the bricks underneath showed in patches. Dawn seemed to break through a smokelike sky——he had opened his eyes on the ceiling of his room growing light with morning.

He had stopped short at the wrinkled pink poster. His glance held to the name as if it were somehow familiar. It implied some memory. But it had an ordinary sound, the bulging letters might just as well have read 'Fletcher' or 'Miller,' it suited the billboard of a carnival. There was the dream, he had recollected abruptly, calmly. Like a reel of pictures, a sheet of water, fragments of clouds, the face of the Rev. Edward Owen, S.J., passed through his mind, a wall of stucco fallen into ruin. Walking toward the bank, with caution, barely consenting in his will, he had patched the thing together. The furtive procedure seemed in some way shameful. Yet the fading images hung together in sequence of a sort. Or he could pretend to think so, if he wished to amuse himself.

The unashamed silliness—in sleep his brain, like an old peasant woman's, was free to delve into distinctions of spiritual prestige. His pride had not ventured beyond ambiguity, at any rate. The man conjured up to be his spiritual equation was merely a phantasm with a blank face called by a common name. The dream had been of use in showing up the energy of his pride. Was it permitted to inquire into any further function? If the featureless, reedy gray figure and the diver were to be taken for one and the same man, if he confronted him, if—the argument was abominable —the man in the carnival might have some imagined bearing on himself, what then? Sitting on the side of the bed, the priest pressed his palm against his chin cautiously, with distaste. With no reaction of shame he was almost imagining a dream to be supernatural intimation. Like a gypsy or a table-rapper. Like the gulls

39

of gypsies, the female dupes of crystal globes and ten-cent horoscopes. And his eyes could have fallen on the poster without his knowing; he might have passed it ten times unawares, read a name at random, forgotten it again, then in the witless adventuring of sleep drawn it back into consciousness to trick out the furnishings of a dream—in that case, none of it meant anything at all.

He gave a brief, almost inaudible laugh and got to his feet. Against this overweaning parable or dream he kept one last argument. He was not willing to submit to its terms. To touch on premises which equated him with a man hired to entertain mobs by feats of self-display. The inference was beside the point. Favoring a man, God hardly cared whether he was literate or clean or skilled or of pleasing address.

With his fingers knit together Father Cawder glanced at the crucifix on the wall. He drew his hands apart in impatience. It was time to cut short this self-important casuistry. For a Christian it was more becoming to regard what could not inconceivably be a motion of God's will with a child's unfidgeting trust. As a child listens to the voice of his father. As if God, like a man, had no idea of His own causes or effects!

As he pulled back the bedclothes he felt a springing joy. He was free not to commit himself. All he need do was to see this man; he could go, expecting nothing, desiring nothing. It was good to refuse scruples, hairsplittings which to God must only be proof of man's cloddish impertinence. It was proper to be ready to accept the terms, the possible terms, of God without condition, like a child, like a servant attentive to the nod of his master. In the night as he lay asleep it could, not impossibly, have been God's will that his dull understanding should be cleft by a spark from the blinding day of His being, grossly interpreted as a landscape of rock and cloud, a lake, a silent man. He felt the joyful calm diffusing through him like a flow of cool wind. He switched off the light, aware, in his mind, in his body, of a shock of bliss, a piercing pathos. He could end, if he wanted, this comical indecision. He could go without subterfuge to look at this man. His actions not binding God, in spite of what he did or did not do, God's will would still be done.

He stretched himself out on the planks covered with blankets and shut his eyes. I will go and see for myself, he thought, with no plan, without scruples, like a child.

7

MRS. GIRARD GLIMPSED FATHER CAWDER
ahead of her. As he paused to settle his hat in the
rocking wind, she hurried forward. She meant to over-
take him at the corner of the street. The gypsy woman,
she noticed, lounged with splayed feet in front of her
shop. She was making ready to spit, inevitably, a li-
censed fortuneteller dressed in filthy green silks. Mrs.
Girard saw the priest turning toward the litter of bottles and rusting buckets around Ella Johnston's shack.
By the time she reached the fence he had disappeared
inside. She laid with care three fingers of a white-
gloved hand on a picket black with damp. It was only
a sick call. He would scarcely stay longer than was required at Ella Johnston's. At the sight of the scaling hut
she felt a flicker of disgust. The shack with its one
window askew looked infectious, breeding mildew,
nameless bacteria. Just to see it seemed to communi-
cate uncleanness. She faced the street. She could wait
a minute or two.

"About the cushions," she would begin. "I've
changed my mind. It's the planting around the church
I'm taking exception to now. How would you like two
dogwood trees on each side of the walk?" Or better, use
a bolder opening and intimidate him. "My dear Father,
I'm giving you two handsome trees, I've decided."
Mrs. Girard's eyes rested on a bedspring rotting to
pieces against the fence. They swung downward to her
shoes.

As if breathing air infected by Ella Johnston were

not enough, she was also spattered now with mud; black drops of it clung to her stockings. Bad pavements were enraging. Life was so full of exasperating grossness, it was curious one could not be spared a petty thing like a puddle. But so God willed, apparently, pinprick after pinprick. Perhaps at her age a biological law determined she should busy herself with the fates of children if she was to take her ease without any twitch of nerves. She was a woman whom God must consider a failure, biologically speaking, having presented to Him only the two poor little nothings, red rags of flesh obscenely disposed of like a nastiness, the souls of the poor things locked in limbo for all eternity. Now with a big girl on her hands she would have no time to bother about soiled gloves, holes burnt in table tops by cigarettes, the scarcity of leeks, boring middle-class minutiae. It would be soothing to have a girl to dress in virginal washable white, a blond virgin with ignorant eyes fresh from the Sacred Heart, to put to rout ineligible presuming bounders, to launch a plot with mothers and aunts to carry off exactly the right broad-shouldered rich Catholic young man to bed with her girl for life, a young man not too bookish, not money-grubbing, certainly not a broker, not painfully horsy. Mrs. Rozier's nephew Dan, since he was heir to Nanjemoy, would do to begin with, in spite of droopy eyes. It would have been amusing to conceive of deviling old Mrs. Rozier, by means of a pretty daughter, right out of her manorial halls. But her mind, in its silly way, ran on. A poor time of life to be marrying off nonexistent daughters. Certainly it was now sixteen years since a man, since Ben, that is, had taken it into his head for the last time to slip between her sheets, unhumorously disposing her legs with his cold narrow feet.

Inside the shack Ella Johnston lay in Ben's mother's beetling walnut bed. "Poor old body," Mrs. Girard murmured. Poor creature, lying inside like a mongrel cur nobody wants. Twenty years before she had been a

43

good cook, expert with popovers. Before she got in trouble with men, slashed and carried shouting off to jail. Now she was not tolerable even in the privacy of a kitchen, less like a woman than a rank evil-smelling gorilla. Doubtless she drank as well. The two things usually went together. A cook who was both loose and a drunkard could hardly be kept on even by a saint.

Disease was killing the woman. Syphilis, fleshly sentence meted out by providence to violators of the moral law! At any rate, of a sizable bit of the moral law. A case of syphilis could be edifying in a sense, it occurred to Mrs. Girard. The sin of fornication, fallen to in the bins of vulgar brothels, was followed by a punishment which was physical and almost mechanical. Divine justice assumed for once an Old-Testament simplicity.

"The poor woman," she said under her breath, "she'll be better off dead."

And Father Cawder, wasting himself on syphilitic Negresses, ready like Saint Catherine of Genoa to minister to lepers or anyone else sufficiently repulsive. It was all in a way part of his style, the flair of the zealot. But to visit the sick and the dying is a command of our Lord. Such activities therefore are proper to zealous clergymen. She brought to mind the only gift she had ever made to Father Cawder, just after he arrived, eight short years before. It had been a fat capon, baked to perfection, plumped up in a pretty basket beside a bottle of the three-dollar sherry. A gesture which would have drawn from old Father Magruder many a cheerful smile and protest of old-fashioned flattery. Father Magruder's successor was of a different stamp. The following day the sexton brought the basket back, chicken and all, with a civil note. The note made as if to thank her for her kind intention. At the same time it rebuffed an attempt to ply the clergy with inappropriate luxuries. It had been too stupidly insulting. He could have sent the chicken to some old in-

44

valid or worthy widow. Clownishly returning a gift of welcome! She had decided to call on him.

To make apology for her lapse of taste. She went primed to put the man in his place. A little priest meaning to dress her down, and she sprung from a race of land-owning squires who had defended the faith with renown for eight hundred years, in Lancashire no less than in Calvert County! She remembered coming to a halt just beyond the door saddle. His hard, blue, somewhat menacing stare confused her. She probably stammered some pointless compliment. She was given a rather dry homily on self-denial, the season of the year being, it seemed, the lesser fast of Advent. She had instantly been pleased against her will. She had been wrong about him. He cared for no niceties, he was not worldly, that was all. With no respect for persons. Like God he was unpleasantly democratic. He perceived no gradations between her and Mr. Birdseye, president of a bank and grandson of a hotel proprietor, between Birdseye and a dirty Negro begot by slaves.

He is taking a deal of time, Mrs. Girard said to herself. She looked round toward the window of the shack. A light was being shifted inside. He had perhaps brought the woman the viaticum. He would be unwilling to chat about cushions and dogwood trees if he was carrying the Sacrament. She was not sure, in that case, what to do. In France she would be expected to kneel down in the street, warned by the boy with a bell. Kneeling here on the bricks was possible, her stocking being already ruined by the mud. On the other hand he had no use for singularity, anything like affectation in these matters. There were still the chops to buy, she thought all at once, since Nancy Poe was coming to dinner, rib chops, now that Nancy, like all old maids untempered by male complacency, was getting so fussy. Waiting like a seamstress on the streets, how absurd she was, taken up with priests and shrubs. She had still many things to do before four o'clock. A

45

thimble to be bought, kitchen soap, a fifth of bourbon, a new lipstick, some fresh salmon. Salmon forked over with lemon juice and plenty of good honest home-made mayonnaise. On the side, vegetables in aspic and lots of watercress.

Mrs. Girard adjusted round her neck two sable pelts. As she did so, a man who was bearing down on her along the pickets touched his hand to his hat. The slipshod gesture! Worse than no greeting at all, it seemed to her, the ample proportions of politeness reduced to this slovenly pecking.

"Father Moran!" she exclaimed with a smile. "I didn't see it was you! I'm waiting here for Father Cawder. I hope he doesn't plan to spend the whole afternoon in there with old Ella."

"How have you been, Mrs. Girard?" Above a shiny and probably celluloid Roman collar, the boyish face smiled back at her. "Ella's got a lot weaker. Father Cawder stopped in to see her a day or so ago. I expect he's gone back to give her Communion. I don't think she'll last much longer. It will be a blessing for her when she goes."

"Poor old Ella!" Her voice rose to a higher key. "Oh dear! If he's anointing Ella, I'll see him another time. He wouldn't want to stop to talk now. Anyway, it wasn't important."

"Shall I tell him you want to see him?"

"Lord, no. It's nothing that can't wait. I was wandering the streets like a lost soul and I saw him and thought I'd waylay him. What about your bank? Have you planted it yet?"

"My bank, Mrs. Girard?"

"The bank along the apse. You did ask my advice, you know. What have you done with it?"

"Father Cawder had ivy put on it."

"It'll never thrive, mark my word. Far too much sun. Dwarf cotoneaster is what I'd have put. But no one does as I say. I'm terribly chagrined. Arctostaphylos uva-ursi would be nice too."

46

"What is that?"

"Oh, a plant, a divine little thing. Well, when your ivy dies I'll advise you all over again." Mrs. Girard, smiling, moved off a step. "Good day, Father," she called out with a graceful brightness.

8

REACHING ACROSS THE ALTAR, FATHER
Cawder thrust the pyx into the darkness between the
curtains, shut the door of the tabernacle and turned
the key. He stood still with his eyes raised to the windows. The last of daylight glimmered in them—watery
blue and green, dusky reds. The dim air seemed to lap
over him in soundless waves. It was like, after a day
spent in the burning sun, coming into some thickset
grove. He breathed suddenly with relief. Now for the
first time since morning he could feel himself free of
small compulsions, of the duty to expel wayward or unprofitable impulses, also to exhibit patience at the un-
reason of members of the foolish human race. They
were fools in a scriptural sense, fools who asserted in
their most secret thoughts, for all their unction, that
there was no God, idolaters of molecules and nervous
reactions. Sometimes like poor Father Moran, merely
womanish. "Have mercy on us, Jesus!" Looking at the
altar he moved his lips. Then he genuflected toward
the tabernacle and went down the five marble steps.

The trailer had been gliding round the corner of the
street. Recollecting the scene, Father Cawder passed
through the gate in the communion-rail and shut it
after him. Barred by the gate in Ella's fence, still hearing her mumbling slow contralto voice, he had turned
and seen it. Slightly aslant it had dipped behind the
trees on the curb, become foreshortened, vanished in-
distinctly into the leaves of hedges. The name DIA-
MOND was painted in white letters across its side.

And in the car to which it was fastened there had been a man—at least, he had for an instant seen a head, a dark patch, recognizable, the outline of a human being. His eyes had followed the trailer with nothing more than surprise, he imagined. It was an ordinary feeling. Mere surprise that the man existed. He was startled that the diver, the carnival, any of it, had as real an existence as himself. Up to now, apparently, he had never believed that Diamond was a living man. Yet the diver had a life which might be supposed to be as intricate, as immediate as his own, so it seemed—he had discovered that the man possessed a shiny black car, that his name was painted outlandishly on the steel walls of a trailer. These facts strangely assumed an importance. Father Cawder stopped beside the first pew.

If he felt surprise on learning that the man existed, he felt little else. He had at this moment no desire to observe him, to question, to weigh answers. All that could wait. At the carnival he would come upon the diver in due course. A spectator like the others in the crowd, he would watch the gyrations of an acrobat. With no more effort than the notice taken of any stranger who might walk in front of him. The priest saw his hand motionless on the finial of the pew. He passed inside it and knelt down.

Old Ella, fearing God, would make a good end. She had stumbled out of bed to her knees to adore the Host he carried in his hands. While bending over her with the spoon he had glanced through the panes of her dirty window. There by the gate stood Mrs. Girard, placid, erect, on the watch for him. She had the good sense to go away; when he looked again the street was empty. Another recollection crossed his mind—the woman smiling from her polished chair, making her offer of cushions. Like everyone whose words she listened to or read, Mrs. Girard was subject to a lust for mere comfort. Upholstered in bed, at table, at work, at the last when lowered to worms in the padded satin

49

of a coffin. As he knelt he pressed his shins against the oak plank with satisfaction; it was hard as rock. The house of God, sanctuary of the Most Holy, was to be upholstered too, carpeted, heated, like the bedrooms of the rich. Not, however, as long as he had power to deny whimsical female perversity. That You should be adored with a fit homage, merciful Jesus!

He was too hard on poor Moran. Moran who schemed to snatch the souls of communists from the burning, who had been near vomiting at mention of an old woman in good accord with God. He spoke to him yesterday without prudence. He had been rough, had acted without motives of charity. The breviary in Father Cawder's hand opened at a place where a card protruded. Have mercy on us, Lord—Increase in us charity and love!

He read a first page and then a second. When he came to the top of the third he closed the book over a forefinger and lifted his head. *"Terris Teresa barbaris Christum datura—"* he muttered softly. *Christum datura aut sanguinem*—the choice had a ring of crudity about it: the child Teresa meant to give the Moors either Christ or her blood. The proposal would have an indecent, even scandalous, sound to those who believed the body's comfort to be a serious matter. It was otherwise with the Spanish woman, hater of half-measures, squeamishness, and upholstery. Teresa stood transfixed in triumphant pain on the summit of Carmel, whirled up to God in a wheel of fire with the prophet Elias. He, Thomas Cawder, priest, was not to face such dilemmas; he would shed no blood for Christ and His Church. But it was possible, with a strong joy, to imagine the effusion of one's blood poured down from the steps of this altar. For Your name's sake, Jesus. At which every knee shall bow. His blood would never be spilled on this floor. There being no need of bloody witnesses to Christ, man and God, in this time and in this place. His neck was safe in a paltry world where bodily ease was preferred to the unbearable words of Christ. *Charitatis victima!* Pray for me and for the congregation of this church, Saint Teresa of Avila.

He took up his breviary and read on until he had finished the office of the day. Then he adjusted the picture between the leaves and shut the book with a snap. He stayed on his knees. The red lamp hung from a cable winked in a tremor of wind. Outside it was sunset. It was dark in the church.

He would not be necessarily at fault now if he went. If he went to the fair grounds not through any motive of giving satisfaction to himself—for he posed no conditions, he was committed to nothing. The trailer was highly polished. Brushed by hanging leaves, it had flashed in the sun like a sheet of water.

Rising from his knees Father Cawder made the sign of the cross and faced the altar. He peered up through the dark air at the glimmer of the brass vases. Behind that weak glitter, layers of textile and metal, incredible humiliation lay secreted in a box. A god submissive to time and space, the Holy One of Israel, Emmanuel, the lion of the tribe of Judah, the Anointed. Jesus, mercy. Lord, have mercy on us! It was shameful, a fearful mystery. The anointed messiah of the Jews, born of a virgin according to the prophet Isaias, He lay concealed in this patched wooden shed, His human flesh distending space, here on the corner of Rozier Street and Winter's Lane, opposite a filling station and a boardinghouse. Shut up in the dark, the savior of Christians and Jews, heretics, communists, atheists, out of sight, basely unattended some ten feet away.

For Your sake, Jesus, king and high priest, it is fitting to punish the body, to offend its soft surfaces, its nerves and muscles. It is suitable to master appetite with watery foods, to choose the hard bed, the short sleep, the long prayer, the thin garment—to bridle the tongue, to check memory, to cross the will. And these things are done in order to appease the justice of God, to atone for the crimes of men, to learn a means

51

of refusing the nothingness of a visible world, of grasping the good of invisible worlds, to have at least a small share in the hard mystery of the cross. Be merciful, dear Lord, to Father Moran and Ella Johnston and Mrs. Girard and old Fenwick. Also to Diamond.

Father Cawder made a genuflection. Once in the aisle he hurried quickly away down the length of the shadowy church.

T HE TWO PRIESTS TURNED INTO THE FAIR
grounds under an arch of green bunting and yellow
electric bulbs. Father Cawder, gazing round him, wondered what he had thought to see. From the turnstile
the carnival had a shabby, on the whole a mournful,
look. The rags of canvas over leaning stalls were limp,
rubbed thin, it seemed, from years of use. A blast of
light like the glare from a furnace beat down on the
packed clay. It fell on currents of moving faces, shifting or staring eyes, exposed each pebble and leaf, burning out suddenly over the tops of the trees. The high
voices—screams, rather—of men waving their arms
behind the counters sounded as mechanical to the
priest as the tremendous tune from the loud-speaker
which drowned them out. They uttered cries, their lips
and fingers worked. But the man beckoning to him had
blank eyes like a frog's. The barker was putting himself through a routine of violent motion. Meanwhile
his brain and his quiet eyes were fastened on some
image which had nothing at all to do with the whirling
wheel behind him.

A knot of half-grown boys lounged against the side
of the stall. They glanced out absently between the
paper festoons to the night beyond. Stolidly observant,
moving abreast in twos and threes, the wives of farmers strolled past them. One pair stopped in the throes
of clacking laughs. Father Cawder took note of their
sallow cheeks, their bare linked arms thin as lengths

of rope. The wind that lifted out of the trees smelt of oil poured over roasting peanuts.

He stepped back from the lane of booths into the shade of a dense tulip poplar. Surrounded by children, Moran was raising a rifle to his shoulder, taking aim at a bull's-eye and a file of white ducks sliding along a belt. He could fend for himself, mildly smiling as he was. Father Cawder watched the crowd uneagerly stirring in front of him. These were, or ought to be, the familiar faces, hardened or flattened out, which he had come to know over eight years. A few, perhaps, he had never seen before. At that, they were recognizable as the grizzled or red scrubbed faces of the men of Nanjemoy County. Diamond would be somewhere beyond, behind the booths, waiting in the half-light of a tent. Like the barkers spinning wheels, shaking dice, such a man would take no pleasure in the nightly grind of this huckstering. All the more if, while hired to exhibit skill, he was also able to illustrate somehow another man's inward life. In a tent or a trailer, a hotel room, the diver could conceal under the disguise of a buffoon an experience of grace. His body contorting in a glare above the heads of a crowd, his spirit moved by a force which perhaps mystified the man himself. The face like a varnished Halloween mask of Mr. Birdseye approached the priest, familiarly grinning. As if to imply the free-masonry of one overlord to another, the banker as he passed patted his arm.

Father Cawder shifted his eyes from the precise pink-gummed smile. He was perhaps being overcautious. Instead of groping by instinct, the diver could be, there was no impossibility, a man pledged to God without reserve. There was the day laborer, Matt Talbot, not long dead, loaded with chains under his overalls, a hod carrier in a brickyard, soon, it was said, to be raised to the altars. The priest felt his skin creep in a shudder of awe. This particular man among freaks and touts could wield in secret the terrible powers of a saint, one who

54

may have looked nakedly on God—a Benedict Labré in a traveling carnival. He could take some thirty or three hundred steps, only turn, it was possible, he would come upon grace culminating and perhaps made plain there before him.

The priest frowned. The dream had posited—if a saint, then it followed he himself . . . A heat prickled suddenly over his neck and cheeks. He stared at, without seeing, the swinging lights of the Ferris wheel. He had guiltily assumed then, must indeed believe—his pride was then a mania, unsuspected in all his desires, the hidden spring of all his thoughts. Through the day, by night while he slept, it lurked in wait, at hand with its idiocies. Was the root of his being only insolence? Pride being insolence to God and of all sins the most irrational. He had supposed he knew himself to be an unprofitable servant. On getting out of bed every morning, he stated to himself the fact that by the eye of God each of his parishioners could be deemed better than he—Ella Johnston, old Fenwick, certainly Mrs. McGovern in her feeble-minded malice. Was his humility, he pondered uneasily, just a form of politeness to God? "Whited sepulchers" is the language used by the Holy Ghost of such men—outside, a seemly polished wall, within, a rotting filth.

Father Cawder became conscious of yells, cries of laughter, the heaving groans of the merry-go-round. His eyes dropped to winking red electric bulbs, to an old man in duck trousers tossing rings into the chicken wire of the nearest stall. What had he thought to effect by waiting in this din? He might have come alone, a minute or two before the scheduled time. Since Moran clearly had no need of company to amuse himself. A vexing mistrust settled over the priest. He stood here idle, without dignity, without reason, put to eyeing these bodies imperturbably propelling themselves back and forth past the booths. Better to search for Moran, talk of crops or loans to a farmer or a banker, wait with due skepticism for the moment of an acrobat's leap into a pool six feet by eight.

For several minutes he had known that from time to time someone at his side glanced deliberately toward him. Turning slowly, he saw that it was Mrs. Girard. A tolerant smile for the odd diversions of mankind seemed to play over her face. Her eyes were invisible in the shadow of her hat; from one arm she carried a basket of vegetables. He felt as if she had been observing him at disadvantage, in some covertly discreditable situation. He measured out his voice.

"Good evening, Mrs. Girard!"

"I was wondering when you were going to speak to me, Father. Don't you like the games?"

"Father Moran is the one who is distributing what we brought for the firemen. I just saw him over at the shooting gallery."

"So did I. He looked most militant. I've been losing at bingo and winning at those wheels. See all my hoard." She held the basket forward, a heap of peppers, tomatoes, acorn squash. "I'm lucky tonight. All this for ten cents."

"I am waiting for the dive. I had wanted to see that."

"Oh, yes. You like that sort of thing?"

"I prefer it to the rest of this."

"Really? It seems so crazy, jumping all that distance. They always break their necks sooner or later, don't they? I find gambling much less of a bore." The shadow of her hat fell sharp and dense across her upper lip. Father Cawder looked out over her head. He saw the phrenologist, Mrs. Ringer, the resident gypsy, at any rate, of Duke Street, and behind her the massive jowls of Mr. and Mrs. Garrity. Far on the right stood Father Moran, placidly inspecting the bingo tables. Mrs. Girard exclaimed:

"I followed you this afternoon right up to Ella's door, Father. I hadn't realized you were bringing her the Sacrament. I wanted to say I renounce the cushions. Next spring I'm going to give you two dogwood trees

56

instead for the side lawn. God could hardly be displeased with them, could He? Our deserving firemen! This year, if they make enough, we're to have a lovely new red fire engine, did you know? Oh, look!"

A faint flash crossed the sky, a searchlight pointing upward above the trees. It jerked to and fro, then swung over the mottled clouds to a white pole. A small ledge near the top of the pole jutted out on a bracket. In the distance the water tower seemed to float, buoyed up by dark air. Father Cawder moved out into the lane. His tone, when he spoke, became abrupt.

"That's the pole. Would you like to get any closer?"

"I don't think so, thank you. I shall see all I want from here."

"If you don't mind, I think I will get a little closer."

"Good lord, Father, please don't be concerned over me. I'm going home any minute now."

He pressed forward behind the unhurrying backs of the others in front of him. As he went past garlands of fluttering green paper he kept his eyes fixed on the pole. It seemed to get shorter; and while the beam of light steadied and increased a man climbed into view, his moving legs and arms flattened against the pale sky, a straw-colored sliver without weight or volume. He mounted slowly, seeming to crawl, like an insect on a stalk. A sudden roaring like a rush of wind crackled through the air. A vast voice spoke:

"Now folks—you've been waiting around and having your fun—now you're going to see what you all came for—I want to take this opportunity now—of getting all you good people acquainted with Diamond—here he is, folks, all set to demonstrate his skill for you—"

The crowd thick around the priest was taking a stand. He was aware of shuffling feet and labored breaths, snatches of half-heard comments that had no meaning. Raising his eyes above the mass of heads he saw a brown line. That was the tank, too far away to be more than a streak of shadow. Squinting, craning

57

his neck, he looked upward. The diver had reached the ledge and took a dancing step across it. A second searchlight focused on him now. He was a small man, his still face was dark, he cast on the earth below an undecipherable glance.

"—life and limb in every town and hamlet of our country, friends—time after time, in rain or shine—and he's ready to risk the same for your pleasure here—he will dive, without any single wire—no net or mechanical device of any description—my friends, he will dive, with his customary luck and skill—from that terrifying height where all of us see him now—down into that little tank of water there—a tank of water just six feet three inches by eight feet zero—now my friends, let's all of us shut up while Diamond gets himself ready—how about it, ladies? Let's all co-operate! Quiet now! Everybody quiet! Quiet, please!"

The hoarse roar ended in a hiss. The Ferris wheel and the merry-go-round were grating to a halt. Somewhere a phonograph was cut off in the middle of a blare of saxophones. The hum of muttering voices dwindled away.

"Ho, Diamond! Are you ready, Diamond?"

A sharp faint sound came from overhead.

"Diamond says he's ready. Quiet, everybody, please! They're all waiting for you, Diamond boy—good luck and the Lord be with you—it's all yours, Diamond!"

The flat shape brilliant with light balanced itself on the bracket, stretched out its arms, advanced, drew back again. Then as a drum rolled and small boys began to scream, it shot to earth. The searchlights were immediately switched off. The people near Father Cawder started to speak, laughed, sauntered leisurely away. Father Moran, he found, was standing behind him.

"Almost anybody can do a dive like that with practice," Father Moran said. "All it takes is practice and nerve. Not much to have waited around for."

He was right, the dive presupposed little more than practice. Any healthy man used to high elevations could jump from a pole into water. On the surface the diver's brief turn was no less dull than the rest of the carnival, rusted Ferris wheels, bingo and rancid peanuts, women with beards, children with two heads. By and large, all were of a piece in their tainted slackness. But the diver vended no stinking food, did not tout with megaphone or dice box in his hand, expose the abnormalities of freaks. Plummeting through the air with something of risk, he merely functioned to strike a moment's easy amazement into the eyes of children and tenant farmers. By comparison there was an economy in this feat of only moderate skill, a pleasing restraint. Ridiculous though it was, Father Cawder realized he had taken pleasure in the instant of impersonal display. He turned to Father Moran.

"Are you going home now?" he asked in an insistent voice.

Moran was throwing a last calm glance over the carnival. He nodded indifferently.

"In that case I'll leave you here. Before I go back I want to see one of the people connected with the carnival."

Father Moran appeared to take no particular notice of this statement. He vaguely waved and hurried off toward the shadowy street.

10

U NDER THE HANGING LANTERNS OF A
tent, two men were counting the dollar bills neatly
stacked across a table. One of them said, "He's got a
trailer. He's got it out there in the parking lot, behind the
freaks." Father Cawder turned back and walked along
the latticed side of the rifle range. The crowd had
thinned out. A heavy soundlessness was noticeable
now that the Ferris wheel and the merry-go-round
had shut down for the night. He came upon small groups
of men as he went between the stalls. They were leaning against posts or squatting on the ground, talking in
low voices of money, presumably, or of corn fields or
heifers or women or times gone by. The empty stalls
in front of him looked like the wrecks of houses in
the dark. He glanced at the bellying canvas picture of
a monstrous child. The sign could be read: "Baby
Brenda, Two Months Old, The Real Baby with Two
Heads." Within would be the customary pickled indecency in a vat of greenish alcohol. The tent of the
freaks, a shadowy mound of flapping walls, abruptly
ended the lane of concessions. The tall grass of a field
rustled beyond. The priest stumbled. The earth under
his feet was pitted with holes, slashed into ruts. Apparently, the field was used as a dumping ground for
rubbish. The glare behind him flickered out over bottles, beds, rotting burlap, slabs of razed brickwork.
At a short distance on his right he saw a cluster of
parked trucks and vans.

The headlights of one topheavy black hulk flared

and covered him with light as he came near it. They flashed off after he passed through the steady double beam into the darkness. On every side of him he heard a shrilling of tree toads. He had reached the middle of the field, he thought. He halted beside the fork of an uprooted tree. A fence or hedge was strung across the slope ahead of him. Where it dipped behind a smudge of saplings he saw a lighted window within a long humped mass. He started toward it. The stream of light gave form to the heaps of rubble thrown down into the grass. He had been walking through the field in a wide arc. Beyond the hedge he could make out the girders of the Ferris wheel, domed clumps of what might have been lindens, a thin wispish pole.

The light fell from an open door in the back of a trailer. Like reflections in dark water, whitish letters spelled the word DIAMOND across its side. As he rounded the flank of the trailer his pace slackened. Huddled in the doorway, someone sat with head inclined forward as if watching him.

He stepped into the light and shielded his eyes with his hand. His heart, he noticed with annoyance, had quickened its beating. The disturbance of his blood, however, was not visible to whoever was sitting on the step. He made himself speak.

"I want to see Mr. Diamond. Is he here?" The words loudly starting from his mouth surprised him with their harsh ring. In a voice which seemed charged with arrogance he added, "I am Father Cawder."

The crouched figure was a woman. She locked her hands against her knees and leaned backward into the light. "Diamond's not around right now." The woman stolidly looked at him. After a short silence she said, "He's gone to the drugstore for something."

The priest turned his nails into the palms of his hands. Having come to a halt a few yards from the woman, he had a feeling of being struck dumb. While she spoke he was unable to move, he imagined for an instant, to effect words with his tongue. He watched her

61

in a breathless panic, at a loss to what actions to put himself. He supposed suddenly he must appear ridiculous, that he was flouting some unsuspected convention of immense importance to the woman. She spoke again.

"I wouldn't like to say just when he'll be back."

Her head hung aslant in shadows. She was looking at his face or at the sky behind him. No plausible phrase came to mind. He had meant to probe the potentialities of an unknown carnival performer. Put bluntly into words, his motive for being there would drive the woman behind her door in fear of a frothing lunatic. While his thoughts eddied in a bewildering flux, he heard his voice heavily sounding:

"If you think he'll be back shortly, I would like to wait a few minutes. I am pastor of the Catholic church here in Lulworth. I saw him dive over at the fair grounds. I wanted to speak with him. If he'll be back soon—"

He raised his head expectantly and stepped forward. He had power of speech, he could deal, it seemed, with this situation well enough. The stifling tension in his chest relaxed. In its place a sensation of easy calm expanded through him. The woman had no quality of perception, she had probably not observed him at all, she had noticed only a man of no special interest asking questions without relevance. She rose to her feet and stretched her arms behind her. "Come in," she said indifferently.

Inside the trailer a sofa was bolted to the wall just beyond the door. The woman lay back against it, her shoulders settling against a pillow covered with ticking. When she motioned slightly toward an armchair beyond the sofa, he passed in front of her and sat down. In the strong light from the ceiling she had a look of being very young—a girl in her teens, the priest thought. Her loose blond hair was almost white. The turn of her body, her thin shoulders and wrists, her school-girlish hair gave her the look of a child still growing. But her

62

face was preposterously painted, he observed. The sharp outline of her lips appeared crudely stenciled, the hollows under her eyes moist and greenish from some outlandish pigment. A sweet perfume came from the girl as she moved. Her glance followed his eyes to a calendar on the wall. It displayed the vaporous breast and rich curls of the Sacred Heart of ecclesiastical commerce.

"Is he a Catholic?" He avoided, he realized, the use of the diver's name, the trite circus alias. The man, likely enough, was served by a totally different name in the workaday world. The girl turned to face him. Under the layer of paints she was, or would be, he supposed, beautiful in a thin, somehow too pointed, way.

"No. You mean that calendar? You just pick them up. Some undertaker or somebody gives them to you and you just tack it up to the wall." She laughed abruptly. "I'll tell you a good one. Once upon a time I was going to marry a parson. He was a Mormon, honest to God. Whee! Them were the days. I was fifteen years old. I really was. Up in Pennsylvania."

While she was speaking Father Cawder glanced to the floor. Her feet were stuck into slippers made of straps of gold kidskin. The soles along the edge were caked with mud. "All that," the girl added in a mocking voice, "was before I decided to go on the stage."

"You take part in the carnival too?"

The girl looked up curiously. She seemed to take stock of him for the first time.

"My God!" Her voice rose. "Me? You do mean me, don't you? Do a turn in this slop of a show? I should say I do not. Me in this buggy carnival, that's a laugh! I got too much self-respect." She pulled out her cigarettes from under the pillow. "There's one thing I can't stand and it's this here carnival. That's God's truth. I can't abide it. You wouldn't catch me signing up with this bunch of tramps. I've gone around with it since Diamond's had this job, but it's getting on my nerves plenty, mister, I can tell you that. Maybe I hadn't better call you mister. Is that wrong?"

She bent her head sideways, smiling, almost shutting her eyes.

"How about reverend? Call you reverend?"

"Father. A priest is called Father."

"Father?" Making game of him the girl let her jaw drop. She was still smiling. "Sounds funny to me somehow. I mean, it's not like I ever saw you before. Father. I feel like a prime fool."

Father Cawder gazed impassively across to the table where a pale fish hung suspended in the water of a glass globe. Raising a thin hand the girl tore off the end of a broken fingernail. "There's another one gone." She spoke slowly and without expression. "You run a church here in this town?"

"Yes. Saint Gregory's."

"Gregory," the girl repeated. "I know a boy named Gregory. He's a friend of a friend of mine. A wop, I guess he is." After a pause she said, "This is sure one funny little dump of a town."

The girl closed her eyes. Father Cawder pulled out his watch. "I came without realizing how late it was getting to be," he said. "I can come by tomorrow sometime during the day."

He saw the girl's shoulders when she leaned forward. She wore a shirt like a man's, made of a thin silk. As she stretched herself it caught the light. Her face was settling to a look of discontent.

"Diamond will be back sometime. Don't you fret. He's not a one to get lost for good. No such luck."

He turned to her in silence. She appeared to be sourly studying him.

"Just what is it you want to see Diamond about?" she asked suddenly. "I can tell him what it is when he comes. You don't have to wait. You can tell me whatever's on your mind and I'll tell him when he comes."

He took time to glance again at the floating fish before he spoke. "It isn't necessary for me to wait, of course. If you'd prefer that I didn't."

"To tell you the truth, I don't just know when he will be back. Sometimes he's gone all night. You can't wait all night for him, can you?" She looked at him with a hostile shrewdness. "If you want to wait here, suit yourself. I don't care." A faint grin slipped into the girl's face as she clasped her hands behind her head. "Diamond a stranger to you?"

"Yes," he said shortly. "I don't know him."

"I have to admit, I don't get it. If you don't know Diamond, how come you have to see him so bad? But maybe you're fooling, maybe you really have got a line on him? That it?"

She kept her discontented face obliquely bent. Her eyes, sharp and blue, watching him, looked mournful. He made no answer.

"It ain't got nothing to do with money, I don't guess." Woodenly, stupidly staring up at him, she moistened her lower lip with her tongue. As he shifted his watch to his left hand and wound the stem, the girl looked away. She stood up and stepped past him. Pulling a brown bottle out of water standing in a sink she held it up in the air.

"Fancy a beer?"

The priest, soundlessly moving his lips, shook his head. She poured the beer into a striped glass and came back to the sofa. She smiled disagreeably.

"You know, I feel sorry for you preachers. Can't even lap up some beer when you're visiting with a lady. I won't breathe a word if you change your mind, cross my heart and hope to die."

He got to his feet. The girl sipped greedily from the glass.

"Beer sure is filthy stuff. It'd be hell to pay if some old woman caught you at it, I reckon."

She raised her chin and the light glittered on her small white teeth. Glancing downward Father Cawder picked his way over her crossed ankles. With his hand lowered to the door knob he turned his head. He saw her bare foot, finely arched, flex itself in the gold sandal.

"I will see him another time. Good night."

"So long, Father."

He stepped out to the wet grass and peered around him. A faint light struck the ground behind the trailer. It came from a street lamp beyond the hedge. He knew at once where he was. By day this was a field into which dwindled a street of sheds and gabled houses between rotting fences and a wash of red clay, behind the water tower, a pasture where a few piebald goats sometimes were tethered. The hedge, he saw, sloped to a break, the corner of a fence. He walked aslant toward the light.

Near the fence he came to a path worn across the grass. It led to a sidewalk of buckled concrete. A dim house rose before him in a yard, pale clapboards in a cluster of privies and chicken runs. The street light feebly glowed a few yards ahead of him. He made out the road below the sidewalk, like a still stream at the bottom of a bank. There was a stable somewhere near; he heard in the darkness the stamps and shuddering movements of a horse. Beyond the lamp post a loping man or boy was coming toward him. He passed the black shape, humming to itself, and the light at the same moment. Almost immediately he stopped and turned back.

"Wait!" he called out in a loud voice. "Excuse me. Are you with the carnival? I want to find Mr. Diamond."

The small figure came back slowly into the light, a dark slight man without a hat. His face was bony and pointed, his eyes sunk within deep shadows. He smiled without speaking, distending a wide thin mouth, making an easy inspection. With his head cocked on one side he laid a finger against his nose.

"Let me think, the carnival, you say. Oh, yes. Yes, I'm with the carnival. You want to find Mr. Diamond."

The man's lips jutted forward as he grinned. The light fell on his black darting eyes. To the priest, his face had a sly foxlike cast. He leaned backward from the waist and held out his hand.

"Easy! If that's all you want. I'm Diamond. Who are you?"

Father Cawder passed from the shadows under the trees into the violet-white glare which lit the fronts of shops. Aware all at once that he was tired, he turned doggedly to the hill, his shoulders raised and narrowed, his head sunk forward. He was in need of sleep, nerves and brain gone stiff, it seemed, in a steely languor. What had he expected, or objectively, had desired? With a stranger a man uses as a matter of course words intended only for concealment or accommodation. From the first it was a fool's errand, the venture of a simpleton possessed by illusion, too witless to allow for the dry formulas of speech. Even if Diamond had been no paltry foxlike tout of a man at all. Even if the quality of the grinning diver had persuaded of the likelihood of God's interventions, of being illustrated in visions! What he felt now was not, possibly, tiredness as much as shame. Even if the dream could still be thought more than a dull duping prank, he evidently supposed he had only to confront an unknown man, in an instant, with a word, abolishing strangeness, custom, the glasslike separateness of human beings. He had meant to glance at whomever he was to find and then to know him, whoever he was, as God knows him. As it happened, a thin swarthy man stopped under a street light, as uncommunicative, as disparate, as any sealed expressionless face seen in a church or bank. He suggested no antecedents. People like the banker, Birdseye, Mrs. McGovern, Mrs. Girard, observed on a street, might point to further associations. Diamond existed in a void.

There was the woman. An infidel without respect or piety, who from her appearance—but he was free to pass no judgment on the woman. Enmity to a priest is

67

an instinct natural enough in the world, and colored greases smeared on a woman's face pointed to nothing beyond the fact of irrational female simplicity, as with Mrs. Girard. The woman, it was possible, was his wife, of unimpeachable repute. He had gone to the trailer to observe. If he observed what was displeasing, a lurking taint, he could then pass judgment, not on the woman in the trailer, but on himself. The man and the woman served only to open before him his own ignorance, ignorance of God and of himself, the abyss of mystery germinating the fates of all men exiled on the earth.

"I am Diamond," he had said. He had shaken hands. With his small head cocked sideways, his bony fingers stroking his cheeks, the man had listened. Attentively, civilly. He listened with deference to the statement that the day after Saturday was Sunday, that there was a Catholic church in Lulworth, that he was being addressed by its pastor—"I am Father Cawder." Being the priest in charge, he had wanted to offer his services, through Diamond, to the carnival people; some, no doubt, were Catholics. That was probably so, Diamond said. Some of the girls who did a dance in the side show were Catholics.

"In that case, can you let them know? Mass at the church is at eight and ten o'clock, High Mass at eleven. In case anyone wants to know."

"Sure, Father, I'll see them, I guess. I'll tell them. I'll see the Costello girl. Sure. Glad you thought to drop around. Won't you come back to the trailer for a bottle of beer?"

There was nothing further to be said. He felt, suddenly, no interest in this deferential sly man. Diamond inclined his head. He gave an impression of watchful guile. He had listened attentively, but with an appearance—not of guile, it was more like a light suspicion. As if he were saying to himself, "Just what does he want? What is this priest doing here on this deserted street petering out in mud? What has this priest been up to?" He turned round again beyond the lamp post, his hand thrown up, extravagantly bowing like a colored waiter caricaturing himself out of mockery.

"Good night to you, Father!"

As the priest paused to latch the gate in his fence, he heard the town-hall clock clang in the distance. The stroke of twelve, on the calendar a new day. He made the sign of the cross.

he...
Fathe...

11

F OR A BRIEF SECOND, FOR FIVE MINUTES
or half an hour, his back flattened on the cot, Father
Cawder watched fragments of memory drift through
his mind as if in a dream. With eyes shut and turned inward, he saw himself move under the glare of hissing
lights, stumble in the dark over bricks. It was surprising now to remember that he had entered the trailer,
had freely chosen to sit in conversation with the girl.
Her shrewd sensual face, framed in yellow hair, floated
before him. A glaze of corruption tainted the unflawed
surface of her skin. He heard again ridiculous words exchanged with a weedy loutish little man grinning
around a lamp post. Disgust caused the priest to open
his eyes. Then he knew he was awake, it was morning.
He threw back the sheet and swung his legs from the
cot, blinded by light beating across the varnished floor.
It was a new day, one which pertained, he seemed to
forget the fact, to the duties of a curé of souls. Already he had found time for the luxury of shifting
these nullities through his brain, the diver, the pale
girl, the unwinding spectacle of the carnival—just as
insignificant, his own inept shameful actions. There
was a certain satisfaction in expelling these images
from his thoughts. It was like spitting from one's
mouth some soft rotting substance. Naked beside the
chair hung with his clothes, he had silently begun to
repeat an Our Father.

In the early evening, after a cold dinner pieced together by the sacristan and Father Moran, Father

Cawder sat in his brown and red parlor. He frowned as he read the faint gray words across a page of *The City of God*. After a while he closed the book and laid it on the table. The day had furnished the usual minute occasions which passed for a priest's functions in Lulworth. Checks deposited, insurance pored over with oriental procrastination, a cat caught between two joists, the plumbers tracked down inside a well a mile beyond town, visits to the hospital and old Mrs. Mareen, the final withdrawal of Mrs. McGovern, ominous with silence and exactly paid. A Mr. Hugo Shea presented a letter from the bishop of Wilmington and shortly afterward was married in the parlor to a girl who dragged at his sleeve with a tight red fist. At the bank he had met Mrs. Girard as she tapped across the gleaming marble. She dropped her head to one side, warned him of the treachery of autumn weather, recommended, as if of deep concern to her, certain precautions against catching cold. And as she left she made inquiries about the health of "dear Father Moran."

His eyes quickly darting, his hands full of notes, Moran had hovered about the door while Mr. and Mrs. Hugo Shea made ready to leave. Once they had gone, he hurried into the room and spread out his diagrams. A complete synopsis of the corporal works of mercy had been plotted in the high spirits of one night. There was to be a guild of ladies to nurse the sick, a drive to buy a tract of timber and a sawmill—those colored people unable to pay for firewood could get it free— and one of the spiritual works of mercy, Instructing the Ignorant, a study club, that is. There was always, Moran sentimentally murmured, his salary if they needed it.

After the guild got under way, there might be a chance of shaping it into an actual clinic. The county had funds only for desperate cases. And the poor hated to be inspected, to sign papers, they were supposed to be deserving at the hospital. What about the sick poor

71

who were not deserving? What was needed was a kind of free consulting service, paid for by the parish since the poor have a right to expect the Church to minister to body as well as to soul.

At the same time perhaps they should aim at a credit union. For the lending of small sums without interest, that is to say, without usury. He had heard of a priest in Nova Scotia who had started one for a fishing village; they had lost hardly anything from bad debts. He would write to a friend whose uncle taught sociology in a seminary in Halifax.

As for the round table, the group for instruction in the teachings of the encyclicals—Moran stammered, explaining. Naturally it would be the pastor's privilege to preside at these doctrinal discussions. However, he himself had many a free evening. If meetings of this kind interfered with plans of Father Cawder, he would not mind at all—

Moran's emotion was without cunning. His eagerness made his hands shake, his voice creaked in its excitement. Father Cawder, glancing at the columns of neat figures, felt a mild, diffuse good will.

"I will consider some such plan," he must have said. "Some parts of it, at least. If your finances work. When you settle on something definite," he added, "I will write the bishop and ask him what he thinks of it."

Moran stared at him intently. "You think it's not bad then, Father," he had said. "You do think we could make some kind of a start, don't you? You want me to keep on with it, don't you?"

It could do no harm to tend the sick, to aid the needy, to debate the words of popes. One could assert it would do good. Although Moran's schemings always began with a concatenation of charts, the bent of his mind was bureaucratic. At least this plan of his would use up his energy. There were priests more suited to the melodrama of running a waterfront mission than to hearing confessions and mortifying the will. God having made Moran as he was, to give play

72

of some sort to his secularized talents was economical. Like the communists and the capitalists he mentioned so frequently, Moran also was a materialist, fearing material evil or desiring material good, busy with corruptible matter. He spoke much of justice. But it was justice to be done to men, himself or another. It was no concern of these millennial enthusiasts that detestable injustices took place every instant against the majesty of God. Failure to worship God was injustice, a denial of just due more shocking in essence than a starving of a million men who were merely the creatures of that God.

The clock in the hall began to strike the hour. At the same moment a bell in the back of the house shrilly pealed. With his eyes shut, pressing his breviary into the palm of his hand, Father Cawder listened to the meaningless sounds. Is not justice a proper order, he was thinking, the order of the universe as willed by God? Then is not rejection of God a violating of that order, of justice? If offenses against God are to be ignored, is it reasonable to take notice of injury to His creatures?

The bell pealed again. Father Cawder laid his breviary on a chair and went out into the hall. He opened the door to the street. At first he frowned into the dark, not recognizing the woman on the steps.

As her hands pulled at the edge of her coat she drew her head abruptly back. Then he saw who she was.

"Good evening." He heard his voice, startled into a rising pitch, with distaste.

"How are you," the woman said. She shook her loose brilliant hair and peered at him coldly. "My name is Stella Swartz. Miss Swartz."

The priest steadied the door with his hand. "Yes, Miss Swartz? You wish to see me?"

Her glance contracted, possibly with suspicion. "Yes," she said stiffly, "I wanted to speak to you about something. About a certain thing."

73

"Come in, Miss Swartz."

He followed her into the parlor and shut the door. During the day he had recollected her face as full-blooded and insinuating, her movements light with an animal grace. He had forgotten how she looked. Seen in the light of his own lamp the girl appeared thin, a meager child with colorless cheeks. She stood in the middle of the room, drawing her scanty black coat closely about her. Her behavior struck the priest as odd. After she had seated herself well forward on a chair, she glanced about the room covertly, absurdly. Full of suspicion, wary of Romish treachery skilled in daggers and trapdoors. Or sorry now she had come. When she lowered her eyes her expression seemed sleepy and ill-tempered.

"Well, Miss Swartz." He seated himself in the armchair beside the table.

The girl looked sidelong at her feet. "I don't just know what I really want to say to you. Haven't had much practice."

Father Cawder watched her over the tips of his fingers. Gradually she began to feel more at her ease. She crossed her legs and raised her head in a level stare.

"I can guess what you're thinking to yourself. I guess you think a person like me is the kind that's not much account, don't you?"

The priest eyed her calmly. "There's no reason for me to have any opinion about you at all, Miss Swartz. To a priest, the chief fact about people is that all of us are made to serve God. If I can be of help to you in any way—"

She took time to make up her mind. After a pause she said, "I don't suppose I was the perfect little lady last night. I didn't mean anything special by it. It's just a way I have. Sometimes I feel like being ornery. If I made you mad, I'm sorry."

"It doesn't matter, Miss Swartz."

Again she took time to decide. "I don't guess you

74

priests miss many tricks," she said at last. "Diamond and me aren't married. You knew that, I guess, didn't you?"

Father Cawder shifted his eyes to the print of the Cowper Madonna. "I didn't know, Miss Swartz."

"Well, this doesn't seem to be getting me anywhere." She began to laugh. She threw open the front of her coat and leaned back in the chair. "Listen, what I wanted to tell you is this. I've got a little girl. I guess she's about six. It's about her. She's not Diamond's kid, she's just mine."

A look of questioning surprise must have crossed his face. She glanced at him and frowned.

"It's about her I wanted to ask you. That's why I'm telling you all this." She stretched out her chin, moistening her small red lips. "You see, I want to get her away from where she is. I've been thinking to myself maybe I could put her into a home. I mean a place where they'd take her in free. A convent or something, I sort of thought. Don't they take in kids free? Convents?"

"Under certain conditions, they do."

"That's what I thought. Well, I never could get around to doing anything—about the kid. And last night I got to thinking after you left. You see, you're the first priest I ever met, in a social kind of a way, that is."

"And you came to ask my advice about your child."

"Yes, that's right." The girl's eyes moved brilliantly in the light from the lamp, her painted lips hung strangely open. Why did she let her mouth hang loose, he wondered. It gave her a nerveless look, slumped sideways as she was, her wide eyes stupidly slanting.

"What I thought was, if I don't see this priest now, meaning you, I might never get another chance to talk to a priest. So I took a chance and came round to see you. I thought to myself it was maybe the only opportunity I'd get to do something about the kid."

"I see." He looked for a moment at the line of sweat

glistening about her mouth. "Has she been brought up in any religion, your little girl?"

She smiled thinly. "She's nothing. She's like me. Just girl, she is."

"Where is she now?"

"With friends in the country." The girl stifled a laugh.

Why did she choose to laugh now, with her vacant stare? She was graceless, without respect. It might have been expected that on a visit to a priest she would have decently clothed herself. The white gauze of her blouse, parting over her pointed breasts, rose and fell with her breathing.

"You would have to give up all claim to the child, you know that," he said tonelessly. "If she went to a home for children. If you paid nothing to keep her there."

"Well—" She studied her glittering fingernails. "Well, that would be okay. I thought maybe I'd have to. All in all, I won't mind about that. It's not like I'd ever been with her much."

"Is the child's father dead?"

"Dead? I don't guess he is. But he never seen the kid. He don't know a thing about her. Why? What has he got to do with it?"

The priest nodded. "And you. Won't you miss your child if you leave her in a convent?"

"I'll get on all right, all right." She tightened her lips and looked at him boldly. "Don't you worry none about me."

"You're not fond of the child, Miss Swartz?"

Her mouth pushed forward. "I don't know. She gives me the creeps. Sometimes it makes me sick to touch that kid."

"Makes you sick?" he repeated. "The child makes you sick?"

"Forget it." She began to swing the leg crossed over her knee. He saw she was wearing the same muddy gold shoes.

"She's an all right kid. But I didn't have any bed of roses when I had her and I want to forget it. She brings it all back when I see her. Anyways I can't take care of her. Moving around like I do. I couldn't pay for her keep in a regular school."

"You want her taken off your hands."

"Somebody ought to take care of the kid." Her voice sounded harsh, grating in her throat. "She's never done any harm to anybody. There ought to be somebody who could take care of her."

"Do you think you've been a good mother to her?" He was using the girl without discretion, without forbearance. While still in the act of asking her this question, he wished the words unsaid. She looked up, startled. Her face tightened in a humorless smile.

"I've got one little piece of advice for you. Don't you dare to pull any line like that on me, don't you dare to! I'm not one of your mollies. I didn't come here for any of your criticism."

Father Cawder rose from his chair. He spoke, he thought, equably. "I didn't invite you here, Miss Swartz. If you have anything more to say to me, take good care how you speak. Otherwise, I must ask you to leave."

She ran a finger over her eyebrows as he moved round the table. "All right, I'm sorry. Forget it. I say I'm sorry."

The clock in the hall began to strike the hour. While its springs throbbed and hissed the priest and the girl looked at each other in silence.

"Ten o'clock," she said.

He took his seat again. "I suggest this. There are convents which take in orphans and other children, like your little girl. I know about four or five. I can write to them. I could let you know if it is possible. There would be a few papers for you to sign, I suppose."

"Papers to sign?"

"Giving up claim to your child."

77

"Oh, sure. I told you I wouldn't mind that. But what about her name in this convent?"

He eyed her with annoyance, as if she might be trying out on him some clumsy prank. "What about it, Miss Swartz? I don't understand."

"I mean what name would they call her by? How would they put it down in the books? Swartz?"

"By the name she has now. Why should it be changed?"

The girl grinned and showed her teeth. "Oh, I don't know. I just thought maybe the nuns might want her to go by a new name. Just to keep everything on the up and up. You'll tell them all about me, won't you?" Her mouth curved upward at one corner.

Father Cawder reached stolidly across the table for his breviary. "I will tell them what you have told me, of course," he said after a silence. "That would only be fair to them."

"I see."

"No matter where the child goes, you would not have to bring her yourself. Someone agreed on by you in advance could come to get her."

"What's wrong with me bringing her? I'm going to see what kind of a place the kid's going to, you can bet your last nickel."

The priest watched her alert eyes narrow. He should choose his words with caution. The woman was willful and full of vanity.

"That might not be the wisest course for your child." He stood up, arranging the ribbons in his breviary.

"Why not? What's wrong with me going along to see the kind of a place it is?" She got to her feet in front of him. Her hands squeezed a little purse of green leather.

"Why not, Miss Swartz?" He seemed to reflect. "Well, in your child's case my advice would be not to learn where she was going to live. I think you would be wise to leave the details to some disinterested person, someone you've not known before. Like myself, for instance. Later on perhaps you might take a fancy to visit

78

your little girl. Your present feeling may change. But you will not be tempted if you don't know where she's gone to live. Because once she is in a household, a convent, it would, you see, be doing her an injustice if you—what I mean is, if you came to where she was living, you would want—"

"All right! All right!" she interrupted. The priest saw her fists clench over the strip of limp green leather. "I guess I get it all right," she exclaimed in a loud voice. She broke into a ringing laugh. "You dirty two-faced preacher! You lousy fake!"

He strode into the hall and flung open the door of the house. Behind him he heard the woman's noisy chuckling. She sauntered from the parlor, smiling at him. She meant to be insolent, he judged. At the door she turned round.

"Just a piece of dirt, so you think. That right?"

Father Cawder felt his anger struck suddenly to an overmastering sadness. He shook his head.

"No, Miss Swartz, no."

With a broad smile she studied his face for a few seconds.

"Oh, well," she said. "Tweet-tweet! Pip-pip!"

She ran down the steps and opened the gate of white pickets into the street. She glanced back over her shoulder as she crossed the dark of the pavement. Black against the yellow light from the hall the priest made no movement. He held himself erect, examining the yellowish misty air blown like smoke across the sky. In the distance a shrill faint clamor of voices sounded. That would be Diamond, plunging in his leap. He closed the door and went back into the parlor.

Only a few seconds had passed since the woman sat opposite the table, talking without propriety but at least not unamicably, he had thought. What had been done amiss? What arrangement of words should he have contrived for this girl? Beside the lamp, his eyes fixed on, without seeing, the magazines scattered over the table, Father Cawder weighed his intentions un-

79

easily. He had then rebuffed her. She was an infidel who had drawn near to the springs of grace by accident. To the unique channel of grace, Christ's Church, sole ark of the new covenant, represented unworthily and for the moment by himself. On the woman's part it was a whim, a notion of fancy, perhaps the first in her life and never to be repeated. He had dealt her a rebuff. Made no allowance for the narrow mischances of her life. It was evident he had failed in charity toward her. And therefore he was responsible; he had driven her away in anger.

When the clock in the hall struck the half-hour he raised his eyes. He pulled out his watch. There was time enough. He hurried from the parlor, snatched his hat off the rack by the door, and left the house. He set off down the street, slipping in his haste over the wet bricks. Fog filled the dark. It rolled in wisps of vapor ahead of him over the rise of the ground.

In sight of the town hall he peered up at the clock. The hands on the glimmering dial pointed only to twenty to eleven. There was time. There was no need to hurry. Nevertheless he walked with long rapid steps. He was out of breath after climbing the hill of King William Street. A pain began to mount under his heart. As the street curved he glimpsed the carnival below in the slit between two thin black houses. It glistened in a smoke of light, layers of moving heads and arms between creaking and rotating wheels. Diamond by now had time to get back to the trailer. The girl would be sitting within as on many a night before, sipping from a glass of beer. For another half-hour the fair grounds were sure to be swarming with boys and aimless couples. He had reached the fluttering arch of bunting. The stitch in his side made his breath come short. He pressed his hand against his ribs.

At the turnstile he threw a glance down the length of wooden fence. There was a lane, a narrow alley, beyond the whitewashed palings. Where it opened into the street a black car with a trailer, about to swing out, was briefly halting. He watched it blink its lights, glide round the corner of the lane. It bore slowly toward him. As it came forward he ran to meet it. "Diamond!" he called at the moment it passed him.

Father Cawder stopped in the middle of the street. The car gathered speed. Twinkling into the fog, the tail light disappeared over the crest of a hill. No one else had noticed the trailer; the men and girls idling about the turnstile had not troubled to look round. He crossed uncertainly to the further curb. Too late, they are gone, he thought dully, an instant before the implication of the fact struck him. Filled suddenly with angry impatience he stared, as if for help, into the misty sky. For undoubtedly he owed a debt to the railing woman; he had weakly allowed her to provoke his pride. Still, the woman was free to act as she pleased, she had freely chosen to provoke him. The child was another matter. He had not remembered the child. Its salvation for a few minutes in his parlor could have depended on him. The will of God in this particular might have meant him to be its instrument. By thrusting away the mother he had thrust the child away too. A young girl, the woman said. If the providence of God was a reality for all, for a sparrow as much as for a man, he was not free to turn aside, withdrawing himself from what God willed.

And in that case he would have to find out where they had gone—the priest's right hand, hanging at his side, impatiently clenched—get Diamond's address or the woman's from whatever man it was who had seen to the carnival concessions. He would have to write her a letter, set in motion the machinery of some house of nuns who took in unwanted children. The little girl would thus be got away from her mother, which in itself would be a kind of amends to Stella Swartz, that being what she wished. It might not be much, after all, to do.

He could send a wire or mail a letter; then he could forget that the pair of them had ever existed. It would

81

have been painful to have had to speak to them, to have had to hear one time more the spite or foolery of their jeering voices. That was one advantage in having missed them—he need never see them again. If God willed him to come to the aid of an unknown, unwanted, ignorant child it could be done perhaps as economically as sending off to Baltimore for a fresh supply of candles. Quickening his steps, imperceptibly beginning to breathe at his ease, Father Cawder turned down the hill toward home.

Part Two

1

FATHER CAWDER REACHED ACROSS THE BED
and turned on the glass lamp with the tattered silk
shade. The weak pink glow made the small room appear somehow less dirty. In the gray afternoon light
the soot-streaked walls, the strings of carpeting, seemed
to him as if filled with an imponderable extension of
the thousand bodies which had stretched exhausted
over this bed before him. But like hot baths, a clean
room is a luxury only less obvious in sensual satisfaction than meat or drink. The laity, believing respectability to be rectitude, had invented the standard of
comfort thought proper for the clergy, but no canon
required the views of lay people to be followed in
choosing a hotel. Having descended the wet wooden
stair from the train tracks overhead, standing in the
rain, he had taken note of the tan block of pebble dash
which might have been an old-fashioned textile mill.
But the flat roof was crenelated and under the tin
battlements was strung a sagging line of letters, *Hotel
Piedmont Running Water in Every Room*. Within, he
had assumed, were a bed, a towel, a cake of soap. If
he liked, he could have a double room for the price
of a single, said a woman behind the desk, scratching
at her scalp with a pencil. When he signed his name
he had had to bend under a plant whose spotted
handlike leaves bristled with a red down.

The priest had moved the telephone from the table
to the bed. With the scrap of paper flat on his knee, his
eyes fell uneasily over the list of numbers. While wait-

ing on a bench for the train in Baltimore, he had already speculated why it seemed necessary to hurry off, precipitately, without facts in hand, imprudently. Nobody in Trenton was known to him. He should first have made inquiries, written to a priest, to some unknown political hack in the mayor's office. If the woman was to be found at all, to whom he persuaded himself he was under some sort of obligation. He had elected to busy himself over a child he could not be sure existed. Some strange prospect of pleasure, it must have been, urged him first to the bus, sent him off to visit two orphan asylums in the Baltimore slums, asking for information to indulge some twist of officious self-conceit.

Mother Imelda the nun was called who presided over a hundred children in a brick tower six stories high. She had shown a decent, prying sympathy. They certainly conducted a house in New Jersey, a foundling home, above Newark—they would be glad to find room if they could for a child whose inhuman mother wanted to abandon it, worse than any wild animal, since the beasts could not be accused of that. But she knew they were crowded. It had pleased God in His infinite mercy, so she said, to burn down their house at Prairie du Chien. At the other asylum Sister John Capistran had compressed her lips, fingering her beads with a plump hand. There was a house of theirs in New York, she had meagerly admitted. But she supposed they had enough to do with the ones on hand without being at the beck and call of every woman who wanted to get rid of an unruly child, especially as he could not state precisely where the unfortunate mother lived. She then smiled humorlessly, as if she had detected an attempt at some unsavory fraud.

Leaning into the light, he added a fifth number to the list he had jotted down. He eased the telephone directory back into the drawer of the unsteady table. He had not thought to find Diamond's name slipped into these money-getting industrious trades, not below "Air-compressors," "Antiques," or "Attorneys," not under "Artists." He had made the one call to "Diamond, A. T." as a matter of course, the name stuck in the column of gray print between "Diagonal Cleaners" and "Di Angelo, Miss Tonietta." The breaking wheeze of an old man came thinly across the wires. The thin voice whined, "Can't help you, mister, can't help you." He was Amos Diamond, speaking from the premises of a livery stable; he knew nothing at all about acrobats, carnivals, or country fairs. "Entertainers" had referred forward to "Theatrical Agencies." That is to say, amusement parks, an ice rink, accordion players, a revolving bar, a wigmaker, and Babs Savarin, songs and specialty skits. Enclosed in black bands here and there on the yellow page were the names of five men who professed to be agents for "theatrical talent," "smart floor shows," "singers and entertainers."

The telephone girl downstairs in the lounge put through each call in turn. After the faint jangling of a bell the same voice, thick with sleep and bad temper, had seemed to answer. A moment of silence followed his first question. Then the voice muttered, "Who is it?" or "Who was it you said?" At the name "Diamond" it trickled off in exhaustion. "Don't know anybody—" then the light click cutting off the still mumbling voice. "Dermot Mulcahy" was the last name on the list; he could provide professional talent of every description, special terms for banquets and smokers, at the service of northern New Jersey for more than forty years.

No sound came from the telephone for a few seconds after the mention of Diamond's name. Then a woman's voice said, "Oh, sure. I know the one you mean."

"He dives from a pole. He travels with carnivals and fairs."

"Sure, I know the man you mean. Why do you ask? You want to get hold of him for something?"

"Does he live here in Trenton? I'd like to get in touch with him."

The woman's voice defined itself with caution. "If you want a diver or some kind of a performer for a picnic or something, that's what we're in business for, mister. We're agents, you know. It's not our policy to give out no names or addresses."

He spoke, he imagined, more slowly. "I'm not interested in hiring an entertainer. I only want to find out where this man can be located. It hasn't anything to do with your business."

"Oh! I see!" The voice cut itself short. Then a sharp laugh vibrated. "It's six of one and half a dozen of the other! I don't know what I was thinking of, mister. I don't have his address, so you see I can't give it to you if I wanted to. In fact I haven't seen him in two or three years. I wasn't thinking. I thought you were looking for an acrobat or something."

"Could you give me the name of anyone who might know where he is?"

"Honest, I'd tell you if I could. But you can't keep your finger on those guys." The voice flattened in a yawn. "I'd tell you if I could. They're a slippery bunch, acrobats."

Having settled the receiver back in place, Father Cawder sat down again on the side of the bed. There was a scent like drugs, he noticed, rising through the air. To track a man down through the hive of a city— Father Felicchi applied the word "sporco," gutturally spat out, to the filth of streets, the sound suggested soot and dung—what was the first step, here in this mean city? At any rate the man was known, had been known, to the civil-spoken illogical clerk of an entertainment agency. Since the woman knew of him, it followed that others had known him, that there were men close at hand who might know where he was at that very instant. The priest took a breath of the stale air. Some slatternly woman, undressing in this room, had left on the table a knot of hair combings about a toothpick. As he rose to his feet the hair fluttered, and he saw that the wrinkled scarf was stuck to the wood with a purplish stain.

Newspapers took care to amass ridiculous files; like the secret agents of dictators, they had their dossiers for classifying the unfortunate or the infamous. A steel box could enclose a card, a scrap of paper, a trace of Diamond, his name or the fact that in a certain year he had been alive, portentously filed under "D." There were the statistics filling ledgers in town halls and courthouses. Or the police, priding themselves on the scrutiny they brought to bear on any city dweller who was unprosperous and without importance.

The priest took his hat from beside a glass bowl stuffed with paper nasturtiums. He crossed to the window and raised the sash a few inches from the sill. After gathering up his coat from the back of a chair he left the room.

Outside the courthouse the day was darkening. Father Cawder let the door of chromium and glass swing to behind him. He glanced up at streamers of cloud solid as cardboard. They cut across the sky over the line of roofs, black against a depth of intense blue. He could now visit in succession, without interest, almost, the polling club at the corner of MacMillan Street and Love Place, the woman called Mrs. Diamond who kept a lunchroom. Since in any event it was like a game, hardly serious if soberly considered —a chase after an acrobat, a puzzle taken up to test his brain. It would have become him more, have been perhaps more prudent, to have resisted scruples over the woman and her child, to have stayed in Lulworth to listen to the presumptuous or silly confessions of idle housewives, paid bills, taught catechism, interviewed plumbers. Rather than pace to no purpose through this city full of sacrilege, greed, and lust. He could have spent the time on his knees before the altar, before the Word made flesh within his own trivial hands. Poplar leaves whirled about him as he walked along a street planted with trees. Behind the black branches a sunset flush widened over the clouds like a stain.

The young man must have seen the Roman collar as he hesitated beside the brown marble column. He— the young politician—came forward smiling, a second smile, it seemed, creased across his pink bulge of forehead. He knew the ins and outs of the courthouse, he worked right across the hall, he was "always happy to render assistance to a member of the clergy." Just an address, was that all? If the address was down in black and white, he certainly knew where to look for it. Father Cawder straightened his arm to avoid the young man's prompting fingers as they passed down polished lobbies. Through air greenishly lit as if under water, into elevators as rich with gold chiselings as a monstrance. Meanwhile discussing the transport union, the Negro vote, the Knights of Columbus. In a vast room behind a grating, like convicts or nuns, a hundred women drummed preposterously away on typewriters. The young man pored over mimeographed records from steel cabinets massed from floor to ceiling, his thumb expertly darted down the names of householders, purchasers, vendors, and trustees. He then entered a cubby-hole high above a landscape of chimneys and tin roofs. He turned the pages of two minute books bound in black leather. He wagged his head over the massive desk, spread apart his clean fleshy fingers. He had come across three Diamonds in all. But one was a Republican and the owner of a livery stable, another one had been dead for six years. The third, a Mrs. Gina Diamond, was a foreigner, not even a citizen, proprietress of a cheap diner, a greasy spoon. She certainly would not be the party. Diamond was by no means her real name, she was an Armenian. He copied her address on a card, slid it across the desk with a look of steady curiosity in his pale eyes.

His thoughts withdrawn from where he was, Father

90

Cawder stepped from the curb as the street lamps started into a flash of gentle light. The pavement bore aslant up a hill.

On the way back through offices, corridors, lobbies of bronze and travertine, the young man—"The name's Redman, Father"—had still supposed that priests unaccustomed to these costly passages were to be steered by jogs to the elbow, pluckings of the sleeve. Beside the chromium door to the street he had reached into his pocket.

"Here's the address of a club, Father. Young Democrats. They've got names we don't have."

"Thank you, Mr. Redman."

"You might learn something from the bishop. Do you know what parish he belongs to?"

"He's not a Catholic."

"Is he a Jew? That could be a Jewish name."

The priest halted as a sign on a lamp post met his eyes across graying air: "MacMillan Street." Redman said the club, polling place, whatever it was, filed the names of voters in the primaries. He turned into a street of shabby houses, each at the top of three white wooden steps.

The taxi ground to a stop at a corner where a network of neon tubes glowed against a two-story building. Pausing on the curb, the priest watched *Cosmos Restaurant* flicker to *Mixed Drinks* across the black bricks, green neon bubbles flashed inside the stem of a champagne glass. He pushed open the shiny slab of metal into a long room. He noticed first only waiters wheeling and darting sideways, men clapping their hands along a bar, angry or possibly merely excited swarthy girls yelling in a foreign language. Then he saw an arbor of artificial ivy and within it a fat woman behind a cash register. He went toward her. Her roving stare fixed on his face. "That's me," she said, "I'm Mrs. Diamond." She shook her head and lowered the lids over her sharp eyes while he was still speaking.

"It must be somebody else. Oh, no! We have no relations here. No, no."

"You have never heard of him?"

"No, no, no. Never. I know nobody else here with that name. And anyhow I was not born in this place, my husband neither. He's dead now, my husband. We were not born here. We are Rumanians."

"I see, Mrs. Diamond. Thank you."

He heard her shout unintelligibly behind him as he opened the door. He turned left on a street brilliant with light. A white glare beat through the plate-glass walls, glittering over stoves, spotted furs, spangled shoes, highlights on steel, cellophane, and leather. He went past a delicatessen, a bar blank with glass bricks, three silver globes above a pawnbroker's. MacMillan Street had been dark, rows of steps with mounds of dirt and leaves swept up against them by the wind. As he searched from house to house his eyes strained at the numbers nailed to walls of buckled wood and imitation brick. Then it started up before him on a corner, a curtained drugstore it looked, wanly lit from an inside room. The MacMillan Street Jefferson Club of Young Democrats. The three men got to their feet from tilted chairs. They made ready to pay deference, to use familiarity. They had never heard of a professional diver, an entertainer, by the name of Diamond. It never showed in the black to bother with entertainers or people like that. They never stayed in one place. Sure, they'd ask around, they'd keep their ears open, just in case. You never can tell. Like the old Jew who set fire to the other fellow's goods. So long, so long, Father, so long!

Light fell now from all sides over the pavement ahead of him. He saw the cheeks of sauntering or rushing people turn orange as they passed under neon signs. He looked into an immense cafeteria lined with white tiles. Within, hunched like children's in a schoolroom, a hundred backs were visible, solemn musing faces intent with greediness or vacuity over their plat-

ters. With silent working jaws they had nothing to
say to one another, nursing their grievances, savoring
the pleasure of meat and grease mixing with the juices
of their mouths. So he and Moran often ate together,
in graceless silence.

When he told him he was going away, Moran had
calmly nodded, even cheerfully. He had not repressed
an impulse to tell Moran it would be his first vacation
of sorts in seven years. In the weakness of human nature, Moran said that since it had been so long he
must take things easy and forget all about Lulworth.
On his return, Moran added, he might be surprised.
He had hopes—Moran's eyelids had fluttered, he had
grinned—he said he had hopes of real progress for
the outline or prospectus he would be working on. He
knew of at least eighteen—twenty!—people (including
six ladies) zealously eager to sit round a table once a
week and discuss the anti-capitalist teachings of Popes
Leo and Pius, of blessed memory. He mentioned he
was still turning over in his mind the possible services
of a nurse one or two days a week for the sick of the
parish, his Negroes, he meant to say. The guild for
firewood was complete on paper. It (or the Saint Vincent de Paul Society) might buy a fifteen-acre piece
of mixed hickory and oak which he had heard of from
a man at the bank. At no more than $30.00 per acre.
Moran had laughed, and a dimple appeared on each
side of his stretched mouth.

A flood of sulphur-colored light burst over Father
Cawder. He stopped in the glare and raised his head.
About a ticket-seller's booth a ramp with brass rails
split in two gleaming arcs. It was the front of a burlesque theatre. Photographs of women naked except
for breasts and loins, tinted and life-size, lined the
vestibule. He noticed a man slouched against the wall.
The red jowls drew haggardly down to a neckband of
dirty shirt, the lips of the old face trembled above a
sloping chin. For an instant the old man's eyes shifted.
They had caught perhaps the white edge of the Roman

93

collar. Slanted sideways in impassive folds of skin the bleared left eye furtively winked. The priest began to walk more quickly. He paused at the corner on the crest of a street sloping steeply away. In the distance he glimpsed the long roof of the railroad station. Swallowed up below him in the night, a gray vaporous hulk, one of the clusters of lights he saw should be the hotel, across the park of cinders with its crescents of dead cannas. He turned and hurried downward.

He knelt to finish his office beside the desk, his fingers crossed upon the blotter. Two lines of doggerel were penciled over it in a hand like a child's:

> You've had your love, You've had your share
> So say good-bye, What do I care

He opened his breviary at the page he had marked on the train. When he came to the end of the last psalm, kneeling rigidly upright, he realized his eyelids were almost shut. He rose to his feet, opened the window and turned off the light. But stretched out on the bed in the dark, he felt sleepy no longer. He lay still, flat on his back, his eyes open and slanted to the night faintly luminous beyond the sash.

He saw himself as if in a scene on a stage for a flickering moment, darting away from the church the Monday after the carnival, thin busybody in a billowing cassock, striding off in the wind. On the round of calls that morning—he had not, naturally, worn a cassock on the street—he had been amazed that not one of them had even talked to Diamond. Jere Fitzhugh, having sublet the fair grounds, printed the posters, contracted for the carnival, could only say when it was over that he knew nothing about it. Diamond, freaks, and Ferris wheel, the whole lot, had been on the road all summer, traveling on a circuit. He just wrote to a man in Lancaster, Fitzhugh said, an old man there had been an agent for years for carnivals and small circuses. Lulworth ended the season for the carnival. The last night, after his dive, Diamond collected his money. A percentage, it was. Then he clamped his trailer to his car and quietly drove off. The man named Billingsley who was hired to sell tickets at the turnstile thought Diamond must come from New York. Diamond and the girl, he said, never seemed very friendly with the rest of them, they kept to themselves. It had then been necessary to see Fitzhugh a second time. The man who sent him the contracts—he first thumbed through a small dirty notebook—was named Grew, he ran a movie theatre in Lancaster.

It took half an hour to reach Grew by telephone. A weak voice had whispered, drowned out in the drumming of a piano—rustling irrelevant sounds. He was inquiring, he repeated, about a diver, about the traveling carnival recently in Lulworth, about a man named Diamond. Then a door in Lancaster slammed and the voice—it was Grew—articulated. This Diamond just walked into his office and he signed him on, never heard his name before he put his head around the door. He came with a trailer and a canvas tank and a pole and a blonde, and all he did was to sign him on for the carnival. He had driven over to Lancaster from Trenton. Why, anything wrong? Scatter some rubber checks? He didn't furnish any address, he just said he'd come in from Trenton. He had a letter with him, from some man with a theatre. What was the take in Lulworth, Grew asked. Did he know what they cleared?

Inert and wakeful, Father Cawder stared at the greenish sky between the stirring curtains. When his eyes closed he had seen, as if from a sheer cliff, wraiths of Diamond and Stella Swartz marching arm in arm through the undersea light of the courthouse corridors. In the morning, he thought, his eyes opened to the night, there would be time to decide: whether to apply to the files of the Trenton *Courier-Dispatch,* which train to take back to Baltimore. His hand slipped under the pillow and he groped mechanically for the rosary beads he had put there on getting into bed.

2

WHILE EATING HIS BREAKFAST IN THE
low grillroom he saw in his mind a scene of crowds
massed in the glare from shops. He remembered the
splayed walls of the theatre, himself hesitating on the
curb, a red-veined eye feebly winking. He had passed
an angle of mirrors, a ramp with curled rails springing
inward under a blaze of mustard-colored light. There
was another particle of memory, he realized, doggedly,
uneasily shuttling through his thoughts. When he tried
to fasten on it, it flickered uncertainly away. It was
something to do with Jere Fitzhugh. Or if not with
him, then with Grew. Rather, it was a phrase used
by Grew, utterance of a disembodied voice addressing
him some hundred of miles away over a wire. With a
sudden effort he defined it. Grew, three days before,
spoke of a theatre. The manager of a theatre, he said,
had vouched for Diamond's professional standing in a
letter. Diamond had brought it with him. The man,
like Diamond—had Grew stated so with certainty?—
lived in Trenton. Grew had surely said that the man
who wrote the letter ran a theatre in Trenton.

Without finishing his coffee, Father Cawder left the
table and paid his bill. He mounted the stairs to the
lounge. Across the room the telephone girl sat behind
a wooden barrier, under a rubber plant. He hurried
to the counter. As she looked up, he spoke brusquely.

"I want to make a call to Lancaster. I want the
Franklin Theatre."

Shut into a booth with an iron door he listened with

impatience to a woman's tired murmurs, "Lancaster, please. Lancaster, please." Almost at once a man's thick voice seemed to answer her.

"Yes? Hello?"

"I'm calling the Franklin Theatre. I want to speak to Asa Grew."

"Yes. Speaking."

"This is Mr. Grew?"

"Right. This is Grew."

"This is Father Cawder. I called you several days ago, Mr. Grew. About a man named Diamond. He came to Lulworth with the carnival."

"Sure. I remember. Did you ever locate the fellow?"

"No. But you told me he brought you a letter from the manager of a theatre. Do you remember the name of the theatre? Was it in Trenton?"

"Did I say that? Well, maybe he did, now. Let me think."

"You said he was recommended to you by a man who ran a theatre."

"Are you in a big hurry? Hold the line a minute."

Grew had a haphazard kind of memory. A few days before he had been able to report what Diamond had said as he went out the door. He remembered that Stella Swartz's wavy hair was dyed, that she wore a man's white silk shirt, he had described the shape of Diamond's thumbs—sign, according to Grew, of one not entirely to be trusted. A small voice clacking in the receiver startled the priest.

"I got it right here, Father. Funny, I thought maybe I'd cleaned it out with a lot of other truck. I found it right where I went to look. It says here the man's name is Kidder. With a K. He runs a theatre up in Trenton; here on this letter it's called the Garden Theatre, 1724 Division Street."

"Kidder, the Garden Theatre. That's what I wanted to find out. Thank you, Mr. Grew."

"Well, I sure hope you come across him. It must be important, all the trouble you're going to."

Frowning, clutching the change given him by the girl, Father Cawder went outside. A taxi was about to turn the corner. He motioned to it and climbed within. For a few blocks he was driven along the flank of a market open to the air. He saw barrows of coconuts under low roofs, stalls heaped with cabbages and Malaga grapes, tables at which butchers were chopping the feet off yellow hens. The taxi spurted up a hill. With a lunge it rocked into a crowded street. It was the same street down which he had walked the night before—windows spread with cheap clothes, pawnshops and cafeterias which had vaguely slipped through his mind while he ate in the grill. The walls of plate glass lost their brilliance by day. In the glare of sun the shops had a ramshackle look. A cloud of dirt swirled up from the gutter and settled slowly over the pavement. Beyond the spiraling dust he glimpsed the sign swaying above the ticket booth of the burlesque theatre. The car slowed down. He expected it to stop in front of the yellow ramp swung inward between mirrors. It came to a halt further along the curb.

Turned about from paying the driver he saw a narrow frontage of green wood and bricks, a cast-iron balcony sagging aslant. "Garden Theatre," the name was spelled out on a kind of frieze, faded letters in the shape of female contortionists. It was smaller, in every way shabbier, than the other theatre gaudy with paint and lights. Its chamfered posts and brackets hung reedily forward from the shell of brick behind. Streaming with sunlight, the hacked doors had a look of being seldom opened. He noticed the scars in all the angles of wood along the street. At some time in the past they had been violently battered. He pressed a white button set into a panel slashed with initials.

In spite of a bloom of dirt across the glass doors the building was being put to use. Two posters and an easel of photographs displayed the bent legs and grins of the cast. The placard beside him showed a strutting Negress, a ruff of black feathers round her hips, her hands stiffly crossed to conceal her breasts. "Minna Wing"—underneath, her name was hugely curled— "And Her 7 Jungle Jazzers." About to push the button again, he heard a sound of scraping feet. The door slid sideways a few inches. Through the crack a short man squinted up at him.

"You want something?" The man's face had massive gray cheeks. He set the knob of his chin tight against the edge of the door.

"Is there a Mr. Kidder here? If he is, I would like to see him."

A janitor, the man looked, in his colorless overalls, a stagehand. His dull eyes settled ahead of him, lusterless as stones.

"What do you want here? What's your name?"

"I've been told a Mr. Kidder is the manager here. If he's inside, tell him Father Cawder wishes to speak to him."

"He's not handing out no more money." The man made no movement. "They came here begging last week. You'll be wasting your time."

"Ask him whether he can see me." Father Cawder glanced away from the man's lumpish nose pitted with black pores. "Tell him my business will not take long."

The man stared in front of him a moment longer. Then he shoved the door back. "This way!" he muttered, padding off. He tramped softly into the dark of a carpeted passage. At the end of a curve of wall he halted under a blue light at the bottom of a spiral staircase.

"This way!"

He went ahead up the narrow iron steps. On the landing he opened a door coated with aluminum paint. The priest entered a small office. A desk and a high wardrobe covered most of the floor. Along the wall stood a row of crated green-glass bottles of some mineral water. At a sound from beyond the wardrobe he looked into an adjoining room. Against the gray oblong of a slit of window a man in a figured shirt was getting unsteadily to his feet from a leather couch. As he came into the office he rubbed his eyes.

"Mr. Kidder?"

"Right. I was having a sweet dream. You woke me up. What can I do for you today?"

"I am Father Cawder. I came here to see you——"

"Glad to make your acquaintance, Father. I hope you don't want any money for a new set of bells. A man came here from some kind of a bye-bye house for bums last week and cleaned me out. It ain't the management's idea to give anything regular, you see."

"I came to ask you whether you have the address of a man named Diamond. I understand you gave him a letter of recommendation before he joined a carnival early in the summer. I thought you might know where he is now."

Rubbing his pointed nose, the man lowered himself slowly into a chair and raised his feet to the edge of the desk. He twisted his face to an expression of mocking shrewdness.

"So you know I gave him a letter, do you? Old Diamond! That little sprat Diamond! You mean Willie Diamond, does a turn into a tub of rain water. Don't know no other."

"Do you know if he's here in Trenton?"

"I used to bum around with the boy once. Before I took things serious. He'll flop without a red cent one of these days. He can't leave hisself alone. A real flimflam."

Kidder cocked his head sharply to the side.

"Who did you say sent you around here?"

"The agent for the carnival gave me your name. Asa Grew, in Lancaster. Diamond left your letter with him."

"Yeah? Diamond ain't owing any money, is he?"

The priest had not taken the chair toward which Kidder had waved a white bony hand. Through the open door at his back he heard the janitor, or whatever he was, shift his feet on the iron plate of the landing. Kidder glanced across at the man and pursed his lips to a silent word.

"I would hardly know about that, Mr. Kidder. Can you tell me where I could find him?"

Two narrow yellow teeth showed in Kidder's smile before it died away. He joggled his little finger vigorously in one ear. "Is Diamond back up here, you think? I heard somebody saw him." He spread his legs and folded his hands over the paunch below his thin waist. "He usually beds down over at May Garrick's. He's stayed with her on and off for years. She might know where he is, anyways. She keeps roomers. She's a real nice old lady, is May, done a mean lot of fancy scratching in her time, the old trotter." His sleepy eyes flickered tentatively over the priest. "Mrs. Garrick's the name."

Father Cawder took a step toward the door. Kidder's skin, he observed, was extremely pale. His cheeks had a granular look, like the surface of a crumbling cake. The priest shifted his eyes. The close air might have caused the slight ache he felt across his forehead. He noticed a sweetish, unpleasant smell wafting out of the adjoining room.

"Where does Mrs. Garrick live?"

"Everybody knows her shop. 302 Montgomery. Not so far, 302 Montgomery."

Kidder lay back in his chair and lazily watched the priest write the name and number on a card. He began to smile.

"Seen our show, reverend? Matinée today. You might stick around, seeing you're inside already."

Father Cawder slipped the card into his wallet. Kidder stretched his arms out over his head. "She's something, that Minna." Meeting the eye of the squat man impassive behind the priest, yawning, he held up a finger. His smile widened.

"Yessir, she's hot. She starts me jumping up here in the balcony. After a good look at Minna I got to run

102

take a sprint around the water tank on the roof. Half French, half crib nigger, Minna."

While his fingers moved methodically to button his coat, Father Cawder paused at the door to the stairs. He had meant to drop his eyes to the face which he supposed was tilted up at him. His glance fastened on the faded roses spotted in bunches over the wall.

"Good-day, Mr. Kidder."

At least he had curbed the pitch of his voice to a tone flat and expressionless. At least he gave no sign that he could deem this husk of a man weighty enough to compel notice of an affront. Dead husk, hulk of carrion behind a desk, blood and muscles moving with corruption to counterfeit something alive, carrion ransomed, so must one believe, by a god.

Kidder stooped to tie his shoelaces. "Take it easy," he said, crouching out of sight. "Show the reverend how to climb out, Fritzy."

The little man went silently ahead of the priest down the coil of stairs. From the room above a sudden skirling of horns sounded as a radio was switched on.

3

WALKING ON HER TOES, UNCERTAINLY smiling, the old woman left the room. She shut the door with extreme care, as if the slightest sound was likely to displease him. When she was gone Father Cawder moved from the chair beside the crumpled bedclothes to a rocker in the bay window. The square room had the look of an old-fashioned parlor, except for the high-backed bed where the old woman slept. At the spindly stove behind the bed she must cook, he thought. There were eggshells, fragments of burnt bread, in a heap on the slate hearth. Above, on the marble shelf, a cut-glass pitcher was crammed with a bunch of dusty holly. He saw a rope strung between pipes across a corner, slack under a load of tattered underwear. The old woman's washing. The pink rags swung in front of a sink.

Mrs. Garrick, on learning he was a priest, had flattened a fleshy hand over her breasts. She pushed back a fringe of hair from her eyes and circled round him with apologies, a lively curiosity spreading into her face. "You'll have to excuse me, I know I look a sight," she had said. And then a moment later, "My poor old room ain't always in such a mess." She drew awkwardly round her shoulders a green silk scarf spotted with yellow birds. "Just you sit yourself down. I'll try to fix this hair of mine a little."

She stood in front of a smudged looking glass, darting her fingers ineffectually about her head. "Have you known them long? Just since last week! My word, that ain't long at all. Oh, they make friends easy. They're real friendly, them two." Diamond always came to her, in work or out. A nice boy, Diamond was, good as gold and just like a son. And Stella, if you treated her right, never made any fuss. There was no harm in her. Of course, she was young.

She had suddenly looked up and groaned. You might think she had put away one too many. But she had clean forgot. Diamond was gone. He went out of the house before eight o'clock. She was standing up eating a bite by the door and she saw him go past. She never thought, she had clean forgot it. That Stella was still in bed as like as not. She never bothered about any breakfast.

"Can't you come back later?" she said in a strangely plaintive voice. "He's sure to be back later on, can't you come back again later?" She dropped her head sideways like a hound, eagerly eying him.

"Since you think Miss Swartz is in," he said, "could you find out whether she can see me?" Perhaps if she could go up and tell her he was downstairs. To see if she was awake and if it would be convenient. Mrs. Garrick gazed over his head a brief while without speaking.

"I could do that," she said at last. "Yes, I guess I could do that." She smiled at him, he thought, almost timidly. Then she left the room and stumped up the stairs.

As he sat in the rocker the house seemed very silent. The only sound he heard was the ticking of a china clock beside the bed. The face of the clock was the bottom of a barrel or keg, sprigged with roses and straddled by a naked girl. He failed to hear Mrs. Garrick when she opened the door. She came up behind him and softly laid a spotted wrinkled hand on his shoulder.

"She's up and decent," she said. "I got her up. She remembered you right off. She says for you to come up."

The old woman's hand startled the priest. He gathered together his coat and hat and stood up. "Thank you, Mrs. Garrick."

"There, did I make you jump? I should have coughed as I came in." With a short hissing laugh she rubbed her palms over her heavy thighs. "I ought to tell you, my name's not Garrick. It's Gurig, G,U,R,I,G. Just thought I'd mention it to you."

"Mrs. Gurig?"

"That's right. May Gurig. I guess you think I'm too old to be telling my first name right off. There's a right time for everything, they say."

"Shall I go up to see Miss Swartz now?"

"Oh, sure." Running her tongue over her creased lips, she glanced pensively at the carpet, as if she had something more to say.

"Do I go up the stairs, Mrs. Gurig?" He looked round at her from the open door.

"Yes, you go right up. You'll see her. Third floor back."

The old woman followed him out into the hall. She was still watching from below, he saw, when he made the turn of the first landing. From the second floor to the third he guided himself up with the rail into the darkness. A woman was waiting at the head of the stairs. Her pale skirt glimmered in the shadows.

"Is that you, Miss Swartz?"

"Hello!" the woman called out. "Excuse me for making you wait. You kind of took me by surprise. I had to take time out to get a coat of enamel on." He recognized no sound of the harsh jocular voice. It rattled out like the smart raps of a little hammer. She went ahead and opened a door. As he entered the room she turned to smile. Her white dress, tied about her waist with a red ribbon, was like a pinafore. Suddenly looking as he had remembered her, she shoved a striped suitcase under the bed, her bare shoulders crossed by starched ruffles.

"I could have died when the old woman said you

106

were downstairs. Reverend, it's rich. What are you doing all the way up here in Trenton anyways? I certainly thought I'd seen the last of you. How did you ever find this dump of old Gurig's?"

She settled herself against the pillows on the bed. Then she pointed at an easy chair covered with a torn square of chintz. Father Cawder sat down.

"I had wanted to see you," he said, "before you left Lulworth. But you had already gone. To talk to you again about your little girl. I wanted to see whether something couldn't be arranged for her."

Stella smiled. "You don't have to bother about her. It don't matter so much."

"You did right to come and see me about your child, Miss Swartz."

The corners of the girl's mouth pulled downward in a faint sneer. She lit a cigarette.

"I can't say I think much of the reception you gave me, reverend."

"You didn't understand me, Miss Swartz."

"If I remember, you practically said I was no lady." She grinned at him with enjoyment. Between her teeth smoke curled out like a trickling liquid.

Watching her smile, he was aware of a weighing melancholy. In spite of his effort to conceal it, it seemed to weigh down the tone of his voice. "I know what I said displeased you, Miss Swartz. I am sorry. It was not altogether as you thought. I was thinking of your daughter. You took what I said in a way I didn't mean."

"Forget it. I wasn't mad long."

"What I said at the time would be true of anyone giving up a child. It had nothing specially to do with you, with you personally."

"Forget it. I've been called names in dizzier towns than that dump Lulworth and I never give a damn. I guess that sweet little place sort of got on my nerves. I must have been feeling sensitive or something." She spread out her fingers, studying her crimson nails.

"Tell me this, how did you ever find this dump of old Gurig's?"

His eyes followed her hands as they wagged slowly back and forth. "The manager of the Garden Theatre here knew Diamond's address. I was told where to find him by a man up in Lancaster."

"You sure get around." She looked at him curiously. "I'd say you're a fast worker. Kidder, you mean. I know who you mean, the sneaking little peddler. He makes me want to run away and die. He's plenty low-down, that Kidder. I hate to see that snake coming up the street." She reached down under the bed and drew up a bottle of nail polish. "I can't get it how you ever got around to him. He likes Diamond. Used to be a time when he saw a lot of Diamond."

The priest wondered how he could have once viewed this girl as a person to whose words it was fitting to take exception. He said to himself, mournfully watching her, he wished her no evil, surely he wished her well.

"You told me in Lulworth you were on the stage, Miss Swartz. Will you take up stage work now that you're back in Trenton?"

Stella softly laughed. She looked at him in a musing surprise. "Did I honestly tell you that? Shame on me! Putting on the dog that way. I'm not on the stage. I don't do anything. Oh, once I came on and kicked in a night club. Two nights I did. Do you think I look like an actress?" She gave a barely perceptible wink.

He considered her with a mild intentness. He felt a foolish pity, as if because of her candid eyes and fresh cheeks she must be innocent and blameless as well. And since he was not empowered to know, possibly she was, as a cat or a squirrel is innocent.

"Yes," he said as if reflecting, meaning to use no irony, "I think perhaps you do. Although I'm not sure that an actress has any special look."

"Coming from you, I don't exactly know just how to take that." She bent affably over the little bottle. She

108

pulled out the stopper and compared the paint on the brush with the red of her nails.

"Will Diamond be back soon?"

"Diamond don't tell me what he's up to. You want to see him too?"

"I thought he would want to know if you decide anything about your daughter."

"He went off to see a man about a job. No jumping act. It's a club or something." She began to dab the red paint at spots on her nails where the dried paste had scaled off.

"Have you made any plans for your little girl? Is she still in the country?"

"It's a funny thing," Stella murmured, "Diamond was talking about you one night. I can't remember what it was he said. I'll tell you something funny about Diamond. He was raised in a convent."

"He was an orphan?"

"Sure he was. Ain't that a laugh, that little monkey in with a bunch of nuns? He stayed in that convent till he was ten years old. He didn't have no relations, some stepfather or somebody put him in that convent."

"In that case, he may have been raised a Catholic."

Stella made a jeering cackle in the back of her throat. "Him? Maybe, if you want to call a kid anything. He didn't waste his time hanging around that convent. He ran away."

She paused to spread out her hair behind her over the pillow.

"It sounds like a bum movie, but he ran away with a traveling carnival. He made tracks with that carnival till he grew up. That's where he got on to that bloody jumping act. Diamond usen't to be so bad once. He was in a vaudeville swing once. Once he put on an act in a circus. But if you ask me this jumping act of his smells pretty high, thrashing around all summer in hick towns into a tub of dirty water. And one fine day he'll break his little neck."

Father Cawder watched Stella's fingers dip toward

the nail polish, dart with the brush and again dip to the little bottle. He hesitated, having no right to question her. Then, his voice rising brusquely, he said, "Have you known Diamond long?"

"Longer than you might think, a long, long time." Stella lay back smiling into the pillows. She waved her hands to dry the polish. "We're just an old respectable couple of mugs by this time."

He searched for the permissible word. He was intervening without prudence. There was something of indecency in questioning this girl. "Have you—" he began.

"When I first took a look at Diamond," Stella was soberly pondering, "I must have thought he was pretty sweet. He was different. I must have been kinda romantic then. I guess he's got his good points. But he's always at me," she exclaimed vehemently. "I'm getting good and sick of the way he is. He won't leave me be for a minute."

She glanced up and uttered a shrill laugh.

"A lot of people I know say I'm so lucky, Diamond will do anything I tell him to, he's off his nut about me, so they say. And he likes to tell me how crazy he is about me. Why can't he think of some way to show it then? He coops me up here in this damned old house without a cent, he's always at me."

Father Cawder exhaled a slow breath. He pushed back his chair. "Have you seen your little girl?"

"I heard how she is. She's all right."

"A few convents near here will take in children like your daughter, Miss Swartz. I made inquiries. If you still are interested. . . . Is the place where she lives near the city?"

"Oh, it's not far a bit." She raised her head suddenly, a finger against her lips. She sprang from the bed and stood erect. She shrugged her shoulders. "I thought I heard something."

After a moment of silence a sound of scratching

110

came from the other side of the door. Stella sharply called out:

"Who is it?"

"It's me," a voice said in a kind of lightly spoken whine. "Open up."

The door of the room was held shut by a brass bolt. Doubling one hand back at her waist Stella stretched out the other and pushed slackly at the pin. Her fingers rattled the metal knob to and fro.

"Sorry I had to get you out of bed, honey," the whining voice quavered.

The bolt shot back as she gave it a violent shake. She wrenched the door open. Diamond, standing motionless in the dark of the hall beyond, quietly looked into the room. Father Cawder got to his feet. Diamond was pale, he appeared old, the priest thought, his sallow face was lined with a faint crisscross of depressions. He could be middle-aged. On the street in Lulworth, his eyes and cheeks black with shadows, he had seemed much younger. He was breathing hard as if he had run up the stairs. Rocking slightly on his heels, he eyed Stella without speaking.

He turned toward the priest and stared stupidly a moment without sign of recognition. "So it's you," he said finally. He knit his eyebrows together. "I remember. You were down there in Lulworth. You're a good ways off base. Do you play on a circuit?"

"You damn fool!" Stella gasped. "Come in and shut the door."

Diamond smiled as he stepped across the door saddle. His voice dropped to a fawning softness. "Why didn't you think to send me a telegram? I always like to be in the know, don't like to miss anything. I could have been here to give you a real welcome. You dropped in, did you? You just happened to drop in?" He had begun to speak in the mocking falsetto he had used outside the door, his eyes fixed on Father Cawder.

"You fool, Diamond!" Stella's voice was loud with

111

anger. "You fool, you. He wants to take the kid, he came up here to take the kid away!"

"To take the kid?"

"Can't you hear? The kid, the brat. He's going to put her away in some convent." Stella lit a cigarette with trembling hands. "Diamond, you make me sick right down to my shoes."

Diamond walked away to the one tall thin window. While he rubbed his chin he glanced up into the sky, his head and shoulders dark against racing wisps of cloud. Stella picked up a hairbrush and studied herself in a looking glass.

"Don't mind the way my little man here behaves. He's peculiar. Sometimes he just goes off his nut. By rights he ought to be up to the big house with the rest of the screwballs. We like to keep him around for the laughs."

Without looking toward her, Diamond crossed the room and stopped in front of the priest. He twisted his mouth, tentatively smiling, as if preparing to urge an excuse.

"I'm glad to see you here, Father. Right at first you kind of surprised me." He held out his hand. "I'm sorry if it looked like I—"

"You're a mess, Diamond," Stella stridently broke in. As she brushed her hair before the mirror she watched his reflection. "You dirty hound, Diamond."

"I'm here in Trenton for a few days." The priest's heavy tone was expressionless. "I wanted to talk to Miss Swartz and you about the little girl."

"At first I didn't rightly see it was you," Diamond said. "If the old woman had just told me—"

"I think a convent near Newark will be willing to take the child. I can make sure tonight. If Miss Swartz still wants to place her with the sisters. I can spend one or two days here, to make arrangements."

"She's at Lily's. That right, Stella?"

Stella leaned close to the mirror and rubbed a finger across an eyebrow. She made no answer.

"The kid's in the country, Father." Diamond tilted his head to one side as if in calculation.

"When could you send for her? I will not be able to stay here much longer." Father Cawder turned to Stella smiling into the glass. "Will your friends in the country bring her here?"

"Stella and me can go get her. We can get her in the car. I've got nothing to keep me. Any day. How about it, Stella? We can go any day."

Stella's smile broadened. "Why ask me? You're so damn smart. You know so much about everything."

"Stella and me can go tomorrow for the kid. Tomorrow morning."

"I will want to see the child before I let the sisters at the convent know. When could you have her here?"

Stella yawned and stretched up her arms. "Why don't you come with us? Come along for the ride."

Diamond pushed his lips forward to one side. "You wouldn't want no part in that ride, Father." His eyes fell on Stella. "It's one long cold dirty ride. Anyhow, you can see the kid better here."

"You come along with us," Stella said. "It's a real pretty ride. Lots of trees, right through the heart of Jersey. Diamond really wants you to come. He's just bashful."

"I don't like to take him in that car. That car's small, the priest don't want to be crowded in with us and a kid too. The kid might get sick on the way, the way she did once before."

"The car holds four easy, Diamond." Stella gave a gasping laugh. "You poor jazzer, why don't you tell him right out you don't want to take him. What's the matter with taking him? Anything wrong with a woman going to get her kid from friends in the country?"

"I can wait to see the child. It will be just as well to see her after you get back."

"It don't matter to me." Diamond glanced from the priest to Stella. "Come along, if you want to, Father."

113

"It would save time perhaps if I came. I will have to see her before I notify the sisters."

"Sure, you come." Stella covered a yawn. "On the way up I'll have a chance to tell you more about Diamond. It's fascinating."

"At what time would you leave?" The priest turned from Stella as if he had not heard her. Diamond clasped his chin, grimacing, as if some secret joke was now shared between them.

"Eight o'clock. Any time. Nine o'clock. What about nine o'clock?"

"We'll pick you up," Stella said. "Where can we find you?"

Father Cawder moved to the door. "I'm at the hotel across from the station. The Piedmont. I can be ready at eight o'clock, or at nine."

"Make it nine. Eight's too early." Stella had sauntered close to Diamond. "You get crow's feet if you get up too early. I've got to keep beautiful if I want to stay in the running."

The priest paused a moment as she rested an arm, long, smooth and white, on Diamond's shoulder. "What is your little girl's name?"

"Marina."

"How old is she, Miss Swartz?" He opened the door.

"Six. No! She's seven."

Stella and Diamond watched Father Cawder begin to tread cautiously down the dark stairs. Crossing the landing on the second floor he heard one of their voices faintly whisper in the shadows above him. The door of Mrs. Gurig's room soundlessly opened as he reached the foot of the steps. The smiling old woman was standing just inside, the slanted insinuating wrinkles were a greeting, he judged. He nodded toward her in silence.

4

DUNKIRK WAS THE NAME OF THE TOWN, painted across a sign on the top of a hill. With a bound the car veered off a street of turreted houses past a whitewashed fence. Father Cawder looked out at yards crammed with gigantic brown sunflowers, at a muddy brook, an arch of black boulders set into the black wall of a graveyard. For an instant a shouting woman beside a ditch beat at a shouting boy with a handful of twigs. The car began to move faster, skirting a pasture where a flock of ragged sheep was grazing. It took the incline of a concrete ramp. Raised now on stilts, the road lay across a marsh. Pools and shaggy grass wavered away out of sight toward a belt of clouds. The marsh at first was rank and green; further along it turned gray, heaped up in scaly folds. A yellow smoke rose from a crack in the shelving earth. The priest saw a small man near the road. He dragged a sack behind him, poking with a stick into a mound. He was about to clamber up a pile of broken crates. But man and crates, smoke, bottles, barrels, flashed behind. They had come to a sheet of gray water. As the car swayed, Stella shouted from the back seat:

"Stop trying to kill the priest and me, Diamond."

Father Cawder glanced toward her. She smiled across at him, her face splattered with the black spots stuck to the mesh of her veil. The smile perhaps was suggested by civility. She wanted him to know that notwithstanding Diamond's uncivil moodiness her own feelings were certainly those of friendly good humor.

Diamond's head fell lower and he drove on in silence. A strong wind lashed the car. It clattered against the windows, whistling and heaving up under the floor.

Beneath the wire parapet the water dwindled into glistening mud on which small boats were beached. The road dropped to a stand of pines. Their thin trunks shook with the wind. Black and wiry at the edge of the concrete they flickered past the car without gaps or clearings. Through the glass Father Cawder drowsily watched their bristling tops, almost with a sleepy pleasure. None of the trees grew tall; the land looked light and sour. No wonder this unthriving soil was desert, waste of pine, scrub oak, knots of brambles. As they raced forward in a straight line, for many minutes, it seemed to him, not once had a man or animal or house come in view. Then a domed silo rose above the thickets. The car buffeted by a country store huddled at the roots of three sycamores, a railroad crossing vague in a gust of grit and leaves. Along the tracks the sandy fields stretched naked under irrigation pipes. Stripped after the last crop, the white sand cut back into the woods. The pines sprang up again at the side of the road, quaking in the wind.

The long fall of the ground flattened to a dead level, and little by little the wind sank down and died away. The priest watched the straight line of concrete vanish behind him like a cord being wound on a spool. All at once he noticed the noiselessness of the air within the car, now that the wind was no longer blowing. Stella had moved. He smelt a sweet scent floating forward over his head.

"It seems a lot longer than it used to, Diamond."

"It hasn't changed none, it's the same old grind. There's Cairo."

The car was passing a clearing. Ruts gouged by wheels in the pale mud curved toward the trees in a tangle of grass. A gutted chimney of brown stones stood beside an old flat-topped pine. Rising from a

116

base shapeless under ivy it was pitted with fireplaces on three levels.

"There used to be an old house here," Diamond said. "Years ago. But they had a bad fire. A great big white house. It was called Cairo."

"That was nowhere near my time," Stella said. "I never saw any house here. But then I'm pretty young. I guess I was just a baby then."

Diamond lit a cigarette. While he blew smoke from his mouth, turning sideways to speak, Stella put her head close to his and whispered.

"What of it?"

"I'd kinda like a beer. I'd just like to drop in for a minute. Just for a real good cry."

"Donegan ain't there any more."

"Who cares!" Stella settled back into the seat.

"Do you mind stopping off ahead there, Father?" Diamond said. "We'll just stop a minute. So Stella can get a beer. One time she used to know the people who ran the place, she used to like to come out here."

He nodded toward a ring of pines clustered about a long bungalow with screened porches. It lay back into the shade of the trees, sheathed with bark cut to look like logs. A peeling sign was raked along the roof. "Sue's Cabin," the priest read, "Beer and Wines 'Neath the Pines." Tall weeds had grown up during the summer in the patches of sandy soil. They stood in withered clumps below the window, against the porch. The car curved to a halt. As the wheels ground noisily over pebbles a woman came to the screen door and looked out. She put her hand over her eyes.

Diamond glanced sharply to one side. "Do you mind getting out, Father?" he said in a low voice. "Come in and have a beer with us. Or maybe you want to wait in the car here?"

Did he think, this ferrety man, to spare him the shock of seeing a woman drink a glass of beer, the priest wondered. He slid his feet downward out of the car. "I won't have anything, but I may as well go with you."

Stella ran ahead up the steps. "Is your beer good and cold?" she called out. The woman smiled, holding back the door with a knotty fist. "Sure." She trudged ahead across an empty dance floor to a round table. With a rag pulled out of her apron pocket she wiped off its top and the seats of the chairs. Her arms were brown and muscular. White hairs sprouting over her chin glistened in the light as she faced the windows. Rubbing her hands on the rag and smiling, she observed Stella with an easy curiosity.

"Now, what'll it be? All of you want beer?"

Father Cawder heard two faint voices wrangling somewhere in the distance. The woman's steady eyes shifted to Diamond.

"Two beers," he said. "Just the two beers."

When the woman left the table Stella gazed round her. "My god, Diamond, this place is scary. I'm sorry we ever came in. It's all changed. They've gone and got rid of all the blue mirrors, did you notice that? And those silk lamps, I don't see them anywhere."

Diamond peered into the shadows lengthening from a pile of stacked chairs. "They get a different trade. They don't do so much business any more. Lily's pulled out of the place—a couple of years ago."

"Lily knew how to make a place look attractive. This place looked real sweet sometimes when Lily had been working over it." Stella turned to the priest. "Lily's my friend who takes care of Marina. She put some cash into this place once upon a time."

"It was an investment," Diamond said.

The woman had come back without their hearing her. She stood waiting behind Diamond with a tray in her hands. While setting the beer bottles on the table she slackly smiled.

"Excuse me for asking, but aren't you Stella Swartz?"

Stella took a sip of beer. "I certainly am, my friend. How did you know who I am?"

118

"I thought I recognized you. When you came in I was looking at you. I seen you here once with Miss Lily Bell. I thought I knew you."

Stella took her glass of beer and got to her feet. She tapped Diamond on the shoulder.

"You wait for me. I want to do a job on my face." She lifted her eyes to the woman's. "Come along to the ladies' ta-ta. You can shove out the goods on Lily while I powder my nose."

The two women walked away toward the back of the room. A shriek of laughter came from Stella as she pushed through a curtained doorway. Diamond's fingers were scratching at the label on a beer bottle. His lowered eyes flickered briefly over the priest.

"You oughtn't to get any wrong idea about Stella," he said in a flat voice.

"Get a wrong idea?" Father Cawder had forgotten for an instant the diver, the girl, the child. He turned his mind to the words with an effort. "Get a wrong idea about her?"

"Yes. I thought you'd got to think things about her. She's just free and easy. It's the way she has. She just likes a good time."

"She—" Father Cawder began. He paused before he went on. "I don't judge people, Diamond. I don't— It's no concern of mine to pass judgment on Stella, on anyone at all." He had called him by his name with familiarity. Diamond may or may not have noticed the patronizing freedom. His black opaque eyes focused searchingly on the priest.

"All right. I thought maybe you might get an idea. Stella's a girl who's had some lean pickings. That's why I don't mind her having a good time. She don't mean any harm by it."

"I have no right or interest in making what you or she does any concern of mine. I think no harm of Stella." Father Cawder broke off uneasily, as if what he said was misleading or too weak. He meant to say that he did not usurp the operations of God, not

119

that he separated himself from their destinies. The strange point apparently had an importance for Diamond. He was still looking fixedly above the top of the beer bottle.

"It's no part of a priest's business to pass on people like a judge. A priest has no means of doing so even if he wished; only God sees people as they are. I have good will toward Stella." Father Cawder gazed over the empty tables. If inadequate, still the statement was not untrue. It was a version adjusted to the man before him. Could he say that a priest wishes to evade mere social relationship, that a man to him is merely an entity whose intellect is to be brought to know God, that he was, or meant to be, bound to that charity which is indifferent to personalities and questions of demerit? Indifferent, that is, to the demerits of everyone except himself. Father Cawder stared through the shadows at a shiny object sparkling in the gloom across the room. He had this intention to Stella, he said to himself. Surely it was charity he felt for her.

Diamond's rasping voice broke through his thoughts.

"It's like we're married, Father," he was saying soberly, uncertainly. "That's the way it's turned out with me and Stella." A lowered pitch to his voice caused the priest to look at him. His eyes gleamed, his lips swerved open, like a fish, like a child, under the stress of some turn of emotion. Father Cawder contracted his forehead into a frown against his will. He spoke out at random.

"If you mean—" he stammered.

"I know what she's like. That's why I take care of her." Diamond stared solemnly as if his choice of words should carry extraordinary weight or suggest some hidden meaning. He threw back his head and drained off his beer. "I don't want nobody to get her wrong."

The priest said nothing. He tried to recall if his manner to Stella had been short. If some careless phrase could have seemed too pointed. By what process, he wondered, could his conduct strike Diamond as important? But then as Diamond functioned irrationally there would be no occasion for rational procedure. He thought of the tone of Diamond's voice a moment before, mournful, drawn out like a groan. He exhibited emotion easily. It was imaginable that painful emotion, once exhibited, gave him something like pleasure, a kind of relief. Behind him Father Cawder heard the clicking of a latch, a note of Stella's shrill laughter. As the two women came toward the table he and Diamond stood up.

"I paid Miss Annie here for the beers," Stella said. "Are we ready to go?"

Diamond walked off to the door. For an instant Stella and the woman looked humorously at each other. They both began to smile.

"Got to run, Miss Annie. Don't let them roll you against the wall. I'll see you sometime."

"You tell Miss Lily Bell I asked after her," the woman said. "Be good, Miss Stella." With a grayish forefinger she dug at the flat skin of her chest, watching Stella cross the porch.

The priest stooped into the car and Diamond, hunched in his corner, started the motor. He waited for Stella to settle herself in the back seat, his eyes raised to the little mirror above his head. The car swung out onto the road. Almost at once it turned off into a lane of sand which dipped forward into the pines. After a little the wood thinned out. Singly or in twos and threes, the pines stood clear against the sweep of a vast mackerel sky. The car climbed a slope, rocked down through fields rippling with pale grass. The land must be close to the sea, Father Cawder thought. They were passing clumps of mallow still in bloom and tufted ponds lay here and there below the level of the lane, round and rankly green like vats of dye. Beyond them he saw a house squarely rising across the long slant of the grass. It looked at first sight like a yellow junk, a blocky ship strung with hawsers. As the car came closer the walls fell back within verandahs, a scaffolding of posts in three tiers, wider than the house. The eaves projected flat and bold over brackets heavily coiled; the green paint of the trim was bleached to a milky bloom. Rusted urns on iron pedestals flanked the steps up to the porch. A dwelling which would be termed, if in a public park, a mansion house. A decayed hotel, possibly, the priest conjectured. Evidently decayed, since under the blotched consoles a weatherboard half as long as the width of the house had fallen away or been ripped off. Diamond stopped the car under an arching tree where the bare earth had perhaps been trampled by animals or by children at play. Three small sheds roofed with tarpaper stood against a wire fence.

Stella walked toward the steps. She began to pull down her spotted veil over her face.

"Your friends don't appear to have ploughed the fields for some time," Father Cawder said. "I suppose the soil here is thin."

"A Miss Bell runs it. The friend I was speaking of. She raises dogs to sell. Chesapeake Bays. That right, Diamond?"

"Sure." Diamond was glancing up at the windows as if he thought to see someone within move into view. "It's a dog kennel. Lily raises the dogs to sell."

"Your child has been living here all the year round then."

"That's right. She's had a good time. She loves dogs and animals."

"She is seven? Could she get to school out here?"

"I'll tell you." Stella halted at the foot of the steps. Across the planks a black hen scurried, beating its wings. "This is how it is. This girl who runs this place, she's a friend of mine and all that, but with the kid getting older, Lily hasn't got the time, out here in the country she can't get to a school—"

"She's the only child here."

"That's right. Just her. That's another reason. She's

122

old enough now to want to meet some other kids her own age."

They started to climb the steps. Two baskets filled with empty Coca-Cola bottles had been left beside the double door. Diamond put his arm round Stella's waist.

"You go wait in the car, baby," he said. "You don't need to come in."

"What are you getting at now, I don't need to come in?" Stella plucked impatiently at his hand. "I came here to get the kid, Diamond."

"You go back to the car. You ought to stay out in the car."

"I've got to see Lily. You know I've got to see Lily, Diamond." She looked angrily toward the priest. "I'm being protected again. He thinks I might get broken or something."

Diamond turned aside, his glance darting out over the fields of broom-sedge ruffled in the wind. "You know what I think." He took his hand from about her waist. "You ought to do what I say."

"You great big bleeding heart, how do you think I got along before you looked in?"

"For Christ's sake, Stella. For Christ's sake!" The girl's brilliant eyes fixed on Diamond's as he swung round again. "Go back to the car. I'll bring Lily out when we find the kid."

She walked to the edge of the porch. "You think I'm just a great big beautiful doll, don't you? I might get my shine rubbed off."

"Sure. That's what I think."

"You poor little thing!" Stella went down the steps and sauntered slowly toward the car.

Diamond grasped the knob of greenish brass. "It's her nerves," he said. "It's bad for her nerves to see much of Lily. They don't get on. That's why I wanted her to go back. She's upset today."

He pushed open one leaf of the door. The light struck past a wall of paneled wood into a murk of shadows. They stepped inside. Diamond called softly,

"Lily! Lily!" As their eyes got used to the dimness the edge of the wainscot stretched off into the center of the house, the ceiling ended at a gap through the floors, galleries, faintly looming, hung out overhead round a stair well. A beam of sunlight fell inward from the door left ajar. It made the dust dropping through the air sparkle like crumbs of steel. Diamond placed a foot on the stairs. "Lily!" he called. He waited, listening.

There was no sound anywhere in the house. Diamond and the priest walked back to the open door, their shoes ringing like stones against the floor boards. "Lily!" Diamond called once more. He peered up at the railings vague in the dark. "Maybe they're gone somewhere for the day. I'm going to take a look around outside for Lily. Maybe she's round in the back with the dogs. I won't be long."

Father Cawder heard Diamond clatter down from the porch. He turned away into the wide well of the stairs. Far above he saw a skylight; the glass, spotted with dirt, let in a grayish glow which spent itself on distant banisters. A sofa had been shoved under the first bend of the staircase. Wads of stuffing bulged through the slashes across its seat. The sight of the dangling matted cotton faintly disgusted the priest. On a small table with wire legs stood a half-full Coca-Cola bottle. He sat down beside it. After feeling in his pocket for his rosary beads, he touched the crucifix and began to recite the creed.

"—*Crucifixus etiam pro nobis, sub Pontio Pilato passus*," he whispered, then was silent. A light scraping had caught his ear, a footfall. Near him, somewhere beneath him, a light foot was ascending stairs, drawing closer. He stood up. Further along the strip of paneling a door creaked. A child came forward carrying a tray, a little girl, sharp-faced, with long hair of no color. When she saw the priest she stumbled.

"You scared me, mister!"

"Is your name Marina?" he asked. "You're Marina, aren't you?"

The little girl nodded. She watched him with a look of wary curiosity. "What do you want?"

"Your mother is here, Marina. She's come to take you away with her."

The child bent over, examining the plates on the tray.

"You remember your mother, don't you?"

"Sure. I remember her. Stella. You're fooling me."

Father Cawder glanced down. The tray held two plates of eggs, cups and a covered bowl, on the edge a steaming pot.

"No, she is outside. She wants you to come out and see her. She is going to take you away with her today."

"I wouldn't mind." The child spoke in a sleepy singsong. She settled the tray against the bone of her hip. "Why did you come to get me?" she said suddenly. "You're not Stella's big time, are you?"

"Your mother wanted me to come and find you." He looked down into sharp pale eyes. The girl's face had a peevish cast. It was like the pinched discontent seen in the mouth of a bad-tempered old woman.

"I got to take Marie her eggs. She gets mad when they're cold."

He followed the child, after hesitating an instant, into the darkness back in the depth of the house. Ahead of him she made a sound as if working the lock of a door. He halted, hearing her cautiously step forward through a darkened room or passage, then again stopping, rattling the china on the tray. From somewhere close at hand came a shrill peal of laughter, a muffled clapping noise. The little girl lightly kicked against, as it seemed, a second door beyond the first. The small scream of laughter died away. "Come in! Come in!" a vibrating voice shouted. Marina must have pushed into a room full of daylight, for a faint brightness cut across the air.

"Where'll I put it?"

The child's murmur was thin and clear. He stood still. "God almighty!" a woman's high voice exclaimed. After

125

a whoop of subsiding laughter the same voice, falling, controlling itself, said, "Put it on the bed, honey." From farther away another voice spoke, a soft drawling that was perhaps a man's. "You old tub," it said.

"Marina! Come here! There's no ketchup!"

Someone took a step. "Come here!" the high voice yelled, suddenly sharp.

"What's the matter, Marie?" The child's words came faltering through the shadows to the priest. "What's wrong, Marie?" For a few moments there was no sound from the room beyond.

"What did I tell you about them eggs?" the woman cried out abruptly. "What did I tell you yesterday?"

"You said, 'Don't let the eggs get fried too much.' "

"Leave her alone." The soft remote voice was certainly a man's. "Eat your damn eggs and leave her alone."

"I said," the woman cried, "not to burn the edges of the damn eggs. Look at them eggs. They're all burnt up." The tray violently rattled. Father Cawder stretched out a hand to the black frame of the door. "Can't you see they're all burned?"

Marina was stuttering, chattering, "O Marie! O Marie!" Her stuttering was drowned out in the woman's crackling voice.

"And what did I say I'd do? You remember? What did I say I'd do?"

The child mumbled, "You said I'd catch it."

There was a noisy laugh. "I said you'd catch it. You certainly are going to catch it, sweetheart, you damned little runt. I'll tell you what I think I'll do, I think I'll smear one of them eggs all over your sneaky little face. How'd you like that? And after I've smeared the egg on your head I think I'll lock you up in that closet there for the rest of the day. After you've kicked and screamed and peed in your pants in that closet for four or five hours, maybe you'll learn how I want my eggs. How'll that be?" The woman laughed again.

126

"Quit picking on her," the man said. He was yawning. "Your coffee'll get cold."

"I ain't picking on her." The woman crossed a bare floor. "She brings me stuff I can't eat. The little monkey does it to rile me."

"I know what's eating you. You're mad she's got a little something you ain't."

"Shut your dirty mouth." All at once the woman was speaking with a slow mildness. "Go get that ketchup, Marina."

"Yeah, it's one little trick you ain't had a good while back. So you take it out on the kid. She's a cute little biddy. Thin, maybe, but she's young."

"You ought to be ashamed." The woman was moving away, her words fell to an easy mutter. "Go on, girl, git."

Marina slipped out soundlessly into the hall. Father Cawder reached for her fingers. If the abominable woman had proceeded to handle the staring spindly child, had then and there laid hands on her, he would have had to pitch himself into the room, to drag her out of the way of the woman's infected touch. This, at least, had not been necessary. He felt an instant of quick relief. She had not seen him standing motionless in the dark, had not forced upon him by some chance the polluting contact of her hands or breath.

"We will go out to find your mother," he said, using an ordinary tone, to the little girl.

"Who's that there?" the woman called out. He heard her heels click through the passage. She stopped short, indistinct against the light behind her, a woman with frizzly hair shapeless in a black wrapper.

"Marina." She lowered her voice. "Who's that with you?"

"She's here with me. I came to get Marina for her mother."

"God!" the woman gasped. "You scared me! What

127

are you doing prowling around in here? We got union hours, sweetheart. Nothing doing this time of day."

"I came to get Marina. For her mother. Her mother's waiting for her outside."

"Her mother," the woman repeated heavily. "Her mother? You mean Stella Swartz? You say she's here?"

"She came for Marina. She is taking her away with her."

"Oh! So that's it." Her voice became careful. "Stella better see Lily. Lily's somewhere around. You better see Lily about it first before you go off anywheres with that kid."

Father Cawder led Marina toward the sunlight sparkling in through the still open door. From the porch he saw Diamond below, stooped on his heels beside the car. A few feet away Stella was talking to a woman whose sleek black head glistened in the sun whenever she moved. Three Chesapeake Bay retrievers brushed against her legs or nosed their muzzles into her hand. As he came down the steps with the child, the two women glanced up.

"You haven't been square with me, Stella, you know it," the woman was saying in a ringing voice. The priest took a stand behind her. Dropping her chin she folded her arms in silence.

Stella knelt down in front of Marina and grinned into her face. "Hello, baby," she said. "Can't you talk? Can't you say hello to your old momma?"

Marina thinly smiled. "Hello, Ma."

"You're going to take a ride with me, honey. You and me are going away together." Stella rose up and motioned with her hands. "Father Cawder, I want you to meet my friend Lily, Miss Bell."

The woman's eyes lifted lightly to the priest. They were black and deliberate. "How do you do," she said. He observed her pale forehead broadly curved under symmetrically waved hair, her pale clasped hands. Her white blouse, her gray skirt and jacket, hung from her body without wrinkles, or even folds. "I see you didn't have any trouble finding the girl." She waited for him to speak. After a silence she turned back to Stella with her fists clenched on her hips.

"You said all along she was mine. You told me to take her, Stella. Well, I've given her a home. I didn't mind. I don't mind doing a favor for a friend. But you said for her to stay here. I wouldn't have taken her in unless she was going to stay here. What do I get out of it? You're not being fair to me, Stella."

"What's the use of all this jabbering back and forth, Lily? I'm taking the kid with me. I'm the kid's mother, and by God she's going where I say."

"Who paid for that doctor? Who paid for that doctor, Stella?"

"You make me laugh, Lily. You'd have looked pretty with a dead woman stuck in your best bed."

"I've had dead women in that bed a sight fancier than you, dearie." Miss Bell shot a glance at Marina. "She's been an expense. She's cost me at least a hundred a year, just for food and wear and tear. Four years, four hundred dollars, just for food. Are you paying me back that four hundred dollars of my good money I've put out, Diamond?"

"Listen, Lily," Diamond said, "you've got no kind of claim on the kid. Stella's giving the kid to a convent. Just write her off as incidental expense. Has she got any clothes?"

"Take her the way you find her, you pair of chiselers. Pay me my four hundred the girl's cost. You might want a good friend one of these days, you two." The woman's voice rose.

Stella and Diamond had each taken one of Marina's hands. They moved away toward the car. "We'd better start now, Father Cawder," Diamond said. Stella pushed Marina ahead of her into the back seat.

"Good-bye, Marina," Miss Bell called out. She turned back to the priest and surveyed him stolidly. "They're a cute couple of tramps, your friends. All of you must be sure to come back real soon."

He got into the front seat beside Diamond. As the car began to swerve in a long arc Miss Bell followed it with her eyes. Diamond swung round toward the lane and drove back within two feet of her. "You dirty tramps!" she shouted. "You dirty chiselers!" Her cold eyes struck into Father Cawder's. She burst into a laugh which, far within the black of her mouth, winked with the glint of gold.

5

A WOMAN SWINGING A BUNDLE IN A SACK of red net knocked against Father Cawder. Without looking up he stepped aside to give her room. "Always pushing and shoving," she muttered. He glanced at her pouched face without interest.

The child had been got from the hands of infidels, at any rate. A child now had the means to live in innocence, he was thinking, as the shadow of a cornice blotted out the sun smarting across his forehead. One who except for him would have been debauched by whores. Hereafter Marina would know that there exists, sustaining the blind dance of matter, He who is called God. Whom she was bound to love and serve. At the two judgments, the particular and the last, the girl need not reckon on the excuse of Invincible Ignorance to avert damnation. To Stella, born in sin and theological error, God was no more than a thin sound—an unmeaning syllable to be murmured when a drop of nail polish spattered on her sleeve. Immovable, she was, in ignorance. Unless a predestined mercy struck her, she was doomed till she was dead to be ignorant of that mercy, of the pure beingness which men have agreed to name God. It was likely that nothing he could think of saying could move this woman. It was possible to suppose that she, being ignorant, was not culpable for a single sin; she breathed and talked and determined her actions in the innocence of animals; she would not be judged responsible.

Or it was equally likely he knew nothing about her

at all—settling a woman's fate by facial expressions, words tossed out like pebbles flung into a pond. The day before, at the moment when the car stopped in front of Mrs. Gurig's, Stella was leaning forward, frowning at her thoughts. A glimmering sullen look passed over her face. As Diamond took the child indoors, she pulled from the palm of her hand under the black glove a knot of dirty dollar bills. "Take it for the kid," she said. It was to assert the respectability of her daughter when she entered a household of nuns. The child was to come with worldly goods provided by its mother. He had hesitated. It was not necessary, he said. "Give it to the sisters, tell them they can spend it any way they like." As he put the money into his wallet he heard Stella's jeering laugh. Maybe Marina would turn out to be a nun. She was thinking, the nuns getting a hold on the girl so young, maybe they'd keep her in the convent for good. He was pushing the wallet back into a pocket. He said it was fortunate the child was going to live with the sisters at her age, she was sure to be raised a Christian. As for being a nun—he looked up to find Stella sharply watching him.

"Don't you think I'm a Christian?" she said. She was staring in amazement. "What do you think I am?"

Her angry blue eyes, her angular parted lips, bewildered him. He spoke without confidence.

"You're a Christian? You believe in Christ?"

"Certainly I do! Certainly I believe in Christ! Just what do you think I am?"

Her mouth still open, she snatched up her gloves and stepped from the car. Having violently slammed the door, she took three rapid strides across the sidewalk to the house. Then she stopped, glanced blankly back and said, "Thanks for seeing about the kid."

A truck, grinding forward, halted Father Cawder on the slant of a gutter. Diamond's nature was simple, the priest considered, he was merely mediocre, suspicious, and lustful. He existed, according to the custom of the world, for the brief sensations of each day, the

132

pleasure to be had in a woman's body, a soft bed, food and drink and pocket money. Like all the millions on the earth, a creature moved like a puppet by his appetites. Beyond a dull disordered mediocrity, nothing more was visible. He had seen Diamond by count three times. It was curious to bring to mind. He treated with the diver, he realized, as if he stood on the footing of a bank clerk or carpenter passed every day on the street. Like Jere Fitzhugh, or the druggist with the tobacco-stained mustache familiar over years of truisms casually exchanged but whose name he had never heard.

"Faith," Father Cawder said, almost aloud. Faith is mysterious, a free gift. Since Diamond did not have —it was to be presumed he did not have faith. Nevertheless, he and Stella might be thought less desperately fixed in a mold of perverse will than the others— their taint somehow differed from the cold avarice which had seemed to glaze Lily's eyes, in some integral way they were different from Kidder, from the harlot in the black wrapper. A potential was perhaps observable, something—the priest was unable to define what he meant. In Diamond it was like a germ of piety, *pietas,* that reverence paid to the order of natural law, to parents, to guests, to men in authority, to the dead, to priests and rites. He was civil. His civility suggested he made acknowledgment of priestly status. As a French freemason takes off his hat to the clergy conducting a hearse, to show his pious respect to natural law and the dead. It was an instinct that signified little.

The setting sun, flashing round a street corner, blinded Father Cawder. He lowered his eyes against the glare. Diamond was a man trapped in sins of flesh. Fornication, however, is one of many vices. Other sins also bear weight. He had forgotten the dream. Would he have inclined to shy from the fancy of a libertine's being equal with him in God's sight—if he had known he could say of Diamond that he had connection with

133

a disreputable woman? Other sins risk damnation: anger, pride, the idolatry of the will, the dry rot of covetousness. Perhaps it could be claimed for him that he was not covetous, not a glutton, nor envious nor a lender of money at interest to the poor in their necessities. But he was subject to anger, willful, able to be tempted to pride. And sloth . . .

Father Cawder stood in front of Mrs. Gurig's door. Aware all at once of the worn slab of brownstone, the cast-iron grapes along the railing, he looked up at a bank of clouds. The uttering of a single word might prove able to unloose the mystery of why two certain men in God's providence come to confront each other, and not one or another man entirely disparate. By a word or tone of voice, God could let it appear that one who had been casually encountered was in reality singled out, that chance served in truth to converging ends. But Diamond and Stella, the people he could hear noisily shuffling behind him along the street, none of these perhaps believed in the providence of God. He laid his hand on the brass ball of the bell. Before he could pull it, the door opened.

Mrs. Gurig, standing sideways for him to enter, faintly smiled. "My! It's you, I see. I never thought to see you tonight."

"Is Diamond at home, Mrs. Gurig?"

"Diamond's out." Her left hand wandered over her cheeks. "And that Stella's got company."

"Do you know when he's coming back?"

The old woman squinted up at him as though reading a line of small print across his forehead. "Just some girl. Some girl's always up there visiting with Stella. I don't mind, I'm sure. She's lively and she's young." She threw back her head, seeming to think someone had called to her.

"This hall of mine's so dirty and drafty, come on into the parlor." Mrs. Gurig stumped across to her room and beckoned. When he had passed inside, crouching forward, she cautiously closed the door. Her face brightened at once with quick expression.

"Diamond's jealous! Did you know that? He's terrible jealous of Stella." She came up to the priest and laid her hand, blotched with brown spots, on his sleeve. "Once he got so mad. It was up in Perth Amboy. Stella had been carrying on. He just grabbed her by her neck. He said if he ever caught her—"

Father Cawder turned toward the door. Should he allow himself, he wondered, even to sit waiting in the hall? He could go back to the hotel for an hour. Or leave a note for Diamond, with the address on it and the time. Scratching at her cheek Mrs. Gurig moved after him. A thread of spittle glistened across her lips.

"She was scared," she hissed in a rapid whisper. "I tell you, Diamond don't miss much. But she can't help it, the poor thing. I say, if she can't help it, she ain't to blame." Her wide mouth worked with sibilants. "Stella Swartz's a young kid. Diamond's crazy to keep her penned up so."

The liveliness died out of Mrs. Gurig's face. As the priest opened the door to the hall, she seemed to be slyly pondering. "I mind my own business, it don't matter to me what the others are up to. You can't blame a girl just because she's human." She lowered her eyes, feebly smirking. "I got to thinking about you getting Stella's kid off her hands for her and all. Anybody's free to take a look at Stella, nothing wrong in that."

She eyed him boldly, her smile deepening, wavering across her pale gums. Father Cawder looked at her in perplexity. Abruptly, as he stared into the old woman's trembling face, a thrill of anger ran through him. Her blinking lids drooped. "Maybe—" she began.

"Be quiet! Unless I speak to you, be quiet!" The old woman had startled him, he realized, into an authority which he thought improper to use on those outside his charge. He strode into the hall.

"The girl, where is she?"

135

"The girl?" Mrs. Gurig mumbled.

"The little girl." He spoke loudly, with impatience. "The child, Marina."

"She's out back, I guess," Mrs. Gurig said slowly. "In the yard. I'll show you."

She went beyond the staircase and pulled up the blind of the single window. The priest followed her. He bent to peer through the grimy glass. A thin evening light was fading from the sky. He barely made out the child in the shadows below. She was sitting on the coping of the steps which led down into the basement. She sat without moving, looking over the yard of black cinders to the high boards, slanting inward, of the old woman's fence. She raised a hand as they watched and began to rub the blade of a snakeplant beside her on the stone.

"Look there! Look at her now!" Mrs. Gurig cried. "Daring to touch my plant! All the livelong day she's been into things, meddling, meddling." She beat on the pane of glass. "Take your hands off! Take your hands off my plant, do you hear?"

The old woman turned away and wrapped her arms over her breasts as if she felt cold. "I'll be glad to get her out of here. I'm too old to be put to mind a kid. It ought to be somebody taking care of me. I can't be taking care of all the meddling brats they bring to this house, imposing on me. I won't stand for it."

"She will be here only for the night. See that she gets her dinner and goes to bed early."

"I'm not well," Mrs. Gurig exclaimed, moving off unsteadily. "I never asked Stella Swartz to bring these dirty meddling kids in here."

Her tongue ran over her lips while the priest pulled on his overcoat, opened the door to the street, adjusted his hat.

"She can't stay here in my house but just one more day. Just one more day!"

The closing door muffled the frantic voice. The twilight was darkening. In front of the house the street lights burned at the center of spheres of mist. Their pale glare across the pavement was dappled with shade from a tall locustlike tree. There was no one in sight. At the opposite curb Father Cawder noticed a car drawn up, its headlights steady through the hazy air. He walked off quickly to the right.

The motor of the parked car throbbed as the priest came abreast of it. It glided out, turned round and came softly behind him, its beam of light filling the concrete with his shadow, suddenly gigantic. It passed ahead and stopped. A voice called faintly, "Father Cawder!"

He went to the open window. "Is that you, Diamond?" Stooping down, he looked inside. "Mrs. Gurig told me you had gone out. I have just come from there."

Diamond opened the door and leaned sideways. "I know, Father. Come get in the car. I saw you when you went in."

"You were driving by?"

"Sure. I saw you when you went in." Diamond cocked his head. "Did you see the old lady?"

"I spoke with her for a moment. I saw the little girl. She was outside in the back yard."

Diamond started the car. "I'll just cruise around. Tell me if you want me to take you somewheres. You didn't see Stella?" He threw his cigarette through the window. After scanning the street he turned round in the dark. "No, she had company," Father Cawder had been about to say. He kept silent.

"Did you see Stella?" Diamond's voice slipped flatly through the shadows. "Or was she busy?" He glanced to the side as if his eyes could pierce with ease into the darkened air around him. Father Cawder opened his mouth to say, "I didn't see her. She was busy." Instead, he stated brusquely, "I saw her just a few seconds."

"You saw her?" It was a straining insistency which flattened Diamond's voice. The priest was aware that

137

the vague unease he felt, a something like fearfulness, had to do with Stella.

"Yes," he said, "I saw her on the stairs for a few minutes. It was you I wanted to talk to. About the little girl, Marina."

"About the girl? Where do I drive, Father? You want to go back to the hotel?"

"That will be all right, drive to the hotel. Do you know the Carmelite convent on Fremont Street?"

"Fremont Street?" Diamond jerked up his head. "Sure, sure. The place with the big stone wall. Sure."

"Tomorrow afternoon Stella can take Marina there. Both of you had better go. You can leave Marina there with the sisters. They'd like you to come around one."

"We're just to leave her, then."

"Yes. Stella must go too. The sister will give her a paper to sign. I'm leaving tomorrow morning as I planned."

"All right. Stella will be there."

"Marina will spend the night with the Carmelites. The next day I've arranged for one of the nuns from Saint Anne's Home in Bantry to come down for her. That will be all there is to do. She will go up to Bantry with the sister. The sisters there are glad they could make room for Marina."

"All right. Everything's settled then about the kid?"

"Yes. After tomorrow."

"I'll tell Stella. We'll be there on the dot." The car passed under a swaying elm and slid between the gateposts of a park. Along the road lawns fell off in gentle slopes, bright with moonlight. "You won't be seeing Stella again then."

"No. I'm taking a morning train. I'll say good-bye to you now."

"Stella's much obliged. For the trouble you went to over the kid. Maybe she didn't say much, but she won't forget it."

"She was right to want to get something done for Marina. It will be a good place for the child to live."

138

"She got to thinking about the kid while we were on the road. Being up there at Lily's place."

The car came to a slow halt under a spreading tree dark from thicknesses of leaves.

"She should not have put the girl there," Father Cawder said abruptly. "She knew what the place was. Both she and you must have known what it was."

"Sure. I knew." Diamond lit a cigarette. Holding the match he smiled meagerly, glancing at the priest. "I told Stella it wouldn't take you long to figure out the setup. Stella thought you'd never notice. It was this way. Stella and Lily are friends from way back. You see, Lily just runs the place. That's why Stella let her have the kid."

"Had Stella been there? Did she know what the place was when the child went there?" Father Cawder watched the slanting grass brighten as the moon flared from behind a mass of clouds.

Diamond softly whistled. "You don't seem to get it about me and Stella, Father," he said quietly. He turned halfway round in his seat. "You don't know, you just don't get how it is." Turned sideways he seemed to be keeping his eyes on the priest's profile outlined against the window. "Maybe you do at that," he muttered after a silence. "You've had a chance to see what Stella's like. So maybe you do know. Sure, Stella had been to the place. She had to, seeing as how she came from Lily's. She stayed up there at Lily's three years. I went and took her away from the place. Four years ago."

"Since then she has been with you."

"That's right. She's been with me."

As Diamond drew on his cigarette his face was dimly lit by its smoldering end. The priest noticed that his eyes were closed. For a short while neither spoke. When the butt of the cigarette burned down to his fingers, Diamond tossed it through the window. With his foot pressed down and gently racing the motor, he laughed briefly.

"You want to know a lot of things," he said in a

139

bantering voice. "You've asked me a lot of questions, Father. I've got one I want to ask you."

The priest switched his eyes to the road in silence. The car began to move into the moonlight.

"What I'd like to know is this. Just what did you come up here for?"

Father Cawder made an effort to speak without emphasis. It would be foolish to let the tremulous irritation he felt enter his voice. "I came here to see to the change for the little girl," he said impassively. "You know that already. There would have been no reason for me to come except for that." He looked overhead at the clouds sweeping upward in the flood of light. "At the same time I wanted to see you and Stella again," he added evenly. "The thought occurred to me that my meeting with you at the carnival and Stella's coming to see me about Marina were—providential, or could be providential."

"Providential," Diamond repeated.

"Providence. The will of God."

Diamond rubbed his forefinger across his lower lip. "Hah!"

"By the will of God I—"

Diamond interrupted. "All right. I get it." He kept rubbing his lower lip. "Now I'll tell you what I thought. Maybe I oughtn't to tell you, but I will. I didn't catch on to why you came up here. I know Stella went and told you about the kid. That's all right, but I still didn't get what got you started. Do you remember two days ago when you first came round to Gurig's?"

"I remember." The car entered an alley of huge elms. The leaves above their heads shook in a long sigh of wind.

"You were in there talking to Stella. Then I came butting in. I tell you what I thought when I saw it was you. I thought she'd dreamed up some play to get you thinking you could knock down something easy. I got an idea maybe down there in Lulworth she'd—then she started yelling you came to take the kid away. But

140

that's what I thought when I came butting in. I thought she'd had her fun with some fancy proposition and put it to you."

The car slipped forward and came to rest on a small stone bridge. Below in the dark a brook thinly trickled.

"I'm sorry I told you that. It's nothing—" Diamond had suddenly turned. He seemed to be hesitating. "What do you say I've got to do?" His voice grated now. "You say what a man's got to do. When a woman's like her, when you think you can't keep going on with the way she does?"

"You are free to leave her, if you find fault with her. She is free to leave you, if she chooses."

"She'd better not try pulling out. She knows better not to try that. That's one kind of a claim I've got on her." Diamond twisted about as if struck breathless. "Did you tell her to get out? Did you tell her that?"

The priest ponderously shook his head. Was he bound to hear this man, he wondered. Was a duty involved in the hearing of these gibbered confidences?

Diamond's shoulders curved forward. He snuffed in the air with a sound like a snore. "What do you say a man's got to do, seeing you're a priest?"

"Got to do? What do you mean?"

"With Stella. With a woman like her. Any woman. You say what to do. Let myself get kicked around like a piece of dirt?"

"Nothing binds you two to each other." Father Cawder cut his words short with a rankling impatience. "Stella is not accountable to you. You are not bound to her. Why have you asked me what to do?" If this were the confessional, he thought. If I spoke as a priest stoled, forgiving or retaining sin. From under the arch of the bridge a murmuring floated up. Near at hand a singsong of voices faintly quavered. If I spoke judicially, wielding power of forgiveness, the priest repeated to himself.

Diamond was slumped down into the seat. "Christ!" he muttered. "Good Christ!"

He paused to take a breath. "You don't get how it is. She knows what she's doing to me with the way she acts. And by now she knows she's had her last chance. I told her that. She won't get another."

"You have no right of any kind over her," Father Cawder said tonelessly. "If you think she is at fault, instead of frightening her, threatening her—"

He flexed his fingers in uncertainty. He felt a sudden longing to spring from the car, to hurry off under the trees without further speech, to put himself on the instant beyond earshot of the soft railing drone. Why should such a desire give him a feeling of dereliction, an abandonment? Of what, he hesitantly wondered? Of the woman who, if she chose, need not have to do with this man? Was it fear for her? Or was Diamond appealing to him in some extremity? Appealing against his will to be dragged back out of his illusions?

"It is time I got back," he said. "I will get out here and walk." He groped for the handle of the door.

"No, sit still," Diamond muttered. "I'll take you back in a minute. I want you to know what it's all about." He turned off the lights of the car.

"It is getting late. It's time I got back." The priest kept his fingers curled over the blade of the door handle.

"I want to tell you just how it was. So you'll see what I mean. You see, it started when we were up in Jersey City. Up at Smitty's." Diamond spoke in slow dry gasps, his head and shoulders hunched forward. He cleared his throat and went on. "We'd been there at Smitty's about three weeks. One day a man named Otto moved in. One of those German waiters, singing waiters. Old Smitty put a cot for him by the door. We didn't mind Smitty or him. He wasn't in much, most of the time he was asleep or out somewheres. Then he started to hang around during the day. He got a phonograph from a man, and he and Stella'd be dancing all afternoon to the thing—I didn't care. Then I got an idea maybe Stella was falling for this Dutchman. So I watched her. I came back early one afternoon. Old

Smitty opened the door a crack. 'You can't come in,' she yelled. 'I'm dressing.' I could guess what she meant. I'd seen her padding around in her shirt plenty before that. I pushed the door open. I saw—"

"If you think you have a good reason," the priest interrupted, "to tell me about this, be brief. There's no need to speak of these things in detail."

Diamond was silent for a few seconds. When he spoke his voice sounded easier, a low even drawl.

"Smitty was an old woman. We were broke and she rented us a bed. She had a big room with a double bed and she slept in a rocker by the window. She put this Otto near the door. So it wasn't news to me she was getting into her clothes. She had her arms up pulling her dress over her head. 'Help me into this thing,' she said. I pulled it down over her. 'Now you're going out and get me a taxi,' she said. 'Just you run out now and get me a taxi.' I didn't say anything. There was nobody but her in the room. I went out to the areaway. It was in the basement, this room, in the back."

Father Cawder put his face to the wind fluttering in through the window. It must be by some scruple that he believed himself in league with this easy voice—this sounding body, soft, stale shell, jabbering like the mindless rant out of a radio. As if, since he was at hand, it followed he had patience to hear this mumble as of an ape's chamberings in his filthy cage. He could leave without blame, in prudence ought to leave. He could walk toward the haze of light above the trees, a road it must be, a city street. Did Diamond mean him to listen, he suddenly mused, solely because he was a priest? If Diamond believed that forgiveness of sins was communicated, had imaginable connection with a priest. He could intend—but still, this parading of secrets, amalgam of vilenesses . . .

"You don't need to mention these others," he said. "You have no right to tell me these secrets of Stella's."

"I'm telling you so you can see how I stand." A gurgling laugh broke from Diamond. "Secrets!" he whispered, prolonging the word. "Stella's got no secrets. She don't know about secrets. I'm telling you what I did so you can know. I came back from this areaway. Smitty had a little back hall off the room. It had a back stairs in it and a rubbish can and a cupboard under where the stairs went up. I went up to the door. 'No, you don't,' Smitty yelled. 'You stay out of my concerns.' When she stopped yelling I opened the door. It was dark in the hall. There was nobody there. Then I squatted down. After a bit I heard her breathing or something breathing. I gave the boards a kick. It was just a cupboard for buckets and brooms. I could hardly see. When I opened the cupboard door that Otto lit out like a cat. Stella was inside on the floor. She'd fixed up a pallet for herself out of some rugs. She said, 'What are you going to do now, Diamond?' I pulled her up: I said, 'Nothing.' And I didn't. I never laid a hand on her."

Diamond shifted his back and legs. "That day I knew he'd be there." The pitch of his voice sounded to the priest with the exaggerated effects of a politician on a platform, sinking, absurdly rising. "All I said was, try it again. She knows what I mean."

A struck match, whitely flaring, lighted Diamond's rigid face. Against the dark it had a look like the snout of some intent marauding animal. As his lips grinned back, his eyes blankly stared, focused inward on a scene within his mind. Outside in the shrubbery a bird or something live was moving. The leaves and branches rustled.

Concealed again by the dark, Diamond almost whispered. "It's lucky I only caught her once. It's the old woman—Gurig. She's let out a few things. I thought maybe the time when I got stalled up in New York— that's why I've been keeping an eye on the house from around the corner. Or I drive around. To see if she goes out or who goes in. There's a wop she knows— wop or a Greek. She don't go to much trouble. One night I could smell the bay rum that got rubbed off from his hair." His voice dwindled weakly away. Father Cawder twisted back the door handle. Thoughts, words framed on his tongue, were blotted out, as he fumbled, in loathing. The wave of disgust gave the illusion of something physical—a film seeping along his skin, as if a foul moisture fell through the darkness, defiling the air, his lungs and mouth. At his side he heard Diamond's heavy breathing, he seemed to feel its loathsome warmth. He wrenched the door open.

Diamond strained his arms against the steering wheel and made a groaning sound into the spokes. "She's got no right! What does she think I can take? She knows she's got no right!"

The priest swung his legs out onto the concrete. The waste, the deadly squandering nullity! Feeding on their own filthiness, what did either one matter, dogs licking up their vomit, slavering over their malice and egotism and lust, vessels of wrath fitted to destruction.

"Wait." Diamond leaned out through the door. "Wait. Wait a minute, Father. Get in. I'll take you back."

"No. I will walk back. Good night!"

He set off down a path curving under branches toward the pale glare of the city. As moonlight struck the hillside the lawns below him were slashed with the tremendous shadows of trees. He heard no noise of a starting motor. When the path swerved to a lower slope, he saw the bridge. The car was still there, a black humped smudge against the bright night sky.

6

As the door pivoted inward, the hall pleased him with its look of deserted darkness after the rocking of the bus, the hours in the violent racket of the train. But there was a stale smell as of rooms never aired. Stepping inside, Father Cawder lowered his suitcase out of the way against the wall. A slip of paper was stuck into the frame of the "Espousals of the Virgin." It informed whom it might concern that Father Moran had driven over to Mattapan but would get back in time for dinner without fail. Father Cawder's glance wandered restlessly into the parlor where the blinds were still drawn. Stopped in the center of the carpet he felt ill at ease, his will deadened, without desires. When the woman touched Him, He knew that virtue had gone out from Him. A quotation of no relevance to him. The shunting trains, fumes of coal gas and carbon monoxide, had brought about this resemblance to paralysis of will. His brain was clumsily functioning, thoughts stirring slowly as leaves afloat on a pond. Waste! he silently repeated, only this waste, intolerable vanity! He buttoned his coat again on a fresh impulse and left the house.

By the gate he halted to take a deep breath as the wind struck him. He felt the cold air pleasurably tingle against his teeth. Then he started off down the sidewalk of muddy bricks. Looking ahead into a narrow yard he saw that Morzouphlos, that patient Greek, had already completed the loving precise swaddling of his fig tree for the winter. Its trunk and lower branches were bound in brown bandages, like the limbs of a body swathed after some prodigious surgery. Where the brick paving sank out of sight in mud and tufts of brilliant grass, he turned aside onto the cobblestones of the road.

He had chosen to take himself in; so much at least was clear. From the first he had been concerned only to amuse himself. After the carnival, if he had rejected the superstitions of a dream, it was only in order to invent more substantial amusements. He was to effect the rescue of a child! Or present himself to the disreputable pair in some role entirely unimaginable. He had wanted to enact the part of predestined agent, Tobias subserving providence, a priest extending the decrees of God by his own cleverness! What was its innermost source, this self-deception? Underneath all virtuous protests, his principle of will must be founded on the solemn belief that he was without fault—holy as God is holy, effortlessly, through mere being. He blasphemed with every breath, with every beat of his pulse.

Perhaps, however, not quite like that. He had stopped below the iron volutes unwinding against the gate into the cemetery. Above the pinkish bricks, the spikes of yew looked densely black in the clear evening sun. He turned, musing, into the path rising aslant beyond the gateposts. Such a huge sin was more proper to the nature of angels than of men, the flaw of Satan. His own fault would be something meaner. Vanity, not pride. A look into a mirror gave him no pleasure. But to look inwardly at himself, that was another matter, observing moods, interpreting dreams, indulging small unbearable whims. Like a woman gaping idiotically at her face in a looking glass. It was self-love, the core of faithful passion warming every man on earth, except saints, mysteriously, gratuitously, pre-empted, the tender emotion controlling him and Diamond and Stella and Father Moran, Marina and Mrs. Gurig.

Out of vanity he had tracked down a base sharper of a man, obtruded a small girl into a household of nuns,

147

prayed in a vanity of discomfort on his knees before the body of Christ locked away in its marble hut. He had sat long ago by the side of a stream, fishing. Gardner had been with him; the stream was called Pawpaw Creek. Under pale reflections of the sky glinted the world of eels, turtles, carp, water moccasins, perch. A tree had mournfully swished overhead. Far out over the water its trembling leaves swung to and fro, arching down like a weeping willow. It had been a water elm. He sat there all day, caught nothing, not even a bite, and Gardner had eight perch, gleaming yellow against the tin bottom of a lard bucket. When they got home he took out the longest and carried it to his mother. She thought it was his, naturally. And he had not said a word. And when Gardner claimed the fish at the supper table, everybody burst out laughing. His father said he was sly, looking round at him, a boy that would bear watching. Gardner called him a liar. He easily remembered the hot rush of anger and outrage. How unkind they are, he had thought, how disrespectful. With tears running into his mouth he looked across the table at his mother, and she was laughing too. Even then he was controlled by vanity, a puling comic bean pole of a boy. Father Cawder paused on the neat path forking off on each side of a high yew. He went to the left, toward the area of consecrated ground.

Vanity was a root of sin, possibly in his case ineradicable. There was the waste, besides. Time and energy lapsed forever into nothingness. Beyond waste, the intricate illusions. When he had seen that Stella for her own reasons had chosen a brothel in which to leave her child, the fact led to no pertinent deduction. Having entered that brothel, endured familiar address from harlots, he did not begin to use a prudent reserve. When the car drew up to the curb, he had recognized Diamond with a sense of strange amicable confederacy. As the streets rolled under the wheels in moonlight he had inclined to mark in himself, mingled with distaste, with impatience, with faint unthinking fear, this

148

further thing, species of collusion, as if he was bound to some compact. Thus he sat unmoving, bemused with absurd scruples, while Diamond's possessed brain provoked itself with injury to what he believed his rights, with Stella's lover who perhaps did not exist and with the question of whether the latter were a Portuguese or a Jew. In the transports of contemplating his own paltriness, Diamond found a man sitting there by chance a convenience for his egotism. Almost a day had gone by since he had left the car on the stone bridge, swallowed up in the dark. Now as he stood inspecting a granite cross whose surface imitated the bark of a tree, he felt as he remembered feeling then, precipitately walking away from the man behind him in the darkness. Remembering the face twisted with self-pity, the soft or strident voice, he felt the same unreasoning wave of disgust. As if touched by filth, some abominable oozing thing.

The cross carved like a tree was polished in the middle and bore the incised name *Cahill*. Rotting underneath the ivy would be old Margaret Cahill, put away below ground in the same pleated black waist smelling of drugs which she wore to the High Mass every Sunday. A woman renowned for her bulk, for skill in washing a lace curtain, for loud vituperation. Sunk into the side of the hill, a brick vault shut with an iron door drew the eyes of the priest. He studied without interest the marble block set over the arch, cut with a coat of arms. A damp green stain blotched one side of the stone. It was the cavern into which Mrs. Rozier of Nanjemoy would be trundled when at length she succumbed to rich dinners and good works in New York. Mrs. Rozier, when at home, preferred to think of Saint Gregory's as a chapel of ease to the manor's masshouse, built by the slaves of her ancestors. Just as Nanjemoy County contracted to a private park in the middle of which she could domineer from lofty historical rooms. He had dined one Sunday with Mrs. Rozier. He had been asked to say grace, he sat at the end of a

149

long table, and except for the Negro proffering a succession of silver dishes no one addressed three consecutive words to him. With the old woman safe in New York the county expanded, beyond the influence of looming busts, swords of heroes and manorial parchments, the bed known to have been occupied by General Washington, Louis Philippe, and the infanta Eulalia.

Mrs. Girard was subject with the rest to the same process of expansion. Father Cawder, descending the hillside, surveyed the modest tombstone, lettered in a fine script, of her husband. Mrs. Girard expanded too, with Mrs. Rozier out of the way, fancying in her turn some delusion of dominance, as if Lulworth might be made to contract under the influence of her china, her grandfather the admiral, and her cheerful pride. Fenced in with iron rungs, the Girards' plot appeared full. When the time came she would find a narrow enough room beside the late Benedict Otwell Girard. In a corner lay a child's grave, marked with a marble lamb like an albino mole. The priest straightened up above it and looked away from the steep slope of tombstones. Slowly breathing the sharp air blown against him, he turned homeward.

The walk through the cold wind had quickened his blood. As he left the graveyard he set his lips in a line of hard composure. If he was vain, foolish, sinful, he was not obliged, therefore, to exhibit any misgiving to the two blond girls who were approaching in evening light up the road, to Father Moran. When he reached the front of the church he saw Moran's black Ford drawn up in the driveway. Old Fenwick would now be bumbling about the kitchen, piecing together the evening meal for two priests, senilely muttering. He felt no desire for food. He closed the door of the house and meant to go up to his room. But Father Moran was coming down the stairs. He called out in his affable voice, flinging up his arm.

"I saw your suitcase, so I knew you'd got back. Did

you have a good trip? Did you ever come across the people you were after?"

"I found them, after a search. The child has gone to a foundling home. Did you get along all right, Father?"

A mild smile was playing over Father Moran's face. The drive over from Mattapan had drawn up the blood into two red spots on his cheeks. He backed off to the doorway into the parlor and leaned against the jamb.

"I've been busy every minute. I hardly knew you were gone." He laughed at his impertinence. "I've got quite a lot here I want to show you. It's really down in black and white this time." He gestured into the parlor toward the round table. "Do you feel like taking a brief look before supper? Can I give you a brief idea?"

Without moving Father Cawder glanced past him to the table spread with neat stacks of paper.

"Those are your notes?"

"Yes. You can see them now if you want. Or if you think after supper would be better." His fingers eagerly wriggled.

Father Cawder's eyes fastened on the stone from the Holy Sepulcher holding down one of the piles of paper. "After we eat," he said quietly. "That will be time enough. I'm going up now to wash."

He was surprised that the meal served up by old Fenwick was orderly and on time. Only a platter of cold chicken wings had been set down in front of Father Moran as his meat, but the old man had taken pains over the vegetables. He had used a sparing hand, a change from Mrs. McGovern's blowsy wastefulness, and he carried in the dishes silently, his grizzled face glum and respectful. It might be that he would do on a permanent footing. Or a colored man might be more sensible than another experiment with a devout widow woman, with her novenas and bad temper. Father Moran hurried through his dessert, gobbling up the cherries in quick spoonfuls. He walked ahead into the parlor. "Now," he said firmly, turning on the lamp sur-

151

rounded by blank pads, diagrams, columns of figures.

Sitting in the armchair, Father Cawder felt his muscles slacken, his cold legs weigh against the floor. As he watched Father Moran fasten together a handful of curling scraps the blurred, aged, sentimental voice of Mother Assumpta again struck his ear. "Yes, Father," the voice had feebly stated to the telephone. "Yes, Father. She's here. They brought her. She's a dear, Father. So quiet and gentle. She's had a bath. We'll take good care of her." It had been only prudent, before he left Trenton, to telephone the Carmelites. It appeared that Diamond and Stella had penetrated to the convent grille without difficulty. The child, already playing on the sympathies of aged foolish nuns, was disposed of, at any rate. Father Cawder looked up to find Father Moran patiently observing him. "What have you there, Father?" he said.

Father Moran waved his notes and seated himself on a cane-bottomed chair. "I did a lot of thinking while you were gone," he began. "Some reading, too. And I've written for data to some friends of mine. I think I've improved on my ideas a good deal. In fact," he smiled somewhat sheepishly, "I don't think the first idea I had was so good. I have some better ones now."

"You mean ideas on almsgiving."

"Of course, Father. But I think I've got them broken down to fundamentals. I've kept in mind the way you seem to feel about not doing things by deputy." He spoke hurriedly. "I think we ought to try some way of appealing to all the people in the parish, plan for participation, that is, from everybody, if possible."

"And what are these plans of yours now?" If it happened he took no lively pleasure in compassionating the poor, would this priest still show the same zeal, Father Cawder wondered. Father Moran stretched out an arm to snap up a piece of paper.

"—If we make a radical change," he was saying, "and I think any change we make ought to be radical.

152

As I see the picture, charity in the parish ought to be functionalized into three main groups or areas of activity. First, for women, maybe a maternity guild, a sort of practical sodality, under the patronage of the Blessed Virgin. To look out for women having babies, help out with the bills if necessary, see to their families while they're still in bed. And also, any routine visits to sick people in general. Then after we got going, maybe we could see our way clear to branch out with a clinic, whatever we could afford. Oh, say a practical nurse two days a week. Secondly, for the men, a reorientation to bring the Saint Vincent de Paul Society up to date, not only with handouts to men out of work, food, that kind of thing, but to get together and discuss, weekly meetings, opened with prayers, of course—so we can keep an eye peeled on farm and labor conditions, represent members maybe with employers or landlords. It would be like a study club with active social functions. Later on we could aim for a communal farm, to get the Church back on the land. Then, third, something that strikes me as basic if the Church has got to co-exist with finance-capitalism and still has to try to make things tolerable for people—a credit union for everybody in the parish to belong to, to make small loans without collateral and without interest. I've been reading some material I have filed away. I don't think it would be right to put off the credit union till later. It's essential. We could do it; if they can build one up in a fishing village in Nova Scotia, we certainly could have one too. But I need to get more details. There's the legal angle. I'll hear shortly from some of my friends who are interested in the credit union movement."

While Father Moran was speaking Father Cawder's eyes had drifted slowly down the length of picture molding. For an instant, thinking of Stella's face glimpsed briefly as she had turned once to Diamond, he remembered its daydreaming mildness, lids drooped and seeming to shed a childlike, unbelievable innocence;

153

he looked down to the carpet. He felt very tired, he realized. His skin felt as if sticky with sweat and grime, as it had when he stepped down from the Baltimore bus into the streets of Lulworth.

"Don't you think," Father Moran said, "this approach could be made into something to work on? Couldn't we begin with this as a basis for a sensible way to reorganize?"

Father Cawder's eyes were fixed to the floor. They lifted to meet the blank reflections steadily flashed from Father Moran's gold-rimmed glasses. "I know I told you to go ahead with all this," he said. "I know that." He paused and looked away. "To begin with, it still seems to me you don't entirely understand what I had in mind. I doubt, in fact, whether I'll be able to go very far along with you on these plans of yours, Father."

Father Moran licked his lips and smiled. "How do you mean? Do you think it's too ambitious right at first? Or is it actual details? I have it worked out—" He fluttered his notes.

"You seem to have taken what I said last week in a more positive sense than I had in mind." Father Cawder spoke heavily, with a slow distaste. "No doubt loan societies do much good in some situations. But I never had in mind all this ramification. Lulworth, you know, is a small country town. We have no room for all this."

Father Moran's smile ended in a coughlike laugh. "Women have babies here. They still have to pay bills here. People still die in Lulworth."

"Such societies are mechanisms; they have to be staffed," Father Cawder resumed without haste. "They need bookkeepers, treasurers, they depend on a flow of cash. What I was interested in was something essentially different—how to aid the poor through the actual services of people in the parish, getting rid of cash and mere doles. The running expenses of your plan would be heavy, Father."

Moran twisted in his chair and drew down the corners of his mouth. "What am I to understand, then?" he said in a quavering voice. "Are there any changes I could make in it? Or don't you want anything like this at all?"

"I can't see the need for organized social service here, Father Moran. That is really just the opposite of what I had in mind."

"In other words you want none of it!" Sharply exclaiming, Father Moran gestured toward the littered table.

"At any rate put it aside for the present." The lids of Father Cawder's eyes were hot and seemed to scratch against his eyeballs. He stretched them open. "We can take it up another time. I will be thinking it over. I didn't know," he glanced at the strewn table, "you would be giving so much time to it."

Father Moran watched the face of his pastor with a gloating attention. While he sat without swerving, his body inclined forward, he lowered his hands to his lap and wiped the moisture from his palms onto his trouser legs. Finally he laughed again, a coughing bird-like noise. He rose and left the room.

Father Cawder shut his eyes. He heard no sound as Father Moran came back into the parlor. He turned his head at the crackling of papers which Father Moran, blocking the light of the lamp, was gathering into a single pile. "I saw you had left your notes," he said. "I was going to bring them up to you."

Having made a neat stack, Father Moran leaned over to roll it up, fumbling with a rubber band. When the band snapped into place he still held himself pressed against the table, looking down into the reflections of its surface. Father Cawder opened the breviary he had pulled from his pocket. "Fenwick did pretty well to-night," he said, turning a page.

"I understand." Father Moran spoke in a grinding, unrecognizable tone. He lunged away as if to leave, then stood still again. "You fast twice in the week," he

155

exclaimed in the same grinding voice, "you give tithes of all you possess. You can thank God—" He appeared to be addressing his reflection in the top of the table. As his lips came together they pursed themselves downward in a narrow wedge. He crossed the room into the hall without looking round.

Father Cawder glanced dully after him. Father Moran was free to hold whatever random ideas his convenient impulses suggested. Like any professional zealot he could persuade himself of betrayal by anyone who did not happen, for good or bad reasons, to fall in with his vagaries—even when that one was his canonical superior. He did probably what he imagined to be his duty. His angry piping words—it was charitable to think he had been startled into speech in the grip of anger—his words, it was satisfactory to find, could be listened to without emotion. It was not necessary to feel resentment over the indiscipline of poor Moran. Certainly, if he himself was vain, foolish, pervasively sinful, it would not become him to condemn Moran because he too sopped himself with illusions. He prayed daily for Father Moran, he wished him well, he wished to use him with charity. More becoming than resentment over Moran would be contrition for his own egotism. Penance, fasting, cold, night watches, silence. These were the means employed to master ill will and illusion by Trappists in their freezing cells, by the ten thousand monks who had stood in prayer through the night in the caves of Egypt. On hot sand, cold rocks, peaks of niter, the desert fathers curbed malice with thirst and hunger, adoring the goodness of God. He could desire, like them, to take possession of the spring of his will, to be drawn to no masking instinct, muse on no image concealing within it nothing but love of himself. There were penances of the will. But mere steel, even, had served these ends, chains, shirts of hair, the flesh scraped to force the will to remember that it was defectible as long as the body breathed. Limned in the complex of secular lives around him, he was possibly beginning to be tainted by their futility. Since all the idolaters agreed that self-inflicted pain was scandalous—the worshipers of their senses or of power or a nation or a class—he was tempted to dismiss the crudity of a chain. Too barbaric, too externalized, chains, hair shirts, and whips. There was a small length of flat chain in the tool box in the kitchen, saved from some broken gear or pulley. Tightened round waist or arm it would be suitable to remind him of the motives urging his perverse will. Thomas More, chancellor of England, wore a hair shirt under his robes of office without extravagance. Pascal was said—but he made too much of it. Better, if he felt inclined to it, to get the chain, knot it round without argumentation; the question was itself of no interest. Father Cawder heaved himself out of his chair. "I should be thinking of God, not myself," he murmured, half-aloud. He moved off toward the stairs.

He heard the light knock as he was winding up his watch. He opened the door and stood aside, but Father Moran shook his head. He had taken off his coat and collar. Although his eyes were placidly, modestly, lowered, his voice still grated, strained to an earnest pitch.

"I won't come in. I wanted to see you before you went to sleep. To apologize for what I said downstairs. I know I have no right to speak to you, to anybody, the way I did and I apologize."

Father Cawder listened without attention. What did anger or apology matter? As if refinements of human respect were worth these careful frettings. He turned back into the room.

"I won't think any more about it, Father Moran."

"I was wrong to question your motives," Father Moran went on in his contending voice. "I am sorry."

"It's not of any importance. We can both forget about it." This easy exchange might be thought to be enough. Moran's straight lips were inaudibly quivering as if he was framing a set of words. He stood silent and frowned.

"There is another thing," he said at last. "I think I ought to speak about it now."

Father Cawder studied the priest's stiff flushed face with a benumbed melancholy. How hard he took these trifles. I have good will to you, he thought, I am disposed to charity toward you. "What is it?" he said as Moran again opened his mouth without speaking.

"I've been thinking about my work here," he blurted out. "I wanted to tell you I know I'm not of much help to you here, Father Cawder."

"I think you do your best, Father Moran. You may expect too much of your post here."

"I don't think I'm suited to our parish here—Lulworth. In a city I might not show up so badly, since that's what I'm used to, but I don't fit in a place in the country like this. And it seems to me you ought to have an assistant here who would be able to smooth things out for you. I don't seem able to do that." Father Moran's eyes shifted as if he had noticed too bold a speciousness in what he said. "I've been thinking about this for some time. It really has nothing to do with tonight."

Father Cawder began to unbutton his coat. "Why do you tell all this to me, Father? Why not go and tell the bishop how you feel?"

"I don't want to do that. It might look like I was making a complaint about you or the parish here. It's just that I think it would be better for me and the parish both if I were somewhere else."

"You don't choose to tell him and yet you tell this to me? Do you expect me to make complaints to the bishop?"

"No, I don't." After a pause Father Moran added, "Do you think you'll see the bishop soon?"

"I intend to write to him about confirmation. But I am planning to go up to Cecilton to see Father Sims."

"I was wondering if you'd mind letting the bishop

know how I feel, sometime when you're up there, if it was convenient."

"I'm not sure whether the bishop would approve of discussing these feelings of yours with me, Father. It would strike him as somewhat irregular." Father Cawder moved toward the green curtain hanging across a corner.

"It's just that I'm requesting you to see him about me. I don't see why he would mind listening to you if he knew I'd requested you to come to see him."

Having pulled off his coat Father Cawder reached behind the curtain for a wire coat-hanger. "If this is what you want me to do, I'll go and talk to the bishop. I can see you have given the matter thought. It's getting late, Father Moran."

"Then you'll see him when you go up to Cecilton?"

Father Cawder slipped the coat-hanger through the curtain and caught it on a rod. It would be generous to make Father Moran some plain statement of good will. It was evident he had worked himself up to view the situation as of an enormous seriousness. When all he wanted was a change of scene, scope!

"I will be going to Cecilton soon. I'll let him know what you've told me."

"Good night, Father Cawder."

Father Moran dropped his pale uncordial eyes and walked away. Father Cawder gently closed the door. How can he dislike me so much, he said to himself; I bear him no ill will.

7

IT WAS QUIET IN MRS. GURIG'S ROOM. THE air had gradually darkened with the early evening of winter. All at once the street lamps flashed on. As a thin bar of light shot over the carpet to Mrs. Gurig's feet, she breathed in sharply. She had seated herself on the edge of a chair, craning forward, one arm loose along the table, her head sagging, her eyes opened wide. For a while she did not move. To her straining ears the house had become very still. There was only the rattling of the china clock, racing away on the mantelshelf. At least ten minutes, it seemed to her, had passed. Her bent head sank with a lunge further downward. From far away she heard a noise, softened beyond recognition by boards, ceilings, sheaths of plaster. Something had been dragged over a floor, a chair or a trunk. Softly, from somewhere above her, came another light sound, a feathery tapping. Was that footsteps? Or a hand swinging free and idly drumming on the floor or a table? Then she heard, faint but unmistakable, a woman's shrill laugh. Mrs. Gurig caught her breath. Lowering her head to her knees she wrapped her arms about her legs. Her heart began to leap and flutter.

Except for the rise and fall of her breasts, the old woman kept herself motionless. It must be a full fifteen minutes, she thought, that was more than enough. Maybe it had been half an hour. The excitement of her heart seemed to have muffled her hearing. Certainly she had heard nothing for the last few seconds. No sound within the house. The thin hum in the distance came from the cars on the avenue deadened by space and bricks and plaster to be barely audible. She caught at the table and pulled herself up. Slightly raising each leg in turn she shook her shoes loose and kicked them aside. Then she opened the door to the hall, listening and standing rigid in the dark. There was the sound of a dog somewhere snapping and snarling. There was nothing else. She padded soundlessly, cautiously over to the stairs.

She guided herself up with one hand on the rail. She had been smart to remember, after her bite of sardines, to switch off the lights in the hall. Sixteen steps there were to the landing, then five more up to the second floor. She reached the top of the stairs and dragged her hand across the wall until it met the frame of a door. Then she wheeled about in the dark, grasped the rail slanting up along the second flight. There were fifteen steps to the landing below the third floor. On the fourteenth step, as she stumbled, she caught at the banisters. A crackling noise, loud as a pistol-shot to the old woman, started suddenly from the board under her feet. The staircase seemed to heave under a tremendous shock. She clutched at the rail in terror. Her painfully pounding heart prevented her from breathing; a sweat broke out over her fingers and palms. They could hear that, they must surely have heard that, she thought. For several minutes, breathing heavily, she stood still. No sound of any kind came from above. She hauled herself up to the landing and knelt down on the bottom step of the turn. She stared past the edge of floor on a level with her eyes. That long black slit, darker than the wall, that was the door. She was close enough.

The climb up the stairs had put a strain on her legs. She felt sick with weakness. As she waited she leaned forward on her elbows. She could still see the top of that darker patch of black which was the door of the room. A slow rustling from beyond caused her to straighten her back. She raised herself, pulling at the

161

steps above her, one heel pressed against the base-board, her neck stretching sideways. Still she could hear a delicate rustling. It could be the rasping cuff on a man's shirt, something lined with tissue paper, the friction of a shoe. Then her slack breasts flattened against the nosing of a step, a voice sounded, and her heart seemed to stop dead. It was a whimpering cry, close above her head, a woman's rapid moaning, frantic and meaningless. Kneeling on the stairs Mrs. Gurig trembled with excitement. A piercing joy seized her, filling her with a painful, pleasurable alarm. "Cooing! Like a pigeon!" she whispered. "Like a nasty squatting cat!" She got to her feet with care, her muscles all at once relaxed. Throwing back her shoulders she breathed freely and deeply. She clutched the handrail. With caution, as fast as she was able, she turned and hobbled downward in the dark.

She kept her eyes on the open door of her room while coming down the last flight of stairs. She hurried in. She fumbled under the table for her shoes. The smudge of black on the bed was her coat. She snatched it up and dug her hands violently into the armholes, ripping the lining. She began to glance wildly from side to side. The dark mound of her hat was nowhere in sight. Then she remembered it was in the hall. She rushed from the room and gathered it up from a chair. Her pocketbook lay underneath. She stumbled out into the street.

Her hat was still squeezed in her hand when she reached the delicatessen. She brushed past the woman at the counter and shut herself into the phone booth. The nickel was ready, wet from being cupped in her palm. She dialed the number. Five times the telephone at the other end of the city rang. What was the matter now, she thought, they were sure to be open for hours yet. Then a man's voice said, "Yeah? Who is it?"

Mrs. Gurig, gasping, for a moment was unable to speak.

"Who's there? Do you want somebody?"

"I want to speak to Diamond," she said in a whisper.

"Wait a minute." She heard footsteps ring over a concrete floor. Then someone came back to the telephone.

"Is that you, Diamond?" she stammered. She rapidly licked her lips. "It's me. May Gurig."

"I didn't know it was you. What do you want?"

"I was just in here to Gordon's for some cold cuts. I thought I'd give you a ring."

"What about? Anything special?"

She paused before answering. "No," she said, in a changed voice, slow and vigorous. "Nothing special, Diamond. I just thought I'd ring you up. Thought maybe you'd want me to get you something here at Gordon's. Since your manager's in town for the day. I thought maybe you'd want something for a snack."

"What is this? What do you mean, manager? Is this just a bum joke?"

"Well, ain't he your manager or your agent or something?" Mrs. Gurig's slow voice broke into a plaintive flutter. "That's what I thought she said he was, being so friendly and all. I just thought maybe you'd want to know. So you'd have time to get away and see him before he left."

"Where's Stella now?"

"She's up at home. They're both at the house. I just thought I could get you some beer or something." Diamond made no answer. She wondered whether he was still listening. After a few seconds she heard the other phone remotely click.

When she left the booth the little woman behind the counter was filling a flat dish with potato salad. She looked up with black sharp eyes. "Get your party?"

Mrs. Gurig nodded. She felt a tightening rancor as she watched the little woman's hands. Prying, prying, she thought, always meddling into what's no concern of theirs, these dirty Jews. She rested her arms on the counter.

"Give me two bottles of beer," she said.

8

MONSIGNOR MOON FOLDED HIS OVER-
coat over a chair and laid his Homburg on the desk. "I
hope you've not had to wait long, Father," he said. He
was pulling off a pair of doeskin gloves stitched with
black silk. With a rapid smile delayed until his gloves
were entirely removed, he held out his right hand.

"It's Father Cawder, isn't it? Of course, of course.
Lulworth, Saint Gregory's." He shook hands heartily.
While he smiled above his purplish chin, his eyes
glittered over Father Cawder minutely.

"Sit down, Father, please sit down. I'll be right with
you in a moment." His scrubbed well-pared fingers
unscrewed his fountain pen and made three neat no-
tations on a pad in the middle of the desk. "Well, how
are things proceeding in Lulworth?" he exclaimed,
swiveling in his chair.

"Quietly. About the same as when you were there,
Monsignor Moon."

"So I was, wasn't I? August a year ago. I remember
perfectly. A very pleasant little visit. Excuse me,
Father." At that instant a short man in shirt sleeves
brushed past the desk. Breathing hard, he flung a slip
of pink paper onto the blotter.

"Just take a look here at this bill, Monsignor, just
take a look at it," he cried, his high voice shrill with
excitement.

Monsignor Moon glanced down. "What is it?" he
said in a sudden tonelessness.

"It's the bill from the printer. For those Advent
164

handouts. Sixteen dollars over what it ought to be. Sixteen dollars! They can't do that to us!"

Without moving his head Monsignor Moon handed back the bill over his shoulder. "Isn't there a flat rate down in the contract, Dunn? I understood a flat rate was always put into the contract." He shook a cigarette out of a yellow leather case.

"Sure it is!" the man said. "It's a flat rate. That's what I mean."

"Well, then. Take it back. Tell the printer the bill is wrong."

"All right, all right! That's what I wanted to know." The man jerked up and rushed away through the door left open when he entered.

"I'm sorry to be keeping you this way, Father." Monsignor Moon crossed the red carpet without hurry to shut the door. "All day long, one long series of interruptions. Can't keep them out. They have some idea the chancery office is a kind of club. They'd like me to install a couple of slot machines in here."

"I wanted to know when the bishop could come to confirm. We can be ready any time. Now or in the spring. It was shortly after Lent the last time he came."

Monsignor Moon had already found and was flicking through the pages of a loose-leaf notebook. "Winter's really very bad," he murmured. "After Lent there's Wicomico. Do you like May?"

"Any Sunday in May will be all right."

"Let us say the first Sunday in May. May third, that is. That will suit you, will it?" Monsignor Moon's eye wandered down from Father Cawder's cuffs and fixed on his socks and shoelaces.

"Very well. The first Sunday in May."

"And now was there anything else I could see to, Father? If not, I'm very much afraid—" Clutching the rim of the desk, Monsignor Moon smiled and made as if to rise.

"No, nothing at all. But I wrote the bishop several days ago. I told him I would like to see him this afternoon if he found it convenient. Do you know whether he's in?"

"He will be, any minute now. You're sure it's nothing I could be of any help with?" Monsignor Moon's lustrous black eyes bore momentarily into Father Cawder's. "But if he's expecting you. Oh, he will be back any minute." He went to the door and threw it open. "I'm sorry to be so rushed today. Come with me. I'll see the bishop is told you're here to see him."

He crossed the hall and pushed in the door opposite that to his office. "Just make yourself at home here, Father."

Father Cawder stepped inside. As Monsignor Moon prepared to draw backward he looked round an instant longer. "Splendid showing the other week from Lulworth, Father! For Propaganda Fide! Splendid!" The door shut soundlessly. His heels rattled away over the marble paving.

He had shown Father Cawder into the bishop's parlor, a room of repute in devout circles of the diocese. Crimson wallpaper, stamped with swags of acanthus leaves, covered the walls, fading at the windows to a rusty brown. The ranks of armchairs were tufted with plush of authentic episcopal purple, the gift of a distiller's widow now dead for more than fifty years. Dust appeared to dull gilt moldings, a gas chandelier glinting with lusters. Father Cawder's eyes rested on the row of pictures hanging forward in heavy frames, blackened beaked heads, miters and rabats, the portraits of prelates. He moved to view them more closely. The one above him was, of course, old Darnell, a waxy face with red cheeks like cherries. Tasseled curtains bellied out from a greenish Tuscan column; beyond was a stormy sky livid with clouds. It was reported that Darnell, first bishop of Cecilton, was deemed a saint in Ursuline convents. The sisters were said to ask his suffrages in their private devotions and to have broached his cause at Rome. Between the second and fourth bishops of Cecilton hung a painting of Pio Nono. A white shapely hand was raised in blessing. He sat beside a table spread with damask and littered with parchment, the decrees of the Council, the Syllabus, the Bull of the Immaculate Conception. The fluttering papers were held down by a pair of keys and a gibbous gilded tiara. Too bold, too princely an eye, the priest reflected, for these latter days of prudence and disaster. A high priest without fear, pronouncing anathema on the whoredoms of the nineteenth century, one who not merely asserted but believed that the Mother of God wielded powers greater than Cavour, Napoleon III, the Prussian army, the British navy. Beyond Pius the Ninth he paused under heads of Cardinal de Cheverus, Archbishop Eccleston of Baltimore, Morissey, third bishop of Cecilton. He walked slowly down the length of the wall. As he halted at a parrot-like, peevish face blackened by time and varnish he heard a door open behind him. At the end of the parlor, against the light, stood a short man. Father Cawder went up to him and knelt down on one knee.

"Your excellency." He brushed the stone in the bishop's ring with his lips.

"I'm sorry you were made to wait, Father Cawder. I had just got back from my walk. They make me walk a half-hour a day now. They tell me I'm too old not to take any exercise." The bishop indicated the open door. "Come in, Father."

He passed ahead into a small square room brilliant with sunshine. He sat down and gazed across his desk. "I don't think you're looking as well as you did," he said. "I don't like to see you looking so tired. How are they treating you in Lulworth?"

The bishop's eyes were round and blue. Although he was evidently old, his face appeared also strangely juvenile to Father Cawder, like that of a rosy child. His pink cheeks seamed with vertical furrows had an unwasted bloom, his white silky hair was like a tow-headed boy's. Father Cawder glanced away to the sunlight dancing reflected on the wall.

"I am perfectly well, your excellency. Everything in Lulworth goes along about as usual. A few more children to confirm this time. I just saw Monsignor Moon about confirmation. We'll have a big class for you when you come."

"That is good. Very, very good. See that the children know what the answers mean. Sometimes I find the children don't seem to understand what they have to say. The priests are too busy, I suppose. But see that yours know."

"I will see that they do, your excellency. I wanted to talk to you—"

The bishop leaned forward with a brightening face. "I hear such good reports of your choir at Saint Gregory's, Father, the singing. The real Gregorian, so I am told. That's very, very good. Our rites continue the liturgy of the old law, you know, Father, the chants of Solomon and Zorobabel, fulfilled now in holy Mass. God is pleased when we take pains to praise Him well."

Father Cawder straightened his back against the chair. "There's a certain matter I wanted to talk over with you today."

"Yes, Father, yes. What matter is that?"

Father Cawder looked off into the spangled gloom of the parlor. "Father Moran, my assistant, asked me to talk to you when I next came to Cecilton. He has told me he is dissatisfied with a post such as Saint Gregory's, in a small country town—or to put it more justly, he does not believe himself to be well-fitted to a parish like Lulworth. He believes he can do more good in another kind of community. Also he seems to think another man in his place might be able to co-operate more easily with me. There's been no disagreement," Father Cawder added quickly, "of any importance between us."

"These poor young men." The bishop raised his eyebrows. "So he asked you to see me. Why didn't he come himself?"

"He didn't want to put himself forward as making a

168

complaint, I think. Apparently, all he wants is for you to know what his opinions are with regard to his own work. And I think he didn't want to appear to be going over my head. In making what you might consider a censure of me."

"I see. I see. Punctilious, he must be. He spares his pastor." The bishop vaguely smiled. "And what do you think of all this, Father Cawder? Do you agree with him? Would he do better elsewhere?"

"I think Father Moran is apt to mistake the stress of his emotions for the force of logic." While he spoke, the priest felt a blush hotly spreading over his cheeks. In spite of steeling himself to state no more than fact to the bishop, he was using, it seemed, words which sounded with an unpleasing irony. "I mean to say Father Moran can very well be mistaken as to his unsuitability to the work at Saint Gregory's. He is hardworking, conscientious, he does what he can. He would, of course, feel more at his ease in a big city. Father Moran has many ideas hard to put into practice in Lulworth."

"Ideas?" the bishop murmured.

"Father Moran is a great student of the encyclicals." Father Cawder heard and tried to transform the faint sarcasm flattening his voice. "He is greatly interested in changing the existing social order. Father Moran fears capitalism more than sin, it seems to me sometimes."

The bishop's face became melancholy. "Avarice is a frightful sin, Father. A frightful sin. Avarice and grinding the poor. They cry to heaven for vengeance. The Holy Ghost tells us that."

Father Cawder moved his feet with a twitch of impatience. "I may have been unjust to Father Moran. I don't question ideas of his which are drawn from the encyclicals. I disagree in applying them at Saint Gregory's. Lulworth is a market for farms, a small country town."

The bishop looked down to his blotting pad. A pitch

169

of coldness had modified his voice. "There is avarice everywhere, Father, avarice, grinding the faces of the poor, laborers defrauded of their hire. Our Lord is crucified again every hour, everywhere."

"Father Moran," Father Cawder said on an abrupt impulse, "wished to start a credit union in Lulworth. I didn't agree it was desirable. He was disappointed over this."

"I see, I see." The bishop was studying his blotter. "Well, Father, you may tell Father Moran I will give due consideration to what you've told me on his behalf. But I believe at present he is best left where he is. I think he will do much good with you there." Musing, the bishop raised his eyes. "I recall Father Moran. He impressed me favorably. I will consider duly what you have told me."

The bishop's words seemed to have come to an end of whatever he thought proper to say about Father Moran, but he made no motion of dismissal. He sat as if pondering, gently breathing, and Father Cawder watched him in silence. He lifted his blotting pad and pulled out a letter. For a few moments his eyes lightly ran over the typewritten lines. "Do you want another priest put in Father Moran's place?" he said.

Father Cawder frowned. "I have no preferences of any kind. I am satisfied with Father Moran. I advised him to make the best of Lulworth."

The bishop nodded absently. "This letter reminded me of another young priest, Father Freck here in Cecilton. You read perhaps that he died last week. Happy for him, but a sad loss to us. He was going to leave this diocese for Philadelphia, to take over an old city parish. One he was born in. *Requiescat in pace.* Did you know him?" The bishop looked up.

"I read his name and that he had died."

"He was younger than you. The church he was going to be pastor of in Philadelphia is an old Bohemian parish, very run-down, in the heart of the city, very poor, drying up, people moving away, not large or prosperous enough for more than one priest. Father Freck was born in the parish, and it was thought that he could keep it alive because of his familiarity with conditions. It would have been a holy sacrifice on Father Freck's part. No money to work with, a life's work perhaps, burying himself, as the world judges, for the good of souls."

The bishop, pausing, again looked across the desk with a musing expectancy. "I was asked," he went on, "to give up Father Freck to Saint Ludmilla's—that is the name of the church—because of the difficulty of finding a proper man for such a parish, and of course, because Father Freck was willing to go. But God has taken it out of our hands, and the chancery in Philadelphia must make a new search. Saint Ludmilla was a martyr, strangled, I believe, by her own daughter-in-law, who was a pagan. She was Saint Wenceslaus' grandmother."

The bishop raised his mild eyes to the priest. "How many years is it now you have been at Saint Gregory's, Father?"

Father Cawder ran his hands restlessly over the arms of his chair. "It's been eight years, nine years in August, your excellency."

"So long as that? I had forgotten." The bishop looked down at the letter and spread it out. "I am really getting old, Father Cawder, for a minute or two I was daydreaming. I had thought perhaps a parish such as I described might have bearing on your own case in Lulworth. It could be arranged, you see, the transfer beyond my jurisdiction to another diocese."

"You meant for Father Moran?"

"I meant for yourself," the bishop murmured. "But I was forgetting that a parish like Saint Ludmilla's could not seem attractive to you in any way; I was forgetting you desire no change, as far as I know, and that I would seem to be requiting your able services in Lulworth with what others would certainly deem a demotion. As the world judges, and the clergy at

171

times too, I am afraid. I would like to be free to recommend opportunities of self-sacrifice and abnegation to my priests. But when I remember, I know that they cannot be moved about without seeming in some cases to be undergoing public correction. Besides, I would lose you. That, too, I did not remember. I have no wish to see my priests unfairly treated, Father Cawder, and you must excuse my wandering old wits. Whoever goes there, Saint Ludmilla's will be no sinecure."

Father Cawder rose from his chair. "I have no special reason to want to leave Lulworth. Did I rightly understand you? Are you advising me to consider some kind of change, your excellency?"

The bishop also rose. He held up his hands. "No, Father. No, no, not at all. It was just a fancy of mine, pure and simple. You are satisfied to stay in Lulworth, are you not? And with Father Moran?"

"I am satisfied." Father Cawder felt a slight impulse of guilt. His terseness was a form of deceit. He went on, "I didn't mean you to suppose he and I are on bad terms."

"I do not suppose you are." The bishop moved to the door behind his desk. "And if you are content, so am I. Even if you were not, you certainly don't have to expect to be burdened with a parish of poor Czechs. You must tell Father Moran not to trouble himself. Let him come talk to me if he wishes."

"I will tell him what you say, your excellency." Father Cawder bent his knee to the ring held out to him. On getting to his feet he found himself uneasily returning the bishop's level scrutiny.

"When I speak to those of you who are in my charge, it is not with guile, Father. Now that I am old I think aloud, that is how it is with me now. Pray for me, my son."

The bishop's eyes, wavering, took in the hall and Father Cawder turned aside. Shuffling legs and arms, bobbing heads, seemed to block his way. Tramping noisily over the black and white marble squares were men in overalls carrying two tilted palmlike plants, a bald friar, a Negro boy in a white jacket, three squat men smoking cigars who looked like Greeks or Syrians. A whoop of laughter burst from Monsignor Moon's office as he went by. The colored boy darted ahead to open the door to the street.

On each side of the bishop's steps, workmen were stooping over the box bushes, clamping down frames to protect them during the winter. Father Cawder groped for his watch. There was time to make his confession. He could walk to Father Sims' church of crumbling stone green like moldy cheese. He could go on foot and still have time to interview Mrs. Orde, "an experienced economical cook-housekeeper," before the train left. Watching the workmen while he buttoned his coat, he held his back to the stiff pressure of wind. Then he faced about and pushed forward against it, close to the walls of granite blocks sparkling in the sunlight with mica.

An hour later, on his way back to the bishop's, as he passed again in front of the six granite houses, he was walking more slowly. At the clumps of box bulging now out of their crates, he came to a halt, his eyes sinking from the bishop's door and its silver knob to the pavement at his feet. Contriving an arrangement of facts, making omission for the bishop's bemusement, he had, himself, made use of guile. He had taken no overt exception to the bishop's too civil phrases; he had not desired to speak truth about himself. And if a priest here and another there considered that sudden unexplained removal to another diocese connoted demotion, perhaps disgraceful correction, was the proposal to be rejected any the more for being a species of penance? Would he always be unready to endure injury or disgrace in patience? He thought of the unemphatic voice of the bishop, with his unoffending, undeceived child's eyes. Since it was irrelevant to make refusal of a thing on the grounds that it was hard. He could at least make inquiry, de-

173

clare himself ready to be disposed of by this man who professed to act not with guile, at the least submit himself as to a blessing when it was suggested that he should choose to live in difficulty and professional suspicion for the love of God.

When Father Cawder knocked on the green door it was opened at once by the bishop's colored boy. Monsignor Moon was passing through the hall. He eyed Father Cawder sharply.

"Back again, Father? I thought you had seen the bishop."

"I want to see him again," Father Cawder said. "For a few minutes."

Part Three

1

THE DINGY SNOW WAS MELTING IN THE warm spring air. Walking less briskly, the two nuns edged round a puddle and turned toward the side street. When they came to the gutter, with a simultaneous movement they gathered up their skirts with their left hands. Behind them the street with the shops had been full of people. Here it was quiet; no one passed them. The black windows of three small houses had a vacant look; one of the doors was splashed with radiator gilt. Across the concrete was a fence and behind that a wreckage of junked cars. The nuns walked to the corner of the street in silence. They stopped at a patch of black mud, again pulling at their skirts. The short nun concentrated her sallow face and said,

"We should have taken a taxi, Sister Jane Mary."

The red-faced nun with glasses was testing the mud with the toe of her polished shoes.

"Why, Sister? Are you tired? It can't be much farther. The next block's the three hundreds."

"I'm not tired. It's not that. It's just that this neighborhood's—"

Skirting a drift of slush at the curb the short nun broke off her words. Sister Jane Mary had sprung across with a vigorous jump.

"Oh, nonsense, Sister Victorine! What's the matter? Too dirty?"

"Not that at all, Sister. Only I think this neighborhood's not really suitable for walking in. For us to be seen in, I mean."

177

"Pshaw, Sister! Jesus is king, Jesus reigns!"

"Forever and ever amen! But I don't think it looks quite the right thing. It's not as if we were begging sisters."

"I'm surprised at you, Sister Victorine. It's just a poor neighborhood. I know all about that. The trouble with you, Sister, if you don't mind my saying so, is you've led too sheltered a life. When I was in the world I lived for years on a street just like this. And I never saw anything I shouldn't. Cast your care upon the Lord. Saint Joseph's watching out for us."

"You don't need to remind me, Sister. I've been praying to him ever since we started. However, I'll say no more about it."

"Nobody wants to bother a religious. They have respect for our habit."

Sister Victorine forced her mouth into an expression of patience. After a minute she said:

"I was thinking more of Reverend Mother than of us, Sister Jane Mary. I think she would have wanted us to come in a taxi. It would be the prudent way."

"Well, Sister Victorine, we don't know that and what you don't know can't hurt you."

The clatter of a passing truck put an end to the possibility of conversation. The two nuns stepped with nicety through the wet of the cross-street and went on without speaking. In the middle of the block Sister Jane Mary pulled a piece of green paper from her sleeve.

"302. It must be there on the corner."

Sister Victorine made no comment. "Sweet Jesus!" she said to herself. "Immaculate Heart of Mary, pray for us! Saint Joseph, foster-father of the Blessed Infant, pray for us who have recourse to thee!"

Sister Jane Mary stopped, inspected the slip of paper once again, and threw back her shoulders. Her hands came together and disappeared into her sleeves.

"There's the house," she said. "The one with the steps."

178

Sister Victorine's eyes rose slowly up the brown flaking wall. The curtains in the windows were limp and dirty.

"Yes. Now I see it I understand. Poor Marina!"

"She's come right along, considering what she was."

"She's too quiet. But it can't be helped. Early associations."

Or as Saint Paul said, bad companions. Sister Victorine saw Marina in a vague blur of memory. The wind blowing the child's mousy hair as she curled her leg around an iron pillar, dreaming awake, her eyes blind, moonily frowning as the other girls screamed and ran past her—a woolgathering, unresponsive child. Sister Jane Mary, making for the steps, raised a knitted glove.

"Come, Sister. We will simply wait at the door and inquire. There'll be no question of going inside. Shall I do the talking or shall you?"

"Mother gave you the instructions. It seems she wanted you to do the talking."

"Yes."

The nuns climbed up to the door side by side. Sister Jane Mary reached for a metal knob blackened by weather. It came forward, when she pulled it, with a sudden jerk. Sister Victorine turned to observe the street. A dirty baby crouched on a brownstone step and an old woman was dragging a toy wagon into an alley. There were two trees, starved and black but with all their twigs brushed with green. The ends of the branches were already thrusting out buds of leaves.

"Pentecost is the nicest time of the year. Soon our tulips will be up."

"I don't hear a thing," Sister Jane Mary murmured. "I wonder if it works."

She pulled at the bell again. A tall boy in a sweater glanced up curiously as he passed the house. Sister Victorine lifted her gaze above his head and pivoted round on her heels. The wood of the doorframe was badly in need of paint. It was black with a crust of soot.

"Maybe it's empty," Sister Jane Mary said. "The child's mother wrote it was a boardinghouse. But if it's empty that would account for things."

"Hark!" Sister Victorine exclaimed.

"What?"

"I thought I heard something."

It had been a noise like a window closing somewhere over their heads. Sister Victorine cast her eyes up the face of the house. All the windows were shut. Each showed a blank rectangle of glass, a sheet of watery glare. There was no one looking out at them.

"It sounded like a window coming down."

"Maybe they're hard of hearing." Sister Jane Mary grasped the knob of the bell and shook it in its socket. "They ought to hear that."

"Sister, I think perhaps we'd better go. We've come and rung the bell. There's no one here. We've done what we could."

The door opened gently as she spoke. A woman stood inside with her hand pressed to pallid reddish hair, watching them from pale eyes. She had a narrow face and a snub nose, pale lips, yellowish eyebrows. She was wearing a gingham housecoat. Her voice was low and diffident.

"What do you want?"

Sister Jane Mary fixed the woman, as she thought, competently through her glasses.

"You are Mrs. Gurig?"

"No."

"Isn't this Mrs. Gurig's house?"

"Sure. This is her house. Did you want her?"

Sister Jane Mary cleared her throat. She noticed the film of dirt on the woman's cheeks. Standing a step below her, the nun, to meet her eyes, had to look up.

"We did indeed, yes. Or Mrs. Swartz. I'm Sister Jane Mary and this is Sister Victorine. We're from the Holy

180

Infant up in Bantry. We wanted to find out about Mrs. Swartz."

The woman's face was empty of expression. She gazed down at the nuns vacantly out of dilated pupils.

"Well, Mrs. Gurig's not around today. Gone to spend the day in New York. You want to leave a message?"

"No, indeed. That will not be necessary." The nun smiled symmetrically and her glasses flashed. "Maybe you could tell us."

Sister Victorine said, "All we came for is information."

"Do you live here yourself?" Sister Jane Mary's smile faded. The woman in the doorway had not moved, she scarcely seemed to breathe. She answered abruptly:

"Sure, I live here. What kind of information?"

"About a lady who lives here. We'd like to find out if she's still here. This was her last address."

"She was here in this house?"

"Yes. Mrs. Swartz her name is."

"Nobody here by that name."

"She was here, she wrote to us from here. You see, we have taken charge of her little girl. She wanted to come up to see the child. But she never answered our letters and the last one was sent back."

"She ain't here now."

"But she was here. Wasn't she?"

"What name was it?"

"Swartz."

The woman lowered her eyelids. She was perhaps searching her memory. After a few seconds she said:

"What was she like? Blond? Sharp nose?"

Sister Victorine and Sister Jane Mary said together, "We do not know her."

The woman looked sideways judicially and the door swung further open. The nuns confronted a dark tunnel of hall running back to a gray window.

"I think that's the one. Swartz. Yeah, that was her name, now I come to think about it. I recollect her.

Kinda young. And dyed her hair. She's been gone away from here a long while."

"Oh, she's not here! But you remember her. She was here then."

"I never saw the woman you mean. She left here a good while before I came."

Sister Victorine shot a glance into the woman's weak eyes. "But you said you recollected her. You described her."

"Yeah." The woman gave a little yawn. "But that was from hearing Mrs. Gurig talk about her. I think she must be owing a bill. I think that's how it was. I never knew this Mrs. Swartz. Sorry, Sisters."

Sister Jane Mary had kept her face persistently upturned to the woman. "Where did she go?" she asked brusquely. "Don't you know where she went? She wrote she wanted to come see her child but we can't seem to get in touch with her."

"Oh, we don't have any address of hers."

"But the lady of the house ought to know. You see, our last letter to her was returned from here."

"We ain't got no address. Mrs. Gurig don't know nothing about where she is now."

Sister Victorine stepped behind Sister Jane Mary and studied a purple bruise on the woman's neck. She said in a thin voice, "How do you know that?"

"Because Mrs. Gurig told me, Sister." The woman's brows for a moment sullenly knotted. "I told you she owed a bill. She's been gone the best part of a year. She just lit out."

The two nuns stood motionless in easy silence. Sister Jane Mary said at last,

"There was also a certain man. By the name of Diamond, I believe."

The woman shook her head with impatience. The door swung back. "Never heard the name. Not since I been here. Nobody here now with that name."

"I see." Sister Jane Mary lightly settled the glasses on the bridge of her nose. "Thank you so much. We wanted to find out. We had written to Mrs. Gurig but she hadn't answered us. We just wanted to keep in touch with Mrs. Swartz. Thank you."

The woman's lips moved in a half-smile. "No use you writing her. Her hands are too crippled up to write any letters. I don't reckon she could tell you anything anyways."

"Thank you again. Good afternoon."

Sister Victorine smiled with definiteness, Sister Jane Mary gripped the iron railing to descend the steps. The woman waited within the doorframe until the nuns arranged themselves at each other's side and paced off along the curb. How black they look in those hoods, she thought. She had felt uneasy while talking to them, very faintly she had felt afraid of them, all in black like undertakers. She shut the door and walked to the back of the hall. Mrs. Gurig was still sitting on the trunk under the slant of the staircase. After a yawn the woman said:

"Did that suit you? Did you hear? They wanted to know about Swartz."

Mrs. Gurig grasped the edge of the trunk and pushed herself up. In the darkness her frizzled head looked unnaturally large to the other woman.

"I know, I know. I heard them. Writing letters to me. My stars, I've got plenty to do the way it is without writing letters to strangers."

"How did I do?"

"You did okay. Thanks."

Mrs. Gurig's voice dropped. The red-haired woman's hands hung listlessly at her sides. She watched Mrs. Gurig's fleshy back move off along the wall.

"What did you say?"

"I said thanks."

"What's the idea? Why didn't you see them yourself? You could have told them straight out. No call to make me tell them all that stuff."

At the door of her room Mrs. Gurig had paused, her head at an angle, her gaze dreamily held to a crack between the floor-boards. She appeared not to be listening to the woman.

"I said, why tell them all that stuff? What's the big idea? It's no skin off you."

Mrs. Gurig's shoulders slowly rose, the wrinkles round her eyes expanded as she glanced at the woman.

"No, but I'm not well. My nerves bother me. I don't want to be bothered about things. Makes no kind of difference. I don't have to be annoyed this way."

At the foot of the stairs the younger woman turned and said, "They asked about Diamond too." Mrs. Gurig moistened her upper and lower lips with a circular sweep of her tongue. With her head cocked, staring into the air, she did not seem to have heard. But rousing herself, she spoke out all at once in a heavy voice.

"About that bill you been owing me, Mrs. Gonzalez. If you pay me sure by the first of the month I guess it will be all right. I'm sure I don't wish to be hard on you."

The other woman said something under her breath and ran up the stairs. Indistinct in the shadows Mrs. Gurig suddenly sighed. She laced her fingers together, squeezing the knobs of their swollen joints. "Me write letters to strangers," she muttered.

Beyond the house, at the corner of the street, the two nuns came to a halt. Sister Victorine waved to the driver of a taxi.

"I'd feel much better about it," she said. "I don't think Reverend Mother had any idea what kind of a jaunt it would be."

Sister Jane Mary saw that the taxi was about to turn in its tracks. Meeting the driver's eyes she lowered her own with composure. "I have a dollar sixty cents," she said, "left over from what Mother gave us. But she didn't say anything about cabs."

Sister Victorine was clutching her blowing veil. "If

Mother had had any idea she'd have sent Mr. Mahaffy. It really wasn't just the thing for us. And we didn't learn anything."

"It didn't do any harm. Seeing as we were here today anyway. As Mother Fidelis used to say, 'Better to grin than to growl.' Well, here's your cab. Get in."

"After you, Sister."

The two nuns, raising their skirts above the slime in the gutter, stepped forward into the taxi.

2

DIAMOND PRESSED HIS SHOULDER TO THE
wall of glass. His unblinking eyes slowly made out the
shop-window. It was a display of women's hats; the
whorls of straw and flowers had been dropped on sight-
less plaster heads with slashed red mouths. As the man
drew near, Diamond held his breath; he heard the
scrape of soles against the concrete. There was a shuffling to the steady gait. Diamond stared at a hat with
two black spangled horns; the price tag read $8.95.
The sound of the steps struck behind his back and he
turned. He saw the slope of a dark coat, long swinging arms, a flash of an old, sad, unshaved face. A
black lunch-box rocked to and fro in the man's hand.
He had not glanced up, he had kept on, walking with
an even, heavy shuffle; he seemed wholly unaware of
having passed another human being. From behind he
was harmless, a nonentity. Still, who could trust how a
man looked? Diamond shifted round again to the
gleaming plate glass. It was just as well to be on the
safe side. He could wait for two minutes, count up to
two hundred. And keep an eye on the old man, to see
what he did next. His gaze fell from two overblown
green roses to a wreath of green grapes.

He counted steadily from one to a hundred. Starting
from one again he moved his head to bring the street
back into sight. There the man was, in the middle of
the streetcar tracks. He was walking down the platform.
He never once cast a glance behind him. He was a nobody, on his way home from work, had never seen the

other man in front of him whom he had doggedly followed for two blocks and then down here past the intersection. Diamond fitted a cigarette to his lips and struck a match into flame with his thumbnail. All of it had been in his mind; it was nothing. Although it had shown good sense to wait for the man, get a look at him, watch to see what he was going to do. A streetcar clanged. It halted in front of the man and hid him from view. When it went on again the platform was empty. A warm fresh breeze blew up the street.

It blew from the east, from the sea. Diamond felt within him vague relaxing longings. For what? Possibly it was just weather, warmth of spring, faint recollection of forty or so summers. He would like, he thought, to be at some beach, still and senseless on gray sand in the sun, gazing from a boardwalk into evening light on little waves, purplish, greenish, milky, with nothing to do, ease in his body, nothing at all in his mind. Perhaps if he went off to Seaside or Atlantic City, for a week or two. There was just as likely to be work there as here. And it might be easier than here. He could bang on the keys somewhere. Or peddle turtles, little green shells painted with candy-stripe lighthouses. Dust blew into his face and he sneezed.

These dirty streets, he thought, I ought to get away, this place confuses me. It was not like New York where nobody knew you and nobody cared what you did; it was strange and vast and yet it closed you in, and because it was strange, also threatening, it was full of busybodies, fat ugly faces, sharp hateful eyes. It would have shown sense never to have come here in the first place. But a man had to live somewhere.

Was the longing he felt just in his body? Maybe what I miss is a woman, he said to himself. A vague uncheerful lust seemed to touch his nerves. Did he need a woman? How long had it been? He began to calculate days, months, then flattened out his lips and spat over the concrete toward the gutter. No, it was something else, he wanted no woman, it was nothing so easy. His eyes had swerved to a bar on the other side of the street. A name in neon tubes, a long strip of curtained window, a door set in glass veneer. He went toward it across the asphalt.

The barroom was dark and full of mirrors. Padded seats ran along three sides; it was a place for women. He was conscious of their heads and faces slanted over tables. But their opening mouths spoke very quietly, he could hardly hear the sound of voices. He went and sat at the bar. When the gin buck was put down in front of him he looked into the mirror. The sight faintly surprised him. He always expected to see a man about thirty or so. But the brown, almost smirking face in the mirror could be fifty. He looked like an old jockey. An old scrounger too old to do anything but run a hotel for bookies and horse-traders. His face was like brown leather; his clothes were lumpy and out of shape. He switched his eyes to the room reflected from behind his back.

Against the wall in the corner was a woman with whitey-blond hair. Her head gleamed against the dark cushion. She sat with her shoulders hunched and turned sideways, talking to the man she was with. Another couple faced them across the table—a girl with black hair lank over her ears, a man with a neck red as meat. Drinking from her glass the blond girl raised her chin. Her pale cheeks were slightly hollow, her scarlet lips, neither full nor thin, began to smile lazily at something the man beside her said. Apparently she thought her hair had fallen forward. As if to fling it back she gave her head a shake; the movement had a kind of grace, easy and knowing. She put a hand to her forehead and touched the palm to the curve of her temple. Diamond observed her lifted arm. It was thin but oddly sinuous, long with small wrists, white, powdered probably, but what did that matter, indescribably smooth, a queer color, pearly—a short bunch of green sleeve fell over it above the elbow. It was strangely like Stella's arm. The girl's face, her curling lips, her bleached hair, everything about her reminded him a little of Stella. The slow way she moved herself. He had realized it when he first caught a glimpse of her. For an instant it had been like, from a corner of his eye, actually seeing Stella. Diamond furtively drew his gaze back to his own reflection. His mouth was hanging open. Startled, he pulled the glass of gin up to his lips. A puddle of water lay on the bar. He bent over to examine it.

When he glanced to the mirror again he saw that the second man had left the table. The two girls were turning toward each other. The blond one's hair was parted in the middle. Loops of it, glittering and silky, now hung down against her neck. Her eyebrows were long and black; her eyes were dark—brown, hazel, or they were a smoky blue. Stella's eyes had reminded him of wheels, wheels of blue ice with dark spokes, jet-black in the center and around the edges a kind of smoky feathering. The girl's hand lay on the table beside the man's. While the two girls talked he sipped from a stemmed glass, saying nothing. His coat was gray plaid with squared shoulders; he looked rich, stuffed with food, and sleepy. He was just buying the girl a drink. He was nothing special to her, had maybe never taken her out before. When he spoke without moving his lips the girl laughed. Not one of the tables near them was empty, Diamond noticed. All at once he smiled. He was getting too smart for himself. Without knowing it he was getting himself ready to make a play, give the girl a chance to get a good look at him. "Why not?" he seemed to whisper. If the man got up for a minute or two. If he was sitting somewhere near. He could flip his glass up, say offhand, "You girls aren't around much lately. Haven't seen you here for a good long while."

The girl moved and he was dumbfounded to find her eyes fixed straight on his own. But not as if she saw him; he was a watery shadow in the glass and the girl kept her eyes on him because she was tired of the sight of all the other things in the room. The man was craning forward, gesturing at her with spread hands; a bright stone winked on the little finger. He was a gambler, a stockbroker, maybe a moneylender. The girl still peered into Diamond's stare. And perhaps she did see him, perhaps while the man beside her talked she was lazily, idly thinking of the brown goggling face in the mirror over the bar, for very gradually, very slightly she smiled. A waiter cut through the reflection. He had brought more drinks to the table. The girl picked up what might have been a daiquiri.

That one year, Diamond thought, he had been happy and the joke of it was that at the time he had never known it. Probably it was the only happy year of his life. Stella and he sat on the verandah, the summer breeze blew the tablecloth, each of them had five whisky sours and then they had the regular dinner, a whole fried chicken apiece and a big platter of sliced tomatoes and cole slaw, that was all there was, two dollars per person, the hotel faced the pier and in the distance they could hear the merry-go-round and they looked at all the old women rocking away in rockers and they had laughed and laughed, the hotel was such a dump, ceilings twenty feet high with electric fans like propellers hanging down on the ends of black pipes, but the chicken was wonderful and they drank all those whisky sours and the wind came down on the choppy water with little spanking slaps and when they walked on the pier they could see the jellyfish floating by, bluish, milky, and on the end of the pier Stella put her arm around his waist under his coat, they could hear behind them, faint and screechy, the music from the dance hall in back of the trees. At the time it had just been another day. Maybe it was the happiest day of his life. That was something you could never tell about. Diamond turned back to the mirror. The girl had drunk half her drink, her chin rested on her clasped hands. The black-haired girl lurched sideways to cross her legs. There was nobody sitting now at the table beyond her arm.

190

He left the bar and with his drink in his hand started in between the chairs. The tune on the radio was changing from gourds and rattles to thin piano notes. Knocking against a chair leg he felt sad and now that he was on his feet, afraid. He was afraid of the girl. Supposing—it was horrible to think of—she was just like Stella. But that was crazy, she would not be the same. He knew what to do, whether the man left or stayed where he was, it was just a question of a look; the girl would see him and if she wanted him to speak he could tell from the way she met, or did not meet, his eyes. He reached for the empty chair, pulled it out, set his drink down on a disc of cork. If he turned his head he could look right into the girl's face. He took up the coaster and spun it on its edge. Above its rim he saw the cloth on the girl's table, they were perhaps getting ready to eat; he saw a glass of water, a woman's bag of dull black silk.

The man's voice was both soft and cracked. It said:

"Oh, him. He's left those McKinneys. He's gone over to that Chevrolet place. Doing not so bad, I heard."

"I always liked Marion—" It was the dark girl; straining his eyes sideways, Diamond made out the moving of her lips. "Funny name for him to have. But I do, I like him a lot. A while back we went places quite a bit. We'd have dinner, then dance somewhere. He's okay by me. He's the generous type."

"That so? You're the generous type too, aren't you? Didn't you ever do anything for him?"

"Oh, I prattled away. He thinks I'm funny. Haven't heard from him now, though, for quite a while."

"Don't guess you were funny enough. I wouldn't worry. There's lots of big-hearted, open-handed guys. Like me. I'm the generous type too. That's so, isn't it?"

"If you say so, dear. And you can start right now. I'm hungry."

"Do you ever see that girl he used to go with—" it was the blond girl's voice, halting, slow, full of stress; Diamond listened incredulously, it was nothing at all

191

like Stella's voice. "O my God, what a sight. I run into her all the time. You know who I mean, don't you, Kay?"

"You mean that girl with the big bust and all the hair—Jean something."

"Girls, girls."

"Yeah, that's the one." The voice was heavy, made up of gasps, as if she was afraid her breath might give out before she finished. "Jean Minnawitz or Minkititz or something like that. My God, what a figure. I don't see how any man who'd want to take out a girl like you ever saw anything in a girl like that. I honestly don't. She looks like somebody's mother with her wrinkled old baggy face and all her fat hanging down in front, my god."

"He hasn't seen her for two or three years. I know that for a fact."

"I should hope not—" The blond girl had lost interest in what she was saying; her words uncertainly dragged. "It looks bad to see a man going around with an old bag like that. Old enough to be his own mother."

Maybe if he turned to watch her, Diamond thought, it would come back. It might sound different if he was watching her face, he might forget the slow gasping voice. She, seen between half-shut eyelids, might remind him, might almost for an instant seem to be Stella—the woman's voice came again in a sudden cry.

"Oh, Kay! You didn't come up to see the dress. I wanted you to see it. Kay, it's just heaven on me."

"What's the color?"

"Oh, black. But gee, it's pretty. It's got a sort of a panel on the side. And the neckline's just right for me, if I say so myself. Sort of square with rounded corners. Do you know what I mean?"

"Like a boat neck, you mean."

"Yeah, but the neckline's quite low. I'll have to keep it for parties, it's sort of formal looking. It's got a belt of beads, twisted like—"

Diamond saw the blond girl's hand move across the

table to its edge. He studied it. It was reddish, not whi...
The fingers were thick and stubby, the thumb was as
muscular as a man's. The red nails appeared to have
been bitten down to the quick. He glanced up suddenly
to her face—her mouth was open, she was saying, "—a
lovely blue one, rayon taffeta, but after—" an immense mouth smeared with lipstick like house paint,
the teeth, worn away, dwindled downward to the gums,
the nostrils above were black and flattened out over
the girl's cheeks. He must have shown his disgust. Or
disappointment. He felt like crying, he was staring
crazily at the gabbing girls. He became aware that all
three were angrily staring back at him. He got to his
feet.

"Some fresh ape. Some drunk."

The dark girl spoke behind him. On the other side
of the room his hat was hanging from a silver peg.
Stumbling over nothing, he made his way toward it.

M RS. GIRARD, HER CHEEK PRESSED INTO the pillow, was peering down into her garden when she knew she was not asleep. The effortless stages into wakening had left her filled with strange refreshment. Almost a kind of happiness. She looked out from the sleeping porch at the copper beech. A blue haze drenched its humps of leaves. Its shadow seeped across the grass, gray in the rich shade with dew. For a moment or two an illusion of washed air could be enjoyed, of blue shade and glittering leaves, inexplicable physical peace it seemed—one could call it happiness. Larghetto. Like being borne along through blue water to a slow movement of Mozart's.

The shutters were already fending off the first hot glare of sun. Like a frog in a well she could lie still in the cool dark within doors until the sun set. Ben would have delighted in such a summer morning. He would have rubbed his chest with witch hazel and put on a white linen suit. During the whole of her life she had been lucky, even in a husband. You have been very good to me, dear Lord, she murmured silently. Thank You for Your bounty to me, dear Lord. Mrs. Girard made the sign of the cross. Suddenly she looked at her wrist watch and kicked the sheet to the floor. She remembered she must wash and dress, make herself coffee, hurry to the bus station to see Father Cawder off to Philadelphia.

But the bus did not get in till seven. She slipped her hands under her cheek and closed her eyes. To take leave of a cleric who was not at all the kind she liked. Her tastes were Jesuitical. She liked a priest who drew virtue out of mortal failings, accommodating himself to the world for the greater glory of God. Thus this feeling was surprising. She was touched by some irrational sympathy with Father Cawder, now that he was leaving forever. On the Sunday in April when he announced the bishop's devious manipulations, standing red-faced under the concave shell of the pulpit, tears, it was very ridiculous, had come into her eyes. So he was to leave and they would never see him again. It was almost as if she had been expecting mere acquaintance with Father Cawder to turn, unnaturally, into friendship, the kind one understands the word to mean when one is a child but which thereafter one never experiences. It was love, she thought, she must feel for Father Cawder. Chaste enough, God knew. No doubt the maternal impulses which God and nature had decided, in her case, to leave without employment, like the vermiform appendix. All poor Ben could find was a worthless womb in which to spend his seed with such perseverance. He had been good about it, a man without an heir.

Did new pastors always seem a degeneration from the old? After Father Magruder died she had not been pleased, she remembered, when Father Cawder came to take his place. And now that Father Cawder was going they were to be left with Father Moran. He was earnest, "sincere" it was called, a hustler, the low businessman's phrase adapted to the cut of Holy Mother Church. It was queer one never came across a priest any more who was a gentleman. Once she had met a priest who was also an archduke—in Styria, down a country lane full of geese, she had curtsied—a doddering, rather wild-eyed old man. Turkey suppers and machine-lace surplices would be the order of the day now that it had pleased the bishop to make a pastor out of poor Father Moran. All his words and gestures had a hearty, moderate, sheepish, lower-middle-class kind of tinge. And he was not conscious of this at all

195

and quite happy, poor young man, to be as he was. He was a serious person. As Father Cawder, of course, was too. Worrying over one's sins, taking things so hard, they both exhausted one. Opening her eyes, Mrs. Girard brushed at a fly which had settled on her chin. Reminders of the bliss of heaven, the pangs of hell, rehearsed every Sunday of one's life, projected at times too large a perspective. "I'm tired of tragedy and common people," she said aloud.

The air in the sleeping porch was growing warmer. She pulled off her nightgown and dropped it on the floor. Raising her right leg she scanned the pale bony shin. Nowadays the young girls had legs like boxers; they ate too many vitamins. She had the good fortune to have had a mother who knew nothing of dietary values. Consequently her bones were small, as a woman's should be. Formally speaking, she was an old woman, but she had good ankles. Everyone had always said so. They are pretty, she repeated to herself, really pretty, a lady's fine bones. If you saw only her legs you might certainly think her a young girl. Mrs. Girard fitted a pair of mules to her feet and opened the French window into the house. How silly she was, horrible too, dawdling naked on a cot. She wanted to have time to make Father Cawder some chicken sandwiches. Also a slice of orange cake would go nicely. She could breakfast herself off a raw egg in a wineglass.

The street had a clean peaceful look. There was only an old colored man abroad, shambling uncertainly toward her. Mrs. Girard began to walk briskly in his direction; she passed two fingers under the string of her parcel. Because it was empty of the deformities of the human race, the paving glistened with silky light; in spite of the heat it looked washed in dew. I am almost happy, she thought and said an instant later, "Good morning, Charles." The old Negro pulled off his hat, mumbled incoherently as his habit was.

If I had only known during the winter, she was thinking, that in July he would be leaving. She re-

196

membered planning to have Father Cawder frequently for dinner, to bully him into feeding at a plentiful board at least once every month. All winter long he looked gaunt and miserable. But except feebly and only once, studying his lined face across the tea table, she had never mentioned meals to him at all. He had not been to her house since that fiasco of an afternoon—it would be decent to wait a month or so after Father Cawder's departure before renewing the offer of the cushions to Father Moran. Especially as she had conveniently forgotten all about ordering any dogwood trees. Since that day, it must have been in October, she had seen him only at the altar or out of doors, once, just after Easter, at Maud Dorsey's party for the Englishman, the bespectacled editor of the London Thingumbob, that invaluable Catholic weekly.

Perhaps she was not really on very good terms with Father Cawder. Not good friend enough to be rising at dawn to take him a lunch of chicken sandwiches. It was possible she was cutting a comical figure, a church hen pattering after a priest with dainties and offers to remember him in her prayers. On the crest of Prince Street she stood still to get her breath. She saw below her the shed of the bus station, a flat roof quivering with heat. No people seemed about. My gray linen suit, my off-blue bangkok sailor, she said to herself, are not the grease-spotted black serge of any church hen. Anyway, my father was John Norton of Macomico Hall and I am Mrs. Girard of Lulworth, I do as I please.

The little dirty waiting room was empty when she reached the door of the bus station. Lifting her chin, composing her face, she went round to the back where a covered platform flanked the driveway. Along the curb two strange men and an unknown woman with a baby were standing in a group, and then a little beyond, Father Cawder beside his black suitcase. He saw her and frowned, not with displeasure, she supposed, but with surprise. He took a step forward and shook her hand.

"Good morning, Mrs. Girard. You are going to Baltimore too?" He still frowned in perplexity.

"Certainly not, Father!" Mrs. Girard arched her eyebrows. "On a day like this? No, indeed. This beastly day, what a shame you have to travel in this weather. No, Father, it's simply that I thought I would like to come down to say good-bye to you." She turned to glance at the stolid faces of the men behind her. "Where is Father Moran?" she murmured.

"He drove me down, but I asked him not to wait for the bus. He had the seven-thirty Mass to say."

"I see." Mrs. Girard held up the neat brown-paper parcel, faintly smiling. "Do you remember a long while ago, years, just after you came to Lulworth, I officiously sent you a chicken? Naturally, you had never heard of me and you chose to send it back. I think you said pastors were not to be tempted to gluttony by their parishioners. Possibly you meant when they were completely unidentified women. Anyway, I've fixed a few sandwiches here in case you get hungry on your journey. I hoped you know me well enough now not to mind." The troubled look entering Father Cawder's face amused Mrs. Girard. She handed him the parcel. He held it awkwardly in front of him, studying it with wholly unnecessary seriousness.

"That was kind of you, Mrs. Girard," he said with no humor or lightness. "That was very good of you. You should not have bothered bringing me anything."

"It was no sort of bother." She wanted a cigarette, but she had a prejudice against smoking in places of free access to the public. "I came prepared to take leave of you, Father. I know it will be forever. Until Judgment Day, possibly. You will never come back again to see us. I have a feeling you will never be south of the Mason-Dixon Line again. Try to come down sometime to see us."

"I shall probably be back at one time or another,"

he said mildly. "Perhaps some summer it may be possible to come back to see you all again."

Whom would you come back to see, Mrs. Girard was thinking, who in Lulworth will ever want to see you again? "I hope you will write and report your impressions of Philadelpha, the new parish," she said. "In particular, you must let me know if you think of anything I can do for you here. You may have forgotten to get your shoes from the cobbler. I can send them to you."

He looked at her queerly, turning over something in his mind. "There is nothing to do," he said vaguely with a glance out over her head. "I suppose Philadelphia will turn out to be very different from Lulworth. My church is an old Bohemian parish, down in the old part of the city."

"So Father Moran described it." A parish of shoddy foreigners would be a more appropriate field for a good priest, and perhaps more pleasing, than this peat-bog of clodhoppers. Bogtrotters they were, graceless and loutish, shamefully letting him go off in this way without a gesture of leave-taking. "I suspect you will be glad, really, of the change. I should think the lot of us here must get terribly dull to a priest. We're a tiresome, dreary lot. Professionally, how we must have bored you."

"No, Mrs. Girard. You are mistaken." He of course agreed with her, ready as he was to offer instant rebuke. "It is easy to be taken in by appearances. Possibly I always seemed to be making demands while I was here. If there have been deficiencies—all of you have been much better to me than I deserved."

"You can't expect me to believe that, Father." Mrs. Girard briefly laughed. How unnecessary to feel himself obliged to these protests of humility, this hard-eyed proud priest. Why do I feel this pity for him, this sentimental queerness, she wondered, watching him as he looked off up the street. He seemed a competent, cold enough figure of a man, with his hard

199

mouth and his eyes like marbles. "If I were a priest I would have much higher standards than you. I find myself and the rest of us here in Lulworth quite terribly boring."

Father Cawder, appearing to smile, eyed her. "It is not the same for a priest. A country town can provide quite the same problems as a parish of gangsters in Chicago, spiritually speaking."

Mrs. Girard's eyes roved away. "You will be much happier in Philadelphia, Father. Philadelphia is the North. Temperamentally, I think you are more suited to living in the North than in this dull little frog pond of a place."

"I was born in Kentucky; my mother's parents were Marylanders." Father Cawder turned again to face the rise of the street.

"That doesn't matter, Father. Spiritually you are a Northerner. In the North it is what you *do* that counts. They believe in good works. Southerners are pagans, you know; it's what you *are* that's important. I don't think you find us congenial. That's why I think you'll be happier away from us. Am I being very impertinent?"

"No, Mrs. Girard," he said easily and shook his head. In the same breath he went on, "Here comes the bus." With her bundle lodged in the crook of his arm he turned to pick up his suitcase. Pressing forward, the woman with the baby felt impelled to push along the curb. As though a seat on the bus was a reward for shoving into someone before boarding it. Mrs. Girard stepped back to give Father Cawder room.

He took her hand and seemed to stare solemnly into her face. "Good-bye, good-bye, Father!" She heard her trembling voice lost in the screeching of brakes as the bus drew to the side of the platform. "Good-bye, I hope you'll be charmed with Philadelphia."

He considered her severely. "Good-bye, Mrs. Girard. Thank you for coming down." Unbending to the last—although what more in fact would another man have said, taking congé of a slight acquaintance? She watched a moment while he and the woman and the two men stooped forward into the throbbing bus. What had she expected him to say? Lord, I am silly, she thought to herself. She walked off along the arc of concrete. He excites pity and I had a desire to do him some kind of good turn, some insignificant, unparticularized benefit. There he goes off, sunk into the disgusting plush-covered entrails of a bus. He does not know how I feel and he needs no pity. Why should he care what I think? A drop of sweat, under her slip, slowly trickled from her armpit to her waist. Dear Lord, it was hot. And the street now had eased back again into its usual dusty swelter, full of men in blue denim or seersucker off to work to earn their bread. Also, the wherewithal for their wives to surpass other men's wives in the acquirement of radios, electric washing machines, and rayon draperies. The unwashed gypsy, Mrs. Ringer, was on hand, she saw, beetling in her doorway, waiting to pounce on any foolish farm woman who might idle by her shop. The creature had seen her, she was beginning to grin in her bold brazen way. Lazily, thickly, with no accent of deference, the woman said as she passed:

"How're you today, lady?"

"Good morning, Mrs. Ringer."

With her thumbnail Mrs. Girard flicked off a smut which had lodged on her gloved left hand. The hot day was settling down. The happiness which she had felt when climbing the hill had now, she found, quite vanished away.

Part Four

1

AT THE CHANCERY MONSIGNOR HOLLIS
had blandly gazed over the expanse of a table. Along
its edge had been ranged a potted begonia, a dicta-
phone, and a small china skull. He had gently pronounced, "Well then, you had best be off. The little
priest from the seminary is waiting for you there at
the church. Your bags are with you? Bully. He'll be
on hand when you get there. Ben venuto, Father
Cawder. Look in again next week."

Father Cawder halted at the bed which now was his,
black and high with protuberances like melons, the
double bed of a pastor. On the floor below him the
little priest, fidgety and apologetic, was on tenterhooks
about his train. So it was necessary to go downstairs
again, to return thanks, to hear last-minute details
about the monthly cost of coal. He dropped his hat
on the bed and studied the room over the old woman's
back. She had heaved his suitcase to rest beside a
wardrobe, panting from the climb up the stairs. The
high walls were stained by the drip of leaks; the
room was crowded with another man's collection of
castoff furniture, each chair just where it was when he
died. A bundle of palm stuck out from behind a picture, the fronds were plaited, knotted into chains of
diminishing links, ringletted, tied with a purple ribbon—some convent's Easter greeting to his predeces-
sor.

The old woman's blue eyes were eagerly staring. "It
is all right to leave your valise here, Father?"

"That is all right."

She started herself toward the door. Looking round over her shoulder, possibly for no reason at all, she was still smiling.

"You are Mrs. Hoffer?"

"Yes, Father Cawder. I was here the whole time with Father Angelis."

"When you go down tell Father Blanchard I will join him in a few minutes."

"Yes, Father Cawder." Her daft smile widened as she backed away. He heard her clump off to the steps and begin to descend them. He crossed the room to a wash-basin of black-veined marble behind the wardrobe.

When he had washed the soot of the streets from his face and hands he went downstairs. The young priest with his chin stubbled with beard was still where he had left him, vacantly eying the hall, his loose lips open over his jutting teeth.

"We really thought you'd get here this morning," he said. "I must get back to Saint Thomas More's by dark and my train leaves in an hour. So you'll excuse me if I seem to be rushing you. There's just one more thing I forgot to bring to your attention, I think."

Father Blanchard, opening the parlor door, stood politely aside. He halted first at a leather armchair and pressed his hands on its tufted back by way of invitation. Then he seated himself at the desk and unlocked a drawer. Light fell over him from a pointed window. It showed up the spots of food faintly dried on his lapel, two narrow creases in the middle of his sallow cheeks. Father Cawder looked aside to the bellying black mantelpiece. Above it a huge print displayed rows of heads of all the popes.

"One last thing about the cash on hand, Father." With his hand raising aloft a red notebook, Father Blanchard showed his teeth more in a grimace of pain, it seemed, than a smile. "When I came there was an outstanding account for the flashing and roof repairs. I paid it, but you'll see it didn't leave you with

206

much of a reserve. Everything was so mixed up when Father Angelis died. I hope you'll approve of what I did. I just spent the week ends here, you see."

"Don't feel you must make excuses to me, Father Blanchard. You had a right to do as you saw fit."

Father Blanchard put the notebook down beside the inkwell. A jumble of dusty papers lay behind it, bills, empty envelopes, circulars and holy cards, a cardboard box crammed with the strings of scapulars.

"I told you about this book, Father. It's the addresses. All the ones Father Angelis used are in it, the plumber, church goods, and so on. I added in back what I thought you'd need. This"—he touched a piece of paper held down by a glass prism—"is what I forgot to give you—the combination of the safe. You'll find the bank book, the old mortgages, and the registers all there inside."

Father Cawder noticed a bottle of wine on the desk while the priest was talking. It rose out of a stack of clippings and curled photographs. Idly observing he read the label, *Desiderio Muscatel,* below, a pink hand squeezing a cluster of blue grapes. Beside it was a dusty glass.

"You've made things very easy for me, Father. If I find there's still something I forgot to ask you I can telephone. About Mrs. Hoffer. Does she live here?"

"That's right, she lives here. She has a room off the kitchen. She does all the housework and the marketing. She goes down to the big markets as soon as they open, sometimes before five in the morning. I've found her a great help."

"What wages does she get?"

"She gets twenty dollars a month. It's really out of charity she stays on here. She's very good and devout, a daily communicant. But of course there's no money available here for higher wages."

"And is there a sexton or some man for the church?"

"None paid. An old man named Hiss comes to clean

207

sometimes. He hasn't been around now for a month. I was ashamed to have you see the church so dirty. Mrs. Hoffer and I did what we could yesterday, but we couldn't do very much. It will be hard to run this parish as you'd like. I hope you don't expect too much."

"I expect nothing at all, Father."

Father Blanchard had glanced furtively at his wrist watch. "I really haven't so much more time. I don't think there's anything else I can—" He broke off and suddenly swept loose envelopes from the top of a red book like a ledger. "Oh, there's this! I put it here so I would remember. It's the baptismal entries." He turned the pages rapidly to the middle of the book and thrust it into Father Cawder's hands.

"You see, from here on all these entries are mine. Father Angelis never made any baptismal entries his last year. He wrote them down on scraps of paper and put them in the front of the book. I've copied them in where they belong. I wanted to explain in case you wondered. It's now all up to date."

"I understand, Father. The entries seem all in good order now."

"The baptismal records are usually kept in the safe. I just took them out to show you."

"Father Blanchard! Father Cawder! Can I just interrupt for a minute?" At the loud hissing whisper, the two priests turned round. Clasping her hands over her breasts Mrs. Hoffer stood still and pushed her neck forward. "There's a visitor, Father Blanchard. Mrs. Fleming. She's asked for you. She's in the dining room. What will I say?"

Father Blanchard drew his long fingers down his worried face. "I know her, Father Cawder. She's been here a couple of times before. Do you want me to see her? She's one of the parishioners."

Father Cawder closed the register and put it down on the desk. "No. Not unless you think it necessary, Father Blanchard. You haven't much time to make your train. Tell Mrs. Fleming I will see her shortly, Mrs. Hoffer."

An intense smile spread over Father Blanchard's face. In his joy his tongue lolled between his large lips. "Then I will be leaving right away, Father Cawder. You can reach me by telephone as you said, if I forgot anything. Mrs. Hoffer really knows as much as I do about the parish."

Father Cawder went ahead to the door and opened it. Shaking hands, he looked into Father Blanchard's brown-spotted eyes. They were not observing him, he knew; they were brightening over objects miles beyond this high musty room. He saw the chance of escape—back to friends, the tempered orderliness of classroom and refectory, the leisurely contemplation of the ways of God unalloyed with Mrs. Hoffer and a daily discussion of the price of meat. "I'm making a special study of Saint Ephraim and the church of Nisibis," he had said.

"Thank you for taking the trouble to go over things, Father Blanchard. I will call you at the seminary if I have to get in touch with you. Excuse me for not seeing you out. I will see what this woman wants."

As he smoothed down his rabat under his coat, almost immediately, he heard the sound of feet pattering down the stone steps to the street. He opened the door into the dining room. A middle-aged woman, thin, with narrow shoulders, sat erect at the table. Under a felt hat spangled with metal flowers her lined, rouged face lifted toward him in surprise. She was gnawing gently at her lower lip.

"I am Father Cawder, your new pastor, Mrs. Fleming. Please come into the parlor."

The woman rose to her feet and stared at him. "Oh! I see! I expected to see Father Blanchard."

"He has gone back to the seminary. He was only here temporarily, Mrs. Fleming."

The woman opened her mouth and slowly distended it before speaking. "I wanted to talk to some-

209

one. But you see, I know Father Blanchard. That's why I expected to talk to him. He knows about my case."

"Come into the parlor, Mrs. Fleming." He followed her across the carpet toward the desk. He waited until she had taken the chair drawn up beside it, sweeping the room with her eyes, rhythmically biting at her lips. "Your case?"

"Oh." Her voice prolonged the sound into a kind of growl. "I've been here with my troubles before, Father. It's just that Father Blanchard knew all about it and, naturally, it's not much fun for me to be going over it all again. I've always kept things in. It shames me to have to come to a priest like this."

"I'm your pastor now, Mrs. Fleming; I want to be of any help I can. What was it you came about?"

"If I'd known I'd have had to go into it all again, Father, I don't think I'd have come. I'd have just managed somehow, I guess. Begged from a neighbor. It's very humiliating to me. I'm not used to it, I wasn't brought up to do it."

"You're in need of money, Mrs. Fleming? Is that it?"

"That's just it, Father. It's my husband, Aleck. I try not to blame him, I don't think a wife should, but he's got a bad heart, and so he can hardly ever get any work he can do, he drinks, he goes off and stays away for days at a time. Sometimes I'm at my wits' end with all I have to see to."

"You mean for your family?"

"Not that exactly." Mrs. Fleming, leaning back until her head rested on the tufts of the chair, for a moment shut her eyes. "We were never blessed with any children. Maybe it's just as well, seeing what my life is like now. No, I meant just the house. I rent out two apartments. We own our house. If it wasn't for that we'd be out on the street. But that makes it bad in other ways."

"Owning your house?"

"Why, sure. That's why Aleck can't ever get any relief—he's put down as a property owner and of course he'll never be able to draw anything for unemployment. That's the way it's been, for years now."

"Is there no one in your husband's family, or yours, you can go to? It's their duty to help you, you know, Mrs. Fleming, when you're in trouble."

Mrs. Fleming examined the walls from the corners of her eyes as she spoke. "We haven't got any relations, no one to fall back on at all. Something just happens and then when I get in a little money from the house I'm in debt and it all goes to pay what I owe. That's the fix I'm in now. I'd been saving ten dollars out, I put it in a teapot. That man got hold of it and out he flew. I'll never know where he's gone. When he gets back he won't have a cent. And what are we going to live on for the next ten days? I don't know. I thought Father Blanchard might help me, so I came here. He was very kind and understanding the time before."

Mrs. Fleming's eyebrows had been shaved or plucked out. Where they had once grown a thread of black had been penciled, arching down to her temples. The priest watched them rise and fall. Her eyes, flitting from object to object, came to rest on the top of the desk. With a clumsy motion the woman plucked at her crocheted gloves and peeled them off.

"I'm not very well, for one thing. I've had to spend an awful lot on medicine. With me it's anemia and low blood pressure and you probably know what vitamin pills cost. The pinch comes with Aleck not being able to draw relief on account of owning the house. I sometimes feel I just haven't got what it takes to go on. I was wondering"—her voice became stridently affirming—"I see there's a little wine left in that bottle there, Father, could you let me have just a taste? Coming over here and going over it all again, it's made me feel weak, I feel drawn out. I had no lunch before I came."

Father Cawder noticed her writhing hands; two little rings pressed on the knuckle of a bony finger, one set with an opal, the other with a garnet. "Certainly, Mrs. Fleming. There's no clean glass here. Mrs. Hoffer will bring you one."

He got to his feet. Mrs. Fleming took up the bottle by its neck and twisted the cork.

"Oh, don't you bother about that. This will do. It's just dust."

She rapidly whisked the inside of the glass with a handkerchief. She filled the tumbler half-full and fitted the cork back into the bottle. With the glass raised in her right hand a sharp smile moved her lips for the first time.

"I really needed this, Father. I felt weak as water."

She drank in slow steady gulps. Father Cawder took four dollar bills from his wallet and laid them on the desk.

"I can let you have this much, Mrs. Fleming. I hope it will help to tide you over."

Mrs. Fleming set down the glass, rolled up the bills into a thin tube and, balancing them in the palm of her hand, drew on one of her gloves.

"This will do nicely, Father, till I get something from my tenants, and I don't know how I will ever thank you. I just had the carfare to get home. I would have just hated to beg from a stranger. But I didn't mind telling you."

With a twisting stride, Mrs. Fleming made for the door of the room.

"Don't you come with me, Father. I know my way out. And thank you again."

"Wait a moment, Mrs. Fleming. Give me your address."

"My address?" Mrs. Fleming stood still and frowned. "You want to know how you can reach me?"

"In a few days I'll stop in to see how you are."

"I live at 700 Oglethorpe. It's the yellow double-decker on the corner. Wish you could let me know before you come. I'd like everything to be looking its best for you."

"I will just drop by to see how you are making out. Perhaps I could meet your husband."

"Oh, sure! If he's there." The woman stared at him in thought. "I wouldn't hand him any advice, though, Father, much as he needs it. It wouldn't do any good and just make it worse for me. He's not a believer in anything. Sometimes he says terrible things about religion." She stepped quickly out of the room and, looking back inside, worked her mouth into a strange grin. "Stay where you are, Father. I can get out all right. Good-bye and thanks ever so much."

She darted beyond the jamb. At the bang of the street door Father Cawder came slowly back to the desk. He had a desire to begin sorting the papers scattered in layers over the scarred black leather. At least calendars, begging letters, and advertisements could be torn once across, dropped into the wastebasket. He glanced at and turned away from the wine bottle precariously left on the corner of the wood. The print of Mrs. Fleming's fingers was plain on the dusty green glass. Glib and sly, the woman was a liar —how would she have fared with Blanchard directing on her his unsure toothy smile? Would he have shamed whatever weak chicanery the woman had decided upon by an exhibition of uncensorious love? Probably not. But to Father Blanchard she would have lied with uneasy reserve. With himself that was not necessary. He too was a liar. Recognizing her own kind Mrs. Fleming could cynically, listlessly, speak whatever came into her thoughts. If she was a liar, her deceit at any rate was practiced on a man willing all his life to lie to God.

The light from the cloudy sky was failing. Father Cawder went into the dining room. The table was already laid with one place at its head. He passed through the pantry into the kitchen. As the door swung behind him Mrs. Hoffer shrilly cried out,

"Oh, Father! I didn't want you to see! Your first dinner here! I wanted so much to surprise you!"

"To surprise me how, Mrs. Hoffer?"

"With this!" The old woman's red hands clenched themselves over a platter of cream-puffs. "I'm known up and down in this parish for my pastry. They were a surprise! And now you know. I have been known for my cream-puffs for years and years."

"Well, you have surprised me with them now. It is almost the same. I'm sure they'll turn out to be very good. When do you have dinner here?"

"At six, Father. It is too early? Too late?"

"Six is just right, Mrs. Hoffer."

He paused beside the table of pale scrubbed oak. The old woman dipped a spoon into a bowl of chocolate icing and, deftly twirling it, covered the cream-puffs with shining spirals.

"They are easy to make. They are really nothing at all." She turned her flushed face toward him with a childish exuberance.

He supposed he need make no further comment. At the back of the table lay a dish filled with silver pellets like shot. Mrs. Hoffer delicately lifted one of the pellets and dropped it on the top of a cream-puff. He knew, when she was finished, flaunting a thrown-out arm, she would display the garnished plate and again extravagantly exclaim. Meaning to move away in silence, he stood awkwardly watching her.

2

FATHER CAWDER LEFT THE VESTMENTS TO the boy with the cropped head and went back into the church. The tabernacle door had been left unlocked. He had to remember that churches in Northern cities are the resort of thieves, lurking to pick purses, rob poor boxes, carry off the sacred vessels in sacrilegious hands—certainly sacrilegious, since, if caught, they would prove to be the sons of pious bead-telling Silesian or Calabrian widow-women. When he had locked the little gilded door he genuflected and looked upward over the altar. Now for the rest of his life when he stood there his eyes would be pulled in spite of himself to the topheavy fretwork—red-cheeked saints, wooden clouds, niches and crockets. Forty feet in the air the spikes rose, the whole heavenly court according to Bohemian taste in 1866. In the center Saint Ludmilla, duchess and martyr, varnished and trimmed with lace of punched tin. Whatever the parish had fallen to, in the beginning it had been able to foot the cost of this gaudy church. Was the retina of an eye able to fix on the priest against these gimcracks? Holding up the host, his hands would dissolve into winking stencils behind him, he would be absorbed, just another posturing plaster cast. Slovakians had perhaps a prejudice against a plane surface; they imagined a jigsaw scaffold could express the multitudinous epiphanies of God. In four or five months some way might be found to dismantle the pine spindles without shock to the mulish conservatism of the laity.

Father Cawder dipped his hand into holy water at the arch into the sacristy. Changes should be feasible, now that the parish was Czech no longer. What had happened to the Bohemians of 1870? Except for Mrs. Hoffer they had sunk without trace into the city, their children turned into brachycephalic Bakers, Marshalls, Millers, their crocketed pews knelt in by a few sallow slum inhabitants who spoke, instead of Czech, merely the homely variant of English used by the proletarians of Philadelphia.

The boy had finished folding away the vestments into the press. He was waiting, cap in hand, by the door to the yard.

"You want me same time tomorrow, Father?"

"Yes, the same time. Thank you for coming, Joe." Father Cawder put on his biretta and entered the inclined passage to the priest's house. Smells of mackerel and coffee floated from the dining room as he came into the hall. Mrs. Hoffer planned to test him again with a delicacy. After the first two weeks he had given up trying to control the crafty good-nature of Mrs. Hoffer in the morning. The omelet, the bacon, today the mackerel, always turned out to be something left unused from materials for her own breakfast. She had just put it there on his plate, since there it was and it seemed a sin to let it go to waste, and maybe he would take just a bite of it. Stubbornness underlay the old woman's meek smiling. For thirty days he had eaten his roll and coffee, had left the bacon or the wedge of fish on his plate. She would be ready again after Mass tomorrow, setting down bacon or a sausage in front of him, lying with faded candid eyes, "I chust had this left over, Father. Eat it, meat iss so strengthening."

She started to pour the coffee as he entered the room, flourishing the pot high above the cup, one hand in her apron pocket. "Good morning, my dear Father," she exclaimed. While he said grace she fluttered a cloth at invisible dust on the seat of his chair. Having taken the roll and broken it in half, he pushed the platter with the mackerel half an inch away. Mrs. Hoffer was waiting for this gesture. She turned away to the kitchen with a loud sigh. He heard her pause at the door and her respectful voice addressing the back of his head. "I tink you owe to God to make yourself strong, Father Cawder. I know fish iss good. Good for nerves and brain-work." He made no answer. He knew that as she left the room she was throwing up her hands, shrugging her shoulders.

Before he came he would, he judged, have found intolerable an old woman's brooding female familiarity, like a protective hen's, before he first saw her round Moravian face, stuck against the pane of a window as a taxi set him down in front of the house. She had grasped his hand with a gentle pressure and had been stopped with his knuckles only an inch from her lips. In Moravia it was immemorial custom to kiss a priest's hands. She had then only recently arrived from Moravia? No, no, she cried out excitedly, she was ten years old when she left, she remembered nothing about Moravia. But it had been the custom, she understood, in certain places to kiss ladies' hands, some, to speak uncharitably, who were surely not saints, so why not a priest's? Still, if he objected . . . She had picked up his suitcase, extravagantly smiling, and gone ahead up the stairs. It was odd to feel no displeasure at the old woman's familiarity. From the first day he saw her, five weeks before, he had permitted her deferential gabbling, answering her little, perceiving no incongruity, even at ease within hearing of her sharp unspiteful observations.

On the third morning after his arrival he had given Mrs. Hoffer a rebuff, he remembered. It was fitting, he must have decided, for a priest to be served by his housekeeper in self-effacing silence. He spoke in fact against his inclination. He was, strangely, convinced of no indignity in her free manners. But he said that since he was undertaking the management of a new

217

parish and since she, his housekeeper, was sufficiently charged with her own duties, he would like her to leave the room when he ate his meals; her cries and questions distracted him from his thoughts. She had bent her head, following his words with care, and then only a crooked smile. The new pastor had one more oddity for her to exercise upon. Forcing her voice from low to high notes and then down again, she said cheerfully that although she was only his servant God did not love her any the less for that and although he was a learned, holy priest—she had the impertinence to use the word "holy"—she loved him, even without understanding everything he said. She would chat with him no longer at mealtime, she had indulgently added.

Love from her was not of a kind that flattered its object. Father Cawder crunched the last fragment of roll between his teeth. With Mrs. Hoffer love was a disposition, like a good digestion. It fell on all alike, even strangers, like a kind of indifferent infra-red ray. It was not concerned with personality or response. He had come upon her in the kitchen setting a meal before an unshaved man with black hands and shifty eyes. At sight of a cassock he gobbled down the food and slunk out the door. "What man was that?" he had asked. "Who knows?" Mrs. Hoffer replied, while she wiped off the splashed table, a tramp, a man, somebody. She was so fortunate, she had said, idiotically smiling. Tramps, it seemed, had amazing means of communication. When one got a meal at a house, the rest learned about it, and they all came in turn to be fed. How lucky she was, tramps were always coming to the door, asking for food, thanks be to the good God. He had permitted himself to say, "You have a special liking then for tramps, Mrs. Hoffer?" Oh, yes, she said, naturally, they were harmless good creatures, astonishingly hungry. In any event, would it be wise not to receive them hospitably? Some of those who came were not, she suspected, men at all. They were angels.

He could hear her noisily clanking with pots and

218

pans as he went out into the hall. He took up his hat from the scarred Gothic chair whose seat had been repaired with the slats of an orange crate. Since she was out of sight, there was fortunately no need to solicit her advice by telling her where he was going. By now the old ladies had had a chance to amass a conventional number of backbitings and uncharitable thoughts—two weeks had passed since he had first gone to Saint Edith's Catholic Ladies' Home. The best part of the morning it might take, he supposed, closing the door to the street, his face stung with a gust of dirt blown up at him from the concrete. Ten or twelve confessions of nothing at all they would be, the muttered scruples of women unwilling while alive to give in to a God who caused them to subsist on charity in their old age.

A knot of boys crouching over the sidewalk fell apart to let him pass, no light of civil greeting in their eyes like lead weights. In spite of running noses and dirty mouths he remembered having seen two of their faces below him as he read gospel and epistle from the dusty cuckoo-clock of a pulpit. Their parents could have warned them to beware of priests outside the church, those men notorious for greed, lust of power, and subservience to the rich. On the whole it was more probable that greetings between those of unequal status had fallen into disuse in these slums. The boys, seeing he was a priest, viewed him as some transparent phantom entirely without meaning. Hats are not doffed to thin air. The downward trickle of gentility ended here at higher levels than in Lulworth, poverty and politeness being apparently incompatible in a metropolis. It was nothing for him to mind, he repeated to himself as he crossed the street to a square laid out in strips of lawn trampled into mud. He had not left the graceful trees and cautious sins of Lulworth to look for human respect in a city slum. So much the better if he was reviled in this evil-living city after years of corrupting deference in a village of farmers and genteel widows.

The suspicious men, the white-faced women with grinding jaws—was it possible they thought fit to chew gum during the sacrifice of the altar?—these shifty raddled faces which he had seen below the pulpit now for four Sundays, turned up whitely to receive the Host, eyes rolled back as if in a torturing despair, foreheads pressed like the heads of corpses against the grille of the confessional. These people would never consider him with sufficient attention to want to revile him. There were no grounds for imputing enmity to their dull eyes, their dull vegetable functionings. To them he was merely a shape without a face, moving from side to side before a chalice, making certain necessary motions with his hands, actuating rites to which they came on Sunday mornings from long habit, because they had promised mothers and wives, because there was nowhere else to go, because at home they had been struck blows across the face, because they wanted a quiet place in which to weigh a venture into adultery, because sometimes when money was low there would always be the priest's house to fall back on for five dollars.

The bishop had been right about him, whatever his intentions. In front of the arch into Willing's Alley he raised his hat, silently pronouncing, "Have mercy, Jesus," to the Host behind walls at the end of the dark passage. At the corner he turned off into a street of lawyers' offices. But the bishop, even if he only thought to smooth the workings of a wearisome country parish, had been right. Lulworth was no fit place for him. Even if unhappy here he would at the same time be happier. And in spite of eight years in Lulworth he had done no good to them. A priest with a vice of metaphysical egomania did not disturb Lulworth, lapped in secular vanities, bank accounts, estimable birth, the price of winter wheat, the profits of calves and hogs—and under the orderly sins of white people,

220

the Negroes, with less profit, deviled with blood-spilling, cheap whisky, and the dope of sex. He had done no good to old black Ella Johnston, anyone could bury a dead woman; he did no good to Birdseye at the bank as he made loans on land certain to be foreclosed in six months; no good to Mrs. Bileski in the sodality, feeding her secret thoughts on hatred of her husband and her own unspotted freedom from sins of the flesh. It was thinkable that all these might have more chance of salvation under Moran. It was clear they liked him. And even Birdseye, theoretically the sinister usurer— there was evidence of curious mutual affinity whenever Moran and the banker stopped for a moment's raillery on the street. He himself, whom they did not like, how could he have done good if he had stayed in Lulworth? Why should they have liked him, sinning in vanity, a ridiculous priest? This new parish, he said to himself, is in every respect disgusting, thus I react in sympathy, since I myself arouse disgust; here I feel at home.

Moran had been slow to relent. He had listened to a repetition of the bishop's views on retaining him in Lulworth with eyes cast down, emitting a chuckle of spiritless laughter. So Cawder would get a bustling city parish while he, thus he must have thought, was to be promoted to oversee the backwash of Lulworth, the bishop having been so favorably impressed by him. He had said, smiling, that the bishop meant, it seemed, to haul him into line, but it didn't matter, he liked Lulworth well enough. Before the bishop made up his mind—rather, over the months before the bishop sent formal notice—an innocent transformation was to be observed in Father Moran. He became cheerful again and easy and forgot to leave the room whenever his pastor sat down beside the table spread with copies of the *Catholic Worker*. It was obvious, he had been taken up to the pinnacle of the temple and shown the scintillations of the lot shortly to be his in Lulworth. With elephantine tact he made no reference now to his guilds and his credit union. At his own desk, possibly, he expanded his notes, planned an assault on capitalism, sermons, societies, when he should have a free rein, when in the potency of a pastor he could denounce, order letterheads, commence an inflammatory correspondence with the famous Monsignor Trevulzi! He had weakened in June, after the bishop came. He had said he had arranged—unfortunately, after he, Cawder, would have left—for Monsignor Trevulzi of Alabama to come in October and talk to them about farming communes. He hoped, in doing so, he had not taken anything on himself, prematurely, he meant. That dawn in July, Father Moran, saying goodbye forever, vigorously shaking hands, beamed, almost cried, with pleasure. "He is gone at last, I am rid of him," he should have said but certainly did not even think. What he said was, "You must come back and spend a vacation here, Father."

Certainly he would take no vacation, he would not see again, unless by chance, the neat red and white streets of Lulworth. That morning, in the heat, Mrs. Girard, eagerly advancing, clean, veiled, painted and affable, had taken him off guard. It had not been she whom he might have thought to find paying the conventional flattery of a leave-taking. He had vaguely supposed Mrs. Garrity might waylay him, her enormous breasts spread with beads, or Mrs. Bileski, black-suited like a nun or a black hen. It was Mrs. Girard who dressed herself in her girlish clothes to bring him food. He had eaten the cake; the sandwiches he gave to a man sitting behind him in the daycoach. What had been the matter with her, with nothing to say to him, her swimming eyes expressing—regret, it seemed, facile female disquiet. Because he fancied he could detect in Mrs. Girard's gray eyes no hearty acquiescence in his leaving Lulworth, therefore he too succumbed to sentiment—he had got into the bus saying inaudibly, inanely, "She has good intentions, she's a woman who is easily misjudged." When he meant nothing more than the fact that, moved by unknown considerations, she had risen early to say good-bye to him while all the rest of Lulworth lay still in bed. Mrs. Girard, being an individualist, had chosen to indulge a mood of no significance beyond its being an exercise of her will, ten minutes later the whole thing would have been forgotten. He must have been pleased, anxious, to think, then, that one person in Lulworth regretted his going. Under the illusions of strength was nothing but a tangle of weaknesses. How had he believed himself strong when a woman's regretful or merely facile eyes could deflect him? When shall I be done with illusions, he repeated to himself, when can I see myself as I am? But beneath the illusion, cast off like the skin of a snake, lay a deeper one, and under that, again illusion.

At the end of the row of houses a mournful brown-nosed woman was climbing up the steps bedded into a slope of ivy. She saw him approaching and waited under the transom with its worn gilt lettering. As he came up the steps she fitted a key into the lock and opened the door. She went ahead over a length of carpet rubbed away to oval holes. Ironically smiling, she pointed into the parlor. "There they are, Father, waiting for you." They rose as he entered, turned their heads toward him, aged affronted faces, a dozen female paupers ready to confess they were sinners.

Sitting in a chair to which a small black curtain was attached, Father Cawder absolved the old women one after the other of what they pretended to imagine were their offenses. They were even unable to confess to eating meat on Friday since their diet was managed by Mrs. Prendergast, a woman perfectly conversant with the recurrence of fasts and Ember days. Old Mrs. Rossiter, who whispered into his ear for twenty minutes, could recall no spiritual lapse at all, not even the prevailing forgetfulness about morning prayers. She was the victim of a conspiracy. There were those there, whose names she could mention if she wished to lower herself, who hated her, savage spiteful women who had never had anything, who had come up from nothing, from a rubbish heap, who hated anyone a cut above them, anyone who had once had a loving father and mother who rode in their own carriage, who had been cherished by a husband of substance and who, once, had had sons and a small-waisted, fair-haired, incomparable daughter. Because she had once known good fortune, now they wished to torment her, to mock her and to kill her. When she spoke to anybody in the hall, they opened their bedroom doors on the floor above, shamelessly listening; they laughed in horrible glee because she pronounced "tomato" and "chauffeur" like a lady; and one morning they had left milk spilled where they knew she would be treading down the stairs, cruelly hoping she would slip and fall to a bloody painful death. He had to wait, as she wept silently into a ragged handkerchief, before giving her absolution. She followed him to the front door. "Seeing me talking so long to you, they'll make me suffer for it," she whispered. "They're so jealous, so mean and jealous! Come please soon again to see me, Father, please do. What I know! What I couldn't tell you!"

He turned homeward by the same street as he had come. He meant to avoid the shorter route taken on his first visit to the old women. That afternoon he had walked through a kind of court, houses with broken panes of glass and unhinged doors, and at the corner a passing woman—she was a dark sallow girl—muttering some foulness under her breath had spat from a rigid face onto his shoes. A pain diffusing itself across his back drove the woman's malicious frown from his memory. The dull ache reminded him of the four months' experiment with the piece of chain. He had knotted it about him, settled its flat edges against his skin on the day he returned from his call on the bishop. Shortly after Lent, standing over the fresh earth dug up to make room for Ella Johnston's coffin, he remembered a suspicion striking him at the tug of metal.

The crude penance for pride and egotism was in itself a goad to pride. While he was wearing it he had not been inclined to humility at the sight of Moran's crinkling face, he had urged himself to no love for Moran or old Ella Johnston. Although no eyes but his own had seen the red print of links below his ribs, still a supererogatory pain could yield pleasure, a secret dandling conceit. But if penance nourished pride the fault lay in himself, not in innocent steel. He had put the chain back in the box with the tacks and nails. Since it was of no effect, since, when he felt it drag against his flesh, he failed to mark the pleasure he still took in his evil will. He stepped from the pavement, watching for a chance to make his way between cars and trucks. "Forgive us our iniquities, son of God," he said within his mind as he reached the curb. He threw a glance over the gray painted bricks of the church, defaced by boys with streaks of chalk.

A man hunched up in a black suit was leaning against the wall of the church. He had pulled his coat collar forward over his chin. The turn of his head seemed not unfamiliar to the priest. As he came closer, the man looked aside. He would be one of those on whom his eye had vaguely rested an instant—colorless faces that fell back into a floor of mottled nonentity when surveyed Sunday morning from a pulpit. In front of his door Father Cawder noticed the three marble steps. Mrs. Hoffer must have just been scrubbing them. Until a film of soot, to be washed off on the following day, was precipitated, they would glisten now for an hour or two.

Diamond watched the priest's back as he mounted the three steps, worked his key into a stiff lock, opened the door painted to imitate the grain of oak. He hunched himself against the bricks, his eyes sharply black in a face smudged and indeterminate from the grime of city air, a day's growth of beard. After the priest went inside, for a brief while Diamond looked up

225

intently at the closed door. Then he lowered his head and walked rapidly away, stooping against the wind with his hands dug into his pockets. He reached a street of shops. Secondhand shirts, spilled out on racks onto the sidewalk, flapped round him like flags. He brushed through them. At the corner a trolley car was about to move off. He ran forward onto the cobblestones and climbed aboard.

The car made a stop before crossing a bridge over a railroad cut. Diamond got off and entered an alley. A parapet of black stones ran along one side, the top of an embankment which rose as high as a tree above the train tracks. On the other side he passed tilted yards blowing with wet sheets and thin lilac bushes, wire fences strung between low sheds, long ladderlike stairs up to the kitchens of red three-story houses. He came to the dead end of a street and hurried on into the next alley. In the middle of the block he darted into a yard and up the steps of a narrow house.

As he stepped into the kitchen, a short man beside the stove turned quietly round. Stirring a fork about in a frying pan, he stood in his undershirt and drawers, his bare feet splayed wide apart, his paunchy belly flattened against the oven. His left hand pulled at his purplish double chin.

"Hey, Diamond!" He lifted the pan yellow with egg across to the sink.

"What's the good word, Peachy?"

"Nothing much." The man raised up a lump of egg on his fork and blew on it.

"What about the little guy with the shoes?" Diamond opened the door into the turn of a cramped staircase. "No sign of him?"

"He kept to hisself if he ever came." While his shiny jaws moved the man shifted his eyes over Diamond. "I ain't been noticing who came and who went. What are you worrying for? Did you ever see him before?"

Diamond started up the stairs. "I ain't worrying,

226

Peachy." Entering a room at the head of the steps he heard a snorting sound rise from the kitchen as a fork scraped over metal. "No, sure you're not," the voice muttered. "You ain't worrying." With a sharp gasp of breath he took off his coat and sat down on the bed. His shoulders slumped. He let them fall backward to the mattress. Breathing gently, he lay staring up into the ceiling. It was peaceful in the small not-too-bright room. No thoughts passed through his mind. He was conscious, not daring to move, only of the easy pulsing of his heart, the rhythmical pleasure of the rising and falling of his chest, tempered light, still air soft on his face, silence broken by no imminent step or passionate voice.

3

THE ROOM WAS BRIGHT WITH A DAZZLE OF
sunshine as Diamond opened the door. When he had
left it that morning it must have been daybreak. He
had put his clothes on in the dark. Even ducked behind the bed to light a cigarette, he remembered, still
half-dozing, afraid somebody could be there outside on
the pavement, softly patrolling up and down to get a
glimpse of a struck match through the window. Now
from the look of the sun it was close on noon. His
feet clattering into the house, up the stairs, must have
awakened Peachy. He could hear his chair creak, his
wheezing coming closer, the moccasins slapping as his
feet padded up to the door and stopped.

"Hey, Diamond!" His voice rasped, out of practice
from sleep.

"Hey, Peachy!" Sitting on the edge of the bed, Diamond leaned back on his elbows.

"Your chum with the shoes was here."

Diamond spread out his hands till the joints of his
fingers were resting loosely on the sheet. "Walked by,
you mean?"

"He came right up to the door and started to talk.
Said he sold bags and mattress flock, wanted to rent a
room. I told him to get the hell out of here."

"Did you do that, Peachy?" Diamond, looking intently at the pinpoint of light within the glass door
knob, listened to the heavy wheeze, like a distant hiss
of steam, from the other side of the door. "That's fine,
Peachy. Thanks for letting me know."

"Okay, boy." The footsteps pounded off. He heard the snap of a lock, the crackling of the wicker rocker pressed under a fat man's weight. The sun hot on the green carpet all at once drew his eyes. He sprang up and pulled down the blinds at the two windows. Then he turned on the bulb hung from a black cord over the washstand. He spread out the little newspaper clipping flat on the varnished board and read it again. The crazy thing was the fact that he had come at the bit at all, stuck on the inside sheet, a page about sermons on brotherly love and Salvation Army revivals. He had started in to read maybe after a glance at the headline. *Maryland Priest Takes Over Old Church* ran across the top. He could have got a glimpse of the name.

The Rev. Thos. B. Cawder of Lulworth, Md., has been appointed as pastor of St. Ludmilla's, West Caroline St., according to a recent announcement of Msgr. T. Hollis, Chancellor of the Archdiocese. Father Cawder takes over his new duties Sunday, July 29th. He succeeds the Rev. P. Angelis who until his sudden death last fall had been in charge of the parish for many years. St. Ludmilla's, known as the Old Bohemian Church, was founded in 1863 largely through the efforts of Father Stanislaus Brenek. Rev. Brenek returned to Europe and was made Bishop of Zevecim in what is now Czechoslovakia. The parish has grown less populous than formerly, due to encroachment of commercial interests, but St. Ludmilla's is still noted among art lovers for its pure French Gothic architecture.

After he read the clipping a second time, he rolled it in a ball and stuffed it into a pocket. The sun on the edges of the blinds filled the room with streaks of light. He switched off the pale bulb swinging above his head like a pendulum. He stepped toward the bed, meaning to pull the sheet tight, to take off his shoes, to throw himself face downward across the covers. As he lifted his hat from the pillow he changed his mind. He left the room and went below to the kitchen. On the stove a pot of coffee was being kept hot over a low flame. He poured some into a cup and drank it in quick mouthfuls. Then, slipping over the wet treads of the steps, he hurried down to the yard. He unlatched the wire gate to the alley. First, he looked without haste to each side. But there was no one at all, only a spotted cur rooting in a toppled can. He walked off rapidly along the parapet.

His eyes were fixed on the house half a block away. He was standing with his heels against a locksmith's cellar window when the door moved and swung inward. It must have been two full hours by now. Somewhere a clock had struck three as he started in to plod back and forth within sight of the door beyond the church, stamping his feet to get the blood running through them, pressing his arms in against his ribs whenever the wind clamped down between the walls of houses. The wind knocked his shoulders now while he waited to see who was coming out. It was the priest. He paused a moment on the top step, got up all in black like a turkey buzzard. Diamond crossed the street and hurried forward at an angle. He took a stand near the church. When the priest came abreast of him he turned his head.

"Don't you remember me, Father Cawder?" he said lightly. He watched the shift of expression on the priest's face. At first there was no sign he remembered. Then his eyes lightened, he stopped with his mouth open a little. It certainly looked like he had surprised him. Certainly, from the way the priest stared he never had a thought of running up against him on a Philadelphia street.

"How are you, Diamond? I didn't recognize you at first."

"I happened to be walking this way, Father. I was
230

wondering if maybe I'd see you. I heard you'd come to this church."

"You heard so?"

"It was in the papers." Diamond contrived to laugh as he thought suddenly that his taut face must be marked with no trace of friendliness toward the priest. "Didn't you see it in one of the papers?"

"I didn't know about it. You read it in a Philadelphia paper?"

"Sure. You see, I live here now." He had no look as though he knew anything, Diamond said to himself, unless he was sharp enough to be playing it slow. He was stretching his blue eyes open, goggling like he was learning something hard to understand. But in no special way did he give any sign of having ever chanced upon, ever surmised, the fact without form or quality which Diamond held down quiet in the bottom of his mind and which never, if he took care in time, he need remember. Diamond forced back his chin and laughed again.

"Father, it's funny meeting up with you like this. I thought maybe sometime I'd run into you but I never expected to meet you so soon. I'm on my way up the street to get an early dinner. I'm wondering maybe if you couldn't come and have something to eat with me? Or is it too early? There's a pretty good place around the corner. Nice clean place."

Father Cawder slowly turned and gazed across the street. "I don't think I can do that, Diamond. My own dinner will be ready soon. My housekeeper is fixing me something now."

"Sure." Staring at the priest, Diamond drew up his lips, he believed, into an easy grin. "I don't know much about these things, Father. You're a priest, of course, and maybe it wouldn't be right for anybody to see you eating with people like me. I can understand a thing like that. I just had the thought. Meeting you like this I thought I'd like to ask you to have dinner with me.

231

I haven't forgot all the trouble you went to up in Trenton."

The grin relaxed as Diamond stopped speaking. With a frown Father Cawder watched a pigeon alight on the curb. "Nothing like that," he said evenly, "has any bearing on whether or not I eat a meal with you." He paused, and his glance rose with the pigeon spiraling up from the concrete. "As a matter of fact, I seldom or never eat away from home. Come to my house there some afternoon. I'm almost always in."

"Maybe." After he smiled again Diamond added, "Which means never, I guess, most of the time. Here I run into you and it looked like a pretty good idea. It don't matter. Anyway I just got time to get myself a bite. I'm glad I happened to see you, Father."

Diamond felt that his trembling hand was being inspected by the priest's sidelong eyes. "If you're going close by, I will come and eat with you, Diamond. But not for dinner, just for coffee or a sandwich. Wait here a minute. I want to speak to my housekeeper."

As he walked off Diamond faced the street, his fists clenched and pressed against his hip bones, strained into his coat pockets. What am I doing? Am I getting crazy? he heard his mind question silently, fearfully. Crazily waiting on a street for a priest. Acting like a man out of his head. Mucking with priests who get everything soft, free food and beds, drinks and cars, giving orders, men with stale bodies mingled with no woman's and proud of it, laying down the law to suit themselves for all the rest who could just get by in sweat and danger. He knew nothing maybe, if he had never gone back, never read newspapers, never bothered to hold in his brain a man he had seen just for a day or two. It did not have to be the priest, it could be some man or woman he had not come across or thought about for years. Somebody wanted to jab them, start them off. Even only a boy, or a busybody of a woman, sneaking behind a curtain, who spied out of a window, saw the shoes heels up and bloody on the cinders, blabbing off her mouth when she saw a chance to get paid for a vote by the cop on the beat. Somebody who asked a question, wrote a letter, starting them to sniff around. And all the time old Gurig stuffed her cash into a bolster, taking care of herself, salting it away, licking another envelope with her nasty mouth to send him. "Dear Diamond, I hope this finds you real well. A little bird told me about you changing off to work at the Old Mill. It's a shame to have to be asking you this way, but I have another payment on my loan coming up." If it was not Cawder, not old Gurig, who could have it in for him, who could hate that much to see him alive? And the priest had seen how he used to live, he was able to remember, if he saw it in a newspaper, he could have put two and two together. As Diamond heard the sound of heels behind him he wheeled about, his teeth grinding in a smile. I must get out what he knows, he thought with an instant of rage, with fear.

"We go this way, Father. It's just a couple of blocks."

They set off together down the street.

The littered sidewalk of old clothes, old furniture, old magazines, was crowded with people on their way home from work. Diamond walked in front of the priest. He pushed through the gaps in the mass of jostling backs, the unfocused daydreaming faces. When he reached the end of the block, he halted at the top of a flight of steps. They led steeply down to a basement door on which was printed in a flourish of gilt, "Schriml's Rathskeller." The letters ran aslant white curtains bunched in the middle by yellow bows.

"Here we are, Father. It's not so bad once you get in."

Diamond went ahead down the steps. While holding the door open for the priest he glanced hastily inside. All the tables were empty. Their tops gleamed out of loose clusters of chairs like pools of black water. Three men were drinking in silence at the bar. Beyond them the bartender, leaning out, was talking to an old woman in a long black coat. He flipped up his hand.

"Hi, Diamond."

"How are you, Larry?"

Father Cawder stopped beside the case of cigar boxes. Overhead a flash of light came from cardboard candles stuck on iron hoops. One after another, lanterns were switched on along the wainscot; the dark room brightened. It looked like an excavation, Diamond thought, like the sweating walls of a deep ditch. Brown as mustard now the curdled plaster seemed to glisten with moisture. It could be the dingy yellow glow, kept weak to save money; the dull light bothered his eyes. Worst of all was the chocolate-colored paper castle above the bar, its gate and the slits in its shiny stones lighted from within behind red cellophane. The little ugly thing, he hated the sight of it. He touched the priest's arm.

"Come on this way."

He circled between the tables and went up three steps to a higher level. A balustrade painted to look like marble ran along the edge. It fenced off a row of pointed arches hung with shaggy curtains. At the middle arch Diamond turned to signal a waiter standing idle near the bar. Then he entered a small square room. The table in the center was already set with plates and glasses for a meal.

Father Cawder laid his coat on a chair. All the time, Diamond saw, he was looking round him, slowly and carefully. Before he sat down, looking around the box stall for dirt, maybe. His eyes like a cod's were flicking over the old painted fancy figures, red-faced dwarfs sitting on barrels and chipped from the wall, spurting wine bottles and notes of music, blistered tags of German songs about roses and the month of May. The private stalls looked just the same, probably, when the place was started; behind the curtains here they thought a new coat of paint would just be a waste. Cawder, rubbing up against the table, could be thinking the sour smell of old grease and lager was too ripe for the likes of him to eat in. Diamond drew back a chair.

"Take a seat, Father. I came up here to get out of the way. In these stalls you're private. Is this all right with you?"

A long-armed waiter with grizzled hair brushed through the green curtains. He carried a bill of fare and a glass mug full of beer. Diamond snatched the mug from his hand and began to drink.

"A lot of what they have is all ready. Tell Sam here what you think you want. I want a bowl of soup and shrimps. I'm not hungry. But you order a regular-size dinner."

"Bring me a bowl of soup too." Father Cawder sat down and handed the bill of fare back without reading it. "Soup is all I want."

"Just soup? They've got good crabs, plenty of meat. But today's the day for lentil soup if you like that. They're known here for their lentil soup."

Diamond held up a finger as the waiter turned to leave. "Another beer, Sam, when you bring the shrimp." He kept his hands clumsily at work over the lighting of a cigarette. Then he lifted his head with caution, expecting to be met by a shrewd or at least careful stare from across the table. But Cawder was only fishily eying the bar through the arch, thinking hard about something behind the slash of his mouth, his tight cheeks and big nose.

"I guess Philly is some change for you, Father," he decided to say. "After the cows and the chickens down there in the country."

Cawder's nostrils moved a little. He started to frown, he was just coming out of his thoughts. "Most parishes turn out to be more or less alike," he said, his mouth twitching, trying to look human. "It hasn't been a change in every way. My present parish is smaller, in fact, than the one I had in Lulworth. You have not mentioned yourself. Do you like it here?"

"Here?" Diamond threw out an arm toward the curtains. Schriml's, did he mean? How could he know about Schriml's? Unless he had been nosing around. "You mean this place?"

"Here in Philadelphia, I meant. When was it you came here?"

"I've been here all year, ever since last winter. I thought you meant here at Schriml's. I worked here for a while, you see, when I first came down." The priest would try to be keeping the dead easy look on his face, if he was bent on spying something out, feeling his way. To sit here talking to him in one of Schriml's back rooms was a comical crazy thing. Diamond felt his lips begin to smile foolishly.

"The waiters know you here then."

"Sure. For four or five weeks I played the piano here. Kettler who runs this place likes to have a piano at night. They get a big crowd here then." Cawder, without a doubt, never knew he worked for Kettler. He only nodded his head like any man would. "I guess I've been down here in Philly eight or nine months. Haven't been back to Trenton more than twice. Did you ever get back again, Father?"

The priest had been about to speak. He changed his mind and spread out his napkin, Diamond noticed, when he saw Sam swinging behind his chair. Just like any waiter, Sam put priests on the same shelf with ward bosses and baseball players. He was showing off, grunting and diving while he flipped down squares of butter, passed a basket of rolls and buns. But Cawder paid no heed to him, glancing over the bowl of black soup spotted with sausage. Waiting, he was. Turning his head to watch Sam leave, he said, offhand, "Oh, no. There was no reason for me to go back to Trenton."

"I guess you're tied down now more than you were, with a church in the city."

Fool. Wasting a day jockeying to talk to a priest. Soft-headed, like a crazy man, he had got to be. What did this priest care about him? The priest got Trenton

236

off his mind one minute after the train left the yard. How had he come to think the priest remembered what he saw, what he heard, or cared? Thinking the priest was worrying to keep track of a small-time, ex-vaudeville end man, a cat-house jazzer, a carnival tramp and his blonde.

"A small parish like mine," the priest said, "is like one in the country. Most of the people know each other. It's not like a big city church. With the changes in the business district it's got much smaller than it used to be."

"They're foreigners, are they?"

"Some are. Some are Poles, Italians, a few Mexicans. A few Negro families. Years ago it used to be a Bohemian parish."

"Foreigners like this dirty old town. I guess it makes them feel at home."

"Have you heard anything about the little girl?"

Diamond tasted a spoonful of soup, wondering if he should look surprised. "No," he said. Without any need to, cat-brained dribbling bloody fool, he added, "Not about the girl." He watched the priest's eyebrows come together.

"Marina, the little girl up in Bantry with the sisters."

"Sure, I know. Not a word. I've never been up there."

Diamond split apart a green-seeded roll. Sooner or later, the priest would want to know. Feeding like clockwork now, he was, saying nothing but all the time inside his bony skull he could be thinking. A crazy thing, to sit here with the priest and not wanting to say a single word to him, and all the time he could be batting his brains about a blond woman he once rode thirty miles with, pouring soup into his craw, suspicious and thinking how to begin, how he could hack into another man's head and find out what was there. He was taking his time, easy, he looked, at keeping quiet. Cleaning up the soup he left the slices of sausage in a heap at the bottom of the dish. It was some saint's day or a fast day, running the risk of hell over no little lump of pork. Priests with their quiet ways to get the goods from women, getting women to wait on them and make things soft, all the time with a piece of his own like a railbird, like as not, stuck away in a bin somewhere.

Father Cawder buttered a roll. "You were right about the soup, Diamond. It was very good. I would like to have heard how the little girl is. No doubt she's getting along all right."

"Sure she is, Father." The priest could be going slow. He could be hedging off from questions, if he had heard. He might wait to see if he was going to be told. The soup bowls, Diamond noticed, had been cleared away. He had never seen Sam come back. He began to tap his feet gently against the floor. His blood still was not moving. Now that the rest of him was warm, his feet were just as cold as they had been out on the street. He watched Sam swing the tray into the room. Grunting and shaping his lips behind the priest's back the old freak seemed to want to say something. But he set the beer and the platter of shrimp down without a word. The curtains swung together behind him. Before going away he craned his neck inside around their edge and rolled his eyes.

"You want chili, Diamond?"

"No, thanks, Sam."

Diamond glanced up covertly while he bent the scales back from a shrimp. The priest's hand, corded with veins, lay at rest on the tablecloth. If he asked no questions now then it meant he had a plan for keeping silent. He had gabbled away alone with Stella in the trailer, up at Gurig's, he had seen her at Lily's, he had not forgotten her. He had got some idea in his head, trying like a cop or a lawyer to see how far he could get saying nothing.

"You never asked about Stella, Father. Maybe you hadn't heard."

"How is Stella?" He was looking sharp and level now.

238

His eyeballs could be just glass, Diamond thought, dry blue paint under glass, like the unsocketed eyes left lying about on an eye-doctor's table.

"Stella's dead, Father. I was thinking all along maybe you heard. Of course there wasn't any way for you to know. Stella died last winter up in Trenton." Diamond heard his voice lift and fall. It sounded like a man talking about a politician or a race horse, not about a woman he said he used to love. That is the funny part, he said to himself, I did love her, I loved her, all the time I loved her, even when she was using me the way she did. "It was pretty sad," he said in a tone which slipped out too soft. "It was a good shock to me all right."

"It was during the winter? Was it sudden?"

He had no call to take on, looking like he had a nasty surprise, Diamond thought, this priest looking down his nose, his dry lips pressed together. What was she to him but a tramp bumming her two bits in a doorway; he had never paid her doctor's bills, fixed her coffee and eggs when she was laid up, carried her in drunk and washed her face and put her to bed, felt her cool light hand on his body, he had never pushed his cheek rough with beard against her good-smelling small breasts white as snow, skin like frost over veins blue like flowers. Diamond held up the shell he had stripped from a sliver of shrimp.

"It was an accident. It was sudden, all right."

"An accident," the priest repeated. "A car, was it?" Stiff behind his black bib he was glaring at the tablecloth. What was his trouble, just like he had never heard tell of a dead woman before? He knew nothing, that was certain. He had not known about Stella, he had never taken it into his head to go back up to Trenton, there had never been any reason for running down the priest at all.

"A traffic accident." Diamond paused to lift the scale from a shrimp with his thumbnail. "The poor kid got caught walking up an alley by a truck. It didn't see

239

her. She slipped under the wheels and it dragged her. I didn't know till the next day."

That was fair enough. No law said he had to break down and howl just for the priest sitting here; he could remember, if he wanted, how he had felt when he saw them stretch her out. "They picked her up, but she never regained consciousness. That was way back last November."

"Not long after I was there." The priest struck Diamond now as watching him very steadily. "You say it was a car."

"A car?" Diamond said, too loudly, too queerly. "No, I said she was hit by a truck. A truck full of coal, in sacks. It backed into her." It would look like a natural thing to do, to finish up the shrimps, to stop his mouth with bread, to make his hands pick up a knife. Instead, he knew he had begun to stare across the red scales scattered in front of him over the cloth, his fingers clutched to the edge of the table. What made the priest keep looking? With his slashed shark's mouth drawn down he was still watching. But he had nothing to say for himself.

Diamond pushed back his chair and stood up. He pulled the hairy green curtain aside. He could see Sam's head bobbing behind the bar. He could make a sign for him to come up, order coffee, a gin buck. He turned his head toward the table.

"I'm going to get Sam up here. Have something more to eat, Father. How about a cup of coffee?"

The priest's back was humped over. He straightened his shoulders as his tight frown slipped away and his mouth stretched and widened over his teeth. Diamond looked again at the bar. The crazy priest, grinning now like a terrier. He had heard him talk, say what he wanted to, without a hitch, without any excitement, it was good enough, women are killed by trucks, no man had to howl because a woman was killed a year before.

He listened to the priest clear his throat and say, "I am glad you told me about it. I will remember her

240

tomorrow in my Mass." After a stop he started up again, his voice flat and hard. "Unlike you and me Stella is dead; there's nothing she can do for herself about her sins, whatever they may be."

Diamond felt the curtain against his face scratch his cheek. He suddenly smiled. He had a longing to stamp, rocking with laughter, to push the priest backward in his chair while his own chest burst with laughing. Since he knew, now, the priest, what did any of it matter? The priest had thought to make a guess, watching his face, noticing the way his hand trembled. He had guessed, his ears cocked for the lie, too loud or too soft. He had the knack, trained to it, he was, of listening for a lie. And now he knew, blabbing his mouth off about sins. Crazy pimping fool, he had given himself away to the priest. Diamond shifted his head back from the curtains and swung about on his heels. No fluttering fear, he realized, filled his throat now. When he killed her he had had his rights, tiptoeing through the door, breathless when he saw her, dozing sideways on the pillows with a smile, the poor bitch, the slopped lying trash. The priest could speak for himself if he wanted to blab about sin.

Now he too seemed ready to laugh, at least with his chin sunk, sitting easy in his chair, the priest had his lips pulled apart, his teeth showing, the skin under his eyes crinkled, the eyes themselves steady and bright. Let him look any way he wants, Diamond thought, let him say his prayers for dead women, I made no slip, even if this man knew, maybe there was still nothing to be afraid of, what was real about the priest black behind a platter of shrimps? He himself could get to thinking he was in a dream, light-headed now, with no fear, wanting to laugh.

"I can see"—the dry sliding sound of the words caused Diamond to turn back warily against the curtain—"that her death would have been a shock to you, necessarily, as you said, apart from the way it happened."

241

"That's what I told you. It was bad right at first."

"It is always hard to get used to the change when anyone has died."

"Sure."

"All the same, it was worse for her than for you, in my opinion." The priest folded his napkin exactly. "For the living, the changes made by a death are not much more than inconvenience, when all is said and done."

"Maybe. Why not?"

Diamond held the glance of the priest an instant. Thick as thieves, they were. For once he was looking human; tired out he looked, almost cheerful, almost ready to smile, knowing now, with the brass to say he was sorry for her and not for him. Diamond's eyes shifted to the gray-haired waiter's back and followed him among the tables.

A short heavy man was sitting near the bar. His shoes could just be glimpsed under the folds of the checked tablecloth, firmly splayed on the floor, white shoes with black tips. The man raised a glass of beer to his mouth with a quick grab and crunched a pretzel, champing his jaws from side to side. He seemed to be watching a spot on the wall somewhere above the bar, his fleshy head as wide as his thick brown neck below. Diamond drew back within the curtains. He had left four shrimps on the plate, he noticed. The priest sat with his head cocked, his brain busy, planning to clear out maybe, now that he was sure that a dead woman had not been run down by a truck at all.

"There's something I remembered I wanted to speak about to the bartender," Diamond said. "I'm going to tell him before I forget. I'll just be a minute." He pulled a dirty handkerchief from his pocket and stepped through the arch.

Father Cawder observed the curtains incuriously after Diamond left. The stuff was like an animal's pelt, hides of a goat or dog dyed green and strung together. Beyond, the air had filled with blue smoke. He heard a hum of voices, forks and knives knocking against crockery. As the old waiter pushed through the curtains with a tray, he stood up.

The waiter began to clear away the dishes. "Diamond," he said, "the man you was eating with, gave me a message. He told me to say he had to go. Some call he had to make. It's all paid for, Father."

Father Cawder stopped against the painted balustrade while he buttoned his coat. No one had ever been deceived into thinking the balusters were stone, yellow as cheese and veined with blue scratches. The floor below was crowded now with people eating dinner. Their chairs closed in the spaces between the tables. Walking sideways, circling the arcs of backs bowed over plates, he went toward the door. At the tobacco stand two women with their hair hanging to their shoulders collided against him. They nudged each other at the sight of his collar, his black hat and coat. Their tolerant smiles implied that they had found him out, whoever he was, a priest off on the sly to get his tipple. Could he be charged with giving scandal to inadequate intellects, letting himself be seen in a public eating place of no particular character? If our Lord was to be imitated, priests would be found at table with thieves, harlots, and beggars, also with politicians of ill repute. Our Lord, nevertheless, was not formally stated to have broken bread with a man who had probably, or certainly, done murder. The smoke milky on the air eddied back from the opening door. Father Cawder stepped outside.

4

AGREEING WITH MRS. GIRARD, FATHER
Cawder nodded his head. He gazed at her with an
absurd sense that the image reflected in his eye was
illusion, she was not there. Yet her chin tilted upward
and she moved her small shoes of alligator hide. A
trembling pheasant feather was stuck into the ribbon
of her brown felt hat. When the doorbell rang, the
pen in his hand had poised motionless over the ruled
paper. Then he heard a woman's voice. Mrs. Fleming
it was, or worse still, Mrs. Manuelo—the voice had
a certain richness—Mrs. Manuelo, gibbering, grinning, her slant eyes orientally cast down in the presence of a man. The door had opened, the cordial, lined
face was both familiar and strange.

Father Cawder compelled himself to speak. "It's
sound enough. It was built some time in the sixties, I
believe. Shortly after the Civil War."

Plainly if remotely smiling, Mrs. Girard had used
the interval of silence to scan the room. Dust lay
thick on the feet of the desk. But then, priests
waited on by superannuated old chars were doomed
to live in dust. She saw a fern in a china jar, a
mantelpiece that appeared to be made of licorice. It
was an interior of the world as it was seventy years
ago. The fern stood on a rather pretty little table
with four straight thin legs. She could use that herself. Just outside the study door to hold the little
Chelsea bowl. And a few bulbs of narcissus, the kind
with pairs of yellow flowers.

She said easily, "This room is perfect; it's like the set for a wonderful play. Something very strong by Mr. O'Neill."

Father Cawder said, "The house is much too large, just for me. And then too, it's a burden on Mrs. Hoffer to keep it clean."

"Oh, she does splendidly for you, I can see that. How fortunate she was here when you came. She's a foreigner, is she not?"

"She was born in Czechoslovakia. But she's lived here almost her whole life."

"Really, I'm so glad about her and I shall tell Father Moran. He will be so curious about everything here. I'm afraid he thinks Lulworth's rather tame compared to an old wicked city parish like this. It is wicked, isn't it?"

Father Cawder did not return her grin. "The human race is wicked so I suppose it is, Mrs. Girard. Of course, the people here seem to have harder lives, more privations than most of those in Lulworth. But why that should be so for them and not for others, no one can say."

She looked at him soberly. "Of course, Father. I didn't mean to be so silly. You know, I've often wondered about myself. I've had so little suffering in my life. My parents died and my husband, but I don't mean that kind. Is it a sign that God doesn't love me, do you think?"

"We know it could not be that, Mrs. Girard."

"It may be I'm just very callous. I always tend to think other people are so, I notice."

"God manages these things to suit Himself. Certainly suffering must play a special part in His plans, as we know from His own example."

"Yes, I see that." Mrs. Girard's thoughts took a new turn and her face suddenly brightened. "Oh, I have a message for you. Mrs. Bileski heard somehow I might see you, I guess Father Moran told her, she drew me aside conspiratorially"—the word pleased Mrs. Girard, her amusement deepened—"on the street and said I was to tell you she's finished making the nine first Saturdays and that her favor was granted. I don't know at all what she was talking about but you do, so it doesn't matter. Poor little woman, she's quite lost without you, Father. Father Moran is so bustling and florid, he doesn't make at all the same appeal to her sympathies. She's sure you're cooking your own meals up here and living off pickles and tea. She'll be delighted to hear of worthy Mrs. Hoffer."

Father Cawder listened with a mordant smile that was also disapproving; he was not giving her his full attention. He was as always a difficult man for small talk. In his mind he seemed to be making allowances for her idle chatter. He said quietly:

"Well, remember me to Mrs. Bileski. And thank Father Moran, if you see him, for the books. It was kind of you to carry them all the way up to me."

"Oh, I didn't come on account of the books. Oh, no. I was stopping off in Philadelphia anyway. Father Moran heard I was coming up, so he asked me to bring them. But I was determined to pay you a visit. And not only for the satisfaction of seeing you. You see, in Lulworth we simply can't imagine what your new parish is like. I shall have so much to tell Mrs. Bileski and Mrs. Garrity and the other good ladies. 'He has a fern,' I can tell them, 'that goes all the way down to the floor.' That's the sort of fact we like to know in Lulworth. Things have changed. Father Moran's favorites are Major O'Brien and Miss Mudd. We are being indoctrinated, did you know?"

"In the encyclicals?"

"I suppose so. Last Sunday I learned that if I sell meat I can't lop two cents off the price of a brisket to take business away from my competitors. I must remember that when I set up my little counter for notions and rock candy."

"What is that, Mrs. Girard? You're planning to open a little shop, are you?"

246

Mrs. Girard concealed her stupefaction in a laugh. "Not really, Father. Though I think of it sometimes. Merchants seem to have so much money. I suppose that's why Father Moran doesn't quite approve of them. Oh, he has got so expansive! We have raffles of hams and I hesitate to think of the bridge parties I'll have to pay for and not go to this winter. Father Moran is concocting something! Something, oh, extraordinary! I wish I knew him better so I could tell you what it was."

"Do you mean buying that piece of woodland by Manokin Branch? A parish co-operative for firewood, wasn't it to be? It seemed to me like a good idea." The memory of a landscape of scrub oak and muddy water faded into a recollection of Schriml's Rathskeller—the priest saw Diamond steal again through the curtains, muffling his mouth in a handkerchief. He had run away, in fear perhaps; his tense smile and his goggling eyes, he must have thought, had betrayed too much of himself.

Mrs. Girard exclaimed, "Oh, that, yes, it's a lovely idea. I hate for anyone to be cold in the wintertime. And colored people get so very, very cold. The boys plan to camp there in summer. But I didn't mean that. Something else. I just hear rumors. Something radical, something red—a clinic, is it?"

Surely he must see, from the extent of her stretching lips, that she was joking. And no doubt he did this time; he was merely surveying her with inattentive mildness.

"It could be a clinic. Something of the kind. Father Moran has always felt the need for something of the sort. There are certainly people in the county who're unable to help themselves very much."

Mrs. Girard eyed him in impatience. "Oh, Father Cawder, I wish you hadn't left us. Father Moran is good and kind but he is so exhausting. And once in a while I'd like to hear about God for a change."

He pretended to laugh, without interest; he was not

to be drawn out. "Everyone," he said, "has his own way of going about things. Father Moran sees God in the poor. And he must be right, for the Church agrees with him."

His voice sounded tired, he took no interest in her remarks. The spacious dingy room all at once oppressed Mrs. Girard. She glanced at her gloves, touched her hat, got to her feet with deliberation. "I know I'm keeping you from a thousand things. I must go," she said. "One should never call in the morning. I resent it terribly. You were very nice to see me, Father Cawder."

"I am glad you came, that I could see you again. Are you going to the station? To meet a train, I mean?"

"Oh, not immediately. I'm killing two birds with one stone, Father. I have an old friend here. She went to the convent with me a hundred years ago and usually going up to New York I stop off and have lunch with her, as I'll do today. We talk about hats and other people's business and have a most pleasant unedifying time."

"But don't you want me to telephone for a taxi?"

Conscious that he seemed to be hurrying her away, Father Cawder walked behind her at a slower pace. Mrs. Girard passed into the hall and touched the brown parcel on the window sill.

"Your books," she murmured. "No, I'll walk, I think. I have so much time and it's not too far. Just to the Bellevue. Not too far for a country woman. I love walking in Philadelphia. It's such a fantastically mean-looking city."

A sound of scraping came from outside as he opened the door of the house. They saw Mrs. Hoffer doubled over on her knees scrubbing a marble step. A steaming bucket was behind her. She pushed herself upright with the dripping brush.

"It was time I got to these steps. So much dirt gets tramped into them. I skipped them yesterday."

Masking the abyss between Mrs. Hoffer and herself with an affable regard, Mrs. Girard nodded. "I know, Mrs. Hoffer. It's all this soft coal they use. And marble does show everything up." While she was speaking she descended the three spotless steps. Mrs. Hoffer backed away to one side.

"I peeped into the church before I came in. Rather astonishing, isn't it? All those statues. But it's very cheerful, I'm like a peasant, I like it." Mrs. Girard was securing her veil. "Well, good day, Father. So really good to see you. Good day, Mrs. Hoffer." She moved off, pulling on her gloves, her sharp profile already pointed to inspect the scene ahead of her. Clutching the brush and a rag tight in her hand Mrs. Hoffer asked diffidently,

"That lady is one of your old parishioners, Father?"

"Yes."

"She is nice. Pretty, too, for an old lady. She has nice clothes. She is rich?" Her voice had fallen to a discreet whisper. No answer was made to her question, so she stooped to pick up the bucket; as she bent down, her pinned-up skirt bunched over swelling calves. Father Cawder stepped inside the house.

He carried the bundle of books to the round table in the parlor. He snapped the string and folded back the brown paper. A blank envelope lay on top of the books. One was a collection of Newman's sermons, another a tattered translation of Chateaubriand which had been a prize of some kind at school—he did not remember having seen it in twenty years. The two books on the bottom had black leather labels, *De Conscientia, S. Alphonsi M. de Liguori*. Mrs. Girard could have spared herself. It seemed improbable he would ever open one of them again. Except perhaps for the Newman. He ripped open the envelope and turned toward the light from the window. The note inside was written in a large pale script which he would never have recognized. "Dear Father Cawder," he read—

Here are a few books you left behind. I would have mailed them but thought I could bring them to you myself as I had planned to attend the NCRV congress at St. Radbert's. At the last moment I couldn't get away (summer school). Mrs. Girard says she will be in Philadelphia Tuesday so I've asked her if she wouldn't mind taking them up to you. She said she planned to come and see you anyway.

I hope you're getting settled all right. I'm beginning to get the hang of things and am not doing too badly, I hope. We had a pretty good Forty Hours. Got relays in to watch through the night with less trouble than last year. I'm giving a course of Sunday sermons on "The Just Price and a Living Wage." That way I thought it would get both working people and the entrepreneurs at one fell swoop, so to speak. Nobody has objected but I can't say there's been much of a response as yet. I guess it's got to be gradual. My new assistant, Fr. R. T. Dillon, comes next week. That will be a big help. He was three years at Buckeystown.

Mrs. Garrity asks to be remembered to you. Mrs. Girard has just offered to upholster all our pews. That's very nice of her, I think. In October I want to take my vacation with a group at the farming commune up in Chester. If so I'll try to drop in on you.

> Hoping this finds you in good health,
> Faithfully yours in Christ,
> Martin Y. Moran

Mrs. Girard had had her way with him, cunningly biding her time. Now she could say her prayers with the complacent knowledge that she had freely given back to God a portion of what He had given her. The priest's lips slightly curled and he laid the letter flat on the topmost book. The capital I's, vertical jabs of the pen, sprinkled the page like a pattern. Moran, feeling his powers, was enjoying himself. And he was not one, it was clear, to harbor resentment. Curiously, Father Cawder realized, the letter pleased him. Yet it took an effort even to recall Moran's face. The friendliness of the words had an odd ring. For it seemed to him to be the letter of a stranger. If not a stranger, then someone dead. As if a long duration of months and years had intervened since the time he had last spoken to Moran. It was hardly an interval of time at all, merely a distance of a hundred or so miles. At the prospect of seeing him again he felt, he discovered, nothing at all.

5

"I HAVE SHOES TO BUY, SHOES, SHOES"——THE woman uttered a scream somehow reduced to a whisper—"for the kids, not me, there's still that car that's got to be paid on and that old mangy fur coat, what in the name of God do you know about food, buying for a priest and one old woman, you can eat, sure, and get fat, look at you, fixing whatever comes into your head, you and your prayers, you make me sick! You've got the grocery money, give me five dollars, how can you let me come here and beg you for it this way?"

The steady singsong had been sputtering up from the kitchen through the hot-air register. For half an hour Father Cawder read his office and heard the drone like an insect's, a woman's voice gasping with complaints or anger. As he came down the stairs the sounds were plainer, words spat out in a hoarse whisper through some kind of discretion, it would seem. A faint murmur reached him, Mrs. Hoffer making some tremulous reply. His hand grasped the newel post. His heels against the steps should have been loud enough for the woman, whoever she was. But the angry voice broke out again.

"You ought to be getting twenty dollars every week, a strong woman like you, and you could easy with those priests out in the suburbs, they've got their fingers thick with bills, just you let me rustle up a job, you'd have a bathroom all to yourself and you could do your duty by your own flesh and blood instead of being a drudge and getting no thanks for it here in this dirty old dark house with the rats and all the dirt. Why stay here—you never saw this new priest before—it's all going out and nothing coming in."

"Darling." Mrs. Hoffer's voice seemed old, even timid. "Darling, I have a little bit here. Not much. You take it all. It is mine, my dear child, take it."

There came a hissing laugh. "This? This? You've got the nerve to think I can get any good out of this?" A clash of coins flung down and spinning sounded as the woman laughed again. Father Cawder stepped into the dining room. "Mrs. Hoffer!"

"Yes, Father Cawder. In just one minute."

Someone had moved. A chair was pushed aside with a noise of creakings and rustlings. "I'm going now," the visitor said aloud, speaking in a normal tone for the first time. She had opened the kitchen door, a sudden gust of air blew into the house. "I don't know why I ever come. Talk as much as you like, it's what people do that counts. I'll be back next week. Don't come to the house. The kids get too excited."

"Good-bye, my dear girl. There'll be something here for you."

The kitchen door slammed. Father Cawder saw a tall middle-aged woman pass the windows on her way to the street. She wore a high green hat narrower than her round white face, her wide shoulders swinging as she walked under a bushy fur. "Margareta," Mrs. Hoffer murmured at his elbow. "My married daughter. She comes to see me once a week. Poor girl. She has had troubles."

"Your daughter, Mrs. Hoffer? I didn't know. I didn't know you had children."

"Yes, yes, yes." Mrs. Hoffer's voice was restored to vigor now that her daughter had left. "Children? Yes indeed. One is a nun. And Margareta. And I have a son. But him I don't see, he is in California. And there were two more. But God wanted to have them too. After a little while He took them back again."

He noticed that although broadly smiling she had not yet taken time to wipe off a trickle of tears under her red eyes. She began to rub her face with her apron when she saw his glance rest on her cheeks. "Always I am silly, Father Cawder. Even now with me an old woman. Tears of joy! Tears of joy! I cry for joy whenever my poor child comes to see me."

"It's time now for me to hear confessions. There won't be many. You can have dinner at the usual hour."

He walked away to the back of the hall. He heard her, already in the kitchen, take a pan from the wall with a clatter, her old woman's voice reedily raising itself, a thin soprano.

"Mater amata—Intemera-a-ata!"

Opening the door to the sacristy he sneezed as the church's smell of cold dust slipped sharply through his nose. He put on a surplice and a stole, entered the church, and made a genuflection toward the altar. Only school children, he saw, were waiting for him. Two or three old women, one nondescript man, the two dozen squirming, giggling girls and boys. They caught sight of him at the gate to the aisle and rushed to form a queue, pushing at each other's backs, stumbling over their feet along the bright red and blue tiles. Without looking at them he walked to the confessional and took his seat inside. After he drew the curtain across the quatrefoil of screening in the door, he hung his watch from a nail. The children were hushing themselves, now that he was there, composing catalogues of sins to be glibly mumbled into his ear, making recollection of missing Mass, striking their mothers, telling lies, stealing from grocers, practicing filthy experiments on the bodies of themselves and animals. Beyond the match-boarding on his right he heard a slight bumping, certainly a child restless on its knees. He set his chin straight ahead and pulled open the wicket on his left. Whoever it was said nothing, merely peered in at him. As the quiet breathing paused and a word or two were muttered, he turned sideways to the grille. A dark head filled the middle of the opening; it was certainly a man.

"I can't hear you. Speak clearly, my son."

The man pressed his peering face close to the grille. "Can't you see who I am?" he muttered. "This is Diamond. I've got to talk to you."

Holding his breath, Father Cawder tried to force his eyes to pierce the dark. "Diamond," he murmured. On his knees? Kneeling there, assuming guilt? A thrill of dread ran over him. He felt his scalp stiffen. Was this grace, the thought darted through his mind, grace throwing a man down to ask for mercy? He could still see only the crown of Diamond's head, a dark blurred patch.

"I'm here to talk to you. I wanted to see you alone. Can I wait here till these kids have gone?"

"Lower your voice," the priest whispered. "What is it you want? I'm waiting to hear the children's confessions."

"I can wait till you're through." A faint light was reflected from Diamond's teeth. "I want to see you alone."

"You can't wait here. Wait in a pew till I have finished. Or go next door to my house."

"I won't do that." Diamond's voice crackled in the silent air. "I've been around here all day waiting. I'm not going out on the street. I'll be up in the loft under the organ. I've been there all morning. I'll wait for you to get through."

Father Cawder put his hand to the wicket. Diamond was still eying him. Muttering on a rising note, he added, "I don't guess you've got any idea what I want to see you about, have you?"

With his hand still on the knob of the sliding panel Father Cawder bent his head toward the grille. "You can tell me now what it is you have to say, Diamond. The children can wait a few minutes."

"I'll come down when you come out. I can see if

255

you're through from up there." Diamond slowly drew himself up. The darkness lightened for an instant as he lifted the curtain and went out into the aisle.

The priest shot the wicket back into place. He listened to the footsteps lightly clinking on the tiles, dying away into the church. Then he opened the wicket on the right. It was a little girl. A weak precise murmur said, "Bless me, Father, for I have sinned. It's been a month since my last confession. I missed Mass once. . . . I took the name of the Lord in vain, once. . . . I disobeyed my mother two times"—the voice insensibly sank—"Once I took pleasure in an impure thought. . . ."

He had heard and released the sins of eighteen children, five women, and two men. He pulled his watch off the nail as the last, a quavering old man, rose to his feet to go out. At ease with themselves, most of them had seemed, untroubled by the imbecility of their whispered secrets. They feared hell, but damnation need not be the compelling motive. Was it more than recurring habit that prompted them to say, "Bless me, for I have sinned"? They could stolidly itemize the occasions of giving their bodies up to uncleanness; why was it that they declined to accuse themselves of malice? Or was a lack of charity so fundamental a sin that a priest was meant to assume its presence without special mention? Father Cawder wound up his watch. It was just five. There might be a straggler; he would wait a few minutes more. If Diamond chose for reasons of his own to spend a morning in the dark of a choir loft, he could bear to stay there another quarter of an hour. He could sit in the dark under the painting of *Saint Aloysius Reforming the Court of Mantua* and meditate on the vanity of vengeance. Revenging himself on a woman because he was not God who alone can take certain possession of His creatures. Doubtless he had hated her—he would describe the emotion to himself as "love"—for refusing to subserve his egotism. Made to be possessed by God, Stella chose to pass herself from one man's hands to another's and now was dead. Without doubt, the priest stated to himself, Diamond had had a share in her dying. Hiding now in a church, on the point perhaps of demanding money, crazily lurking in a confessional. She had been killed, the thin yellow-haired girl, with a gun, with a pillow, thrown under a truck, because she had not kept faith with a man who chanced, over certain years, to use her body, because she was not capable of absolute possession, being a creature of God, killed finally because a lustful man had seen that she too was subject to lust. However she died, God's, no man's, eye observed her spirit slip from flesh, God whose mercy is scarcely to be compromised by the death of a whore. He had worsted more cunning antagonists than Stella Swartz.

The priest put his hand to the knob of the door. It was time, now that no more were coming, to signal to the man beadily watching the floor of the church between the curtains on brass rails. With his fingers closed on the knob he sat still. It was curious to be glad to sit boxed in a confessional, to inhabit an evil decaying city, curious to be glad to be even unhappy here—if not precisely unhappy, then with no peace, clenched as by teeth in a trap of steel—after the ordered years in Lulworth. And there, he supposed, it had not been what could in any way be defined as happiness, only an equilibrium, arrangement of habits. Here habit was less strong since pain, trivial counterfeit of unhappiness, swelled, shifted, waned, somewhere far within his mind, lightly pressing, as long as he was awake. It was true he was pleased to be here in this church; the eight symmetrical years in Lulworth recurred now like the tags of some winking dream. He was satisfied to be unhappy. This pain, which was not in his body, not even in his mind, when he tried to locate it, had no apparent cause. Unless it was the knowledge of being

257

touched by nothing, locked up away even from air as if frozen within a block of ice, like the cold void pressing on the living after a death. What Diamond did or did not feel with Stella dead, cessation of all pleasure, good offices, and delight.

But no one who concerned him had died. It was like the loss of something, or abandonment. He felt himself rejected. But he could not say by whom or by what. Not by God, since it is of faith that God loves and wishes to possess every creature. It was a feeling of desperation, worse from the shame of being made subject to mere feeling. One conceived that God might turn aside because He had no further use for one. And in return you did not care, you could perform habitual gestures, but you no longer made the pretense, the insult to God of pretending, that you served Him. As if my serving God, he said to himself, was at any time more than deceit; I have no merit, I can only enact the motions prescribed for someone else. How irrational it was, to feel pain, to grind the teeth, to feel abandonment where there had never been possession, the dupe of nothing more than self-interest. "Have mercy on Diamond, have mercy on Stella and Diamond," he suddenly prayed. Dupe that I am, he thought, what I mean is, "Have mercy on me, have care for me, merciful Jesus!"—dupe of egotism and irrational emotion, without love. He stood up and opened the door of the confessional.

The church had already become dark. Outside, beyond the glass, it was twilight. One old woman was humped on her knees before the red lamps of the miraculous Infant of Prague. The priest turned his back on the empty pews and glanced upward toward the organ. However, Diamond had already seen him. From the dense shadow cast by the overhanging loft there came a sound of quick footsteps.

258

6

FATHER CAWDER MOVED ROUND HIS DESK. He looked up as the floor of the parlor trembled. The shock made the chandelier sway, its glass shades rang together. Diamond waited until the rumble of the truck died away. Then he closed the folding shutters across the bottom halves of the two windows. His face now was brightly lit by the five bulbs above his head. His cheeks had a greenish tinge under the streaks of dirt. Spatterings of dried mud laced the edges of his trousers. At the sound of Mrs. Hoffer's feet striking across the dining room, he turned sharply about.

"Who's that there?"

"My housekeeper. She's getting dinner."

"She won't have to know I'm here."

He whispered, as if making a confidence. With his foot he pushed the black door softly shut. His hands thrust into his pockets, his eyes restlessly or indifferently glancing over the room, he swung round on his heels. Did he think no explanation was in order? Or was he busy rounding off some too simple or too tangled fiction? This rocking wordless posturing, the priest thought, like an actor clownishly reeling across a stage.

"You can tell me now what you came to see me about."

"It wasn't just to tell you something." Diamond began to pace back and forth between the desk and the window. "It looks like I'm in a kind of a fix—a little difficulty, you might call it. I haven't got the hang of what

259

it's all about myself. But there's been a detective down here from Trenton with time on his hands, he's been acting like he wanted to get together with me." He watched the priest with a sharp mournful stare. "Did you ever see him, a snout-faced cop in a brown suit and white shoes, fat as a hog? He's never dropped in on you, I don't guess."

Father Cawder saw a shred of green caught in Diamond's lapel, the withered stem of a flower. He was hardly expected to take notice of these rhetorical devices. Intending to keep silent, he said abruptly, "No. Naturally not."

"I was just wondering." Diamond spoke heavily, watching from dull steady eyes. "No harm in that. Once or twice I thought maybe you could have seen your way clear to mention my name, in an offhand way. After you found out I was here." His voice rose, and his mouth pointed in a smile. "But when I stopped to think, I didn't see how you'd want to do that. First of all, seeing you wouldn't know about this thing anyways."

"You haven't told me yet why you came here."

Diamond lowered his head in a fit of coughing. "I know you weren't the one, Father. It's just some old admirer with a sense of humor, wants to see me hop. To slip out from under themselves, maybe. I guess it's somebody up in Trenton."

Father Cawder reached across the desk to pull off the top sheet of a small calendar. "You mean you thought I made some report on you to the police? Is that what you had to tell me? Or did you come here to ask my advice?"

Diamond sat down on the empty chair. "First let me tell you what I know. It's not much. You see, at one time I knew a man up in Trenton by the name of French. He worked the wards over up there for years. It seems he got in where he wasn't wanted. So to turn him out, he's been got at on a charge of bribes. They tell me he's in deep for getting taxes lowered for his friends and a lot of other dirty business. I haven't seen or heard tell of him for years. But somebody has it in for me, or they think I'm the one to take the rap. They've put through a story I did French's dirty work for him. The whole time I've been right here in Philly."

The priest looked at Diamond's fingers hooked over the beading along the desk; the cuff of his shirt was raveled and black with grime. "I don't think I understand you. Didn't you say you thought I might have gone to the police? You thought I knew of this man in Trenton?" The sleeve of the coat, he saw, was worn smooth, a shiny pattern of gray chevrons.

Diamond laughed. "I'm not such a fool as that. I didn't think you'd have gone on your own. Only, I thought, they could have come around to see you, after I ran up against you in the street, if anybody saw you with me. It's somebody up in Trenton. That's why that tramp of a cop is down here, flat-footing around. The other night at Schriml's I saw him. That's why I never came back to the table. I've seen him pounding the curb up in Trenton for twenty years."

Father Cawder studied the fern in front of the window, watered every other day by Mrs. Hoffer, vegetable continuity of the dead man who had lived in this house before him. "I advise you to go up to Trenton and see a lawyer about it. You have nothing to fear. If none of this has anything to do with you. No charge can be proved against you."

Rubbing his hands together, Diamond smiled. "Proof don't come very high. At a lot of shops it costs about five dollars and fifty cents. Whoever he is, he'd just as soon show a canceled check and swear I got it running French's errands for him. I want to get clear of it. In six months it'll all blow over."

"You spent the day in the church?" Father Cawder suddenly asked.

"I was going to tell you. You see, day before yesterday, I saw the cop again, dressed in his store-bought suit. I saw him shifting his flat feet up and down, waiting for a little talk. I went the other way. A little talk in a hotel room sometimes don't turn out so nice. You see, he'd already learned where I'd been living."

"So you came to the church."

"Yes. You see, I've got no car now. I didn't have a chance of clearing out right off. They work in with the railroads. So I thought to myself—what's wrong with the church here? I've been over there all day and all night. Anyways, I wanted to talk to you."

"I've told you already what I think. To hide in this way will only make it worse for you in the end. You say you had nothing to do with this bribery."

"You don't understand." Diamond's tongue swept over his lips. "It don't matter I wasn't there when all this business was going on."

"It was after Stella died. After you moved away from Trenton and came here."

No sudden wariness crossed Diamond's face. He said evenly, "It all happened a long time after I came here. It was just last month this French got in all the mess." He paused at a sudden inhalation of breath. "What I wanted to ask you was whether I couldn't stay here two or three days—any place, an empty room, in a coalbin. Till I get a chance of clearing out. I never would have bothered you, but I don't know where else to go. It'd just be to keep out of sight a day or two."

"In your opinion, I don't need to know any more than what you have just told me." The priest eyed Diamond appraisingly.

"I just know what I've picked up, you see. But if it was anything to do with me I wouldn't have asked you this way. If I can stay somewhere for two days—I didn't know where to go when I came here."

Father Cawder slid his palms to and fro over the arms of the chair. The lie, meager and slipshod, was not of interest. Diamond himself had no bearing on the question. But there was the premise that men who took refuge with the Church had a claim, of some sort, to her protection. Since the duty of loving beneficence to all followed from no man-made law. Since the Church was called, in an exact sense, our holy mother, and a priest's functions were somewhat different from those of a detective eager to close in on a murderer. There was also the virtue which theologians termed prudence. If he gave a murderer leave to stay —if, more honestly, he concealed him—no final good would follow, merely an evil delayed, increased perhaps until it fastened on himself. And on the Church too, thrust by fault of his into public scandal. The sword of the magistrate, he believed, was the sword of God. Why then was its edge to be held back from Diamond? By choice of an easy sentimentality there was the risk of doing no more than injuring himself— a criminal caught and hanged, a priest detected in a witless fraud. Yet if prudence was the science of right actions, it could not persuade against the chance of grace and mercy. Supposing that Diamond, hunted, taking shelter here—

"You are probably hungry, Diamond."

"I could eat something."

The priest rose and opened the door behind him. "Wait here. I'll see what I can get you." He went through the dining room to the kitchen. Mrs. Hoffer flung up her hands in a cloud of steam. As he lifted a bottle of milk out of the icebox, her voice sounded in an incredulous treble. "You want some milk now, Father? Now? You wish something? Dinner is almost ready. What can I fix you?"

"Cut me two slices of bread, Mrs. Hoffer." He poured the milk into a glass.

"Certainly. How wonderful. You want something to eat." Mrs. Hoffer sliced the bread and put it on a plate with a piece of butter. "Where will you have it? Here? In the dining room?"

"I'll take it into the parlor."

"In just one half-hour!" she called after him. "Dinner! You will not spoil your appetite, if you please, Father."

Diamond was standing in the middle of the floor when he came back into the room. He set the bread and milk on the claw-footed table.

"You can eat this now if you're hungry."

Bending over the table Diamond took a gulp of the milk, clumsily chipped the butter onto the bread. After the first mouthful he ate with quick noisy swallows. Father Cawder sat down and opened his breviary. He kept his eyes moving steadily across the Latin, listening as he read a psalm, to the smack of working jaws. At the bottom of a page, abruptly hearing only the sound of his own breathing, he looked up. The plate was empty. Diamond was staring into the carpet, his arms hanging loosely down.

"When I saw it was you there in the church"— hesitating over his words, Father Cawder was aware of the awkward pause—"at first I thought you had come for confession."

"Confession of what?"

The priest got to his feet. Diamond jerked back his head. His voice, sounding again, sank on a pitch level with derision. "I told you how it was. What makes you think I'm the one for any confession?"

For a few moments Father Cawder looked sideways over Diamond's head at the wall. "What I meant," he spoke with a cold reserve, "was confession of sins. Since you are a man, you have committed sins, presumably, like other men." He turned toward the door. "You may stay here, if that is what you want."

Diamond ran his fingers through his lank hair. He seemed suddenly to be cringing, his quick eyes timidly shifting. "Just for a day and one night, maybe. So nobody knows I'm here. I don't want your housekeeper to see me."

The priest stepped out into the hall. "Come with me. She is busy in the kitchen." He walked ahead up the stairs. Diamond's footfalls thinly sounded behind

264

him. The dark of twilight filled the high narrow passage. At the glimmering jamb of the empty room he reached within to press a light switch. Once inside, Diamond looked steadily around him, at the glinting balls on the brass bed, across the floor to the love seat of cane and chipped gilt.

"You can stay in here. I'll bring you something hot to eat after Mrs. Hoffer has got out of the kitchen."

Diamond might not have heard. He was studying the domes and freshets of the New Jerusalem, worked in beads by a female relative of some long-dead priest, its frame of gold acorns leaning out insecurely from the wall. Father Cawder shut the door and went downstairs. Mrs. Hoffer's head, shining with hair combed to the viscous brightness of taffy, was circling about the table. "Dinner is just ready," she said on her way back to the kitchen.

A smell of frying pork drifted on the air, meat for a peasant woman whose piety easily comprehended a daily self-indulgence in matters of diet. With his back to the windows, Father Cawder watched the old woman pace to and fro through the pantry door. She carried in a bowl of cucumber salad and added it to the symmetrical arc of dishes about his place. "There now," she exclaimed. When she had left the room he took his seat. He helped himself methodically to the omelet, the peas and onions in a milk sauce, the salad sprinkled with black seeds. She was listening, while he ate, at her post behind the door. At the precisely right instant, just as he laid down his fork, she came in to clear the table. She put down two peaches rolling round the rim of a dinner plate. "Fine fruit now, Father, real nice fancy peaches," she asserted vigorously. He peeled and ate the one with a yellow skin, the other with a blush could do, he thought, for the man hiding overhead, at pains to make no sound. He looked down at the cloth while she bustled about him, energetically brushing crumbs into a napkin. Back in the kitchen her tramping, muscular and aimless, beat

265

across the planks. A small evening meal for one man was the cause, it seemed, of this immoderate activity, like a wild beast's lashing in its cage. He sat still. For a while he heard the rush of water and the scraping of metal against the sink. When there was no sound for a lengthening minute, he thought the old woman must have already left the house. But her head, wrapped in a black shawl, pushed abruptly into the room from the pantry. "I'm going to church early, Father," she said, "to make the stations. You don't need me for anything just now?"

He waited for the bang of the back door, the flat tapping of her shoes on the concrete walk. Then, unaware of an effort to step softly, he went into the kitchen. Enough was left for Diamond, a fried pork chop shiny with cold grease, peas saved for another meal in a broken cup. He reached down a tray, measured out coffee, heated the chop and peas in saucepans over the fire. As the coffee came to a boil he remembered the peach. He wedged it on the tray against the milk pitcher. At that moment there was a cry behind him like a child's muffled voice. It was a pigeon, perched outside the window, throatily murmuring, peering in with red glassy eyes before it flew off with a whir. He tilted the coffeepot behind the peach. He carried the tray into the dining room and set it down on the table.

With Mrs. Hoffer out of the house Diamond need not lurk in an upper room. No risk would be run if he came down a flight of stairs and sat unmelodramatically in a priest's armchair to eat his dinner. Father Cawder drew the blinds at the window. Diamond in fact could have heated a chop and made coffee just as well as himself. Hesitating, he went out into the hall. He came back again, picked up the tray and crossed to the stairs.

As he entered the room with the clinking dishes, Diamond, stretched out on the bed, lifted his head. He leaned up on an elbow. "I was asleep," he said.

"What time is it?" The priest, lowering the tray to the seat of a chair, watched his face, stupid with sleep, in uncertainty. Why have I done this, he thought, what is the good, providing asylum, feeding a criminal, striking a pose to please myself? What has my self-dramatization to do with this man?

"It is seven-thirty."

"I've been asleep. I didn't know where I was, I was dreaming."

"Here is something more to eat."

"I was dreaming I was in Atlantic City. Going up the boardwalk in a rolling chair. Only there weren't any buildings, just big marshes going off on both sides. I had on a panama hat and an ugly old nigger walked alongside of me with a box of coronas. He kept saying, 'Here's your cigar, boss, here's your cigar.' I didn't like his looks."

"I am going to the church to hear confessions. I'll see you when I get back."

Sliding his hand over his head Diamond looked down at the tray on the seat of the chair. "You've brought up a real dinner. I didn't need all of this." He got to his feet with a wavering smile. "You ought to put in a call now to the boys up in Trenton, just to be on the safe side—let them know how I'm doing."

"How long will you want to stay here? Two days?"

"That's time enough. Sure, two days." Diamond dragged the rocker toward the tray and sat down on its edge. About to cut into the chop he raised his eyes. "Is that too long? If you can't have me here, tell me." He crammed the meat into his mouth, the knife in his hand trembling over the plate while he munched.

"You are free to stay here. If you still think two days here will make it any better for you when you leave."

A ludicrous comment, the priest considered with a faint misgiving. He was making, ineffectively, attempts at insinuation. He watched Diamond's greasy lips

267

tighten with caution. A fragment of meat slipped downward from the corner of his mouth.

"It won't be too hard. I can get down to Mexico. Or
Florida, maybe. I can get a job easy in Florida or
Cuba." Diamond drank half the coffee in one gulp.
"You went to too much trouble," he said over the cup.
"I can eat anything. Bread is all I need. I don't need
a room like this. I can make a bed on a couple of
sacks down in the cellar somewhere."

"This room is not used."

Father Cawder made a start toward the hall. But as
he turned to leave he lingered, held back all at once
in bewilderment. He felt himself in the grip of a longing
which seemed to have neither terms nor object. It was
an emotion like remorse, an unspeakable regret that
racked while it also strangely, serenely exalted. These
meager phrases he spoke—they were without effect on
Diamond. If he functioned as a priest should, he would
know what to say now, the due arrangement of sounds,
to unlock guilt, to concur with grace. A horrible impulse urged him to fall on his knees, to cry out with
hands interlocked, to declaim shamelessly, "I too am
guilty! I share your guilt, Diamond! Ask God to have
mercy on us, Diamond!"

"I will see you when I get back," he said.

Diamond glanced to the side as his jaws ground
over the last of the meat. "I've been wanting to tell
you I appreciate you letting me stay here. I'm in the
clear anyway, so nobody's going to—it's just one of
those things, some meddler looking for an easy way
out." The priest wished Diamond's mouth, lifting as
he spoke, would slacken from its feeble grinning. The
wrinkling lips sharpened with a rapid twist. "You don't
look to me somehow like you believed me."

The priest stepped to the door. "No. You are right.
I don't believe you." Diamond's questioning smile
widened. "I'm not compelled to believe what you say.
Do you think only a man who speaks the truth can
268

come into this house?" Father Cawder felt his breath shorten with anger.

Diamond scraped at the peach with his teeth. "Truth about what? What are you driving at now?"

"I don't know what your reason was for leaving Trenton—whether it was because of Stella or for some other reason. I don't have to know about these things. You are free to stay here."

His eyes quickly darting, Diamond wiped his fingers, glistening with the juice of the peach, on his shirt. "You mentioned Stella." He had a look of making an experiment. "I can see all right what you're easing round to now. You think anything you want, Father Cawder. Maybe though, you've got too slick for yourself. Maybe there's still a thing or two you haven't figured out yet. Could be." He made an attempt to hold his eyes to a mocking shrewdness. After an instant they wavered, blinking, out over the room.

"What I think about Stella's death is another matter—" His voice, the priest knew, sounded too angry, too didactic. "You came here to the church. The Church exists as much for you as for anybody."

"I don't guess I feel much like hearing about that," Diamond broke in softly. It was a suffusing malice, the priest observed, that seemed to cause the pulling of his features. "Don't you fret yourself. I know the whole routine you could rattle off about me and Stella. I don't blame you priests, living the way you do, getting it soft, cooped up like hens. How do you know what it was like for me? What do you know about the five years she bummed off me, licking it up and dishing it out? Turn the other cheek, pimp! Sure! I'm on to the noises you priests have to make. Christ!"

Father Cawder turned away from Diamond's glittering eyes, from his mouth pressed out with rancor and a sound like an animal's. "Then you think it was a good thing for her to have died," he stated. "Good for her, that is."

"Where do I come into this? Who'll make it up to

me for all I took? Good Christ." Diamond wrenched his body sideways and stood up. "I can just about figure out what you're thinking." He began to laugh silently as he swung round. "If you'd just been on hand, you're thinking, if you'd just done something you forgot to do, said a little prayer, she'd be alive yet, that's what you've got on your mind."

Against his will, Father Cawder stared at Diamond's hands. They shook like those of a trembling old man, blunt black nails shivering on the ends of stiff fingers. His face had become lively with cunning.

"Father Cawder, I want to tell you something. I've found out something about you. I think I'm getting on to you. At first you had me fooled. But you can't stand to lose a trick, can you? You just can't stand to lose out, can you?"

With a prancing step across the carpet Diamond stretched his legs. The priest felt the spurt of anger within him falling away into nothing. He stood there stupidly watchful, he knew, dully saying no word, making no movement, unmanned, it might seem, in some bodily seizure. This sharp access could be shock at his own weakness, he being joined at last in complicity with this man exultant over bloodshed. He salvaged nothing, it was evident; he did nothing at all for another man that was of profit.

His glancing eyes rested briefly on Diamond who looked as if he was going to speak. Father Cawder shut the door and walked quickly away.

When the last man left the confessional and went to kneel at the altar, Father Cawder made a round of the church. He switched off lights, blew out the red and green vigil lamps banked under plaster images. He climbed to the loft to fasten the tilted pane in the rose window. Without haste he passed down the dim nave. He meant to allow Mrs. Hoffer ample time to shut herself into the kitchen, to disappear for the night into her tunnel of a room beyond the icebox. He paused on the flagstones raised above the street, waiting for the spiked iron gate to clang shut behind him. As the crash of metal died away he turned slowly toward the house. A beam of light slanted downward from a window onto the pavement; inside, it fell over Diamond, scared of the fact of death, content to have taken life. He mounted the steps and fitted his key into the lock. Above the roofs across the street a reddish star seemed to dance. A moist, burgeoning freshness lay on the air, a smell like thawing earth; it was Indian summer. The fresh smells would be gone by morning, blown away in the chill of the night. He went inside.

At the head of the staircase he folded his coat over the banisters. For an instant he hesitated. Then he trod softly down the length of hall. He heard no sound within the house. With his hand raised to knock, he changed his mind and opened the door. Across the bed Diamond lay asleep in his clothes. His feet in pointed muddy shoes were drawn up, his breath forced out in a rhythm of hissing gasps, his eyes not quite closed and the lids faintly fluttering in the glare of the lights. The priest watched him from the shadows of the hall. It was very strange. He felt no sympathy, he had hardly good will to this man. Yet he was willing to bear his guilt, to suffer punishment in his stead, to assume another's act of blood. He wished, could pray even, that it might be so. God might then incline to Diamond, might crush him to his knees at the bending of His glance, that weightless bolt which fell with suavity and terror. Diamond stirred as if restless at being observed. He flung his hand back against his mouth. Father Cawder groped for the switch and turned off the lights. The sudden darkness blinded him. Touching the wall with one hand he felt his way to his room.

In the morning, on his way to the eight o'clock Mass, he took care to make no sound along the thin carpet in the hall. When he reached the stairs he saw Mrs. Hoffer below, sitting on the bottom step, her beads dangling from her hands.

"Your friend," she began. She pulled herself to her feet. "The one who spent the night. He had to go before you got up. He told me I should thank you for him. He was sorry he left before you got up. He told me to tell you." She was dressed in her Sunday suit of plain broadcloth. As always, an alert anxiety showed in her face as she looked at him.

"When did he leave? It must have been early."

Mrs. Hoffer put a finger on her forehead. "Oh, five-thirty it was, six maybe, it was real early. I thought it was you at first. He scared me, coming up on me in the dark. Then I fixed him some breakfast. He knows how to look after himself, your friend, he ate and ate, everything I put on the table."

"That was all he said to tell me, nothing more?"

"That was all he said. He helped me unlock the church and then he left. But we had a talk while he ate. He told me about circuses, Father. He knew all about the way they are. They are dangerous for the circus people, especially the horses."

Since the priest was silent she went on, "He told me about the dogs they train to jump through fire. And the lions too. Lots of the animals are dangerous."

Father Cawder had picked up his biretta from the seat of a chair. He turned his back and walked away while she was still speaking.

7

THE BOY CALLED JOE, WHO LOOKED LIKE a Czech and whose last name he had never asked, helped him take off his vestments. Serving Mass the boy had gabbled the Latin with practiced speed. Now he was arranging the folds of green satin with the same mechanized economy of effort. His dirty hands moved with precision. After smoothing the alb down into a drawer he said stolidly:

"Can I go now?"

"Yes, Joe. I'll see you tomorrow morning."

"Okay, Father."

The boy darted from the room. Father Cawder crossed the sacristy to the sink. He let the water run until it was cold and drank a tumblerful. No more than a second seemed to have gone by when the boy rushed in from the church, stopped short in the archway, out of breath from running. The priest was wiping his fingers on a towel. Turning, he met the boy's piercing black eyes.

"Oh, Father!"

"Yes?"

"Father, come quick!" The boy gasped to get his breath. "A guy's been shot!"

"Shot? What do you mean, Joe? Where?"

"I think he's dead. Outside the church. Come quick, Father. He's shot, he's dead."

Father Cawder wrenched the purple stole off its hook as he passed, striding into the sanctuary. Joe had run off ahead. While genuflecting before the tabernacle he heard the boy's heels pound the floor of an aisle. The gate in the communion-rail had been flung back. Over the tiles a cold glare of daylight spread from the open door. Father Cawder hurried down the middle aisle, the stole in his hands flapping against the pews. An unlikely hum of voices wafted in from the street. How had a man been shot here, he wondered. Or was it suicide? He had heard no report, no sound of scuffling or shouts. When he reached the door he stopped. He had suddenly thought, the man may be Diamond.

A knot of people glanced up at him. A few figures in dingy black or brown, two or three policemen. He had expected to see a clamoring mob. The women on the flagstones looked familiar; they must have just come from Mass. Joe crouched staring past a policeman's leg. Behind the policemen the thing covered up with something brown flat on the concrete was a body. A short one; it could be Diamond. Mechanically but with a pounding heart Father Cawder swung the stole over his head. One of the policemen was coming forward. At the foot of the steps he saluted.

"It's a bad business here, Father."

"Is the man dead?"

"You're too late, Father. He's as dead as a doornail. Killed right off."

"Who was he?"

"Well, now, Father, I can't rightly say. I just got here. Some gunman they were after, Lynch said. Hope he ain't one of yours."

"But how did it happen? Who were after him?"

"Why, the police, Father. It was a man with a record. He was hiding there in the church."

"I'd like to see him."

"Certainly, Father."

An old woman drew herself lingeringly backward; a second policeman stooped to raise an end of canvas. The dead man's face rested on its side. Because it was so strangely placid, mysteriously musing the man seemed, or because the skin was so pale, for an instant

274

Father Cawder imagined he was mistaken. Then he recognized Diamond's black, dry, tufted hair, his bony chin slanting to a bony jaw. A bloodstain was darkening across his collar. The policeman holding up the canvas swayed to keep himself from pitching forward.

"Seen enough?" he said.

"Do you know him, Father?" said the other one. "Is he one of yours?"

Father Cawder looked down at the canvas fallen back over the curbstone. At his side the old woman was cunningly, stupidly watching him.

"Yes, I know him. He didn't belong in this parish."

"Well, that's something."

"How exactly did this happen?"

"I wasn't here. You'd better ask the captain, Father. He's coming back. Any minute now. We're waiting for him."

The old woman cleared her throat. "What a shame you weren't here when it happened, Father. When he was still breathing, I mean. He might have confessed and got the oils and all. It's surely too bad, Father."

He felt no repugnance at seeing the dead body that had been Diamond. Just as if now it was suddenly without relevance. Father Cawder touched the stole around his neck. He had come prepared to absolve a man dying outside his door on the street. But he was forgetting—with Diamond, that opportunity could not perhaps have arisen. He glanced at the old woman. Her soft hanging cheeks were white as lard.

"Were you here when he was shot?"

"Oh, Father, after Mass I was saying a prayer to the Infant and I heard all the noise and rushed out and here he was down on the street and the cop with a gun in his hands. Oh, it gave me a fright. I thought my heart was going to give out on me."

Her voice was strong and impassive. The wail of a siren came frantically from a side street. Reaching round the woman, the policeman dragged the priest backward by his arm.

"Here's all the rest of them, Father. The captain's with them. Just you wait a minute and I'll get him. He'll tell you anything you want to know."

Father Cawder eyed the man in surprise at his denseness.

"No, don't bother. There's nothing to be done now."

The ring of watchful eyes gave way. Hurrying past the faces turned after him, he went toward the door of his house.

8

ANXIOUS TO LINGER NEAR THE TABLE, Mrs. Hoffer moved the pot of coffee. The shrilling of the doorbell made her start. Clutching at her apron she began to wipe her hands. She turned to arch her eyebrows as she swung round to the hall. The priest heard the whine of hinges, then her youthful voice sinking in a foreign cadence. "Just sit in here, sir, if you please." She crossed the floor with a heavy tread, followed by the vigorous steps of a man. "I'll go tell the Father you're here." She came back into the room through the door behind his chair.

"Mr. Creessfield," she said with painstaking caution. "He'll be waiting to see you in the parlor, Father." Craning forward, significantly staring, she whispered, "Police!" and frowned at the walls of the adjoining room. She started toward the kitchen. Above the clapping of her shoes a voice sounded through the closed door. It was answered by a brief mumble. Father Cawder looked at the half of broken roll. In spite of Diamond, in spite of policemen, it was his duty to eat. Strangely, he seemed to be hungry. He reached for the butter and raised the knife. For an instant his lifted hand did not move. Beyond him a tenor quaver seemed to stress vague words. An unhurrying conversation was in progress.

Father Cawder stirred his cup of coffee. It had a sour taste, like metal. The body had been shoved into a small van which could have been a delivery truck for a laundry. He had thought they would send an ambulance. But of course he was dead. There was no need for an ambulance.

"Dan, Dan." The rich voice, humorously chiding, broke into intelligible sounds. "You'll never get rich, you're that pigheaded. There's Merritt Beach and there's Gawley Beach and Annandale, Gideon Neck, Joppa—" the words sank again to a muffled singsong. The man had shifted his position.

The organism producing these rich tones would be sleek with ease and animal vigor, Father Cawder mused. At ease with itself and with the world, a citizen who upheld the law. The two men desired perhaps to be heard; they were establishing themselves with respectable banter. At home in the priest's house, finding his parlor a convenience for the chaff and drivel of a moment's leisure. He should have expected them here where a dead murderer had been harbored. The day before perhaps they had watched Diamond, knew he was hiding in the loft beneath the organ, observed him, as the morning sky lightened, push open the church door, try the street, slip back again into the dark of the nave. That was a few hours before—Father Cawder frowned with a small turn of wonder—a few minutes' time. After Mass, as soon as Diamond edged out with the others they must have followed, felt under their coats for their revolvers.

Father Cawder pushed his chair from the table. At the noise of its scraping the high voice made itself distinct. "Yesterday, Dan, I ran into the little Peretti lad. There he was, large as life, holding up the front of the Weschler Building. He saw me coming and tried to duck." The speaker gave a quick, glancing laugh. The priest, turned toward the parlor, had paused to say grace. "He was a sight, bobbing into the arcade there with his little pasty face. I says to him, 'Peretti, my boy, is it high-hatting your old friends you are? Maybe I'll have to take steps,' I says. 'I'll have to take steps to make sure I've got my hook in you.' Lord love us, the little rat was shaking like a leaf."

A sluggish voice answered, "Mr. Crisfield, if you want my opinion, you'll ship him in. Those dumbheads aren't—" The priest opened the door and stepped into the parlor. Two men, lounging a moment before, sprang at once to their feet.

"Father Cawder!" a cordial bray pronounced. A man in a tan suit swung toward him with outstretched hand. "You don't know me, Father, and I've never had the pleasure, but I'm Eddie Crisfield." His florid cheeks broke into a smile which displayed below a small Roman nose a band of regular white teeth. He slipped a bright piece of metal from his pocket, cupped in the center of a pink palm. "We've been representing the city for a number of years now, Father, in our own retiring way, sure enough." He glanced at the man behind him and laughed. "This is my star pupil, Dan Mulvaney. He's been detailed to your end of town here; you'll surely be seeing enough of him over the months if the mayor don't get on to any of his shenanigans." A bulky man with a long upper lip reached out for the priest's hand, foolishly grinning.

"Glad to make your acquaintance, Father."

Crisfield said, "I trust we're not keeping you back from any of your Sunday duties, Father."

"There's only the one Mass here. I was finishing breakfast when you came in. Sit down, gentlemen."

Mulvaney backed away to the window where he had been sitting on a piano stool. Crisfield plucked at the arm of a bulging chair. He began to inch it sideways with his knees. "What an hour of the day for these two dicks to be rousting me out, I'll wager you're saying to yourself, Father." His small eyes surveyed the room while his mouth wavered with smiles. "But it's not me you have to put the blame on, Father. It's this Danny boy here bouncing on his toes at the crack of dawn. He's got his eye peeled for a promotion he thinks he's got a title to."

Mulvaney folded his hands and cautiously smirked.

"Cut it out, you're making a fool out of me to the Father here, Eddie."

Slumped into the chair, Crisfield put his thumbs into his vest pockets. "I'm glad for this opportunity to meet you, Father." His smile suddenly contracted. "I've always had a soft spot in my heart for this old parish here. A boy's years are the happiest, when he still has his mother and the home he was reared in. You see, this was where I grew up, in this parish. A boy's thoughts are long, long thoughts, isn't that what the poem says? I'll always have a kindly thought for old Saint Ludmilla's. Many, many a happy hour I whiled away here, Father, with little thought of the cares of the world afterwards."

Father Cawder's attention wandered from the man's scarlet ears to the tangled yellow and blue of his tie. Policemen, he was to suppose, visited the clergy early in the morning to sentimentalize over their mothers, their innocent childhoods. The easy words were preamble. They were getting round to the corpse in the gutter in their own good time.

"Then you knew the priest who was pastor here before me," he said. "Father Angelis. He was here at Saint Ludmilla's for many years, I understand. Fifteen years or so."

Crisfield shook his head. "Angelis? Was that what he was called? I knew him when I saw him. But that was way after my time. The times I was speaking of were thirty, forty years ago. Old Father DeLacy was here then. Oh, Father, you wouldn't believe the difference. This parish here isn't anything at all now to what it was then. It's no news to you, you can see the evidence of decay all around you. The city hereabouts has changed. It was a decent, hard-working, pious community in those days. Then the lumberyards took to moving in and the rooming houses and worse, I don't need to tell you what, and the decent people moved out. It's all nothing but riffraff now, we know them, foreigners, flophouse trash up to every dirty dodge. Do we know them, eh, Danny?" He twisted to wink over his shoulder.

"This church was started by Bohemians. Wasn't it still a Bohemian parish when you were here?"

Crisfield leaned back to call across the room. "Mulvaney, the reverend father thinks I'm Methuselah. Father, Father, that was a hundred years ago when those Bohemians came here. No, when I mean, thirty years ago, there weren't a lot of them left, few foreigners of any kind to be seen at all. The whole district around here was as quiet and respectable as you'd want, God-fearing, hard-working people. None of this crime, this rape and thieving, you read of now. Maybe some of the boys took a tiny bit more than was good for them now and again, Saturday night and such. But many's the working man's family I knew, on their knees every night with the rosary. Where do you ever see that now?"

"That particular custom is still to be found here. I know of several families who say the rosary together every evening. One of them is a Filipino family; they came to this country just a few months ago."

"Is that so? I'm glad to hear that. Oh, but it's the outings we had too that I'm remembering, down the river. Lively outdoor get-togethers for the boys and girls. Two or three hundred people. You see, Father, I was the one that made all the arrangements. We chartered a boat. I've bought a thousand crabs at one fling, bought and paid for right off the trawlers. It kept the lads off the street, gave them the chance to meet a decent girl they could count on to make a good wife and mother. Many's the dancing blue eye I can remember on those outings down the bay. To speak the truth, I first met Mrs. Crisfield on a picnic from the church here. Vanished happy days! If she could hear me this minute she'd have a strap across my back before you could count."

The detective uttered a peal of laughter. As the blood died out of his cheeks and his mouth closed,

Father Cawder stood up. "I won't be able to give you much more of my time, Mr. Crisfield. Was it about the man who was killed you came?"

"Well, it was, Father." Crisfield pulled a card from inside his coat. "Just a bit of routine. We wanted to know if you knew the man. Willie Diamond. Does the name mean anything to you? It's only a routine question."

"I knew him." The priest lowered his hands to the back of the chair from which he had just risen.

"You did know him! We wondered if you did. You see, Father, we found your name and address scribbled on a piece of paper in his pants pocket. Also an old newspaper clipping about you. So we wondered, you see."

"Was it you that shot him?"

Crisfield made a noise against his teeth. "Oh dear no, Father. It was one of the regular boys. You see, they had lost him somewhere in this vicinity Friday evening and there they were, hearing Mass, and they saw him. That's how it was. They went after him, maybe a mite too fast, the chief's not going to like it. But he had his gun out as he ran. So it goes. Did you know him well, Father?" He peered up over his brightening smile.

"Not well. Last year while in Trenton I saw to a certain child's getting into an orphanage. Diamond was concerned in the arrangements I made on account of the child's mother."

The two detectives exchanged a look of amused understanding. "Ah yes," Crisfield murmured. "Stella Swartz, she was called. She's dead too, you know, Father. We know now this Diamond killed her. He murdered her. That's what it's all about."

"You know it to have been murder?"

"Oh, sure, Father, definitely. One of the boys from Trenton had been here on and off for a month with his hook out for Diamond. When the girl up in Trenton died, you see, this Diamond dreamed up an alibi that

282

was right as rain, just in case. An old woman saw him kill the girl. But at first this old woman swore he'd never been near the place and he'd fixed it up with the punks in some joint to say he'd been with them till kingdom come. It was made to look like an accident. Sure, it could have looked like an accident easy enough."

"Then you know how the girl was killed."

"She fell from a balcony, Father, from a fire escape, broke her neck in a back yard. By which you'll understand that this Diamond flung her down. He struggled with her and flung her down, the old woman says. The old woman kept the rooming house where the pair of them lived."

"Her name is Mrs. Gurig."

"That may be, Father." Crisfield eyed the priest very keenly. "I hadn't heard the name myself."

"I saw her when I was in Trenton about Stella Swartz's little girl."

"To be sure, Father. She was the one who got the boys up in Trenton interested, you see. What she says was that at first she lied about this Diamond being in the house at the time of the murder because, says she, he'd put her in fear and mortal terror of her life. She swears he threatened her life. The truth of the matter, at least so the boys up in Trenton have reason to believe, she sold her silence to this Diamond for a good-size monthly bonus. When she'd bled the sucker dry, off she goes to the station house with this tale of her mortal terror. She took the risk of collusion but she seems to have had it in for the lad. She gave in a true bill at last all right. She says she was below in her basement door. He rushed the girl and grabbed her and flung her off."

Father Cawder dropped his eyes as if examining his fingers crooked over the chair. For a brief while he heard only the slow rhythm of Crisfield's breath. Then the planks in the hall creaked as a foot struck them. It was Mrs. Hoffer lumbering past. The footsteps halted.

283

She had paused, he supposed, to look out of the window.

"When the death was entered in the books," Crisfield's light voice began again, "as an act of God you might say, well, this Diamond beat it down here to Philly. He was thinking, the poor chump, to drop out of the running. The better part of valor, they say. Well, his sins found him out." He got to his feet, brightly directing a glance at the priest. "We just came to check. It's routine. The case is closed, naturally. But tell me, Father, did you see the lad here at any time?"

"I saw him twice. Once about ten days ago and yesterday when he came here to the church."

"You don't say, Father. And that would be the last time you saw him."

"He was here last night. I saw him then for the last time."

"You don't say. Then he must have been lurking around till daylight. With the case closed I'd have no call to inquire further as to what brought him to see you, Father. But maybe you wouldn't mind saying, if it don't touch on the seal of the confessional."

"I think I know the reason why he came." Father Cawder felt the skin across his cheeks tighten. Whatever it was, the expression on his face, it seemed to arrest the other's lively grin. Crisfield's small mouth relaxed. "He knew he was being searched for. I think at first he had a suspicion that I had gone to the police about him. He wanted to find out if I was the one responsible. Also he was afraid to go back to the place where he was living."

"So that's how it was, Father! The Lord love us—he thought, did he, you'd gone to give him in? Wherever would we be, the lot of us, if the priests turned informers! Did you ever hear the like, Dan?"

He beckoned to Mulvaney without looking at him. Vigorously shaking his head to signify amazement he moved toward the hall. "Lord, what'll they think of next?"

Father Cawder followed them to the front door. "There was nothing else you wanted to know, Mr. Crisfield?"

"Oh no, Father. Where would be the good of it now? They're taken care of, that pair. It's at a different bar of justice they must plead now, isn't it so, Father? Mulvaney and me, we're both thankful for the way you have co-operated with us. Send me word any time now, Father, if you need us. Any hour of the day or night. There's rough play sometimes in this here bailiwick. Maybe you'll be wanting to see us back again sooner than you think."

The priest shook their hands. He held the door open while Crisfield, twirling the gold cross of his watch chain, balanced lightly on his toes.

"Good-bye then, Father. I hope you'll allow me to pay my respects from time to time. I frequently pass by here. It's good to know there's a priest like yourself in the old parish once again, with a name you can pronounce. I'll be seeing you, Father."

With his back to the closed door Father Cawder could still hear good-humored laughter as their steps rang along the concrete. He clasped his hands slackly behind him. Why did he stand here inert, he wondered, like a thing of stone. Yet not precisely that, also he feared something, felt almost an alarm. Was it just the fact of having seen a corpse, a piece of canvas wet with blood? Dead now a whole hour. Diamond, shorn of flesh and bones, had been judged for some sixty minutes. The spectacle of a dead body did not terrify; that was something ordinary. But while he watched, Diamond had slipped, like a plummet, from the flux of life into the rigor of judgment. Perhaps what he felt was consternation. Partitions weak as paper had separated Diamond from the finality of his lot—thin walls of flesh, fragile bones, blood spilled as cheaply as water. And now to be judged—he, everyone—more strictly it might be than any man had conceived. Yet by the merits of Christ with mercy too that was inconceivable. As usual he was thinking of himself; if the catastrophe disturbed him, it was only on his own account. Tomorrow he would offer up his Mass for Diamond. Father Cawder straightened his head as he saw Mrs. Hoffer come out of the dining room. She had put her hand in uncertainty to her cheek.

"I wanted to ask you about dinner, Father. I have apples. I have time to bake a pie. Or shall I make apple snow?" Catching sight of his face she fixed a questioning look on him. "They came about that man, then, did they, Father?"

His state was plain to her, some sign across his features of the physical unrest that shook his heart like the grip of a compressing hand. He forced his jaws together and wiped his fingers on his handkerchief.

"They had questions to ask. The man who was killed was the one who stayed here last night."

"Last night! Your friend, you mean, Father?"

"Yes. A policeman shot him. He was wanted for murder."

"Holy Virgin!" Mrs. Hoffer made the sign of the cross. "A murderer! He was standing right here this morning, Father, right here on this rug. Why did they shoot him?"

"He was trying to run from them. He had a pistol."

"In the street!" The old woman wagged her head. "Shot and killed! He did not seem to me a rough wild man. He was very nice the whole time, eating up the food I cooked him. A sudden and unprovided death in the street! Poor wicked man. A murderer!"

"Say some prayers for the repose of his soul, Mrs. Hoffer. And for the woman he killed."

"I will certainly do that, Father. It was a woman! I'll say my beads while I get the dinner started. Right here on this spot he was standing. An unprovided death!"

Mrs. Hoffer turned away. Father Cawder stood motionless till he heard the sound of water gushing into the kitchen sink.

9

T HE AFTERNOON BRIGHTENED INTO AN IN-
terval of glancing light and sailing clouds. It was the
fall of the year; a breeze, fresh and wild, rattled at
the windows. Father Cawder had intended to walk as
far as the strip of park. There was nothing for him to
do until benediction at eight o'clock. He got no further than the front of the church. He put his back to
the two gates of sheet iron hung between high arches,
the platform of granite flags—he wanted to look,
without intelligence, without reflection, at the street.
At the length of curb, the blank expanse of pavement.
He had thought that one or two curious men, morbid
women, would be straggling by, clucking and whisper-
ing, a photographer from a paper. But no one passed.
They were all somewhere else, driving into the country, supine across a bed, crouched before a radio—it
was Sunday afternoon. And there was nothing to suggest that anything had ever happened here. The mac-
adamized surface was a uniform black-blue, the red
streak on the curbstone was paint, not blood. There
was no outward sign at all of a man's dying at this
spot early in the morning. He wondered what he looked
to see, not blood, not stone smashed by a bullet. And
he did not, now that he was here, want to walk anywhere. He turned back to the house. Something glimmered behind the panes of the window. It was Mrs.
Hoffer keeping vigil, watching to see who went by,
watching and speculating as she saw him halt, ap-

proach the church, covertly regard the smooth surface of a gutter.

He mounted the steps and opened the door into the hall. Abreast of Mrs. Hoffer he meant to say nothing, but he stopped and raised his head without looking at her.

"What are you doing, Mrs. Hoffer? Why do you stand here?"

"Why? Shouldn't I, Father? I was just saying a prayer. For that man." Her voice was soft with unmistakable melancholy.

"But why stand here? Why not go to your room?"

"I will do that if you wish me to."

Hanging up his coat and hat he had his face to the tan paint of the wall. "Father!" she called out. Insistently raising her voice she made him turn round. "Father! Do you think before he died he may have been sorry for his sins?" She peered at him with a grimace, almost absurd, of eagerness dragging down her mouth. "Did he have the time to repent, Father, you think?"

He eyed her stonily, feeling a sharp gust of anger. "That need not concern you or me, Mrs. Hoffer. Such matters can be safely left to God."

"Yes, Father." The old woman's gaze instantly dropped. She drew the shade at the window. As she went off to the kitchen the beads in her hands faintly clicked.

Father Cawder crossed the hall and shut himself into the passage. "Dead and buried," he murmured, in silence and for no reason, striding up the incline to the sacristy. Buried in some plot of unconsecrated ground set apart for the carcasses of criminals. In Diamond's case certain to be unconsecrated. But possibly burial was not immediate. The body would be lying on a table in a white-tiled room. Shut into a refrigerator like a side of beef trussed up for carving in some barracks kitchen, ready to be claimed by relatives and friends who would never appear. Saying his office in a patch of sunlight he had got clear, for half

288

an hour or so, of the perturbation strangely raised in him since morning. Whatever its source, it stirred again inside him now like a palsy, a mortal weakness. He entered the sacristy.

He heard water dripping, a sound like slivers of glass hitting together in steady rhythm. He moved automatically to the sink braced against the wall. While he twisted the cold faucets he observed the high ceiling. Once white, with a boss of Gothic ivy leaves cut from plaster in the center, it was black now, or so it seemed, above the gloss of green walls, blackened by fifty years of incense fumes, coal dust, smoke from the wicks of guttering candles. "Why did I come here?" he thought. He pressed his hands together, looking round the cold-smelling room without attention. He had supposed himself to be not quite as he was. Last night he had heard Diamond with meekness. And when visited by Mrs. Girard he imagined he had dealt with her creditably, he had bridled his tongue, he had, it seemed to him, felt pity for her, a vain woman distracting herself with vanities. He had found himself well disposed to Father Moran. Then goggling at him from the window Mrs. Hoffer had startled him, expressing her own style of pity. Surprised into anger against an old woman, taking pleasure merely out of malice in rebuking an old woman's charitable misgivings. Had it been the easy instinct of good will on Mrs. Hoffer's part which irritated him? She made no difficulties over unreasoning responses of pity; she was ready to love murderers and their victims, her covetous daughter and foul-mouthed boys in the street, mangy dogs snuffling in garbage and rats running over her feet in the dark.

It could be this dread like a panic that had made him face the old woman in an instant of hatred. It was an apprehension, bodily fear—but of what? He unlocked a cupboard and saw vestments hanging on racks, damask copes, orphreys of gold lace tarnished and unraveled. Closing the cupboard he listened to the

289

hoot of a distant train. He moved away into the shadowy angle of wall abutting against the church. The pointed black door was partly open; he halted on the threshold. He could see the marble blocks, waxy and blue-veined, behind the altar, a plaster dove furry under soot, the frayed zigzag of red carpet over the altar steps. What had he to fear? Why should fear make his throat dry, convince him in a species of desperation that all strength and all courage were draining out of him? As if a wound had been ripped open, letting blood in a pulsing stream.

He got down on his knees as a draft blew over him into the church beyond. It was hard to understand how a random instance of death had power to unnerve. Objectively considered, it was the sudden and unprovided death, in Mrs. Hoffer's words, of a man barely known by sight, of a woman little more than a name. They were like people knocked against with small exchange of comments in a bus, strangers whose confidences are overheard from behind a seat in a train. How did their dying have an influence on him? He had concern for their welfare when they were alive. But now that they were blotted out in the intricacies designed for them by God and by themselves, good will toward them was no longer of any moment. Their bad ends could not well move him, since he had no love for these two. According to natural premises, there had never been reason for him to love this man or this woman. Even to feel pity—he was not sure. Alone in a sacristy, behind an altar, he did not need to be tempted to deceit. He was not prepared to assert even pity for the girl smashed on cinders, the man shot down as he ran.

It was then only the abstraction of death which filled him with dread. Not the pitiable felling of a known man, but the observation that life, in a given case, had come to a certain end. Extinction, fear of extinction, corrupted in him possibly like despair. By another's bloody death he experienced something of

290

his own supersession. When, cut off from the potential of grace and life, his ignoble spirit would harden in eternity to a worthless crystal for God's infinitely long inspection. Without good works, without merit, why should a man not fear the instant which fixed him forever into the mediocrity of his will?

He bent suddenly forward, leaning his head against the doorjamb and shutting his eyes. God does not give grace to His creatures in equal measure. With such a man God in His turn would deal with a minimum of love, just to the last farthing. Beneath this tabernacle it was not required, not conceivable, to lie—he, it was understood, did not love God. He deferred to His power, respecting the fact of God's existence, a fact like gravity or the sun, necessarily assented to, no other course being comprehensible. But it was of no benefit to oneself, it was not pleasing to God, to pretend to love when no such faculty was present. Grinding his teeth together, opening his eyes, Father Cawder knelt erect. He briefly watched the light in the empty church, tawny from passing through amber glass, darken as a cloud covered the sun and then, like an exhalation, grow bright again. As if, in the colored air, God breathed.

God defined as Being, Truth, Justice, and along with those terms, power, immensity, a quality like terror, the attributes logically following from the great negative of God, since He is all that men are not, and yet now that He too has been born a man, mercy joined to flesh, love subjected to the rhythms of a human heart and circulating blood—if God is such, how strange for His unclean creatures to feel no fear, as indeed he felt none. Not of God, only fear for his own destruction, the imagined freezing void. How strange that he felt no fear to kneel at a point in time and space where the absolute of good descended, a god who was also a man born of a woman, here within this altar.

Father Cawder looked fixedly at the marble massed

291

in front of him, as if by staring he could see into the stone, into the black cube of air within the tabernacle, through to the gilded pyx and the Host inside. He did not fear God. In the dry depths of his mind there merely persisted awareness of reality, like a cloud vastly hovering, terrible unflagging scrutinizing merciful innocence arched over streets and trains and dusty rooms, tables and beds, railing mouths, spattering blood. If only faith justified alone, he thought abruptly. Without sound his mouth worked to a stretched smile, his fingers locked together. It is immaterial, he said to himself, whether I kneel here or not. Since I am nothing. Since in the face of the mystery which pervades all matter like unconsuming fire I can say only, Lord, I believe that You exist.

If, like many a man, he had not known this, then finding no particle of good in himself, no seed of joy or generosity or compassion, he could put an end both to himself and his disgust. But God, above and below, on every side of his wasting cells and guilty spirit, pressed, holding him in being to some foreseen economy, it being his duty to live in spite of himself. God, termless and beyond quantity, a flood of darkness. But death would be no evil to those capable of love —plunged into that gulf, annihilated, so it might seem, with fruition of bliss in that darkness—dense night inverting to human weakness the incandescence of God's being. If death was that, who could fear it? To rest suspended in that sun poorly named love, wisdom, beauty, like a disc of glass pierced by rays until the outline of the disc vanished into the burning dazzle —some saint had written thus of bliss—one remained oneself and one transmitted, a creature made from nothing, the unspending radiance of God. The burdening identity of oneself blazed indistinguishable from the sun in which one was lost forever. I am trivial and abominable, he pondered, I can envy the joy of those who love God, I who cannot love even another man.

He licked his lips. *"Aufer a nobis, Domine,"* he muttered aloud, *"iniquitates nostras ut ad Sancta sanctorum puris mereamur mentibus—"* His voice died away.

Finding himself suddenly cold, he got to his feet. He had felt the chill of stone enter his legs while he knelt on the gray pattern of slate. He turned round and walked quickly to the door of the passage. He had begun to shiver. His fingers, opening and closing, ached, tingling with cold as if they had been pressed in snow.

Afterword

In the caves of Egypt, during the glory of primitive Christianity, desert monks would stand erect through nights of prayer, curbing their vanity and malice with bodily mortification. Had Father Thomas Cawder lived in that era of ecstasy, he would surely have stood among them, blistering his feet on the hot sands and freezing them on cold rocks, as he tightened chains of iron around his fleshless body. But it is the misfortune of Father Cawder to have been born in a later age, our age of indifference and skepticism, when the faith is weak and, even in its occasional strength, corrupted by comfort. It is further his misfortune to be moldering as the pastor of Lulworth, a mild and sleepy town in Maryland, where the ethic of marytrdom is not so much denied as unrecognized.

Father Cawder, whom I believe to be one of the most powerful characterizations in American fiction, is the central figure of *The Encounter*. First published in 1950 by a new but not young writer, this novel was neglected by public and critics alike. It sold meagerly; it was barely reviewed even in the serious journals; and only among a few literary people, the kind who enjoy making and sharing discoveries on their own, did it gain an "underground" reputation. Its fate was the fate of too large a portion of serious American writing: to be buried beneath the flood of books, most of them trivial and not worth an hour of attention, that comes pouring off the presses each year. As for the author of *The Encounter,* all one could learn about Mr. Crawford Power was that he is an architect by profession, lives in Virginia and, to his credit, has no interest in literary publicity.

Now, fifteen years later, *The Encounter* appears once more, as if to sustain the great American dream of a second chance, a second life. Reading the book again, I find myself as stirred and impressed as when first I came upon it. My earlier judgment, I am convinced, was not merely a sign of youthful enthusiasm: this *is* a distinguished novel, one of the small number published during the past twenty-five years in this country.

Like all original works, *The Encounter* evades familiar description. It is too harsh and violent to be called a novel of sensibility, too delicate and reflective to be called a naturalistic novel, and so free from parochial concerns as to be something more and better than what we usually take to be a religious novel. Its hero is a Catholic priest, his *agon* a crisis in conscience, his antagonists members of his own faith; but the book does not smell of the tract nor speak merely to a parochial community. *The Encounter* is one of the few recent novels which not only command a firm emotional response, but also engage in serious and prolonged reflection. Though starkly plotted in its external action, the true life of the novel is an inner one: the broken rhythms of thought and self-examination which move through the consciousness of Father Cawder.

He is a man of complete dedication. He believes in the truth of God's word, scorns the paltriness of mundane affairs, acknowledges the worm in man's soul. His own dry worm thrives in the stale atmosphere of a righteous self-abasement. First seen in a teatime conversation with a parishioner, the comfortable and comfort-loving Mrs. Girard, Father Cawder appears to be following "some fast of his own invention, a private prohibition of cucumbers." When the sensitive Mrs. Girard offers to donate pew cushions to his church

(God, she supposes, gains no satisfaction from bruised knees), Father Cawder clumsily declines her gift: "It seems to me the Church ought to be kept clear of this cult of comfort. Christians are getting to be very soft."

Mr. Power's touch in this opening scene is beautifully right. Father Cawder speaks the truth, or part of it, yet he is also the "ridiculous priest" Mrs. Girard hastily judges him to be; Mrs. Girard is correct in assuming that significant good is possible this side of martyrdom, yet she does represent the adulteration of the faith Father Cawder harshly judges her to be. The clash between the two figures, while foreshadowing the serious concerns of the novel, is done with a gritty humor and that potential of the ridiculous which always lurks behind an excess of seriousness. Mr. Power's humor is neither charmingly gay nor fashionably "black": it is somber, dry, a measure of his ironic distance from a character with whom a damaging involvement would, for most writers, seem almost inevitable. And Mr. Power's humor is marked—perhaps I should say, contained—by a strong intelligence: he follows Father Cawder into every moral trap which the priest's mixture of Puritan sensibility and Catholic faith can devise, yet he is appropriately respectful of this "ridiculous priest" and his exhausting bouts of self-assault.

Bony and graceless, his mouth slit wide like a shark's, and his body recalling "the violated ugliness of a headless fowl," Father Cawder has eaten no meat for twelve years, and feels no difficulty in supposing that "a strict moralist could find occasion of sin in a daily hot bath." Each of the opening chapters establishes Father Cawder through a precise contrast: first with Mrs. Girard, the agent of ease and cultivation; then with his assistant, Father Moran, a Catholic radical keen to the uses of credit unions but dull to the spirit of Calvary; and then with his housekeeper, Mrs. McGovern, a sly mixture of personal sloth and familiar Mariolatry, neither of which Father Cawder can abide.

In the abstract he is right against all three, for each of them represents some deviation from the faith into worldliness and sentimentalism; but in the immediacy of his voice, his gestures and his bearing, he sins against them through judgment and impatience. And his sins against these people seem as large as theirs against the faith, for by an unmodulated insistence on his single truth he subtly violates their spirits. He cannot see that there may be use, or even goodness, in niceties of custom, or in Father Moran's eagerness to root out poverty, or in Mrs. McGovern's acceptance of her own trivial substance. Straining toward an exalted faith, he yields to the heresy of supposing that the world is merely a burden to be endured, rather than the natural residence of the soul. Life gives him too much offense.

Is there a sin that consists in nothing but a constant concern with God? If so, that is Father Cawder's sin. As a seminary student in his youth, he had been tempted by his friend, the Reverend Edmund Owen— "Ned" the Devil in stately ecclesiastic black—to "learn the degree of his favor with God." In later years, even while grasping the enormity of this temptation, he continues to measure his faith: *he needs always to know where he stands with God*. Not for a moment can he lift from his consciousness the thought of God as a factor of his self or forget the shamefulness of the pride that keeps it there. He commands all the forms of piety except that "natural piety," a reverent ease before the objects of human life, without which no man can safely make his way through the small, lacerating troubles of daily existence.

Steadily, layer by layer, Mr. Power examines the moral and psychological life of Father Cawder; and perhaps the most notable fact about this life is that the priest, entangled though he may be with his intellectual vanity, never lacks in self-awareness. He knows the truth of all that can be said against him, and a good deal more; and because he believes that, even if denial is enjoined upon saints, his own denial masks the stubbornness of his will, he continues to mortify himself all the more. He thereby compounds the very sin from which he struggles earnestly to break loose: that overdeveloped keenness of self-perception which, as it reveals cause for humility, goads him into further presumption. At no point does Mr. Power declare in his own voice that the aching sins of Father Cawder are the familiar troubles of the rest of us; at no point does he need to.

The result, for this intensely religious figure, is a crushing load of guilt: the guilt of being unable to live with one's guilt and of realizing that in some perverse way one enjoys this dilemma; the guilt of knowing that the greatest impertinence for him is to assume that, by himself, he can sustain the weight of guilt. In a sense Father Cawder tries to compete with God by taking upon himself an autonomy that, in the religious scheme, no man should venture. His sinfulness he quickly grants; his unworthiness too; but the fact of limitation and the need to accept it as a step toward love of God while, at the same time, neither glorying nor even acquiescing in it—that is terribly hard. "It was proper," Father Cawder tells himself, "to be ready to accept the terms, the possible terms, of God without condition, like a child, like a servant attentive to the nod of his master." But even as he says this, perhaps through his very need to say it, the priest belies his own statement.

Father Cawder's crisis, which forms the outer action of the novel, is provoked by a dream in which there is revealed to him the possibility that a circus acrobat named Diamond, visiting Lulworth with a carnival, is his worldly double, an invisible brother in spirit. But can one trust a dream? Is it a signal from God, or a trick of mania?

It was not impossible to God. If it was pre-sumptuous to think the finger of God might point out a circus performer as in a parable, an un-knowable portentous gesture—on the other hand, it was not permitted to limit God. Forbidding Him intervention, if such was His will. He could make use of a priest in a country town, allying him in some not unimaginable way with a carnival acrobat. If He wished He could make His will known in intelligible form, projecting analogies on a man inert in sleep, inclining a human will to His mysteries. If it was the will of God! Be-fore he slept, once and for all, it must be dealt with—plaguing doubt, ridiculously possessing him like an ache, like a bodily constriction.

How can a man know? Pride tempts Father Cawder to dismiss the dream as absurd: what link can there be between him and a petty acrobat? Pride leads him to search out Diamond and slowly burrow into the man's life: for could not this circus performer "con-ceal under the disguise of a buffoon an experience of grace?" Nothing about Diamond seems promising, neither a spark of spirit nor a sign of grace: "he was merely mediocre, suspicious and lustful. He existed, according to the custom of the world, for the brief sensations of each day, the pleasures to be had in a woman's body, a soft bed, food and drink and pocket money. Like all the millions of the earth, a creature moved like a puppet by his appetites."

Like all the millions of the earth—the phrase brands Father Cawder, it is the mark by which he would declare himself Diamond's superior. But in a restrained symbolism, the affinity between the two men is gradually displayed. At the carnival where Father Cawder and Mrs. Girard wait for Diamond to perform his stunt of diving from a high platform into a narrow pool of water, he remarks to her that he is "waiting for the dive."

"You like that sort of thing?"

"I prefer it to the rest of this."

"Really? It seems so crazy, jumping all that distance. They always break their necks sooner or later, don't they?"

Preferring "the dive," Father Cawder links himself to Diamond: they share a readiness to "break their necks," as Mrs. Girard prudently remarks, "sooner or later." So there begins a slow interweaving of two lives: priest and diver, consecrated man of God and drifting acrobat. Though a mere "paltry foxlike tout of a man," Diamond soon discovers Father Cawder's weakness, as Smerdyakov sensed the weakness of Ivan Karamazov: that is the traditional role of the double in literature, to embody qualities which lie hidden or dormant in the central figure. If Diamond thus brings to brazen light the element of mediocrity shared by all men—(but that is what Father Cawder cannot bear: to be like all men!)—he also personifies a willingness to live in the world as it is, which Father Cawder scorns and lacks and needs. Between the two characters Mr. Power builds an extremely complex relationship, the full meaning of which I do not find at all easy to grasp; it is a relationship, in any case, which controls the plot and prepares for the climax of the novel.

Father Cawder's passion is God; Diamond's a former prostitute named Stella. For both men, love signifies possession: they cannot adore without wishing to appropriate. "I guess he's got his good points," says the tough- and sometimes mean-spirited Stella about Diamond, "but he's always at me. I'm getting good and sick of the way he is. He won't leave me be for a minute." The nagging jealousy with which Diamond harasses the girl is an equivalent to the tormented exaltation with which Father Cawder seeks his God. At first Father Cawder does not see this parallel—it is one of the few things he does not see immediately—but

300

he is nonetheless driven to enter Diamond's life more and more deeply, helping to find a home for the child Stella has left in a New Jersey brothel and becoming their worldly rather than strictly spiritual advisor.

In some subtle way Father Cawder betrays all of his friends: Mrs. Girard, by refusing her gestures of amiability; Father Moran, by discussing him ironically with their bishop; Stella, by lecturing her on morals; and Diamond too. At the climax of *The Encounter* Diamond comes to Father Cawder's new church—a run-down parish in Philadelphia—seeking protection. He has murdered Stella in an outburst of rage, and now the police are closing in upon him.

Here Mr. Power, through the discipline of craft, escapes the dual temptations of sentimentality and routine piety. Father Cawder does admit Diamond to sanctuary, for as a spiritually disheveled priest he at least commands the imagination to see the grandeur of an act rehearsing the humane gesture of the medieval church. But it is an act which leads neither to a reconciliation of love, nor a liberation of spirit; on the contrary, it sharpens the conflict between the two men. Refusing to accept Diamond's shabby denial that he has committed a crime, Father Cawder tells him: "I'm not compelled to believe what you say. Do you think only a man who speaks the truth can come into this house?"

Ringing with the glory of traditional Christendom, this statement represents the most serious moment in Father Cawder's aspiration toward grace. Yet it is Diamond, wretched murderer though he is, who takes the last word. "I can just about figure out what you're thinking," he tells the priest. "If you'd been on hand . . . if you'd done something you forgot to do, said a little prayer, she'd be alive yet . . . At first you had me fooled. But you can't stand to lose a trick, can you? You just can't stand to lose out, can you?" To this harsh judgment, stripping his sacred office to a scrap of egoism, Father Cawder makes no reply. He has none to make. Diamond, unable to live in love, exposes the priest's inability to live by it. Neither through works nor faith can Father Cawder escape what he is: that much the "foxlike tout of a man" has taught him.

All he can now do is to draw up a balance sheet with himself: he does not love God, he does not fear God, he believes in nothing but the existence of God. "I can envy the joy of those who love God, I who cannot even love another man." With God his struggle must continue; with man it is done. To have lived among other men and yet not with them, was a betrayal; and in his failure with Diamond and Stella he sees a reflection of his failure with God. He is still cut off, this anguished and "ridiculous priest"; but he knows where he stands and who he is. How shall we name his affliction? That "acedia," which Joseph Pieper describes as "the refusal to acquiesce in one's being"? That dismay we all experience at learning how much less we feel than we feel we should? Or perhaps something more terrible: a dryness of soul which neither prayer nor intelligence nor decision can begin to moisten?

Yet at the end of *The Encounter* one wonders—as one might wonder about someone intimately known in life—what final estimate we are to make of Father Cawder. That even in his concluding laceration he still suffers from pride, seems clear enough. But perhaps there is also a kind of bleak grandeur in his knowledge that what he is, so must he remain; his awareness that the utmost discovery of self offers no assured relief from its torment.

The Encounter is the work of a mature and undeluded artist with a seemingly instinctive—which is probably to say, a hard-won and deeply-considered—mastery of form. There are faults. Least important is Mr. Power's annoying mannerism of using too many hanging clauses in place of sentences. More important is the problem of Father Cawder's initial involvement with Diamond, which in a novel otherwise strictly realistic verges on the contrived and allegorical. And most important is a certain disharmony between the controlling scheme of the book, necessarily ambiguous, and the individual episodes, always precise and economical.

These, at most, are flaws in a work of distinction. Perhaps the surest sign of Mr. Power's skill is that he enforces his own pace—slow, "thick" and reflective—upon the reader, demanding strict attention not because of complications in plot or syntax but because of the density of his material. Mr. Power shuttles between two vastly different environments, the bare room in which Father Cawder struggles with himself, and the tawdry streets of Trenton and Philadelphia in which Diamond and Stella squander their lives. The prose of the novel is tense, dark, close-grained, at times so packed and nervous as to create friction with the narrative. Here are a few sentences describing the trip to the New Jersey brothel:

> The car began to move faster, skirting a pasture where a flock of ragged sheep was grazing. It took the incline of a concrete ramp. Raised now on stilts, the road lay across a marsh. Pools and shaggy grass wavered away out of sight toward a belt of clouds. The marsh at first was rank and green; further along it turned gray, heaped up in scaly folds. A yellow smoke rose from a crack in the shelving earth. . . .

The most remarkable achievement in this novel is that Mr. Power succeeds in making dramatic the long passages of Father Cawder's reflections, so that one may say of his writing, as Eliot says of Donne's, that his intellect seems at the tip of his senses. Mr. Power portrays a mind in motion, realizing its tangled impulses in a dialectic of clash and conversion; he shows

303

not merely a thoughtful man but a man in the act of thought; and at every moment one is aware of the numerous ways in which his effort to think is preyed upon by unconscious emotion and the demands of the will.

Crawford Power sees the faith in its glory and its squalor, yet the perilous mixture of the two never betrays him into the sensationalism of a Graham Greene or the snobbery of an Evelyn Waugh. His moral seriousness and something of his tone warrant comparison with François Mauriac, though simply as a novelist he seems to me considerably more pliant and sympathetic than Mauriac. The unbeliever can respond to *The Encounter* with quite as much intensity, if not perhaps the same kind of involvement, as the religious person. To yield oneself to this book one need not assent to any dogma or even translate it into a dogma of one's own. For in the end, the language of art is always the same, and that is the language Mr. Power speaks.

Irving Howe